C...
Ri...

By Toppe...

Æ
APPALACHIAN
EDITIONS

Carla Rising

A Novel by Topper Sherwood

Appalachian Editions
Martinsburg, WV

ISBN 978-0-9627486-7-7

Cover design by Maria Papaefstathiou, www.itsjustme.net
Map and Illustration by Katja Sherwood
Typesetting by Marina Siegemund

Find us on the web: http://www.carlarising.com

*To my family, here and there,
and Lebenskünstler
everywhere.*

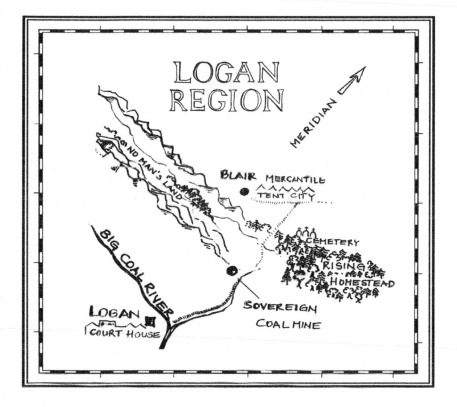

Preface

Carla Rising is a novel I wanted to write, beginning in 1989 when I came to Berlin as a journalist to cover events surrounding the fall of the Wall. I was only able to work on the book after 2007, when I returned to Berlin with my family. I started writing *Carla Rising* in October 2009, and took more than five years to finish it.

Inexperienced as a novelist, I wrote it "the hard way," showing it to tolerant, sympathetic friends, friends of friends, and family members who told me, in various ways, that it wasn't ready. Now, having made it ready, I owe thanks to the following readers, who patiently read and commented on pieces or entire drafts of the book, throughout the process. They include: Gary Nihsen, Kate McComas, Walter Connolly, Gareth Jefferson Jones, Nicole Busse, Suzy Durkacs, Jeannie O'Halloran, Kim Porter O'Connor, James Bell, H. Ferguson, Denise VanDeCruze, Martin Wesson, Wes Rosenberg, Kirstin Simpson, Karla Rempe, Pauline Bugler, David O'Gorman, Aimee Male, John Alexander Williams, John Sayles, Sandra Mesler, Sally Sherwood McDaniel, Max Sherwood and my wife, Katja Sherwood.

Early in the process, I sent a sample and outline to John Ware, a rare New York book agent who – while turning down my proposal – offered a couple of thoughtful suggestions before he died in 2013.

Finally, my deep gratitude goes to the novel's final editor, Suzanne von Engelhardt, whose work revisions and experience quickly made *Carla Rising* a much better book.

I apologize to anyone I've forgotten here.

The many writers whose works, both fiction and nonfiction, supported and inspired this book are too numerous to mention. Those who stand out, however, include David Corbin, with whom I worked on *The West Virginia Mine Wars: An Anthology* (Appalachian Editions) so many years ago; and accomplished historian John Alexander Williams, author of *West Virginia: A History for Beginners,* another of my Appalachian Editions projects.

Throughout his very fine career, John Alexander Williams has taught many, many people that our local stories are often closely tied to a dynamic national (and even global) story. Like many other writers today, I owe John a deep debt of gratitude.

None of these people are responsible, of course, for *Carla Rising's* flaws, my responsibility. For whatever rings true in this novel, however, I remain grateful to great friends, to my patient family, and to all readers and thinkers, who really keep things going.

Topper Sherwood
Berlin, April 2015

Act I

Chapter 1

"Not those! Get the ones off the ground first!"

Instinctively Carla Rising Mandt pretended her attention back to the ground. Edging from her mother's line of sight, she picked through the ripe beetled fruit on the floor of grass and moss, and dropped apples into her gunny sack, one by one. Finally rising to straighten her back, Carla caught a small everyday miracle: The gray clouds broke open, sending sunlight down through the foliage of towering trees, and filled the grove around her with a thousand shades of green. The sudden show of sun drew Mary's attention to the woods.

Seeing this, Carla plucked a second tinted apple from the branch. Spotted brown and red, she slipped it easily into the sack.

Mary Rising's eyes returned to the dozen glass jars circling in the galvanized steel tub of water. The older woman's broad, high-boned face defied scrutiny. Her hair was straight like Carla's, pulled back more severely into a tight twist behind her head. Again, she turned to look to her daughter.

"You forget everything I taught ye?" Mary goaded.

"No, ma'am."

"You growin' a garden of your own yet?"

"No. Not yet."

Carla returned her attention to the ground and set her jaw. Her face was long and firm, like her mother's, framed by a pair of loose-tied braids, the way Mary had always done them for her. Carla could no longer pretend to be a girl, however. At nineteen, she was a married woman. She had Mary's high, wide forehead, his full lips and deep-set eyes – black and open. Eyes that never looked *at* a thing so much as *into* it. Having grown up in the woods, Carla was what her mother called "impetuous." Everything had always fascinated her, from the opossums under the barn to crawdads in the creek. Her father, more than ten years dead, had taught her about turtles and snakes – knowing the good ones from the bad. He'd let her bring them home as pets. Back then, Mary had never minded too much, as long as the work got done.

The satchel full, Carla navigated around and beneath the gnarled branches of the apple trees. Mary pointed to the table on the porch.

"Over here," she said. "Pick out what you want for your people."

Your people. Carla couldn't help but notice her mother's choice of words. Since marrying, she had come to realize that Mary would likely never accept Sid, or Carla's new life with him in Sovereign, the mining community where they lived. How long had it been, Carla wondered, since Mary stopped having people of her own? Mary used to tell a story of how their house had been built by her grandfather, an old man who'd led his family up the mountain, years before, when she was small.

He gave us this place and swore it'd be invisible to outsiders. Some kind of magic, I suppose....

But Carla always knew that this had been a made-up story, a rare fairy-tale that Mary had begun telling soon after the death of Carla's father, Bonner Rising. Carla understood that her own father had been the one who'd actually built the house – along with almost every stick of furniture it contained. Each chair and table bore the marks of Bonner Rising's saw and chisel, having been made around 1902, the year that Carla was born.

Carla watched her mother's powerful hands as they sorted apples. In constant motion, they tossed pieces of fruit this way and that. Always busy, never needing sleep, Mary's hands had spent the past two decades shaping this place. Her touch was everywhere, in the things she made and planted, in the animals they raised. Carla breathed the air, warm and fresh. In such moments, she admitted to herself how she missed her mother's place – the woods and open fields beyond, the hillside springs and all the life coming up from there. As if she'd grown up on a sleeping giant – a thing that could rise, sudden and without warning, carrying them all into unexpected motion.

Carla opened the sack and let new apples rumble across the scarred work table.

"I been asking for it," she said. "The garden, I mean."

Mary looked up.

"What'd they say?"

"They ask why I keep askin'. Everybody else has stopped."

It had been years since anyone had grown anything on the commu-nity plots at Sovereign. Back then, the women had been told to put aside their "farmer ways," that everything they'd ever need could be bought from Sovereign Coal at the company store. Carla couldn't help but feel a knot of frustration to see how the weeds had choked off the remnants of the dead corn stalks, the last hint of any cultivated beds between the rows of miners' houses.

Mary considered. Carla could see the question on her mother's face.

"Even Tildy stopped asking the store manager about it," Carla whispered. "I think Harm maybe got afraid."

Mary frowned at the mention of her sister and brother-in-law.

"I keep asking, though, just the same," Carla continued.

"You'd think they'd want more goods for that piddling store of theirs," her mother scowled.

Carla brushed a twig from her front.

"That's what Tildy tried to tell 'em," she admitted. "The other women, too. But the company just said 'no.' Sharing among people don't come into it with them...."

"They could buy your produce and sell it in the big mercantile, down at Blair," said Mary.

"...and the Blair mercantile's been shuttered up too long," Carla finished. The two women looked at each other in surprise, aware of how their words had just tangled across one another like knotted vines.

"People sure like 'em, though," said Carla, picking up an apple. "Last week, I had one on the porch when a neighbor girl came past. Skinny, runny-nosed thing. I tossed her the apple, and she wolfed it down, seeds and all."

She stared at the apple, wondering whether the changes Sid was trying to bring would ever come to Sovereign. Whether they'd ever have enough to start a family.

Mary's mouth tightened. "Go on, take some with you," she said. "A few shouldn't make no difference."

The two women separated the fruit. Some would be sliced and dried, others made into apple butter. Mary paused in the work, her eyes searching the woods beyond the posts of the wooden fence. Each picket was rived to a point, some of them adorned with upside-down glass jars, hung there to dry. A breeze came through, gently ringing the glasses like Asian chimes.

Mary stepped off the porch and raised her hands to her mouth. She let go with a warbling call, loud and free, cutting through the green curtain of forest. Before long, Nick Rising, a boy of eleven, came trotting down the home path toward his mother and sister. Carla watched her brother loping toward her on the trail, his eyes focused and attentive.

Like a fox, she thought. *These woods belong to him.*

Nick stepped up to the porch, his eyes searching its corners for Carla's bedroll, the sign that she would stay the night. Then, briefly, almost comically, the boy pressed himself into his sister's side without embracing her. He pulled away to reexamine his hand, fingers fluttering before his eyes. Smiling, Carla mussed Nick's tangled locks as Mary examined her son's clothes.

"What have you been into?"

Carla watched her brother stare beyond his fingers into the high green canopy and knew exactly where he'd been. She smiled, seeing the circle of trees beyond the opening of the closed cave, more than a mile away, where he loved to hide. Nick had often taken her to the place, to see some new arrangement of his treasures – mostly rocks and pine cones offset by a row of candle stubs, grown greasy in the afternoon sun. As Carla watched, Nick would light the candles. Then, thinking his own thoughts, he'd sit and stare until their mother called.

"Get yourself washed-up," Mary sighed. "Then put up the rest of these cans."

Nick did as he was told, bathed in a bucket by the spring before returning to the porch. There, he began to move the last of the jars from Mary's washtub to the fence, where he carefully hung them on the posts. He worked in unsurprising silence, never having spoken an intelligible word in his young life.

Mary and Carla hefted two bushel baskets filled with apples and carried them into the house. Setting her load on the kitchen table, Mary opened the small door to the oven and pulled an iron rake across the glowing coals.

"Sid still spreading strike talk?"

"Mama, please," Carla warned, looking sharply at her.

Mary grunted, shaking her head.

"Too many secrets between you two. ...Here. Peel these."

She handed her daughter a paring knife. They peeled together in silence, letting the shavings drop into the dented bucket on the floor. Carla took comfort in the work.

"Sid says the union'll pay us two dollars a week," she said, not looking up.

Mary stooped to retrieve a peel that had missed the bucket.

"You both should get outta there while you can," she said.

Carla stopped, a rash of anger flaring across her young face. Her mother would never understand life at the camp, how good and knit-together people there could be.

"We can't run away," she argued. "Besides, no place else is any better. Not these days. And Sid-. Well, you know: He has a mind to fight it."

Mary placed the knife down on the table, her high-boned face cold and disapproving.

"Same as you, I reckon."

Carla stared at her mother in surprise. She'd never thought of herself as one to fight. Certainly not like Sid.

Now Nick came through the front door and bee-lined to his own dark corner. His hand dug beneath his pillow where he found a piece of quartz, destined for his underground shelf. He blew on it and put his tongue to it, the edges of the rock becoming as familiar as his own teeth. Glancing up at the two women, he put the stone away. His hand returned to the familiar space before his eyes as he hummed, the way he liked to do. It was a rhythmic song, but one without melody, sounding so much like something from the woods that both women stopped their conversation to listen.

Before long, Mary resumed her argument.

"Fighting is the first thing a man thinks to do," she said. "But, sometimes running off is the better deal."

"Tell that to my husband," Carla half smiled, not looking.

Mary snorted.

"No use in that," she muttered. "Can't tell that one anything."

Carla knew her mother didn't care much to speak about her new son-in-law – nor did she have much to say to him. Carla didn't understand this. Sid Mandt was probably the most-liked man in Sovereign. Friends gathered around him easily. If anything, he was too trusting, Carla thought with a smile. Still, Mary judged the lean, angular miner harshly. "Unsettled" was the word she once used, trying to get Carla to see the turbulence behind Sid's smile. Another single-minded man, offering little prospect for a head-strong girl.

They worked on, reunited in their common task. Carla inhaled the sweet-bitter scent of rosemary, bunched and drying in the cabin window. Eying the line of tonic bottles along a kitchen shelf, she recalled the seasons of working like this alongside her mother – spinning yarn, knitting sweaters and kneading bread. Of counting eggs and crafting gloves and hats and other things that she and Mary and Nick had made over the years, or the food they'd pulled or prodded from the earth. Together they had packed countless loads into Mary's wagon to sell their goods to distant families up and down the Big Coal River Valley, people who knew her only as "Trader Mary."

Later, Carla stood on the edge of the porch, her satchel full of apples. In her head, she'd already begun the apportioning at camp: A few for Uncle Harm and Tildy, several for her neighbors, the Bryants and Low-coal Petry.... She struggled to remember the names of all the women and their kids, the ones who never got enough. She turned to face her mother, brushing the last of the apple peelings into the bucket. She waited for Mary to look up, but knew she wouldn't. Carla didn't mind, satisfied to extend this moment-before-leaving.

Then, in the distance, they heard the first toll of the distant bell from Sovereign. With a common instinct, both women knew to fear the worst. Mary stopped her business to look up at her daughter who was grabbing the sack, preparing to run.

"No," the mother said. "Wagon's hitched already. Nick and I will take you."

> The miners use a special lamp to test the air for gas.
> When gas is present in large quantities,
> the flame of the ordinary Davy lamp detects it and burns blue.
> If the flame continues to burn blue with the wick turned to
> its full extension, the miner knows the proportion of gas
> is dangerously high. A good miner tests for gas by poking
> his lamp into all the corners of a room before he sets to work.
>
> – Warden James,
> *The Miners Handbook* (1920)

Chapter 2

At the start of the day, all the men looked different from one another. Even from some distance, each back and set of shoulders appeared alternately long or short, or broad or skinny; black or white, as each man went into the mine. Ten hours of drilling and shoveling coal, however, changed them. A man might be twenty or sixty, but he came out of the mine as if from the same mold as his neighbor, the coal dust having coated every shirtless torso with the same dull cast. Coming up from the tunnels at the end of the day, every thigh and arm and chest seemed to have been reforged – every miner, dark and angular, wrought from the same vein of iron.

They spent their days in the lamp-lit dark, blasting coal and filling an endless line of trams. Mule drivers hitched and unhitched cars, relaying them to other teams. Eventually, a string of two-ton buggies emerged into the daylight and moved across the brief landing to be secured to a chain line for the trip downhill, down the cowled track into the tipple, the preparation plant where all the coal was screened by size and dumped into the waiting rail cars.

Then began the trip that a miner could only envy – a ride into Logan and beyond, to the power plants and factories of Cincinnati, Pittsburgh, Baltimore and New York where a ton of the precious fuel brought fifteen dollars, unheard-of wealth to the men who'd risked their lives to blast and move it for less than one.

Three rows of houses – more than a hundred-fifty identical pasteboard cabins – marched up the angular right-hand fork of Wolfpen Branch. Truman Bryant's place was one. Like all the others, the house was four rooms, wrapped in slate-gray siding and topped by a green tar-paper roof. A lone electric bulb put out just enough light to read the newsprint that covered his kitchen walls. Truman and his wife had been lucky, he said, to get a place on the lower end of the row, one with an indoor toilet and kitchen water that rose to the basin after just four pulls on the pump. Truman told his boys – Gibbs and his older brother, Todd – that the rented house had been "custom-made, just for us," right down to the peeling paint and split window panes he had no time to fix.

"You're living in the lap of luxury," he'd told his sons in better times. "Just like kings in Sovereign."

At the bottom of the hill was "the barn," a large six-sided structure with vertical boards and lathing of oak, inside and out. Although the rough-cut siding looked barn-like, the building's shape made it look more like a giant wooden tent with entrances on three sides. The entire right side of the building was a big community space, where the company held public meetings and the miners and their families could have dances on weekends. The barn's left-hand door led to a medical clinic, staffed by a once-retired doctor who came once a week to set broken bones and hand out pills.

The barn's middle, public door was for the commissary, the company store. New hires came in from places as far away as Jugoslavia, all of them with the same look of surprise. Every one of them had studied the same flier, put out by the Southern Coal Association. Printed on colored paper in different languages, the handout promised new workers a "much better life" in an American industrial town, whose store was fully supplied with "everything a family needs." Every eye grew doubtful, however, upon stepping into the Sovereign commissary, which carried exactly ten items – cornmeal, canned greens, flour, blackstrap, hominy, soap, dry beans, candles, corn syrup and the Bible. Ice-packed meat came on Sundays when those families whose men were not too deep in debt could wait in line and get their cut. Having little choice, the immigrants made the best of it. Wanting to believe in miracles, they suppressed their suspicions that they'd been tricked.

With three men working and no other mouths to feed, Truman Bryant's family was better off than most. They welcomed supper guests on Saturdays, usually Tildy and Harm Fox. Harm was past fifty but could still load coal. He'd worked on Truman's crew since before the boys could remember, long before their mother had died.

"Harm's got his faults," Truman told them. "But there's none better to have behind you, above or below ground."

Most men knew Truman as one of the best miners working in any hole along the Big Coal River. He lived and breathed mining, able to load more ore than almost any three other men. Friends whispered about him, though. They said a strange fixation had come over him after the passing of his wife, fallen victim to the Spanish flu. Like many widowers, Truman had turned to work for solace. Every day, six days a week, he marched down into the black tunnels of the Sovereign Coal Company with a grimace on his face that looked almost like a smile – the kind of smile other men wore only when they were heading home. Watching him go by their houses on his way to the coal, the women shook their heads and commented on the sadness of it, to see a man so "married to the mine."

This was more true than they knew. Truman understood the ways of a coal mine, sensing its moods and inclinations better than most other men knew their wives. His older son, Todd, told his friends the story of how once, years ago, he'd helped their father pull pillars in the "great ballroom" of a section that had been condemned.

The tale had grown into legend. The father-and-son team had drawn the lucky lot to knock down and harvest the last columns of coal – twenty or more giant blocks supporting the roof of the big black space, a room that was just as big as a dance hall, hence the name. In one week, Truman and Todd had removed most of the blocks, replacing them with timbers, where they could. They'd taken so many of the pillars, however, nobody knew just why the ceiling hadn't yet come down. The more the Bryants worked, the closer the roof came to caving in.

"Finally, the walls were poppin' ore," said Todd. "Like somebody throwin' rocks at you – chunks of coal flyin' past my head. You could hear the ribs and timbers bucklin' – cracking like thunder. I figured we were gonna die in there. But Puppy kept on working, shovelin' coal."

Todd held up his massive arms and every man in the circle imagined the buckling timbers.

"Finally, I worked up all my nerve and asked him outright: 'Poppy? Shouldn't we be gettin' out of here?'

"Paw straightens up, kindly irritated, as if to say, 'By god, boy, quit pestering me!' Then, he lifts up his face and closes his eyes, like he might hear the thing comin'."

Todd's listeners grinned at him.

"'Yup!' Paw says. 'Now's the time!'

"By god, how we run! We ran like hell out of that place; and then, just as we get to the main – *boom* – that whole damned roof came down."

Gibbs Bryant had heard the story enough times to be tired of it. At first he'd enjoyed the telling, wanting their father to be the hero – the man who knew exactly when the roof would crack and cave, just from the sound or smell of it – but Truman had long since confessed that the air blast from the falling roof had knocked both men down, ass over teakettle. He'd shown Gibbs the scars on his knees.

Today, Gibbs walked toward his father's room, hearing the resonance of his own breathing and the *tap-tap-tap* of dripping water somewhere. Fifty feet below them came the regular beat of a water pump, its throb echoing through the mine's lattice of passages, empty and hollow and impossibly black. Gibbs wasn't sure why he'd risen so early on this particular day, or why he'd followed his father to the worksite. But, as expected, he found Truman in his room, sitting alone on a crate. The son considered turning off his headlamp, but didn't. Instead he pulled up another crate across from Truman and sat down. He was careful to keep the lamplight down, out of his father's eyes.

"Mornin', Poppy. Catch anything?"

"Nope," said Truman. "Just listening."

"Not sure we're gonna get much work done today," Gibbs ventured. "A lot of the men-. They just ain't feeling right."

He stopped. Sid had said that Todd alone should talk to Truman about the strike. No one else. Gibbs was getting impatient, though. Today *had* to be the day.

"I don't understand it, quite," said Truman.

Gibbs held his breath, hearing the throb of the water pump. His father only let go with a heavy sigh and, together, they watched and listened. Then Truman opened his eyes to look at his youngest son.

"Mining coal is like a holy thing to me," he said. "I can't explain it. It just gets into your blood, mining does."

Gibbs looked away, confounded by his father's patience. Or was it laziness? Gibbs didn't care, his own patience running thin. In this, he knew, he was his brother's opposite. When his mother died, Gibbs became sensitive to every slight, often angry for no apparent reason. He didn't tolerate any boy who poked fun at him, even the bigger ones, and they quickly learned to leave him alone. Gibbs didn't do badly at school. He was quiet about it, though, and eager to join his father and older brother in the mine. As shift boss, Truman knew to give his youngest son plenty of room and time to himself. At fourteen, Gibbs had been put to work with the mules. Five years later, he was still there.

Moving forward on his crate, Gibbs planted his feet flat against the smooth slate floor.

"I don't know, Poppy," he offered. "Things sure aren't getting any easier for us."

Truman talked on, as if he hadn't heard.

"...A mine has its own way. How you set your posts, how you dynamite. It all makes a difference.... A mine has a way of telling you. You can read it, like a newspaper. One way or the other, the mine will let you know."

Gibbs leaned back, his eyes cast at the black ceiling.

"I'm not sure I hear anything," he sighed. "Not like you."

Again, he wished it might be otherwise, wanting to believe that his father could understand the hiss of damp-gas or the random crack of stone. The thought passed.

"It's been hard on the others, especially," Gibbs offered, but let the thought die in silence.

Irritated with himself, he bent down to wheedle a fold from the tongue of his battered boot. His father would not speak, holding to his special abstinence. It was all Gibbs could do to stay quiet. He wanted to stand up and yell, as Sid might. When he was younger, mining coal had been important. An honorable skill that gave a man's life meaning and decent reward. Now, Gibbs felt little better than a slave. What the hell did it matter, at the end of the day, how many tons of rock a man could haul, or how fast he did it? He'd begun to wonder about other places, far from Sovereign, and other work.

By god, we'll never get ahead with this! There's barely enough cash at the end of the month for any of us! We can't even save enough money for a ticket to leave this place!

In his mind, he argued with his father. But, no. He would wait for Todd and Sid, and let them do it. Truman Bryant was a man who loved his job, proud of having risen to shift boss, making him even more distant, unable to see what his own sons were feeling. Couldn't see it, couldn't hear it. At least not from Gibbs. For this job – talking to his father – Sid and Todd were better equipped.

Gibbs knew that his older brother didn't match up to *all* of their father's standards, perhaps, but that didn't seem to matter. Todd took more after Truman. Todd had watched and learned from their father how things got done. More recently, however, Gibbs' older brother was spending more time with Sid. During the past few months, Todd had been going with their friend on his Sunday trips outside camp. Gibbs knew the two were going to other towns to meet with other union men.

He recalled one evening when, under the glare of their kitchen bulb, Todd brought him into his confidence, and let him sign the pledge.

"Will this help us?" Gibbs had asked.

"It sure has in other camps, up north," Todd assured him. "But we have to be tough on it. You ready to fight for it?"

"You know I am."

Todd leaned against the papered wall, tucking Gibbs' pledge into the pocket of his coveralls.

"Well, by god, you'll have your day," he said. "Just don't mess it up. Don't go blabbing it around, or it'll go bad for all of us. Don't you worry, though. I'll let you know. You'll have your day."

Now, as Gibbs sat across from his father in the mine, he wished he could talk about the union.

"You just keep it quiet," Todd had warned him. "Let me and Sid handle it."

At length, Gibbs heard the sound of approaching boots and knew the time was over for listening with his father. Gibbs stood and began the routine of sounding the roof. Raising a Davy lamp to the tunnel ceiling, he squinted anxiously at the mesh; at the safety flame, burning small within its one-way cage of copper gauze. Assured, he set down the lamp and took a nearby ceiling pole. Banging the brass tip against the roof, he listened for the hollow drummy noise, the sound of empty air and latent danger behind the rock.

"That's good," said Truman, and he rose.

Before long, Lowcoal Petry appeared up the tunnel. Gibbs turned to catch his friend in his beam. Lowcoal raised his hand.

"You got your buggies yet?"

"Nope," said Gibbs. "Yours?"

"Ain't no hurry, I guess," Lowcoal muttered. "Not today.... Hi, Truman."

Truman nodded.

"You boys go get your mules," he said.

Gibbs stared at him a moment before turning and heading off, Lowcoal in tow.

Lowcoal Petry was closest to Gibbs in age, if not temperament. While Gibbs tended to be quiet and withdrawn, "Low" volunteered for almost any job, no matter what the risk. No one was quicker than Lowcoal who, it was said, could "beat the fastest tunnel rat" in a race of any distance. He was strong and spry enough to catch a loaded buggy on the fly and could sprag it cold – stop it on the dime – by shoving wooden wedges in its wheels. Standing something less than five feet in his socks,

Lowcoal was sometimes singled out to clear the smaller holes, scrambling into two-foot seams to pull every bit of ore available. The work left its mark on the diminutive miner. The rock had scraped each raised bone on his back, scabs running up his spine like a row of black buttons.

Walking toward the stables, Gibbs and Lowcoal met a small group of men, coming silently down the main tunnel. Todd was among them, a full head taller than any of rest.

"Yo!" he called, and Gibbs started at the sound. At Todd's side was Sid Mandt, surrounded by several other men. Hands were shaken all around.

"Is it me, Low, or do these holes keep gettin' tighter?" drawled Sid.

"Yeah," Lowcoal grinned. "Just like the pay."

Aside from Todd and Sid, there was Harm Fox, the Bryant's neighbor, lanky Ben Tate and "Dix" Mace, a firey southerner. Wordlessly, Gibbs also shook the hand of Darko Dresser, who liked to tell everyone he was "from the Bronx," although everyone knew he'd landed there only briefly; that he'd been raised in far-away Croatia.

Todd greeted his brother, towering over him and all the others, especially Lowcoal Petry, who barely came up to his chest. Todd clapped the smaller man on the back.

"How's she doin', Low?"

"Dark enough, I figure," said Lowcoal, and spat against the black wall.

"Don't you believe it," Sid interjected. "Things are looking up – better every day."

Todd turned to Gibbs.

"Whatcha doin' here so early?" he asked.

"Dead work," said Gibbs. "Checking your room."

Todd nodded.

"Is your daddy there?" asked Sid.

"Yep," Gibbs answered. "He's gone in."

"All right," said Sid. His face looked grim.

Lowcoal voiced the question that had been on everybody's mind.

"You think Truman's gonna walk with us, Sid?"

Sid's blue eyes shown in a half-dozen lamplights.

"Depends on Truman," he said quietly. "More than anyone, we need him on board."

"Will your pa be with us, Todd?" asked Darko.

Gibbs looked over at his brother who seemed to search for an answer. Sid spoke up for him.

"Tru won't let us down," he said, looking at each man in the circle. "Come on, Todd."

The union leader and his deputy moved down the tunnel toward Truman's room. Gibbs watched them, wishing he could be as sure as Sid.

"Why ain't you workin' on your daddy too, Gibbs?" Harm Fox asked.

"I'm not the union boss, that's why," said Gibbs defensively. "I don't rule any of them."

The other men looked down, unwilling to get to work.

"Is it really gonna be today?" Ben Tate whispered. "Is Sid gonna call a strike?"

"We're ready for it," Lowcoal assured him. "Most of 'em are with us – in all the other mines, so they say. But Sid says we need Truman. That would lock it."

"Well, he'd better hurry," Gibbs grumbled. "Harm's not getting any younger."

"Screw you, boy," Harm shot back. "You don't know half of what I can do!"

The men laughed quietly and Gibbs smiled inwardly at the success of his joke. Harm Fox was well-respected, and especially by Sid. Of course, Sid Mandt seemed to like just about everybody. Gibbs had the sense that, with Todd's help, Sid had worked himself in with men from almost every mine in Logan County. This was something, however, that Gibbs knew not to talk about – even with Todd.

"We'd best get to it," he said at last. "Come on, Low. Let's start moving buggies."

Lowcoal nodded his assent.

"Don't put yourself out too hard today," Harm Fox warned. "Be on watch. Be ready."

Waving, the men went their separate ways to find their crews and rooms.

Gibbs and Lowcoal ambled up to their mules, standing hungry and impatient in their stalls. Immediately, Lowcoal held a sugar cube beneath the maul of his favorite animal, Daisy. Another, Stoney, turned expectantly toward Gibbs' lamp. Stoney was skittish and unpredictable, but Gibbs preferred him to the others. He greeted the mule with an easy clap on the shoulder, but knew to withhold the sugar. Not until Gibbs had secured the harness would the animal win his reward.

What conditions make your room dangerous?
Accidents become more likely in mines that might seem
"high and dry," but whose operation is supported by machines.
Danger exists wherever heavy machinery is used,
and where electricity powers an open light;
where temperatures are high, and the coal is "shot"
with dynamite. Where old layers of dust lie, unsprayed,
and the shooting is done by careless men.

– Warden James, *The Miner's Handbook*

Chapter 3

Gibbs moved into the pace of the unusual day. He pulled Stoney through narrower side tunnels, back and forth to the "main line." Four floors deep and more than twenty blocks wide, the Sovereign mine was a city of work, a hive of 150 men who laid new track and extended their tunnels into the earth by hammering, detonating and shoveling walls of coal.

Gibbs guided the mule down a familiar path, where a young trapper rose from his bench. Nodding, the boy pushed open his great, steel ventilation door, its wheels groaning on the track. In the light of his headlamp, the boy shot Gibbs a half-smile, glad for this brief moment of respite from the lonely dark.

"You see the thugs this morning?" the boy asked, his voice sounding anxious.

Gibbs stopped.

"What do you mean?"

"The big one – the one they call *Gow-joe*. Him and another was there when I passed the barn."

Gibbs nodded but asked no more questions. A miner discussed such things only with men he trusted. It would soon be no secret, however, that the Logan sheriff's right-hand man was around – and few would take it as good news. Sid would have to know.

Urging Stoney down the wide hall, Gibbs counted the wooden posts to his father's section. At each juncture, he heard the work of another crew, their voices rising above the rumble of his tram-car wheels, the grinding doors and, everywhere, the strike of steel on stone. He picked up his pace as he approached the room being worked by his father and his men.

"Goddamn it, Tru, we can't wait any longer!"

Gibbs recognized Sid's voice. As he approached his father's room, he coughed to let the men inside know that he was coming. Sid's words, however, rushed on – a turbulent and unbroken stream.

"We were counting on you, Truman! Most of 'em are with us – and not just in Sovereign."

Gibbs froze, surprised at the open risk Sid was taking, his words clearly charged with emotion. At the same time, however, his tone filled Gibbs with admiration for the organizer, hoping that he could finally make Truman understand the growing sense of urgency. The entire mine was filled with men's desire – no, the need – to fix what had been broken for so long. To unleash the storm.

Gibbs listened to Sid remind Truman of all the hardships – of so many men who struggled to keep cash in their pockets. Sid spoke about the sight of their women, gaunt beyond tolerance; and all the kids, so lean and hungry as they made their way to school.

"You know how it is, Truman. Every week, Sovereign Coal comes up with some new way to cheat us out of a fair day's pay, and I'm tellin' you: we're all tired of it!"

From out in the tunnel, Gibbs wondered whether his father would acknowledge the truth of what Sid was saying – or whether he'd continue to ignore the things going on around them every day. Sid *had* to get through to him.

"This is going to happen, Truman," Sid said. "With or without you, it's going to happen."

As if to applaud the speech, Gibbs drummed his empty tram cart with his open palm as he pointed his headlamp into the room. Sid stopped talking and, as he entered, Gibbs peered into Sid's face. Two white points within his coal-dust mask, Sid's eyes shone with admirable fire. Startled by the sudden entry, Truman Bryant turned to his son.

"About time you got here with that," he scolded, nodding to the empty buggy.

Gibbs said nothing, offering no apology. Todd appeared at his brother's side and helped him unhitch the mule.

"Don't let it worry you none," he winked. "We're all running late today. Some kind of illness, slowin' everybody down."

Sid continued.

"Let me show you one more thing, Truman."

Limber as a cat, he crouched down to one of the crates. Pulling a piece of paper from his pocket, he laid it flat against the box and motioned Truman down to him.

"Sovereign took up a collection last year," he said. "You remember? Took our nickels for a statue they said they were putting in the middle of Logan. They said it's gonna have the names of all our fellows, up and down Big Coal – all the boys that was killed in the war." Truman nodded and moved closer, his own headlamp shining on Sid's paper.

"There's better 'n a hunderd names to go on that stone," the young miner continued. "Now, just about that same time, some brothers went up to the statehouse. They found the names of men who've died in accidents. How many names you think are on that list? All of 'em from Logan these past five years?"

Truman inhaled, speaking low.

"I reckon it's several hundred strong," he ventured.

"You're damned right," Sid answered. His eye met those of the older miner as he spoke the names and dates he'd learned by heart.

"Caspar Anthony, hit by a runaway car, outside, died November tenth, last year; John Kelmel, blast shot a board spike through his arm, outside, lockjaw set in, died May 6; Paul Lucinski, killed in a gas explosion, inside, July 12; Furman Sockel, back broke in a rockfall, inside...."

As Sid recited more names, Gibbs could see his father frowning in the bubble of lamplight, nodding at each one.

"I remember Adam Bruges lost both legs that time," Truman broke in. "Somebody saw him in Meridian."

Sid leaned into him.

"He sits on a wheel board by the goddamned First National Bank every day, selling combs and pencils on the sidewalk."

Sid eased back, letting Truman take in the news. He tapped the list on the crate with his finger.

"All these men, dead and injured. Not just men in Sovereign. Hundreds of 'em, maybe thousands, up and down Big Coal."

Gibbs watched his father go stock-still before turning toward his sons.

"You boys're for this?" Truman asked.

Todd exhaled, answering for them both. "Poppy, we got three earners," he said. "Yet, even we're having a harder time of it. A man can't feed his family on what he makes alone. Everyone here is behind. And it just gets worse."

Gibbs leaned against the tunnel wall, glad that his brother was getting the chance to speak.

Lowcoal Petry and Darko Dresser appeared in the doorway. Sid nodded to them as he tucked the paper back into his shirt pocket.

"We all work hard, Truman. You know that's true. But too many are goin' home with nothin' to show for it. Less than nothin'. You've seen how the companies are cribbin' up the sides of our mine cars, counting two tons a load – when we know it's more like three! The manager sits in that commissary, complaining about the cost of everything, even as he charges us prices that blood-suck the poorest widow! They raised our rent and electricity last month with no kind of raise in pay."

Gibbs and the others watched as Sid gathered steam. They exchanged glances and nodded to each other, each trying to read Truman's mind. At length, Todd cleared his throat, a clear signal for Sid to pause and let the old miner speak. Truman turned to Gibbs, who had quietly pulled Stoney around, repositioning the empty car.

"What do you have to say about this, young'un?"

Gibbs froze, disbelieving. His father had rarely asked his opinion on anything. His heart beat fast.

"I'm for it, Poppy," he said. "What-all goes on with us, well.... Like Sid says, it just ain't fair."

"Amen to that," said Lowcoal from the doorway. Several of the others muttered similar words of support.

"The men have made their choice, Tru," said Sid, keeping his voice low. "Practically every man here is gonna walk."

Truman considered the union organizer from across the crate. He rubbed the blackened stubble on his chin.

"Let me tell you something, son," he said. "I don't need to know too much of your business. But, on account of my boys here, I need to ask: Do you think you can win this? And, if so, what's it gonna cost you?"

Sid looked surprised. He glanced at the others there, at Gibbs and Todd, before standing to look Truman in the eye.

"I don't know Tru," he said. "We're demanding union recognition, fairer pay and kicking out the Baldwin Agency police."

Gibbs watched the muscles tighten in his father's jaw.

"We might not win everything," Sid went on. "Not all at once. But we can't sit around and do nothing. We have to try. If you sign with us – and some of these others, like Harm here. It means a lot to us. And, I can tell you, there's much at stake."

Truman stood, balancing his shovel blade on a single nugget of coal. Everyone waited for what he had to say.

"Let me think on it," he said at last. "You'll get my answer at the end of day."

Someone groaned. Sid Mandt's eyes narrowed. He stepped forward and squared his shoulders.

"I'd really like to know just what's keepin' you from decidin' on this, right here and now."

He had tried to keep his voice level, but every man could hear it: Sid's words contained a threat.

Truman straightened and stared at the younger man. Gibbs held his breath, imagining what would happen if it came to blows between the two. At this point, he remembered the trapper-boy's warning about the sheriff's men in Sovereign. He'd only seen one or two, but any number of them could be getting ready, waiting for any excuse to move in.

Truman leaned in toward Sid, and Gibbs' mind raced. Neither man could back down now. Gibbs looked to Todd, who put a firm, supportive hand on his friend's shoulder.

"Hold up a minute, Sid," said Todd.

Sid's lips went tight as he looked around the circle – from Todd to Gibbs, Lowcoal and Darko. His shoulders slackened.

"All right, then, Tru," he said, turning his back to the old miner. "Let me know by lunchtime."

Quietly, Sid turned toward the coal wall. Stooping down, he hefted another box, this one lined with dynamite.

"Come on, boys," he said. "Let's blow some coal."

Grimmacing, Todd pointed his light at Gibbs, holding a tobacco plug beneath Stoney's greedy muzzle. Snorting its pleasure, the mule raised a hind leg and brought it down. Shale chips skittered along the floor.

"One high-class animal," Todd muttered. Gibbs could hear the frustration in his voice.

Truman turned back to his work as Low and Darko looked at each other, disinclined to move. Crouching before the coalface, Todd pulled the drill bit from the borehole. Sid slid in three new pieces of dynamite, the end of the last stick resting just inside the new hole.

"Just like a glove," Sid said.

"We're wiring!" Todd called, and Gibbs prepared to move Stoney fifty yards up the tunnel.

Todd plugged each stick with a blasting charge, letting the yellow fuse lines tumble out.

"Here, let me," said Sid and used his work knife to cut the lines to length. Suddenly, the entire room thumped with a sickening familiarity. Somewhere in a rear hallway, a man-sized ceiling stone had worked itself loose. It crashed to the floor with a tremor that shook the room. The men froze, cold sweat appearing on their faces.

"Sweet Jesus!" said Darko.

Stoney brayed non-stop, raising every heartbeat. The rockfall had happened just five yards up the tunnel. They waited for a second drop. Gibbs stroked the mule's brown coat with a shaking hand. Darko moved out of the doorway.

"Steady, boys," said Truman, as Todd joined Gibbs to face his brother across the cart.

"You all right?"

Gibbs nodded, but his eyes were on Truman, whose chin was down, his face calm. The old miner had quietly laid his shovel aside. Down in a corner, Gibbs' lamp caught sight of a running rat, dashing past their lunch pails. Gibbs got a sickening feeling in the pit of his stomach, almost hearing Truman's call before the words came out.

"Everybody out!"

A safety lamp on the pavement was flaring up.

"White damp!" Gibbs cried, just before the second lamp flashed brightly behind its gauze.

"Grab them Davys!" yelled Truman. "Get 'em out of here!"

Lowcoal took one lamp and ran for the surface. Truman pulled a steel whistle from under his shirt. The old miner blew three short blasts into the deeper sections. The entire mine came alive with shouting men. Boots pounded the mine floor in desperate flight. Gibbs fumbled with Stoney's harness, suddenly seeing that, unlike everybody else, his father was moving away, deeper into the dark.

"Poppy, no!"

"You mind me, boy! Get on out of here!"

With that, Truman Bryant disappeared into the mine, the sound of his two-tone whistle retreating with him.

Sid was scooping handfuls of earth, smothering his fused dynamite at the coal face. Todd ran to the other side of the coal buggy to help Gibbs unhitch the harness. Stoney danced and chafed in a wild panic. Todd responded by wrapping the reins around his left arm, increasing his control. Stoney resisted. Suddenly, the beast lurched back and pushed the empty mine car from the rails. The buggy tipped, sending one steel edge of the bucket directly into Todd's upper chest. The car rim cut deep into his shoulder, pinning him against the wall. Todd screamed.

Gibbs watched in panic as blood surged from his brother's shoulder. Todd howled like an animal as he tried to brace himself against the wall and push the cart away. Caught on the wrong side of the car, Gibbs made a desperate move to yank the buggy back onto the rails. But his angle was wrong; the car, too massive.

Now, Stoney had freed himself and, with an animal's instinct for danger, knew to run. Braying, he tugged at his reins, still wrapped around Todd's forearm. Todd cried in agony and fear as, with a wrenching snap, his bleeding shoulder separated from its socket.

Suddenly Sid appeared, pushing Gibbs aside. With his work knife, he sliced the leather straps that tethered Todd's arm to Stoney. The mule trumpeted up the tunnel, trailing his leather lines.

"Get that lamp!" Sid ordered. "I'll take care of Todd!"

The remaining safety lamp burned intensely, its fires threatening to break through the tube of metal mesh. Grabbing it, Gibbs started up the tunnel. He didn't know how far he'd gotten before he almost slammed into Darko Dresser.

"Here!" he pushed the lamp at Darko who, without a word, took it and dashed toward the surface. Gibbs turned back to rejoin Sid. He found him alongside Todd, whose face had gone pale with pain and loss of blood. In the shaking lamplight, Gibbs saw his brother's knobbed shoulder bone poking up from the open cut, like an egg in a bloody nest.

"Come on and help!" yelled Sid, now working himself into the narrow space between tunnel wall and mine car.

Gibbs scrambled to his side. Together, they shoved the derailed wagon. Slowly – too slowly – it tipped away, and Todd was freed. The miner fell to his side, and immediately started to save himself by crawling up the tunnel on his own. Gibbs was relieved to see the empty wagon move, but its weight carried it too far, tipping over. Before he or Sid could catch it, the buggy had toppled into a wooden post, which keeled. As it fell, the post brought down a ceiling beam.

"Goddamn!" cried Sid, backing up the tunnel with Gibbs.

Their lamps captured more timbers. To Gibbs, they seemed to fall one by one. The three miners watched in horror as new beams came down, followed by great chunks of roof. As they crabbed backward, the unsupported roof knocked down more posts. A large section of ceiling collapsed in a cascade of rock and coal. Gibbs uttered a silent plea as he watched the everything spin out of control.

No. Stop. Please, stop.

It didn't stop. Briefly, Gibbs found himself tangled-up with Todd, both brothers desperately trying to pull themselves away from the disaster. Huge slabs of coal and slate fell down, battering the overturned coal car. Gibbs watched the rockfall and what he saw then made him cry aloud. Across the thunderous curtain of dust and falling earth, a set of headlamps moved. With a sick feeling, Gibbs recognized the two-tone blast of his father's warning whistle above the roar of the falling rock, which suddenly took everything.

"Come on! Come on!"

Sid was pulling Gibbs away. By some miracle, the three were able to get back on their feet. Todd had risen first, and was stumbling up the tunnel. Following as fast as they could, Gibbs and Sid passed another safety lamp, abandoned but still blazing. Further up the tunnel, Gibbs was overcome by the bad air. He sank to his knees. Eyes shut, he pressed his cheek to the tunnel floor and inhaled deeply.

If it's poison, he thought, *I might as well go quick.*

Tasting dust and death, he could see up the tunnel, where Todd moved onward, his headlamp panning wildly. At last, Gibbs felt someone grab him by the arm and pull him up. Puffing, Sid hoisted Gibbs' lean frame onto his shoulders as both headlamps fell to the tunnel floor. Staggering, Sid followed the last trace of Todd's wavering lamp. The next thing Gibbs knew, they had reached the upper hall. Someone – Darko – pulled him from Sid's shoulders and carried him into the blinding light.

On the hillside, Gibbs gradually returned to consciousness. He lay before the tipple, in the shadow of mine-track scaffold. All around him, men ran and shouted, their voices accented by the endless peal of the warning bell. Gibbs marveled at the remarkably clear, blue sky – thought he heard the singing breeze, and wondered that he wasn't dead. He took in more air, as the sounds around him became more familiar. The bell tolled, accenting the bark of men giving orders.

"What section was it?"

"Check who's missing!"

"Mark the time!"

Gibbs listened, reassured to see the crew in gas masks moving toward the mine mouth. Todd lay nearby, coughing and bloodied. Sid leaned over him, pressing someone's shirt against Todd's shoulder.

Surely, Truman would be out soon.

"I'm getting him to the doctor," Sid cried.

Gibbs balled his fists, unable to do anything but watch the two men hobble off together. A feeling of nausea came over him. He fought the urge to be sick, wanting to deny the memory of what had happened, baffled by the utter craziness of it. He closed his eyes, listened beyond the bell, beyond the crisis of the mine: Men moving with their equipment. Everywhere, people's voices – women, now – calling after their own.

Gibbs listened to the ordered panic, certain that these men would save his father. He let the echoless voices take him, understanding a strange order – the order of people working – to the chaotic sounds around him, like some odd, reassuring music, as welcome as the feel of sooty grass against his back and fresh air moving through his lungs.

Chapter 4

Chief Deputy Gaujot stood in the doorway of the Sovereign clinic, idly watching the doctor's work. Outside, the alarm bell pealed, calling miners blindly to the hole. Gaujot's interest, however, was focused on one thing: the suspected agitator, Sid Mandt, who held his writhing friend to the table.

"Don't worry, Todd," Sid was saying. "You're gonna be all right."

The doctor was hunched over the other man's shoulder, his uncombed gray hair falling forward like a hood.

"Hold him still," the physician wheezed, and shot more opiate into the good right arm of the miner, Bryant. The man relaxed, allowing the doctor to move the exposed bone, pushing it with his thumb.

"Well, it ain't broke," he said. "That'll make 'er easier."

"Kid messed hisself up real good, didn't he?" Mouseface whispered.

"Shut up," said Gaujot, wanting to hear.

John "Mouseface" Moler straightened, obediently quiet. With his wide-set eyes, slicked-down hair and long nose, Mouseface was a vain man. He loved working for the Baldwins because of the agency "uniform" – black pants and suit jacket with a matching vest. Mouseface was too distracted by his own appearance for Gaujot's liking. Still, his loyalty to the captain was absolute. And, in Gaujot's world, loyalty was everything.

The big mine guard gazed at the window behind the doctor. Out in the tipple yard, miners climbed into their breathing suits. A flock of fretful women climbed the hill, dragging worried children with them. Gaujot suspected they were there too soon. The suits meant gas, which always slowed things down.

"By god."

Bryant muttered something through the morphine. Gaujot moved forward, as if to get a better view. Mandt continued to hold the man down while the physician set to working on his shoulder. Anchoring himself, the doctor pulled the arm as he thumbed down against the shoulder-ball. The thing went back into its socket with a satisfying pop. Grimacing, Mouseface stayed back by the wall, but Gaujot was almost at the foot of the bed. He watched the doctor close the wound. Twenty-four black sutures. Gaujot had always liked doctors.

Five years with the Baldwin Detective Agency had brought him into contact with some good ones. Looking down, Gaujot opened and turned his fingers, staring at each twice-broken knuckle. Strikers' fists had pugged his nose. Their brickbats had mounded knots of cartilage onto his forehead. The top of his left ear had been sliced away, as if someone had taken a bite from it. All this, plus his size, meant that practically no one argued with him anymore. Few of his own men, excluding Mouseface, even had the guts to speak with him.

Gaujot had been transferred to Logan for his experience. During the war, he'd worked alone, picking up wayward sailors near the docks of Baltimore. The War Department paid twenty-five dollars for each case. When he needed extra cash, Gaujot held a man "on ice" long enough for the AWOL to be called "excessive," paying a double bounty. After a week with the bounty hunter, the meanest marine became meek as a mouse, not daring to breathe a word of what had happened to him, chained and gagged in Gaujot's room.

Gaujot's first work with the Baldwin Detective Agency was in the steam-driven camps of Wyoming and Colorado, where he'd made his name. Mine owners considered him as being among the best, a fearless fighting machine. He was two-hundred-twenty pounds of raw anger, a man whose artistry was measured in pure, unbridled rage. His performance out West had drawn the interest of Sheriff Gore, who brought him to Logan. Here, Gaujot was given command of all the other Baldwin detectives, hired as "mine guards" for all the mining camps, mostly watching everything, keeping union organizers out. In taking his new job, Gaujot was gratified to learn that he would draw not one paycheck but two. The first bore the mark of the Baldwin Detective Agency, drawn on the account of the Southern Coal Association, the coal mine owners. The other check came from Logan County. And Sheriff Riley Gore was the boss who signed both checks. Gaujot couldn't believe his good fortune.

He watched the doctor brush the ailing miner's sewn-up gash with an oily antiseptic. Todd opened his mouth and spoke through his delirium.

"By god, Sid. Did we botch the strike?"

"Shut up," said Sid. "Quiet, now. Quiet. Don't talk."

Todd moaned and Sid was afraid to look around. When he did, he was only somewhat relieved to see that the two Baldwin guards had left.

"Go on, now," the doctor said. "This man needs sleep."

Followed by his long shadow, Sid passed the first few houses on the long row. The last ray of sunlight was gone, tucked behind the western hill, and the cold air made him cough. He shuddered at the memory of the gas and dust in the mine. Sid knew, though, that he had to get back. He was needed there – and he needed to know who, if anyone, was talking to the Baldwin guards. Todd had been right. There could be no strike as long as miners were missing. Sid hoped he could keep a lid on things. They'd come so far, but he still needed the element of surprise.

His leaden feet took him up the steps and through the door of his house. He could hear Carla inside, could use a rest, needed to eat. How would he do anything without Todd?

Sid started across the front room, heading for the kitchen. Suddenly, his arms were pinioned from behind. A pillow case snapped down, over his head. Sid fought, tried to kick one attacker's feet out from under him. Instead he lost his balance and went down hard himself. On the floor, he realized who it was, and knew it was useless to fight. He cursed himself for getting caught alone, but knew this day had been long enough in coming.

"What happened, Red?" a voice asked. "Sabotage go south on you?"

They cuffed his hands behind his back, pulled back the pillow case and stuffed his mouth with his own blue neckerchief. They pinned him to the floor, one man sitting on his back.

"You kill your own?" the smaller one asked. "You might just as well work for us. What do you say?"

He removed the rag, ready to clap it back.

"If I worked with you," Sid choked, "I'd gladly blow us all to hell."

Gaujot interrupted him with one staccato blow to the head. Mouse-face replaced the neckerchief and the hood.

"Man's clearly been drinking on the job," Gaujot said. "Teach him to show better respect for his calling."

Mouseface produced a rubber blackjack, gave the writhing Sid several blows, just to make himself acquainted.

"You want it to show?" he asked, looking up.

"Doesn't matter," Gaujot said. "Not now."

Mouseface went to work, landing blows where he could. It wasn't easy. Even in handcuffs, the hooded man could dodge and move. Mouse-face was eager to make a good impression on his captain, though, delivering the degree of damage he thought should satisfy. Soon his blows were having the desired effect, landing with muffled thuds. Sid became more passive.

Gaujot, however, had begun his search for evidence. Reaching high atop a kitchen cupboard – behind several bottles and jars of home-made goods – he found an American Mineworkers Union handbook. From his own jacket, the mine guard pulled a notepad and pencil, jotting: "contabnd book in possessn of Mandt, S. Sovrine Mine No. 1. Sept 1, 1921."

Standing before the main room shelf, Gaujot examined a framed photograph. Dressed in a suit and tie, Sid grinned as he leaned into his pretty wife, done-up in white. Her hair had been woven into two long braids. Gaujot's granite hand replaced the photo.

Gaujot returned to the main room and found Mouseface, panting. Leaning down, the guard checked Sid's breathing, wondering whether he might have gone too far. Suddenly, Sid reared up, bashing his enemy's face with the back of his head. Pulling back, Mouseface touched his long nose and saw the first drops of blood splash against his fine white shirt. In fury and humiliation, Mouseface landed more blows, grunting each time he connected with Sid's raw flesh. Gaujot watched, pitying the smaller man in his desperation to get even. Mouseface didn't come close to packing the punch that he himself could invest.

"That's good," said Gaujot, and turned to leave. "Get yourself cleaned up."

Mouseface obediently put away his club. Outside, they walked toward the barn. The sun had disappeared behind the high wall of wooded mountains. Mouseface glanced toward the activity around the mine mouth as they walked. He was breathing hard, his scowling face blotched and red.

Inside the mine, the workers were striking the dark rock with energy they didn't know they had. The men hammered at the fallen wall, desperate to get to their friends. None of them knew all the victims. Still, each man dug furiously – each knowing that, one day, the fading life behind the fallen wall might be his own.

The two Baldwins had been gone a quarter hour before Sid was able to pick himself off the floor. He rose and touched his face, checking himself for broken bones. Trying to ignore his aching ribs, he pumped water into a white enamel basin. He knew he'd feel a whole lot worse after sleeping and decided that he wouldn't.

Carla and her mother came in to find him sitting at the tiny kitchen table, nursing his own injuries. He'd soaked a bandana with cold water and clapped it across one eye, which was almost swollen shut. Sid looked up at them, his face masked by angry streaks of sweat and coal. Getting past the initial shock, Carla immediately recognized the source of Sid's anger: He'd been caught and beaten, his long-laid plans gone wrong. She wanted to say something – wanted to go to him; to cry with him. But she knew better. She would do nothing here, not with her mother present.

Mary surprised them both, however, by going straight to the table where Sid sat. With a look that equaled his own for hard-headedness, she took the bandana from him and wrung it into the bowl.

"You got witch hazel, don't you?" she asked.

Carla pulled the white-labeled bottle from her cupboard. Mary dumped its contents into the basin, rinsed the bandana there and handed it back to Sid. Sullenly, he applied it to his face as Mary searched the pocket of her skirt.

"Chew this," she ordered, and pushed a piece of dried root into his hand. Sid held it up, scrutinizing it with his one good eye.

"Sweet flag," Mary told him. "Won't hurt you none."

Sid chewed the soft stem with slow effort as she rinsed and reapplied the rag. Carla pulled the big tub for his bath, but Sid said no, don't bother.

"I'm going back to help," he said.

Mary raised an eyebrow.

"Have you eaten?" Carla asked. Sid stared at her a moment, his jaw working at the root.

"No," he admitted, suddenly remembering his hunger.

Carla went to the bin, pulled a half loaf of bread and began slicing. Now and then, she stole glances at her mother and her husband, neither of whom looked the other in the eye. No two people were closer to her – and so different in their outlook. Each one shared a common bull-head-edness. Carla could feel them fuming, like sapwood soaked in pitch. One spark would be all it took, she figured, to set her whole world on fire. Set all three of them up in one flaming rage.

Sid moved in his chair. He submitted to Mary's administrations, but only just. Finally, the older woman looked him over.

"Is this the worst of it?" she asked.

Sid scowled, his tongue busy with the sweet flag.

"What happened, Sid?" asked Carla, and set the sandwich before him.

Sid sat upright, responding to the food.

"White-damp gas," he said. "Then a roof caved in. Todd come out with a busted shoulder. Doctor has him at the clinic. Gibbs got out, but some others is trapped. Truman's likely one."

Carla leaned back against the countertop, hugging herself at the news, worried for Todd and his father.

"What about Uncle Harm?" she asked.

"He's all right," Sid muttered. "Just saw him headed to the mine. Tildy's up there too."

Fighting back most of her questions, Carla turned to him.

"What's gonna happen, Sid?"

He shot her a warning look and Carla understood. He'd say more when her mother wasn't around. Something new had appeared in Sid's eyes, though, and this was worrying. For the first time, Carla suspected that her husband might be afraid – and not only for himself.

"The thugs found out some of it," he said quietly. "But not everything. They suspect us."

There were no more questions.

Although Carla had been married to Sid less than a year, she felt she knew him just about as well as he knew himself – or even better. He was a kind man, more so than most of his friends suspected, and believed in the worth of other men. But, then, Carla didn't have him around as much as she would have liked. He was so busy, always off to his "Sunday meetings," up and down the Big Coal, what he sometimes called his "other job." Leaving the house in unfamiliar clothes and a hat that hid his face, he took his weekend hikes – meeting with unsettled miners from other camps. Sid didn't talk too much about it, not beyond his general warning, which he repeated often: "We have to be on guard, lest things get rough. If they find out…"

Knowing the stakes – not just for Sid, but for so many others – Carla knew when to ask questions, when to prompt him to tell her things and when to let him keep it to himself.

Sid finished his sandwich and would not wait. Before he could rise, though, Mary leaned into him.

"Nick and I are staying over," she said.

Sid just nodded, and Carla was relieved. After using his finger to blot up crumbs, he jumped up and dropped the plate into the washtub himself. The quickness with which he moved surprised Carla. Almost as if he'd healed completely. But, no, Sid slowed as he walked into the bedroom. Beckoning her to follow, she could see his hesitation. He might hide his pain from others, but not her.

With some effort, Sid went down on his knees and used his pocket knife to pry up the floorboard by the bed. There, he'd hidden a small pile of union books and broadsheets, weighted down by a revolver. Picking up the gun, he placed it on the bed. Carla stared at the fearful thing, black and heavy. She'd known he'd had it, but Sid had never shown it to her before. She'd asked about it, but he'd always waved off her worries, insisting it was "just a little thing."

Now, Carla sat on the bed and stared, blank-faced as he put the weapon in her hands. He pulled a box of bullets from the floorspace and gave that to her too. The girl felt the dark weight of the strange tool.

"Keep it by you at night," Sid told her. "And when you go out."

His voice had gone soft, almost tender, so Mary wouldn't hear. Obediently, Carla tucked the gun into her satchel, hanging by the door.

Replacing the board, Sid pulled on a clean workshirt. He was ready to leave.

Carla reached out to him and his head went down. She laid a gentle hand on his back and rested her head on his shoulder. Sid spoke softly to her.

"Todd's alone," he said. "He's bad-off at the clinic. Somebody should be there with him, just in case."

Carla felt the heat rise to her face.

"How long will you be?" she asked.

Sid backed away and shrugged, frustrated at not knowing. She followed him as he walked through the kitchen. He kissed her in the doorway, then went out, letting the screen door go behind him. A familiar emptiness crept into Carla's consciousness, a void made larger somehow by Mary's gaze. Following her husband, Carla went outside to stand on the porch. She watched him stride up the hill toward the shadow of the mine. Just as Mary joined her daughter on the porch, Sid turned around and called down to them.

"Thanks, Mary!" he said.

Mary grunted, as if insulted, and Carla allowed herself to imagine the smile on her husband's face as he waved and turned away. Still watching him climb the hill, Carla suddenly felt lighter. Once again, Sid Mandt had surprised her – and Mary too – proving himself quick to recover from any wound, either to his body or to his stubborn pride.

Chapter 5

The first thing Carla noticed as she entered the clinic was the pile of clothes – Todd's bloodied coveralls and shirt, crumpled on the floor. She picked them up, intending to take them home. Once washed, they would hang on her clothesline alongside Sid's.

Todd was clearly in bad shape. He lay on the steel-frame bed, his left shoulder bandaged, the injured arm bound across his chest. Light seeped through the line of dingy windows and lit his face. Carla studied it without embarrassment. It was a likable face, she thought. Not as lean as Sid's, but quieter and more thoughtful, with a broad jaw and nose, wide like the beak of a barred owl. Todd's eyes, bright and congenial, were shut tight, shielding him against whatever awful sights he'd seen. Someone – Sid or the doctor – had wiped most of the grime from his cheeks. But not all of it.

Rubbing her forehead, Carla looked for a clean cloth. The doctor had gone to the mine. The whole camp would be there, waiting. Truman Bryant was missing, it was said. How many others? Carla could hear the fearful wives and children, searching for some hope as they sent up their prayers. Wondering whether prayers did any good at all, she watched Todd's chest rise and fall beneath the blanket and was aware of her own whispered voice, thanking the quiet air for his survival – and Sid's too, of course.

Tightening her jaw, she pulled the dark surplus blanket across Todd's bandaged chest. In doing so, she lightly touched his bare shoulder, then stroked it. Of all Sid's friends, Todd had been the kindest to her. She had arrived in Sovereign, new and "green," the previous spring, knowing nothing of life in the camp or in any other industrial town. Some of the men had made fun of her, she knew. Not Todd. A thoughtful man, he came around to visit, even when he and Sid had no business to conduct. Todd seemed to enjoy nothing more than being there for Sid. And for Carla too.

Todd stirred. He turned his head toward her, although his eyes stayed closed. Somewhat self-consciously, Carla put her hand against his cheek. There was no cloth, nor water for it. No, wait: A pitcher was on the bedside table. She poured water into a steel blue cup, and Todd opened his eyes. Recognizing her, he smiled.

"Hey, there," he said through his drug-induced fog.

Carla gripped the water cup with two hands.

"What kind of mess have you been in?" she asked, trying to sound like her mother.

"Damned good 'un, seems like," he said.

"How're you feelin'?"

Todd pondered the question, taking stock of himself. He stared for a long moment at the shadowed ceiling, letting his thoughts wander. When he looked at Carla, his tongue had started working his dry lips. She remembered the cup in her hand.

"Here," she said. "Take this."

Todd closed his eyes and drank, oblivious to the fluid spilling down his neck. Now, passing her fingers across his skin, she thought nothing of it. Todd's eyes closed and Carla felt alone in the room again, though relieved to see he'd be all right. She wondered then when Todd would be able to tell her what had happened in the mine.

A single knock sounded from an adjacent room. Carla looked toward the frosted-glass window of a door. A second staccato *thunk* sounded. She stood and went to the door, believing that maybe the doctor had returned. Instead, she pushed it open and was surprised to see the big mine guard, Gaujot. He was seated in the office chair, his knees spread wide, lobbing his knife into the air and letting it land, sticking into the floorboards.

Looking up at Carla in the doorway, the police guard captain smiled and rose. In that small moment, he seemed to welcome her, as if the office was his own. He retrieved his knife, sheathed it and approached her. Suddenly, he was close. Too close, thought Carla, as she backed against the doorjam. Gaujot's arm wrapped itself around her waist and she exhaled, resisting the urge to call out. There was no one else around, except for Todd.

Carla felt the wind go out of her as Gaujot's arm tightened around her midriff. Instinctively she put her own hands against his arms, but pushing him was like pushing a sycamore. The man was a giant. His bent-up face smiled down at her, his teeth evenly spaced. Then, he moved. Surprisingly, he took Carla and moved her around the room, dancing, as if in a happier family parlor. Carla struggled, but was further disoriented by Gaujot's voice, high and almost feminine. Remarkably, the Baldwin guard had begun to sing.

Tell me, little gypsy, what's my destiny?
I'll cross your palm with silver, if you try to see....

Carla looked away, unable to free herself. Gaujot moved her easily about the doctor's office, his face nuzzling the braids of her hair. He sang softly, enjoying himself in a way that baffled and terrified her.

Will the future bring me anyone?
Someone just for me...?

Carla struggled further, her anger growing. Balling her fist, she hit Gaujot's broad chest once, which seemed to astound him. Then, Carla's fury bubbled up from someplace deep inside, a pure and natural viciousness, as if she'd been born to it. She hit the mine guard again and a third time. She would have hit him more, had Gaujot not pushed her against a cabinet. From behind, Carla heard the sound of tumbling glass – bottles and books dislodged by their combined weight.

"No!" she cried, and was surprised at how short of breath she was. But Gaujot pressed himself closely to her, his nose and lips still moving in her hair.

"*There's a girl for every boy,*" he sang. "*There must be one for me....*"

"Carla?"

Gaujot stopped and they both turned toward the voice. Todd stood there, leaning impossibly against the door jam. He could barely raise his face, that strange dark mask atop his white, bandaged chest. Carla noticed his hands – one bound to his front – like a pair of dark gloves at the ends of his white arms, a painted marionette. Todd frowned at Gaujot with sad, bloodshot eyes. Todd was oblivious to his own appearance – to the coal mask and the fact that he wore no pants. His muscular legs emerged through loose-fitted underwear.

"Carla?" Todd said again, trying to keep his eyes focused. "I'd like your help."

Gaujot stared, his mouth open, then sneered. Prying herself away, Carla went to Todd, the unlikely hero. His tired eyes searched her face, seeking some connection.

"I'll get the doctor," she told him, not daring to look at Gaujot.

Todd nodded and, without looking back, Carla walked out, straightening her blouse, irrationally hoping that the company doctor might somehow come and fix what was happening. Todd teetered unsteadily on his feet. Gaujot considered letting him fall. Instead, he caught him up, accepting his full weight, despite the fact that Todd was almost as tall as

Gaujot himself. Barely conscious, Todd felt himself be taken around the hips and walked toward the bed. By appearances, Gaujot's act was one of compassion, except one hand had snaked around Todd to press against his bandaged elbow. There, Gaujot applied a not-so-gentle squeeze, just to hear his patient groan.

"Stay awake, little bird," the mine guard said. "We love to hear you sing."

Tears came to Todd's eyes as he felt himself dragged back toward his bed.

"Just so's you know," Gaujot whispered. "I can get that red-neck whore anytime I want."

"You son-of-a-bitch," Todd moaned, looking toward the bed. It seemed impossibly far away. "You've got no right."

Close to his ear, he heard Gaujot's high narcotic laugh.

"What can you do to stop me?" he said.

Harm Fox trudged up the creaking steps to his house. He could feel the second step going loose, needing another nail. A better man would have fixed it long ago, but Harm figured it would never happen. Not now. No sense in worrying about a house that didn't belong to him. And never would.

Harm was dog-tired, coming off a long shift of payless dead work. Like the others, he'd dug like crazy, hoping to find Truman and the other victims. How many had they lost this year? Harm couldn't think. He would have liked to have stayed at the mine. His only thought was how tired he was; how much he looked forward to the hot bath that Tildy prepared for him. After that and a few hours' sleep, he'd be able to rejoin the rescue.

Harm was mindful that this was the hardest time of day: at shift's end, well after dusk, when a man's hope tended to fail him. In such times, after his bath, he liked to pull out his banjo and play one of the ballads he knew. He loved the songs of men and women in olden times, whose troubles were of love and the consequences from it – troubles of a far different kind than those of Sovereign's miners whose work seemed never-ending. The hours grew longer even as the pay dwindled, all moving to a point that made Harm's blood boil. Aside from his banjo, Harm knew that hope for the union and a successful strike were the only things to sustain a man. Not just the men around him, in Sovereign, but scores of other mining towns. Up and down Big Coal, miners were being bled dry – and growing tired of it – while company managers kept up the pressure, turned the screws. They'd cheapened work too much, robbing the very life out of the people and their towns, bleeding like the steady discharge of iron-laden "red boy" seeping from the older mines, flowing scarlet into every other woodland creek.

As Harm climbed the steps, Tildy came out to meet him. Landing a sad kiss against his cheek, she hugged her Harm, showing no concern about the black dust that covered him.

"I've boiled two tubs," she said, wiping her eyes as well as her cheeks. "Two baths."

With this, all his anger fell away, and he smiled openly at her.

"Any sign?" Tildy asked him.

"No," said Harm. "Not yet."

Shrugging off the shoulder straps of his coal-encrusted coveralls, Harm shed himself of them, right on the porch, something many miners did to help keep their houses a little cleaner. He peeled off his shirt, handing it to Tildy, then spotted Lowcoal Petry exiting his place, a few doors up the row. Lowcoal waved and, without a word, strode down to plant one boot square against Harm's rickety bottom step. Under Low coal's weight, Harm noted with satisfaction, the plank barely made a creak.

"What news?"

Harm sat down, clasping his loose underwear with a palsied hand. He puffed his words.

"We might be half-way through," he said. "The gas is gone, at least." A new thought occurred to him.

"Did you see Sid? Looks like he got thumped."

"Damn," muttered Lowcoal. "How bad?"

Harm shrugged.

"Hard to say. He ain't talkin' much. Been down there workin' like anything."

"Is he riled?" asked Lowcoal.

"What do you think?"

Harm wiped his chest with his shirt and looked up toward the mine. His thoughts carried him back ten years, to a similar time and place.

"Bad time for this to happen," he said. "I think everything's gettin' ready to bust."

Lowcoal nodded. Having heard what he needed to hear, he pulled his foot from Harm's front step and went quickly up the hill.

Still in his underwear, Harm turned toward his own front door but was surprised to see Mary Rising's blond boy, Nick, staring at him from the next porch.

"Hey, young nugget!" Harm smiled.

Like a squirrel, Nick scrambled over the far porch rail, disappearing from sight. Just then, Mary emerged from Sid's and Carla's door. Frowning at Harm, she dumped basin water over the porch rail, as if she was aiming it at him. Harm turned away, almost running into Tildy, who greeted Mary as soon as she saw her.

"Well, hello, sister!"

Moving past her husband, Tildy tracked down the steps as Mary put the basin down.

Harm watched the two sisters embrace, Mary's face appearing at Tildy's shoulder. He searched her eyes for any hint of recognition, but couldn't find it.

"We're waiting to hear on poor Truman," Tildy told her.

"These are bad times," Mary responded tonelessly. Tildy looked at her.

"It's harder yet," Tildy said. "The men were fixin' to strike today."

Mary's mouth went tight.

"Yours is all for it, I suppose," she said, not looking at Harm.

As if I wasn't here, he thought.

Tildy folded her arms and Harm watched to see whether his wife would rise to take the bait.

"He's been gone close to ten years, Mary. When will you make peace with him?"

Harm's heart swelled with pride. How could anyone stand up to Tildy Fox, his bold lady? But Mary looked away, up the hill, toward the mine.

"Can't say a thing I don't feel," she said. "Best we not discuss it."

Tildy shook her head.

"We're all suffering, Mary," she said. "But how you carry yours about! For years, these men have gotten beat up and down, every way there is. What choice is there, but to fight it?"

Scorn filled Mary's eyes.

"Let 'em," she chided. "But fightin' is no substitute for work. I've worked my land most of these ten years. That's fight enough for me."

Tildy let it pass. She stood, looking sadly at Mary whose face, although younger, seemed twisted up into something old. Sighing, Tildy put her arm on her sister's shoulder and whispered, as if they were children again.

"I was up there most of the morning, with them other women, waiting. Poor Truman Bryant. And the boys. The older one is hurt so bad, and they got no one else. Please, Mary, think of them before you speak your pain."

Mary looked aside, but didn't try to pull away.

"This same-old talk," she scowled.

Smiling sadly, Tildy calmly took Mary's arm. Together, they walked slowly up the steps into Sid and Carla's place.

Harm watched, leaned over the porch rail and coughed for a long moment before spitting into the dirt. He looked himself over: a man of skin and denim, muscle and bone – soiled and ruined by the coal, inside and out.

Damn, he thought, clapping his hand against the post. *My bath's going cold.*

Later that night, Harm had a dream he didn't forget when he woke.

He and Tildy had been out in a meadow, under a stormy gray sky. They'd been lying in the grass, kissing, and Harm would smile to recall this part. How long had it been since he'd had a dream like this?

But, there he was, kissing his wife when a truck drove up beside them. High in the big truck bed, some men called down to him.

"Hop in, Harm!" they said. "Come with us!"

Without a second thought, Tildy jumped into the cab, so Harm climbed up into the back with all the rest. Men and women, all sitting there, greeted him, the same look of expectation on their faces. Now, the truck started to roll across the field, with Tildy at the wheel.

The big machine climbed the hill and kept going up. Then, it rounded the top – but fast. It sailed into the air before tipping downward and landing on the other side with a solid bump. The people sitting in the back just kept talking, but Harm couldn't make out what was being said. Then the truck went up a second hill. Trees floated past, as the machine went off the top, its momentum carrying it off the ground again. The truck sailed up, farther into the sky and Harm could see across a wide distance. He smiled and looked around the truck bed, surprised to see Truman Bryant sitting on the bench beside him.

"You got your lamp, Harm?" Truman smiled. Harm searched all around, looked under his bench and everywhere. His safety lamp was nowhere to be found.

"I don't think I brung it."

By then, the truck was soaring off another hill. Harm felt it rise, tip forward and fall again toward the next green valley. Wind blew in his face. The next mountain came at them, fast. Then, suddenly, the hillside opened up and the truck barreled down, straight into the mine mouth. All around him, people cried out at taking the unexpected ride down into the hole.

Now awake, Harm still heard the voices. Tildy moved in the bed next to him, asleep but fully dressed. Harm rose, plucked a damp pair of denims from the porch line, and strained his ears to hear the shouting. He couldn't pick up any words, but the news was clear enough. One way or another, the missing miners had been found.

Chapter 6

Lowcoal Petry had been the first to squeeze through, puzzling his way around the rocks, nearly cutting himself on the crumpled mine car. He hedged his Davy lamp in first, tipping it sideways into the tunnel and stared, not daring to breathe until he was certain. The flame burned low and steady.

"She's clear!" he called. "I'm goin' in!"

Hopeful and terrified, Gibbs moved forward into the hole, calling his father's name. There was no answer.

He and Sid pried away more rocks, then followed Lowcoal. Together, they scrambled through the hole, then down the pile of rock into the tunnel they'd fled the day before.

Gibbs didn't have to go very far to find the room, filled with stale air and deadly still. Lowcoal waited there, watching. Their lamps reflected sparkling stars from the walls of gleaming coal and the room's rock-shadows changed with every move. Ben Tate and Darko came in behind, followed by Dix Mace and another two, Vick Mattern and Dan Jakes. They all gathered around Gibbs, who stared down at his father's body. It lay with the others, twelve, in all.

"Lord have mercy," Lowcoal muttered.

Ben and Dix went about, checking each man for signs of life. They wandered around the ring of corpses like cautious priests in a sanctuary. Their lights raised, the two miners shook their heads as they lay their hands on the dozen unmoving chests. Making crosses in the air with his blackened fingers, Darko Dresser uttered words in his mother tongue, somehow recognizable to everyone as "Our Father...."

More rescuers crawled in, their headlamps illuminating the strange tableau: The dead men had lain themselves down in a circle, the living spokes of a wheel. At their center, the hub, a smaller ring of lunch pails lay open at their feet. Waiting for their rescuers, the victims clearly had shared a final meal before suffocating in the big black killing jar.

Gibbs picked up Truman's lunch bucket and saw the note his father, or someone else, had scratched into the tin: STRIKE. Gibbs read the word as he heard the unbroken sound of the pump, the dripping water around him, all so much louder to his ear since early that morning. No longer did Gibbs believe that he or his father or anyone had the power to listen to the mine, to hear any kind of genuine warning from the rocks.

The miners stood around the bodies of their friends as Ben Tate crawled up to the entry-way and whispered something past the hole. Immediately, the harsh word spread: "They're found! Twelve men! All dead!"

The men of Sovereign remained silent as the news traveled, amplified, echoing up the tunnel.

"Oh, God.... All dead!"

"...They's all dead...!"

Gibbs crouched down and studied his father's sleeping coal-stained face. Fooled and unsteadied by the wavering light, the young miner instinctively reached out and clasped one cold hand. Something fell from it and rolled metallic along the mine floor: A brass warning whistle. Gibbs picked it up, recalling the last alarm – how Truman had tried to save more men. Life seemed so fragile now. The rancid air grew heavy in Gibbs' lungs. His own breath came short. He didn't feel the mourning, though. Not yet. He looked to his friends, who stood watching him, quieted.

"Come on," said Lowcoal, his voice shaking. "Let's get 'em out."

Registering some undefinable quality of the moment, Sid Mandt straightened.

"While we're at it," he said, "let's pull our tools."

The others looked at him, surprised to hear, at last, the words they'd been waiting for all week.

"Now, Sid?" asked Ben, disbelieving.

"Yeah, buddy. Now's the time."

They stared at him, needing more.

"You want to die like these men here?" Sid asked. "With nothing more than a shovel and beat-up bucket to your name? Cheated at every claim-check, for every ton of coal that should be two? Which one of you men wants to keep on like this? Watching your kids starve to death? Our wives getting mail-order catalogs for all the things we can't never afford? Which of you wants to look back on all this when your time comes?"

"Not me!" Lowcoal chimed.

"Every one of you is signed-up for the union," Sid went on. "And the company's gonna know it soon enough. We need this union, and the only way to get it is to strike. I'm tellin' you, boys: We better turn these lunch pails over now, tonight, because we might not get another chance."

"Amen!" said Lowcoal. "Amen to that!"

He bent down and, performing the workers' rite of protest, turned one of the dead men's lunch containers upside down. Gibbs reached out and reversed his father's dented meal bucket, spilling out an old crust of bread. The scrawled message -- STRIKE -- showed in Gibbs' lamp light, and the others noted it as they went around the inner ring. One by one, they turned the dead men's pails onto their bent rims.

Pull your tools! We're pullin' out! On strike!

Their voices rose through the black mausoleum, the volume growing beyond anyone's control.

Turn your Davys low! By God, we're walkin' out! Pull your tools!

Gibbs tilted his headlamp up to see Sid's face. Beneath the bruises and coal-etched lines of sweat, his friend's eyes were fierce with anger and exhilaration. Electrified, Gibbs heard the sound of his words – *It's a strike! We strike!* – and knew the truth of it: His father lay dead beside him. There was nothing more to lose and everything to gain.

Strike! Strike! Strike!

The more the word was shouted, the more it rang. It gripped the emotions of every man who took it up. The black chamber filled with new life, a thing of passion and rebellious anger. Gibbs clutched his father's warning whistle, a talisman, and Sid let go with a rebel yell. The others joined in and, like a pack of wolves, they shared a common voice. Instantly, men outside howled too. Tilting his head back, Gibbs opened his mouth and joined the chorus of miners whose angry cries soon overcame the dark.

Outside, Carla searched the mine opening for Sid. At last, he appeared amidst the shouting, leading a gang of men toward the houses, all of them marching with their fists raised in rage.

Strike! Strike! Strike!

Sharing the excitement, Carla took in a sudden breath. Sid's devotion to the union had been something he'd held close, and for longer than she'd known him. Carla hardly dared to hope for it, for this new beginning. Things would certainly change now – for him, and her and all their friends. Carla heard the voices of the miners. She wanted to join in, sure that they would win. They had to win. It was the only way that she and Sid could begin the life she'd imagined for them. A better life in a safer place; among good, solid neighbors. With children....

Carla watched the men roust others from their houses, declaring their freedom.

Strike! Strike! No work tomorrow! Rise up!

This was Sid's time, she thought. The result of so much planning. No one had expected it to come like this, though. Not with dead men in the mine. Their moment of liberation was draped in an awful tragedy.

The rough pallbearers came down the hill and lay the twelve corpses, side-by-side, on the sparce grass. Carla turned her attention to the faces around her, to the miserable wives and dazed children. The women drifted reluctantly toward the bodies, each to her own. And yet, Carla saw how each woman continued to respond in subtle ways to the needs of those around her, how each consoled the others. More than anything else, this moved her.

In some of the children, however, she could see a hardness, just forming. She knew their thoughts and shared their sense of life's pure swindle; the unfairness of it, having to mourn a good man who died too young. A good father. As Carla watched, sad survivors eyed the mob -- at the men who now passed among the housing rows. Without warning, a few of the women and kids turned away, and left the hillside. They joined the others, rousing the whole camp and raising the protest. For Carla, the very air shook with the rage of these women and children, furious at the no-hope work that had taken their good, strong men and carried them off to die.

Gibbs Bryant came and found them – Carla, Harm and Tildy Fox -- by the body of his father. They stood together, lit by the harsh industrial light of the arc lamp from the tipple. Gibbs was out of breath from shouting. He stared at the body of his father, smaller and more frail than he remembered. Tildy moved to him, taking Carla with her. Carla found herself mirroring her aunt, reaching out to touch one of Gibbs' shoulders and then, with Tildy, embracing him.

"I'm sorry," she said, trying to make herself heard above the noise.

Strike! Strike!

Gibbs accepted their embraces, then pulled away and thanked them both. To hear his voice, Carla was momentarily surprised. Unlike Sid, Gibbs had never been too emotional, always expressing himself with a silence that became its own unsettling presence, a thing others often interpreted as "meanness." She'd always thought that Gibbs nurtured a silent hostility toward the rest of the world. Now, Carla could see that there was more to him than that.

"I have to go tell Todd," he said, looking first at Tildy and Harm before glancing back toward the houses, at Sid and the angry miners.

Strike! We strike now! Pull your tools! Down with thug rule!

Suddenly, Lowcoal's voice could be heard above the rest.

The Baldwins! There they are, goddamnit!

Two black-suited mine guards had been spotted by the barn. They were just now scrambling into their truck. Carla recognized one as Gaujot, the man who'd grabbed her that day. From someplace deep inside, her fury was rekindled. Some of the angriest miners were moving down the hill, shouting at the truck, and she was glad of it.

There they go! Let's get those bastards!

She turned and Gibbs was watching her. Instantly, she recognized his eagerness to join the chase. Then, with some guilt, his eyes went to the body of his father.

"Go on," said Carla, almost without thinking. "I'll stand with him."

In the next moment, Gibbs was racing down the hill with the others, chasing the fleeing Baldwins.

Gaujot turned in the passenger seat, trying to recognize the men who, having failed to catch the truck, were reduced to throwing rocks at it. Beside him, at the wheel, Mouseface Moler cursed every time a stone connected with the vehicle, slamming against the metal with a loud report. Under a tarp in the truck bed behind them, cowered a terrified – and increasingly bruised – commissary manager. Moler cursed again. "Those sons of bitches have no respect for a good machine!"

"It's not like it's yours," Gaujot said, still turned around in his seat.

Big and fearsome as he was, the Baldwin captain had learned one thing about labor strikes. If your side lacked the manpower, it was best to get out fast. The union men had won. For now, at least. They'd be getting the word out to the other mining camps.

"Goddamn," Mouseface said. "I left my best boots back in that office."

Gaujot shook his head. The truck shook as it crossed another creekbed.

"No going back tonight," he said.

The engine sputtered. Leaning over the steering wheel, Mouseface chafed at their need to hurry.

"I sure don't like to turn tail and run," he said. "Especially from those dirty reds. That sonovabitch."

He glanced down at his bloodstained front, hating to see the stain on his suit, his ruined Baldwin uniform. When the lurching steering wheel allowed it, Mouseface used one hand to touch his tender nose.

"I'd like to get some more of that red," he scowled.

Gaujot grimaced. "Your horse rear up on you, did he?"

Mouseface tensed, bracing himself against the shock of crossing the rocks of another creek. He shifted gears. The motor groaned as they climbed the next hill.

"We'll get all the help we need," Gaujot said. "Tell any friends you've got: Sheriff'll be hiring now."

Gibbs watched the truck lights wobble off, disappearing up the mountain. Turning, he opened the door into the dark infirmary. He found Todd in the clinic. Gibbs was relieved to see a clean bandage across his brother's chest, although some blood had come up through the gauze. Now and then, Todd's expression showed pain, seeping through his medication. For a moment, he lay quiet and Gibbs was reminded of how the men had found their father, sleeping deep in the mine.

"I'm sorry, bo," he said. "We didn't get him out in time."

Pinched and pale, Todd's face turned toward him. At first, Gibbs thought he hadn't understood. His brother's voice was surprisingly quiet and calm.

"Yeah, I figured it," he said. They were both quiet for a long moment before Todd spoke again.

"Life don't give us too many choices, does it?"

Gibbs nodded. Outside, angry miners searched the camp for Baldwins.

"What's all the noise?" Todd asked.

"Sid called the strike," said Gibbs. "Everybody's walkin' out."

Todd nodded as something crashed outside.

"That's Sid and them," Gibbs said. "Finally lettin' off some steam."

Todd frowned, his eyes trying to focus on Gibbs.

"Tell Sid, he should be meeting. Organizing. Getting the word out. Makin' sure others come out with us. Go tell him to get 'em settled down."

Gibbs squinted at the hillside, where Carla Mandt stood watch.

"Damn, Todd," he said. "I can't tell that to Sid. There's hardly any stoppin' them – even if I wanted to."

Todd shook his head.

"Get out of here, then. I'm tired. Need to sleep."

Days later, Sheriff Riley Gore sat comfortably in the back seat of his touring car. He pulled one of the two handkerchiefs he always carried and, despite the cool air, mopped sweat from behind his neck.

"Goddamned heat," he told the driver. "Gonna wilt my collar."

The car's position gave the sheriff a good view up the housing row, where almost thirty guards, half of them green, "cleaned the slate." Gore didn't necessarily enjoy this part of the work. He didn't like watching people get evicted from the properties they had taken to be their own. But right was right. Men had to live with the consequences of their decisions. Clearly, someone at the Sovereign Coal Company had been too indulgent. Now, the damage was done, with troubles broad and deep.

The unionists had gotten the drop on him and his men. But these

37:4

things happened. Gore was confident his men would set things right, helping Sovereign Coal get a new start. It might not be easy, but Riley Gore had no doubt of his ability and his influence. With his force of Baldwin deputies working alongside his uniformed county officers, the Logan sheriff was simply the most effective man around.

Gore pulled a silver flask from his white jacket, unscrewed the lid and took a sip. The warmth coursed through him like an inspiration. He watched up the row, where his guards were moving toward one of the last houses.

"Men're doing all right," he muttered.

The uniformed driver nodded his agreement, looked to one side, touched the bill of his hat to acknowledge the arrival of Captain Gaujot, coming down the hill toward them.

"Men're doing all right," Gore said again for Gaujot's benefit. The big Baldwin captain clasped the sheriff's fleshy hand, extended from the car. Together they watched the black-uniformed Baldwin guards at work. Three teams, each of six men, oversaw the moving of people's belongings, variously tossed or stacked before the last front porches. The sheriff squinted to appraise the nearest pile of things that someone had left behind. Gore shook his head at the pitiful heap: a cracked table, a broken phonograph. Some ragged clothing in a busted suitcase.

"How many are left?" he asked.

"Less than twenty," Gaujot responded. "The men are nailing shut the doors."

"Leave the nail heads high," the sheriff warned. "Company's gonna want to get replacements. Or we'll bunk some of your men in there."

Gaujot gave him a blank look.

"It's called 'personnel management'," the sheriff drawled. "Human-element control, Pearl. Like a doctor removin' a disease. These people have to learn that they can't ignore their contractual obligations. Breaking an agreement with your employer is breaking the law."

At Gore's mention of his first name, Gaujot winced, glancing uneasily at the uniformed deputy in the driver's seat. The sheriff was the only employer ever to call him "Pearl." Ever. Gaujot could have had the name changed long ago, but didn't. It was the only thing from his mother that he'd kept.

Gaujot eyed his men working on the hill. As he watched, one Baldwin grew impatient and kicked a teenage boy. True to their training, the other guards circled, keeping the situation contained. If he'd noticed the melee, Sheriff Gore gave no indication of it, continuing to speak to his own thoughts.

"Bring these workers back to proper values," he was saying. "Any man who bites the hand that feeds him disrupts productivity. They're destroying the very spirit of their company and the community in which they live. Just as bad as destroying property. Or theft."

The miners had no idea, as Sheriff Gore did, of the larger competition in which they were involved. The sheriff had been a manager for the Sovereign Coal Company and was now proud to serve it and all the other members of the Southern Coal Association as Logan County's chief law-enforcement officer. The coal producers, Gore's clients, had been locked in fierce competition against bigger firms from Maryland to Wyoming. For Gore, the principal rule of the game was simple: Keep your costs lower than the other man's. In bad times like this, even a successful coal manager could be traded away like a piece of beef. Good ones trimmed the fat, freeing their employers from unnecessary expenses. Now, since the end of the war, belt-tightening was a must for anyone wanting to survive. Generous end-of-the-year bonuses went to any manager who could turn in high reductions, especially in labor costs.

Gore reopened his flask and, on a sudden whim, offered it to Gaujot. The big officer didn't drink. He knew better, however, than to turn down anything from the most powerful boss he'd ever had. Gaujot faked taking a hit from the flask before handing it back to the sheriff. Riley Gore smiled approvingly and, from his rear seat, stroked the side panel of the car.

Gaujot cleared his throat. "There's something else," he said.

Gore's big chief deputy led him up the quiet housing row, past the work crews digging post holes. Ever the politician, the sheriff waved and greeted everyone he saw. Curious, he followed Gaujot up the steps of one house. Outside, it looked like all the rest.

"We believe this man was one of the union leaders," Gaujot explained.

"Where's your evidence?"

Inside, Gaujot strode to the bedroom, where he'd pried the floorboard free. Reaching down, he pulled out the book and pamphlets, laying them out on the bare bed springs. Gaujot told Gore what he'd learned: The union had been better-organized than anyone had known. The strike was spreading fast. At least twenty-five camps were affected already, although none with participation as high as Sovereign's – good evidence that the subversive activity was centered here. After their company evictions, the strikers were making an encampment at the town of Blair, just beyond the county line. They were setting up camp on the fairground, property held by an independent owner.

Sheriff Gore scowled at the news as he stood with Gaujot in what had been Sid and Carla's living room. The sheriff stared at the wall, shaking his head at the message in the plaster. In rough letters, shot with bullet-holes, it spelled "UNION."

"I can only imagine how it's come to this," Gore said sadly. "Infected. Heart and soul."

He turned to Gaujot.

"Destruction of property, Pearl. We'll have to fix this. Call the way-ward children home."

The sheriff sighed again.

"We'll give this man his day at court. Have Judge Hastie send him a summons. Set it up for Tuesday next."

Chapter 7

Trader Mary drove her pennant-garnished wagon down the rutted road to Blair. Approaching the first wooden bridge, she could see the hard-packed Main Street that bisected the little town. On the left side, a cut-off string of clapboard shops nestled in the shadow of a steep hill chain that people called "Blair Mountain." On the opposite side stretched a line of wooden two-story houses. Once owned by the railroad, every building was painted the same shade of blue.

Even before she reached the bridge, Mary could see people stopping to stare at her wagon, festooned with colorful lines of tapered flags. Well-used to the attention, she kept her eyes forward. Mountain people always came out to greet her and the children when they appeared, the wagon full of corn, eggs, apples, tobacco and handmade goods for sale or trade. Kids ran alongside, their hands reaching out to touch the streamers, the long strings of triangular flags that Nick had once pulled up from the mud of a flooded fairground.

Mary cursed at Swift to quicken his pace and gave Nick a sidelong glance as they crossed the bridge. Immediately, the boy jumped from his seat and ran happily alongside the wagon like a village hound.

Mary turned to check on Todd. The big miner leaned uneasily in the rocking wagon bed, his big boots planted as wide as he was able. His knees knocked against Sid and Carla's things: a rough table, two chairs, a ragged valise. With his eyes tightly shut, Todd tried to hold his shoulder steady, the good arm wrapped around Mary's old camel-back trunk.

She returned her attention to the horse, recalling the time, years ago, when she'd gotten away from her parents for good, landing eventually in Blair. Here, she'd met Bonner Rising who took her up the mountain, to that piece of land he loved. Mary had packed a trunk with her belongings, her wedding dress, since traded away to another drummer.

"You doin' all right?" she asked, interrupting her own thoughts.

"Sure," Todd nodded. His eyes were shut.

Twenty years ago, the town of Blair had been a lively, populated place. It was in a prime location, the meeting point of several narrow-guage rails, each one worming its way up some coal-rich creek or hollow. Every weekend, cars had brought miners from their camps by the hundreds. At night, they lit up the streets, alive with the noise of serious trade and petty larcenies. Blair was the only town around where almost any male, female and pubescent child could get a drink at three saloons.

The mine owners couldn't trust anything they didn't own, however. Workers who came to Blair on a weekend were often slow to return to camp. Mine guards, on the weekend, had to make the rounds at all the bars, picking up men and hauling them off to jail, giving them adequate time to recover by their Monday-morning shifts. Otherwise, mine managers were happy to find and subsidize itinerant preachers, who came in and blanketed the region with self-righteous pamphlets. These became familiar tracts, sermonizing that "good and loyal workers" were well-warned to stay away from Blair.

But Mary, like so many others, had been drawn to the place. She was young and literate, eager to escape the fate of her own mother, who'd married badly. She'd arrived in Blair about a year before meeting Bonner Rising, and was lucky to find decent work. Cleaning rooms at the boarding house hadn't been an easy job, but it was instructional. Mary's country-girl notions were quickly lost. In time, she realized how her background had prepared her, helping her get through a hard day's work without complaint while, somehow, keeping her integrity.

She had first seen Bonner among a circle of friends on the boarded sidewalk before the mercantile. The fact that everyone called him "Bone" did not endear him to her. Yet, Mary saw him as a sober and easy-going man, perhaps a little too happy to chat with any stranger that came along – logger, land attorney, begger or thief. A man was a man to Bonner, and therefore a potential friend. By the time she met him, Blair had become too wild. Mary was past twenty then and had grown tired of the local people, fretting and buzzing like bees; and the men at the boarding house, each one presenting himself as something special, mouthing the same dreams and promises as every other.

In this, Bonner Rising was easier to like than most. Like none of the others, he spoke of wanting a place in the mountains. Here, Mary thought, was someone who could take her away from town, to a home of her own. Who knows why such things happen?

With a sharp tug on the reins, Mary slowed her horse to a trot. She looked around Blair, surprised at the number of people pacing up and down its Main Street. On the left, they passed a succession of shops – a doctor's office, a paint-peeled dress store, a tack and livery place. Todd waved to two friends from Sovereign who stood before the railway station.

Suddenly Nick was back in the wagon bed, settling in beside him. With a satisfied grunt, Nick looped his hand around the miner's good arm and raised his other hand before his face, wiggling his fingers against the sky. Todd smiled down at the boy. Then, wincing, the miner reached into his vest, retrieving a thin glass bottle the doctor had sneaked to him. Awkwardly, Todd used one hand to pull the stopper, licked a single pill from the tilted lip, then replaced the cork and tucked the bottle away. Nick eyed the glass bottle with interest.

Mary slowed and stopped the wagon. Sitting there, she gave herself the luxury of a long look at the old stone building, the last one in the row and standing on a rise, like a white fortress.

Even boarded-up, as it had been for years, the old Holland Mercantile dominated every other place in Blair. Its two floors were marked by even rows of windows, with walls that had been the work of Italian stone masons. The artisans had given the building some hint of their ancient homeland, its two great wings joined, front and back, by two parallel colonnades of pillars, partially visible from the street. Mary remembered the pillared courtyard, open to the sky. There'd been a garden there, in the middle, where Bonner met her after work.

"This used to be the main way into town," she commented to Todd, nodding toward the boarded-up mercantile. She was almost tempted to go up the steps and try the door.

"A man named Holland built it," she said. "He sold things you just couldn't get anywhere else – steel axes and fishing reels, steel ploughs and licorice candy. That was on the right side. On the left, he had the saloon."

She recalled Bonner and his friends. The miners, railroaders and people of all kinds who always filled the store.

"Holland got himself elected mayor," said Mary, half to herself. "They said he worked as much public business in the saloon as he did behind his desk. Finally, around 1913, the Sovereign Coal Company bought him out. They said they'd keep the mercantile open; said they'd even keep the name. But Holland didn't care. He moved to Chicago and the company just boarded up the place. Gave it over to the bugs and rats."

The heart and soul of Blair had died with the closure of the mercantile. It stood, nailed shut, while other businesses limped along – the railroad station, a post office, the restaurant and feed store. Declaring victory, the teetotaling preachers had shut down almost everything but the church, and then abandoned even that, relegating memory of Blair's riotous past to the stuff of their eternal pamphlets.

Getting no response from Todd, Mary turned to look at him. The young man was sitting upright and staring past the town's grand entry-way – a covered bridge, a great red wooden box that spanned the town's second creek. Todd was looking beyond this, however; to the wide fairground on the far side of the brook, where hundreds of miners were busy raising their canvases. The tents were going up slowly, row by row, like a phalanx of flags rising in the sun. Todd seemed ready to hoist himself over the wagon's sideboard, his injured arm be damned.

"You just hold tight," Mary told him flatly, and cursed Swift toward the rust-colored bridge, big and welcoming. The wagon wheels rattled the boards as they crossed beneath the wooden rafters, rolling onto the solid ground of the other side.

"Would you look at this," Todd muttered.

By the creek, teams of men pried and hammered at piles of wooden pallets, re-configuring them as flooring. When a platform was complete, a new crew circled and carried it off, dropping it into place on an empty patch of ground.

Crews of hardened miners and their families shuttled about the field, lugging ragged suitcases and iron stoves. Pairs moved along the tent-lined avenues, cutting canvases for insulated stovepipes. Here and there, chimneys rose from the new flue holes of finished homes, sending up the smell of hotcakes and wood smoke. On the far end of the camp, downstream, men dug latrines and built walls for them. Some grass-lined pathways were already becoming worn, even dusty, with new traffic.

Todd marveled at the sight of miners and their families everywhere he looked, in every stage of moving into camp. Men tightened tent lines and mothers called children away from their wild games of tag. Kids dodged each other among multiplying rows of canvas pyramids or wandered along the banks of Blackberry Creek. Before this moment, Todd had never realized just how big and powerful the union could be. Here was new and visible proof: hundreds of people working together to build a camp – their camp – all around him.

"Looks like we're in this for the long haul," he breathed.

Mary snorted.

"I'll be surprised if any of 'em lasts 'til winter," she said.

She was suddenly reminded of Sid's newest outrage, seeking to borrow her horse and wagon for his union business.

"I don't mind your moving Carla's things," she'd told him. "But not the other. And you should know better than to ask it of me!"

She steered Swift into a gap in the line of cars and carts and parked along the creek.

"You'll find Sid over there," she said and pointed Todd toward the railroad track. He thanked her and climbed down, tousling Nick's hair as he did.

"See you around, young'un."

He made his way along the rising railroad berm and waved to Sid, who stood at the top with several others from Sovereign – Harm Fox, Darko and Lowcoal. To Todd's eye, Sid looked like a general on the battlefield, in consultation with his officers.

"Congratulations, buddy," Sid grinned down as Todd approached.

"What for?"

"You're vice president of the American Mineworkers Union, Sovereign Local 467!"

He reached down to take his friend's good right hand. Todd winced as he allowed himself to be pulled up the railroad berm, joining the others there. He shook hands all around.

"Sid's the president," Lowcoal explained. "I'm the secretary. I beat Darko by ten votes!"

"No Croatian bohunk can be a union officer," Darko grumbled, although Todd could see the European wasn't too disappointed at having lost.

Todd looked over the crews building the tent city. At the end of a line of canvases, he spotted Carla. She wore a long jacket – Sid's jacket, Todd realized. It hung heavily on her, going well past her waist. Todd was aware of the blood pumping in his ears and was immediately embarrassed at the way his heart had begun beating double, just from seeing Carla from across the field. Not for the first time, he worried that Sid might notice.

Todd pretended to scan the field as Carla paused by a tent door, then suddenly turned to one side. He wondered whether she'd seen him arrive. She gave no sign of it. She walked from Tildy's tent across the way, to another canvas where someone was kneeling, hammering a tent stake. It was Gibbs.

"I got Gibbs helpin' the women," Sid smiled at him. "Might even him out some."

Startled, Todd looked at his friend, who eyed the field from beneath his felt slouch hat. Its brim was dipped low, as if Sid didn't care to be recognized. One cheek still showed its purple bruise.

"You boys are bunking across from me and Carla," he told Todd, then turned to Darko.

"Hey, Dark! How d'you say 'cigarette' where you come from?"

"I come from Brooklyn," Darko grinned. "There, we say 'cigarette.'"

Sid rolled his eyes. "Lemme have a smoke," he said.

Darko Dresser enjoyed having tobacco, a luxury he could only imagine years before, landing in New York Harbor without a nickel in his pocket. At age thirteen, Darko had moved in with an uncle, a boxing trainer. Soon, the boy had a job of his own at the gym. He trained there nights, hoping to get into the boxing ring himself one day. In time, he got his bookings and pulled down twenty-five dollars a match, win or lose. Darko believed he'd found his calling, the posters around the Bronx promoting him as 'Dark Horse Dresser,' his fans calling him "another Jack Johnson." It all came to an end, however, when Darko knocked out another fighter who couldn't be revived. Fearing deportation, the big Croatian slipped away, south, to the mines of Appalachia, where he found it easy to become "just another miner from New York."

Sid lit up the cigarette, sending smoke into the air. He was quiet for a moment, watching about twenty men, down in the middle of the field. They worked around a huge marquis canvas, spread out on the ground. Two great poles were moved into place and heavy guy-ropes splayed outward like the legs of a spider. When raised, the thing would be the size of a circus big top, good for community meals and meetings. For now, though, it looked like a giant piece of clothing drying in the sun, as the crew puzzled over the task of raising it.

"Harm," said Sid, turning to the older miner. "Better make sure the meal tables are ready. People're gonna be hungry when that big kitchen's up and running."

Harm nodded and ambled off toward the big tent, passing and waving to a team of men cutting kindling by a row of open stoves.

Todd continued to watch Carla, still talking with Gibbs.

"How's Carla handling it?" he finally asked.

"Hell, she's tougher than any of us around here," Sid snorted, giving Todd a sideways glance. "Just like her mother."

At the mention of Mary, Todd looked back to the wagon. There, Dix Mace and Ben Tate were pulling things off the bed. Sid's eyes moved to the covered bridge.

"Where're they headed?" he wondered aloud, and Todd noticed a new group arriving at the bridge. At the front, a knot of men stopped to stare at the field, looking baffled. The group pressed around them, dropping tied bundles and rolled blankets to the ground.

"I'd say they don't know," said Todd.

"Go meet 'em, Dark," Sid ordered, and Darko scrambled down the hill toward the newcomers.

"You all right?" Sid asked, turning again to Todd.

"Yeah," he said. "I'm tired of doing nothing, though. Ready to get back into it. What do *you* need, Sid?"

"By god," the union leader said. "We need to clean up these coal-fields. Kick the Baldwins' asses clean out of this state. That'd be the first thing on my list. But the union sees things different."

"What are they saying?" asked Todd.

"Tom Kenner and the leadership says we gotta push for union recognition. Get the company to sit down with him and me, as union representatives. Get them to talk, at least, about better pay, about fair weighing of the coal. If we dig a ton, we should get paid for a ton. And something for all the 'dead work' we have to do – checking for gas and putting up ceiling props. It's just as important as blasting and shoveling, but nobody gets paid for it."

"What about getting rid of the company police?" said Todd, glancing at Sid's bruised face. "It ain't right, having the Baldwin guards pushing people around in every coal camp, and the law on their side."

"That's on the list, lower down," sighed Sid. "But union recognition comes first. I don't like it much, but Kenner says that's what we have to do. Hammer on 'union recognition,' they say, and then we can get the rest."

Sid poked the air with his cigarette, trying to make rings. Todd closed his eyes, repeating the points.

"Union recognition. Fair weights and ceiling props. Then, a ban on the thugs...."

Sid smiled as he turned back toward the field. Drawing smoke from his cigarette, he watched Darko, talking with the new arrivals at the bridge.

"Another thing is this," Sid continued, lowering his voice. "We have to make sure the mines stay closed. As soon as we can, we have to get our picketers out to the biggest ones. If the company uses replacement workers to open up those holes again, we lose. We gotta keep the scabs out. You know?"

"Sure," said Todd. Sid glanced at him.

"It's gonna be rough, Todd. I hope we're all up to it."

Todd looked down, feeling suddenly awkward and out-of-place.

"I don't know what I can do to help," he said. "I feel like I almost botched you up already, with my arm and all."

Sid held the cigarette in his teeth, thinking.

"Nah," he said, removing it. "The men like you, Todd. They listen to you. Just keep to the points I told you. Talk to 'em. Make sure they know what's going on. We have to stick together in this. Everybody here, helping each other along and winning the strike. That's the main thing."

They watched as Darko led the new arrivals through the tent city, directing them to a line of lots on the northern edge. Soon, he was climbing back up to join his friends on the mounded railroad.

"It's a local come in from Slatey Fork," he told Sid. "A good many of 'em's Polacks."

Sid squinted down the field.

"You get 'em squared away?" he asked.

Darko nodded.

"Check on them later, will you?" Sid muttered. "They look like good builders. Get 'em working on a big bathhouse. And latrines, over by the far end of the creek."

Darko removed his cap.

"It'd be easier if they spoke good English," he said. "I swear, it sounds like so much gibberish down there."

"That don't matter none," Sid replied. "So long's they all say, 'Union'."

Darko laughed and, together, the three of them watched the work of the camp. Todd couldn't help but gaze over at Gibbs and Carla. Lowcoal had joined them, setting up their tents. Todd watched them work, wondering what they were talking about.

In fact, they were talking about him.

Gibbs looked up at the Blair Ridge, looming high behind the town.

"Did you miss all this – the mountains?" he asked. "Once you moved to Sovereign, I mean."

Carla thought about it and noticed that Lowcoal was listening too.

"I missed my childhood," she said. "Doing things with my father – and with Mama."

She could slaughter a chicken by the time she was twelve. Or even a goat, if her mother required it.

"But when Sid brought me to Sovereign," she said, "I didn't know a time clock from a steel can."

"Folks didn't take to you right away," Lowcoal offered, clearing a patch of grass for a tent stake.

"Folks get scared about something new," said Gibbs.

"Sid said that you boys stopped coming around his place," Carla told them, and looked at Gibbs. Her dark eyes seemed to bore straight into him.

"I know Todd kept coming," Gibbs offered, and Carla's face went blank for a moment.

"That's right," she admitted. "Todd kept coming."

They worked without talking for a moment, and Carla smiled, remembering something she'd heard Tildy say to a neighbor: *Carla can't be blamed for being backward! It's just how she was raised!*

Carla shared the memory with Gibbs and Lowcoal, making them smile.

"And you both made fun of Sid," she went on. "All of you tellin' him how he'd gotten some kind of 'wild catch' from the woods."

"Hell," said Gibbs, reaching for a hammer. "We were only jealous."

He caught himself and, red-faced, shot a glance at Lowcoal, who seemed to be busy with a tent stake, neither conceding nor arguing what he'd said. When he looked at Carla, she gave him a half-smile, taking his words casually – as something coming from a good and honest friend. Yet, Gibbs remained a little irritated with himself for yielding to the un-guarded moment. Exhaling, he gripped the hammer and returned to the job before him.

Later, the men of Sovereign sat down together for the day's hot meal in the meeting tent – sausages and cabbage stew made by a team of women. At the table, Sid talked earnestly about the future of the strike. The men ate their soup in silence, listening and nodding. Then Todd asked a question that had been playing on all their minds.

"What about the warrant, Sid?"

"What of it?"

"Aren't you worried by it?"

"Nope."

Sid pulled the official-looking paper from his pocket, flattened it against the table. Sitting next to him, Lowcoal plucked it up, squinted at it, and slapped it down again.

"I say it's wrote on gingerbread," he grinned. "Let's eat it for dessert."

Up and down the table, everyone laughed, but Sid shook his head.

"Naw," he said. "I'm going to it."

Lowcoal stared at him in disbelief.

"By god, man, are you crazy? They'll throw your ass in jail!"

But Sid leaned back easily, tucking the paper into his jacket.

"Sheriff Gore don't have time for me," he said. "Him and his Bald-wins don't know half of what I done. Besides, I been thinking it might be a way of get someone there to take our side."

Todd shook his head. "You can't do much good from jail, Sid."

"Gore made me a written promise," Sid argued, patting his jacket pocket. "I got 'safe passage' – so long's we don't bring no guns."

Gibbs felt the pressure rise in his chest.

"Goddamn, Sid!" he said. "You can't want to go into Logan without protection."

68

Sid gave him a wry smile. Here was Todd's little brother, who'd never showed so much interest in the union.

"Well, you just come along then," Sid goaded. "You be my protection."

Gibbs stared, unsure whether Sid was making fun of him.

"Damned right, we'll come," Lowcoal shot back. "Every goddamn one of us!"

Sid looked at them a moment. "Sure," he grinned. "A bunch of us going in together might get the sheriff and Sovereign Coal to change their minds."

The camp's pace slowed through the afternoon. Fewer families arrived to raise their tents. People talked about the future.

Sid was happy but exhausted as he joined Carla in their own canvas that evening. She'd been eager to see him, having spent the day putting their new home in order. When Sid finally came through the tent flap, she had just wiped the grime from the lamp glass and lit it, hoping it wouldn't smoke and smell of kerosene.

She told him about her day, showing him where she'd stowed the wood and extra water. Sid listened calmly, nodding at each pause but knowing he'd forget.

"I'm sorry to have been away so much," he said.

It made Carla smile.

"Makes it that much better when you're back," she said, taking his hand. Sid looked down.

"Mary gets on my nerves," he confessed.

"Mama worries. She thinks you put yourself in danger."

"What's it to her, if I do?" asked Sid.

Carla studied her husband's bruised face, a new cut along his jaw.

"It ain't just about you."

She sat on the bed, a tick mattress spread across the bare boards of the platform. Sid slid over next to her, put his arms around her.

"I take care of you," he said.

Carla turned to him, frowning.

"And what do I do if you go to jail?" she asked.

"I won't."

"How do you know?"

Sid grew irritated.

"Gore don't want me in his goddamn jail," he said.

Studying her face, he smiled again.

"We got plenty of things to worry about," he said. "But not tonight."

He got up and went to the doorway. With several short tugs, the door fell shut. Sid moved to the front table and pressed the steel arm of the lamp, lifting the glass globe. Bringing the thing up to his face, he puffed out the flame.

Soon, he was back on the bed, and Carla felt his powerful hands around her midriff. Sid moved on top of her, his palms closing around her breasts.

"I'd be a crazy man without you," he whispered.

Smiling, Carla shut her eyes. She could smell the kerosene, the stove ash and dying embers. The scent of bread came in from somewhere outside. Sid untucked her blouse and placed his calloused fingers against her skin. From the surrounding camp, now dark, she listened to the sounds of new encounters. A man chatted with someone as he re-hammered a tent stake into the ground. At the creek, some girls scrubbed dishes. A mother called a child home from play.

Sid's hands tricked blouse buttons from their slots. He pulled away Carla's clothes, exposing her.

"Get under the blanket," she whispered, aware of the urgency in her voice.

His mouth followed a line below her breasts, his tongue probing downward. There. And there. "Like the French," he'd told her, and Carla did nothing to discourage him.

Her hands alternately pushed and held him, establishing the places and the pace – neither too fast, nor too slow. Sid had surprised her with his ability to accommodate her, to hold himself back. Not like he was for his work and the union, for which he held back nothing.

Carla sighed as she stroked his close-cropped head, his straight jaw. Sid's insistence grew and she abandoned any thought of controlling his need. Or her own. Now, as he moved into her, she no longer noticed the sounds of the village around them, the muted voices, the smell of kerosene, or the flowing water of Blackberry Creek.

As Sid moved with more urgency, Carla opened herself to her own senses. The first hint of feeling returned, like hearing a familiar voice, neither his nor hers, the voice of a disembodied spirit Carla sometimes believed she kept hidden, safe, for the future.

Sid grunted, rocking softly the way she liked it, and Carla's joy grew as he gripped her tighter, grew inside and moaned his pleasure, almost like a cry. The sound aroused her further and Carla moved against him with more determination until her own resolution came.

In the ensuing stillness, she stroked the bruises on Sid's chest and ribs as he murmured the satisfaction preceding sleep – like a child, she thought. From someplace outside, a couple argued. A would-be lover whistled his tune across some distance, hoping it was recognized. A baby cried itself to sleep. Carla listened to these intimate sounds of strangers, excited by the prospect of this new place. She sighed, wondering whether they'd ever win a better life – whether they'd have what they needed to raise a family and Sid would be home more often. Here, with her. Like this.

Carla had sometimes doubted that any of it could come true. But Sid always assured her, always having a ready answer: "Don't worry," he told her. "We can bring the union. All the men are with us and the other side can't beat us when we're together."

He left no room for argument.

All of us, nested here like young squirrels, Carla thought as her husband slept. *Or mice. Or warbling birds at night....*

… Doubtless, the sheriff's power has grown,
along with his popularity. Some call him "King of Logan,"
enjoying close ties with the Southern Coal Association.
The SCA pays about $ 55,000 each year for the services
its members require of Logan's deputies.
"I know one private company that pays a sheriff's deputy $ 45 per
month in addition to his county salary," said one mine owner. "Another
might pay $ 50 for the same service – for escorting payroll or policing
the camps. It's a good arrangement. No one objects to it." ….

– from "Logan Sheriff Rules with Iron Fist"

Baltimore Globe, May 30, 1920

Chapter 8

Sunlight fought its way past the trees of the courthouse square, in Logan Township, although it had little effect on the brittle autumn air. Bundled together in worried knots, more than a hundred people had arrived for what they called "Sid's trial," except it was just a hearing before the magistrate.

Strikers strolled the streets around the courthouse, but not like they did in Blair, some ten miles distant, as the crow flies. The men walked warily, in groups, ambling about the square or idly appraising the brickwork of the buildings or the older sidewalks. Uniformed sheriff's deputies and pairs of black-suited Baldwin detectives sometimes appeared on the street, but never in any numbers and not for very long.

The largest group of Sid's friends waited uncomfortably before the Beacon Restaurant – called "the Bacon" by the locals – where Sid, his wife and friends had ordered coffee.

From their booth, Sid and Carla could see the steps to the courthouse, where three policemen stood and chatted, their hands in their pockets. Carla smelled the eggs and toast but wasn't hungry. Sid smoked a hand-rolled cigarette and laughed with his trio of "bodyguards," Gibbs, Lowcoal and Todd. A week after the mining accident, Todd's arm was still bound to his chest.

"Great day for a hangin', huh?" Sid grinned across the table.

"Dang, Sid," Todd scolded. "That ain't funny."

Carla gave him a look of gratitude.

"You all have got to stop worrying," Sid answered. "I figure we have at least a hundred men outside, and every of 'em ready to speak up for me in that courtroom. That judge will take one look at all of us, take my plca and tell us to go home. Hell, maybe he'll listen to what we have to say! ...Make the company give us our houses back."

Carla looked up to see the waitress by their table, asking whether they liked their coffee.

"Just fine, darling," Sid winked, and Carla made a face at him, drawing a laugh from Gibbs and Lowcoal. Embarrassed at Sid's behavior – and not wanting to look at Carla – Todd stared out the window.

"Uh-oh," he said. "Trouble coming."

The front door struck the bobbling shopkeeper's bell and Gibbs turned in time to see the big mine guard, Gaujot, come in and take a seat two booths away. Then came the other – the one who looked like a possum to Gibbs' eye – and, finally, Sheriff Riley Gore himself, dressed in his signature white suit. Walking in, Gore flashed his politician's smile around the room and waved to someone in the farthest corner.

Gibbs leaned forward, whispering.

"Sid," he asked. "Did you pack your gun?"

"No, dammit. The sheriff and I have a deal."

As if to emphasize the point, Sid nodded to Sheriff Gore, giving him a half-smile. Gore remained standing. "Nothing for us, thanks, Louise," he said loudly, sending the girl into retreat with her paper menus. His two deputies sat at their table, waiting, hands folded before them like schoolboys.

Carla tried to get a clear look at Gaujot. He seemed to stare through her, not seeing. Her hand went to a white parasol she had brought, a silly thing that Aunt Tilly had insisted she take along. Carla could never say no to Tildy. She glanced around the table. Sid eyed the sheriff and his men, quietly drinking his coffee. Carla was certain the lawmen had come to arrest her husband and said as much, whispering the words. Sid shook his head.

"They'd never get me past our men outside," he said, silencing her. "I got no end of protection!" He smiled at Gibbs and Lowcoal as he put down his emptied cup.

Then, without a word, Sheriff Gore and his officers rose. Gore raised his white Homburg hat to the room and, on his way out, used the open door to give the shop-keeper's bell an extra slap.

"Let's get this over with," said Sid, and got up to grab his own hat off the rack.

Todd scooted awkwardly from the booth. Gibbs, the keeper of their "treasury," paid Louise.

"Don't forget your umbrella," the waitress called and handed it to Carla who smiled and, with some effort, thanked her.

Outside, they found one hundred union men on the sidewalk, some with their wives, waiting to stand with Sid in court. Gibbs took his brother's good arm and they waded through the group. Walking along a retaining wall at the bottom of the courthouse hill, they stayed behind Sid and Carla who suddenly smiled and waved.

"Uncle Harm!"

Harm Fox pushed his way through to kiss his niece, then put a big, aging hand on Sid's arm and pulled him off, to one side. Todd, Gibbs and Lowcoal gathered around them, screening away the crowd. Harm produced a small handgun, a thirty-eight. He held it out to Sid.

"I want you to take this," he said, but Sid was looking away, up the hill, stretched on his toes to see the courthouse. Returning his attention to the old miner, he gently pushed the gun back.

"Thanks, Harm," he said. "But I don't need it."

"Take it! Put it in your damned pocket!" Harm insisted. "Just in case...."

But Sid refused.

"Harm," he grinned. "Look at all these folks who showed up to be my witnesses!"

With that, Sid pulled Gibbs over.

"Come 'ere, bodyguard. You explain it to him," Sid said, placing Gibbs between himself and Harm.

Then, Sid pushed ahead with Carla, who switched her handbag and parasol to take his arm. Carla tried to smile at him, but was too afraid. As they came to the long courthouse steps, she thought of turning around, forcing Sid to get back on the train to Blair.

No use in that, she thought, hearing her mother's voice.

Can't tell that man anything.

Left to themselves, Gibbs, Todd and Lowcoal remained in a tight circle centered around the gun, still balanced in Harm's open hand.

"Best put it away, Harm," Todd said. "His mind's made up."

Harm returned the pistol to his pocket.

"By god, he's bull-headed, ain't he?"

"You got that right," said Lowcoal and, together, the four began to work through the crowd again. They were well behind Sid and Carla, and couldn't close the gap before the couple was almost halfway up the steps to the courthouse door.

Carla stopped to look around, and realized that the familiar faces of their friends were gone. All the Sovereign miners, in fact, had been pushed off by a sudden crowd of men, all plainclothes detectives and uniformed deputies. Carla realized she and Sid were walking a gauntlet of Baldwins who had formed a line, two and three deep, all the way to the top of the steps. At a landing, she hesitated, letting go of Sid's arm. Before them, two policemen moved aside, making room for one of the Baldwins who stepped out – the rodent-faced man from the restaurant. His gun was drawn. Carla stopped cold, certain he was putting Sid under arrest. On the opposite side, two more officers drew weapons.

Sid's hand briefly reached for his wife. He turned and looked at her for what seemed like a long moment before pushing her away. Going to his jacket, his hand touched the pocket that, Carla knew, held the sheriff's letter. Then the shooting started.

Carla watched in horror as Mouseface took careful aim with his pistol and fired several shots. The force of the slugs pushed Sid back. As if moved by an invisible hand, he spun away from her. More bullets hit – entering his back and sides, rotating him like a puppet on strings. He turned one full circle before catching himself on a handrail. Steadying himself, Sid started to climb again. Breathing heavily, he charged his attacker, stumbling up the steps, one arm across his face. More shots came and Carla's heart sank as she saw the bullets – *pock-pock-pock* – tear into her husband's sleeve. At this point, she started screaming at the black-suited gunman.

The new volley sent Sid stumbling backward, falling and knocking his head against the concrete landing. Without thinking, Carla ran up the steps and, gripping her handbag, attacked the front man with her parasol. All of Mouseface's attention had been focused on his enemy. The frail parasol struck him twice before he'd even noticed the girl. Only after he was sure that Sid was dead, did he pay attention to his crazed wife. He grabbed the frilly thing from her and threw it. The parasol soared like a butterfly across a long arc, landing in the courthouse lawn. Then, he did his best to melt into the crowd of Baldwin agents and sheriff's deputies.

Carla exploded into a fit of furious screaming. Two policemen appeared and grabbed her by each arm. She fought and cursed at them, wanting to go to Sid. The two officers said nothing as they lifted Carla, practically carrying her up the steps, and disappeared into the courthouse.

Gibbs Bryant stood, tempted to run, but desperate to see and know what was happening to Carla and Sid on the steps. More policemen appeared, guns in hand. They moved with a purpose into the crowd, fanning down the steps and across the hillside, shouting commands as they went.

Get down! ...On the ground! ...Do as I say! ...You there! Get down, I said!

They moved methodically, filling the air with their shouted orders, expertly shielding the crime scene from all view as they forced everyone in reach, both men and women, down onto the ground.

Neither Gibbs nor anyone else would see Sheriff Gore come down the steps and squat next to Sid. The sheriff winced at all the blood as he lifted Sid's left leg and tucked a handgun there. The weapon was warm, as Gore had just used it to fire three shots from Sid's direction into the courthouse wall. For years afterward, the trio of bullet holes would blemish the brownstone building, public evidence of the sheriff's version of events.

It was Todd who finally pulled Gibbs away. Around them, men pressed forward, but Todd pulled his brother back. The older Bryant brother shook Harm and Lowcoal, waking them from their state of shock.

"They've baited him!" cried Gibbs. "They're shooting him!"

Todd pulled harder at his brother.

"They'll get us too if we don't run!"

Realizing, the men turned away from the scene at the courthouse and pushed their way back through the crowd. Reaching the edge, Gibbs was amazed to see some of the bystanders pressing the other way, as if desperate to get close enough to see the work of the sheriff's men, now making arrests. Keeping their heads down, the four miners moved as smoothly as they could. They dug their way through, trying to blend in among local people on the sidewalk.

Across the street, in a second-story window of the Logan Hotel, Pearl Gaujot gritted his teeth. Looking at Sid's broad back through the scope of his high-powered rifle, he'd been prepared to do the job himself if Mouseface couldn't. Around the square, four other sharpshooters watched for Gaujot's signal, each one perched in another upper window. Now, certain the thing was done, Gaujot signaled for them to stand down, leaving the rest to the men on the ground. Gaujot could hear the sheriff giving them orders.

I want that one! And that one! Get him too.

Then Gaujot spotted a big fish slipping through the sheriff's net – Bryant, Sid Mandt's injured lieutenant, was escaping with some others.

Gaujot sited down his rifle. He aimed, tracking Todd, took in a breath and paused.

"No," he said, changing his mind. Quickly, he set aside the rifle and hurried from the room. Downstairs, he called two Baldwins – both in plain clothes.

"You two! You're with me!"

Together, the three officers raced beneath the train bridge arch, heading toward a quiet street of shops. Gaujot stayed in the lead with the taller man.

"They're heading for the train depot," he called.

Three blocks away, the fugitive miners were within sight of the station. Harm Fox held up his hand. Fearing his feet would not stay under him, he stopped to catch his breath. He bent over, rasping ropes of spit.

"Why did we run?" Harm panted, next to him. "They shot Sid!"

"What could we do?" asked Todd.

"Goddamn!" said Gibbs, cursing at the sidewalk. "Goddamn them!"

"Come on, Harm," Todd pleaded. "We have to get out of here."

When he came to the rail station, Gaujot knew the fugitives were likely already aboard one of the waiting trains. The burly mine guard led the way to the nearest platform and climbed into one of the eastbound cars. Walking slowly up the aisle, he returned the glances of nervous passengers. He looked out a window, searching the railyard. Lines of rails weaved among each other, ending in the complex of giant engine shops. Moving through the car, Gaujot approached an old conductor, who scowled as he took a stance in the center of the aisle.

"Ticket!" the old man said.

"Police business," Gaujot said, edging past. Behind his boss's back, the taller Baldwin nodded apologetically. The smaller deputy tried the paneled restroom door. It was locked. The conductor raised an eyebrow at the agent.

"You wait your turn, son!" the man scolded. "That lady gets all the time she needs!"

Behind the door, Harm, Todd and Lowcoal fought to keep their breathing even. Todd shut his eyes tight, as if in prayer. Gaujot scrutinized the conductor who checked his watch.

"We're leaving directly," the man said. "How many tickets do you need?"

Just then, Gibbs darted out from under the train car and made a dash across the open railyard.

"There!" Gaujot shouted. In an instant, the three Baldwin guards had jumped off the train and were after him.

The two younger deputies sprinted across the lot. Gaujot followed, passing a line of open forge doors. Inside, blacksmiths pummeled gentle curves into hot metal, sending sparks skittering across the bricks. The two guards tore through the railyard, causing the iron workers to look up from their anvils, their hammers hovering over red-hot slats. When an engineer's whistle blew a long, single note, more men took notice and emerged from their dark shops.

Gibbs dashed down a wagon-sized passage between two buildings. On either side, the walls loomed overhead. He hoped he might come out on the other end of this curving passageway with someplace good to hide. That hope was extinguished, however, when he came right up against another wall. A blind alley. He was trapped.

He turned to see the two Baldwin deputies come around the bend. Gaujot followed some distance behind. The deputies trained their guns on him. Miserably, Gibbs raised his hands.

"I ain't armed!" he screamed.

"No difference to me," the shorter one said. He approached Gibbs, breathing heavily, as Gaujot came up behind.

"Where'd your buddies go, red?" he panted.

Gibbs said nothing. He didn't know. Gaujot almost smiled.

"No matter. They'll come out fast enough when they hear you screaming."

He aimed his gun at Gibbs' knee.

"Is there a problem here?"

Gaujot turned toward the speaker who stood behind him. A big blacksmith stood there, eying him. The man was joined by a sizable group of surly iron workers. Some still carried the tools they'd been using: mallets, wrenches and iron bars.

Knowing the situation, Gaujot calmly tucked his own gun back into his jacket.

"This man and his friends are criminals," he said, pointing to Gibbs.

The front man's eyebrow went up.

"Is that so?" he said. "What'd he do?"

"Just look at him," said the taller Baldwin. He followed his boss's example and pocketed his own gun. "Anyone can see he's red!"

"I haven't done a damned thing!" Gibbs growled angrily. More trainmen came off the lot, led by an engineer who seemed to be in charge.

"You boys are Baldwin police?" he asked.

"On contract with Sheriff Gore," Gaujot nodded. "We're training some of his deputies here."

"I'll bet," the blacksmith said.

"We've got the man we want," said Gaujot. "We'll have no trouble here."

"No trouble to whip your ass, gun thug," called a voice from the back.

The engineer, however, spoke calmly. He addressed Gaujot's second man, who still had his pistol trained on Gibbs.

"Put that away, son," he warned. "This yard's been union since nineteen and ten. Rail company rules say you Baldwins ain't even allowed on this property. Put it away, goddammit, lest you start a something you can't finish."

The smaller guard hesitated.

"You'd best be careful with that," a blacksmith said. "I believe you got a problem on your barrel."

The Baldwin looked at Gaujot, who stared at Gibbs.

"This man's an expert," the engineer told the Baldwin agent. "Best give him your gun."

The blacksmith took the weapon from the guard and opened the chamber. Six bullets bounced on the bricks like seed grain. Squatting in his sooty coveralls, the man lay the gun on the cobblestones and slammed his powerful hammer down on top of it. Grinning, he handed the weapon to the Baldwin.

"I wouldn't try to fire that," he said. "Barrel's got a dent in it. Might blow back on you."

Gaujot surveyed the mob of trainmen. Finally, he gave a little shrug. Gibbs edged forward, eager to get around his assailants. As he passed, Gaujot leaned forward.

"One of your friends got drilled this morning," the big mine guard growled. "That's a good day's work for us."

At this, Gibbs' anger flared. Without thinking, he wheeled and struck Gaujot's broad scarred face. Gaujot's head moved, then snapped back to focus on the miner, his eyes wide with surprise and rage. His neck muscles tightened, coiled like a snake.

Instinctively, Gibbs backed away, his fists ready. All around him, the railroad men sounded their approval, showing their readiness to join in. They moved in toward the three Baldwins, growling like wolves.

With an effort of will, Gaujot straightened and opened his hands. He appraised Gibbs cooly, as if seeing him for the first time. Gibbs was crouched into his boxer's stance, fists raised. He watched Gaujot, who didn't blink. Around them, the train men gripped their tools.

"You've struck an officer of the Baldwin Detective Agency and a sheriff's deputy," said Gaujot, his voice going soft. "All accounts are reckoned, in the end."

The railroad workers jeered as the mine guard turned and, with his detectives, walked away. As he watched the three black-suited Baldwins cross the yard, Gibbs shuddered, feeling sick to his stomach. He could still hear the gunshots at the courthouse, could still see Sid falling. Gibbs felt dizzy, as if he'd just been thrown into a well, terrifyingly black and deep.

"Come on, son," said the engineer, clapping him on the shoulder. "Let's get you back among your own."

Chapter 9

"Ready?"

Gibbs had been staring into the open boxcar. On the crate, the hand-penciled inscription read: **S. Mandt. Mandt, Union Miner-Blair.**

Gibbs' pronounced Sid's name, scrawled twice by different hands, a fact that riled him.

"You ready?" Darko asked again, without impatience. Gibbs nodded and planted his feet.

Together, they pulled the rope handles. The box came out fast, spilling sawdust from the edge of the train car. It was lighter than either had expected and Gibbs wondered whether Sid was really inside, or whether life had played some mean joke on them.

How tall had he been? How slight?

No one spoke as they slid the sad box onto Trader Mary's wagon, alongside two shovels and a pick. Passersby slowed to gawk at her strange hearse, still decked-out with carnival flags. Nick sat in the back, one arm draped across Sid's coffin.

The reins in her hands, Mary waited with Carla and Todd, their faces blank and pale. She turned toward Sid's friends, some distance off – Lowcoal, Ben and Darko – their heads low, as if in consultation.

"Get in," she called.

"Thanks," they waved and threw their packs into the wagon. They did not get in, though. Gibbs joined them in their choice to walk behind.

"We'll ride!" called Tildy, hurrying with Harm. Mary's mouth pressed into an even line.

"Get in, then," she said, but turned her back on them.

A frost had come the night before, adding weight to the green expanse that hung over the strikers' camp. In a few weeks, the mountain's wall of trees would burst into a variety of reds, oranges and yellows – like Mary's flags. The display would be brilliant for a while, a brief explosion of color before the leaves fell, revealing the mountain's foundation, all solemn granite and gray wood.

The wagon clattered slowly across the bridge. Todd leaned over to Mary, asking her to stop along the road.

"Gibbs and I still have to get our things," he said.

"I ain't waitin' too long," she warned.

Gibbs exchanged a look with Todd, who seemed reluctant to jump down from his place at Carla's side.

"Sit tight," said Gibbs. "I'll go."

Boys' heads poked out from tent flaps as he passed through the camp. Miners came out into the cold for kindling, slapped their arms against the early-morning chill and watched Gibbs through tired eyes. He ducked into the tent he shared with Todd, letting the flap fall closed. Immediately, he started folding changes of clothes into a bedroll. He came across his father's steel warning whistle and, on some quiet inspiration, sought out a cord to tie the thing around his neck.

As he worked, Gibbs tried to calm himself, letting his mind sift through memories of better times. He recalled summer nights on the family porch. His father had been well-rested, ready for another day and his mother hummed. Gibbs closed his eyes a moment, recalling her voice, the ballads she sang – Cuckoo Bird, Pretty Polly and Barbara Allen – songs she'd taught him from some other place and time…. His thoughts turned to the mining accident, then to the courthouse shooting. Could he have done anything? If he had, Sid might still be with them. Gibbs made a fist.

"Gibbs?"

"Huh!"

The sound of Carla's voice startled him.

"You coming?" she called from beyond the flap.

"Yeah!"

He took in his breath. He'd been too slow in packing.

"Just a minute," he said and tied a bundle together.

Outside, Carla glanced toward the wagon. Her mother would leave Gibbs behind if she came back without him. Standing before Gibbs' door, she stared at the line of tents. At the canvas home she'd put together for herself and Sid. She looked away, turning her attention to some children playing by the creek.

"You coming?" she called again, surprised to hear her mother's impatience in her own voice. She opened the tent flap to find Gibbs, sitting on a cot. He held a pistol in his hand, staring at it.

"Harm tried to give this to him," he said. "Sid turned it away."

"Yeah," she said, believing it.

She stood there, mostly outside the tent, watching him. Gibbs looked up at her, his face a mix of emotion, fighting for control. Carla noted how much older he looked now, although they were about the same age. He was different from Todd, she thought. More going on between his ears. In this, he was like Sid....

"It feels like someone pulled the rug out from under us," said Gibbs, struggling to keep his voice under control. "Poppy gone, then Sid. Who's gonna lead us now?"

Carla said nothing, knowing only too well how he felt. She pointed to the gun in his hand.

"Put that away," she said, surprised at how easily she said it. Gibbs nodded and quietly folded the gun into his bedroll.

"It seems like there's something we could've done," he said.

"I know," Carla answered, glad that he was talking. "It wasn't your fault."

She turned away to look up the row, toward the covered bridge. She could see her mother watching from the wagon. Nearby, one of the kids was pulling another up the creek bank. Gibbs pulled his bundle together and looked around for anything he'd forgotten.

"Come on," said Carla. "We have to go."

The wagon resumed its sad, creaking journey. Carla had reclaimed her seat by Mary. Todd had shoved himself into a narrow space with Harm and Tildy in the back, his legs out straight, one hand steadying the shovels and thick handled mattock. He tried to stabilize his aching shoulder; to keep from swaying with the wagon's pitch, not wanting to think of his best friend, lying in the box beside him.

Harm wore his fisherman's cap against the cold and picked at a mud-splash on his white shirt. Lowcoal walked behind the rig with Darko and Gibbs, who wondered why Mary hadn't removed the flags. The decorations turned the wagon into a peculiar hearse, he thought, as he eyed the camp, still waking up. More men were out, chopping wood. Women cooked food and children played in the creek. No one seemed to notice the strange procession, heading away, up the hill. The story of Sid's killing would sift through the tent city, Gibbs figured, but word would spread slowly over days – filtered through a mess of muddled facts in half a dozen foreign tongues.

Nick walked a mourner's pace alongside the horse, whose lip curled at the smell of death. Steel clouds overhead encased the world in gray. None of them had slept.

"It ain't right, us sneakin' off like this," Lowcoal muttered as the tent city receded behind them. Gibbs glanced up at Mary's bolt-upright back.

"It's her land," he said. "It's how she wants it. Quick and quiet."

Well over a thousand miners had joined the strike, but only the men of Sovereign feared its future without Sid Mandt. Even the other union organizers had barely known the mysterious man who'd quietly come to their camps to pass messages and boost their courage before he was cut down. Lowcoal blew snot into the mud, wiped his sleeve across his face.

"It just ain't right," he said again. "There should be more of us."

Gibbs shared a glance with Harm Fox, holding hands with Tildy, her slate-gray hair tied in a brown headscarf.

Mary drove in angry contemplation. At her side, Carla's cheeks were wet with tears. The younger woman stared down at her hands, using them to smooth inconsequential folds in her skirt.

The little procession slogged up the road. Some distance from the camp, they made a left turn, south, off the main highway. Carla took the reins from her mother, wanting to drive. The rough rope felt familiar to her, like the road stretching out before them. The upward grade grew steep, obligating the miners to get behind the rig and push. The party traveled some distance uphill before the path leveled out. Then, the trees thinned and the rutted road disappeared, to be replaced by a less-traveled course, its median thick with thistle.

Soon, the flag-decorated hearse rolled into an open meadow. The mourners waded through waves of iron grass and black-eyed susan, which they combed down behind them in a single, dark wake. At the top, the procession halted. Mary set the wagon brake and they all stood, looking down the grassy hillside.

Alongside them was her family's graveyard, by the ruin of an old chapel. The last visible piece of the church to disappear was a stone arch, once a door frame, over a set of crumbling steps. Behind the arch, a knot of fallen rafters and burned locust beams were concealed in tall grass and tangled briars.

Gibbs stared past the cemetery's iron gate, at the little yard of weeds and stones – not-so-tall markers whose scarred inscriptions were almost worn away.

Halstead. Duty. Bunch.

Gibbs read the words, wondering about the people lying here – people who'd lived here long before the railroad, before the mines and the police.

Well apart from the rest, a tall stone bore the name of Mary's husband. The plot was choked with weeds.

Bonner Rising.

Mary had climbed down to open the gate, but paid the site no special attention.

"Dig there," she said, pointing out a space, two plots removed.

As the others moved the tools, Carla squatted at her father's grave, started pulling weeds. Mary watched her a moment, then turned away to view the field. Others came out of the woods below – just seven men, friends of Sid's who refused to stay away. Without much sound, they matted down the grass and cleared a fire pit, camping like close relatives on Decoration Day.

Todd swung his legs down from the wagon bed. His wounded shoulder would not allow him to do harder work, but he took the shovels in his one powerful arm anyway.

"Is your place far?" Todd asked.

"Back there," Mary pointed into the woods.

"Too far to walk?"

Her sharp eyes scrutinized him.

"You might find it," she said evenly. "But, I doubt you'd find your way out again."

Gibbs accepted the tools from Todd and leaned them against the iron graveyard fence. He stared at Bonner's grave.

"Why's your husband buried so far from your homeplace?" he asked.

Mary scowled.

"He strayed," she said at last.

The distant mountains stretched across the high plateau in a series of rolling saddlebacks. The farthest line of them was barely visible in the morning sun, now bright.

The men took up the pick and shovels as Todd climbed back into the wagon with Nick and Tildy. Carla returned to her seat alongside her mother.

"You'll find a spring down in the cut," Mary called back to them before setting off. Sitting between her mother and her aunt, Carla glanced back one time. Gibbs tried to seek her eye but couldn't see past her little brother. Nick straddled the foot of Sid's wooden box. As the wagon disappeared into the trees, Gibbs saw the boy's hand in motion, waving before his own face.

Gibbs, Darko and Lowcoal shared the digging. Harm busied himself cleaning out the weed-trees that had grown around Bonner's ragged stone. The others watched the old miner, admiring his stamina.

"You knew him, didn't you, Harm?" Darko asked, but Harm kept working, saying nothing, and the Croatian figured he hadn't heard the question.

They alternated with the tools through the rest of the morning, pulling loosened clay and dirt from the sad hole. When the grave was dug, the four of them went down the hill to find Mary's spring, a simple pipe driven into the ground, a tap in the mountain. Spring water splashed from it, then bounced off a gullied stone to spill down through the woods. The men took turns mouthing up the clean water, then washed grime from their stinging hands and necks. Harm discovered an old, polished gourd and used it as a cup.

They waited and relaxed, listening to the thousand sounds of the woods. Gibbs sighed, then began singing. It had been a long time since he sang, but he felt it now. Needed it now. He sang what he could recall of one of his mother's songs.

O, Death! O, Death!
Won't you spare me over 'til another year?
Well, what is this that I can't see,
With ice cold hands takin' hold of me?

As he sang, Carla returned with the wagon. She heard the music drift up to the gravesite from the curtain of woods.

I'm death. I come to take your soul;
Leave your body and leave it cold;
To draw up your flesh, lift it off the frame;
Dirt and worm, both have their claim.
O, Death! O, Death!
Won't you spare me over 'til another year?

Crossing the gate, Carla entered the graveyard and stood before the newly dug grave. She listened to the song, immersed in the ongoing flood of dread and gratitude for it. Turning, she examined the cleared patch of ground and stone that named her father and recalled the last time she'd been alone with him, just before he died. He'd started in the mine, crossing the mountains back and forth to work each day. He came home so late at night and left again so early that Carla had begun to wonder whether he really lived with them anymore at all. She knew now how much the work must have changed him. Her mother too, perhaps.

Carla and Bonner had been walking on the trail together. He'd been telling her about the world beyond the woods – how other people lived and what they did – when Carla heard the rattle. Bonner froze, putting one hand out in warning. The coiled snake lay in the middle of the path. Backing away, Bonner found a strong forked stick. Fast and intentional, he brought it down, pinning the serpent's pitted head to the ground. The brown rattle buzzed angrily as the snake writhed, trapped beneath the stick. Carla was fascinated and appalled to see its fangs unfurl as the animal fought, wrapping its muscular body around her father's ankle. Bonner kept hold of the stick, though. The threatening head tilted up at an angle, its puffed white maw opened in a silent scream.

"Step on it," he ordered. "Crush the head and kill it."

It was the first time that Carla had seen her father angry. She was afraid and didn't want to kill the snake.

"Go on. It's dead already," Bonner muttered, a clear lie. Carla approached the leering head, unable to look away from the coils as they whipped and twined.

"Come, on, girl! Don't think about it. Do it fast."

Carla remembered summoning her pride and balling her fists to work up her courage. Then, lifting one boot , she ground the snake's head into the dirt. She recalled the wave of disgust at the crunch of bones beneath her foot. Her father leaned into his stick, all but severing the thing's neck.

She raised her foot, seeing the snake's head glaring at her through cold eyes. Its torn neck seeped blood into the earth. Bonner nudged the thing with his toe, the fangs frozen in a sideways grin. Then the mouth opened again, sudden and dangerous. The body continued to writhe, refusing to die.

"Don't touch the head," Bonner warned, slipping his foot from a coil.

When the thing had stilled, he took out his knife, cut the rattle from its tail and held it out to her.

"You want it?"

Carla scrutinized the prize. She wanted to be angry at her father for making her do what she'd just done. She scowled at her bloodied boot heel.

"No," she frowned. "Just bury him."

"No sense in that," Bonner smirked. "The pigs'll just come and dig it up."

He stooped and grabbed the body near the tail. More impulses made the long body curl at the end of her father's raised arm. With an easy swing, however, he sent it high over the brush.

In leaving, Gibbs and the other miners raised their cold hands to the little group camped on the hillside, whose campfire they could smell alongside the fresh-dug earth. The sky glowed pink, ignited by the late-afternoon sun, as Carla drove them through the contour of the mountain, over and around two small hills. Gibbs was tired, but the singing had calmed him. He took in the broad-leafed forest around them, the dense trees tapering into stretches of mayapple and Christmas fern. As he ducked to avoid the branch of a leaning alder, he realized they must be near Mary's place. It was as if some woodland door had opened, revealing sudden clusters of berry bushes and chestnut trees, passion fruit and cinnamon plums. Grapevines looped across a thorn fence, edged by deer-nibbled tobacco and merged into a plot of corn with climbing beans and apple trees nearby.

Carla took the rig into the barn lot. The miners climbed out, gawking at the different ways that Mary's homeplace fooled the eye. Almost two stories tall, her broad barn was dwarfed by the towering trees. The house, however, stood in the light, shared by the garden, bordered on the far side by a set of low apple trees. The cabin's aged log walls were gray, more the color of stone than wood.

Carla unhitched Swift and, leading him by the reins, muttered to him the way her mother did. With a satisfied snort, the old horse followed her to a stack of hay by the barn. Although he stood a good twelve hands, the animal looked almost the size of a pony beside the haystack, piled higher than the barn roof.

Nick used a wooden scoop to scatter grain around the lot for chickens, competing with two goats for the food. When he was done, he pushed past the goats and looked toward his mother for approval, his eyes darting.

"Don't go too far," she said, and the boy ran off, into the woods.

"He does that," Carla said. "Got himself a hiding place."

Gibbs joined Todd who stood in the doorway to the barn. Looking inside, they could see Sid's coffin, propped against a low grain crib. Gibbs turned and watched his brother's eyes. They were following Carla as she hung the horse's tack.

"You all right?" Gibbs asked and Todd started, as if caught. He nodded.

Carla returned to the wagon and took the digging tools from Darko. Then, as if by some signal, she came to Todd.

"Let's get you a place to rest," she said.

Exhausted, he didn't argue and, taking his good arm, she led him toward the house. Mary watched their approach from the porch.

"Give him Nick's bed," she said, not opening the door.

"It's too cold there, mama. Him and Gibbs can sleep upstairs, on mine. I'll take a spot by the stove."

Mary pursed her lips, but kept quiet as she followed them inside.

Soon, Mary had dinner cooking for the group. She stoked the fire and fatted two black skillets, always on the stove. She fell into giving Carla orders, as if the girl had never left. Two big jars of goat meat were pulled from the cool place and, soon, it was frying in the pans. Mary stirred, reckoning her guests in meat, potatoes, corn and beans.

After dinner, when the day had slipped past and the light was gone, the company settled on her front porch. Lowcoal and Darko sat together, legs extended, heels planted in the chicken lot. Todd had one leg propped on a rail. He quietly nursed a tumbler of bitter tonic from Mary's cabinet. Nick sat on a wooden bench by Gibbs, fiddling with Truman's warning whistle on the string. When the boy put the thing into his mouth, though, Gibbs gently tugged it back.

"Don't want that now," he said.

Expressionless, Nick hopped from the bench and scampered into the dark.

"Kid ain't quite right, is he?" asked Darko.

On the far end of the porch, Tildy held hands with Harm.

"Ain't nothing wrong with him," she said.

"But he don't talk," said Gibbs.

Harm grimly suggested it had something to do with being raised so far from other kids. Mary's voice scolded them from inside.

"He says plenty," she said, and came out the front door. She frowned down at Gibbs on her way to the garden with a bucket of stove ash.

"You just ain't listenin'," she said.

Then, from the darkness beyond the fence, came the sound of the boy, humming. It wasn't exactly musical; more like a low warbling, akin to the surrounding woods. It made Gibbs think of the sound made by pond peepers, or the crickets' thrum. He looked around the porch. Lowcoal, Darko, Harm Fox and Ben sat together, unmindful of anything but their own talking. Gibbs looked across, to where Carla sat, in a woven chair. He studied her face, drawn and pale and more tired than he'd seen her today, in camp. He knew the world would give a woman in her situation few choices. She'd do well to stay here, with her mother, he thought. She'd be safe here, a far better choice than anything in the miners' camp.

Now Carla rose and lit two kerosene lamps by the cabin door. Moving across the porch, she hung one from a beam in the center, changing the light. Gibbs watched, but didn't see her, still listening to Nick's strange nightsong from someplace beyond the fence. Todd moved into a circle with Lowcoal, Darko and Ben, their tones going low as they do when private things come up.

"I spoke with Tom Kenner, the union chief in Meridian," said Todd quietly. "He didn't care to talk about our boys in jail."

Lowcoal shifted.

"That ain't good," he said. "Must've been more 'n fifty they carried off."

Todd scratched his head.

"I think it's more 'n that," he whispered.

Gibbs glanced at Carla, returned to the double chair with Tildy. He decided, then, to enter into it.

"Every union man should be ready to stand up to them," he said. "We gotta get 'em freed."

The way the other men looked, Gibbs knew they were surprised to hear this, coming from him. He'd never participated in their conversations much before. Not as much as Todd, but this was how he felt.

"Sid would have wanted it," he continued. "We ought to play it as rough with them as they've done with us."

"I swear," said Harm, shaking his head. "This is the worst thing they could've done. Everyone comes together around a thing like this. Just like when they started up the hunting club at Paint Creek."

Darko spat tobacco juice into the dark.

"What's that, Harm?"

The old miner looked grave.

"Years ago, in the Paint Creek strike, the guards killed two of ours," he said. "The men spread the word and formed the 'Miners Hunting Club' against it. Before long, they had a couple hundred men, all with guns, reddied-up to have a turkey shoot. Guards took notice, then."

"As if you didn't have your fill of it!" Mary was stepping through the gate, carrying the empty ash bucket by its rim. Scowling at Harm, she came up to the porch and stood before the hanging lantern. Her straight and sturdy form blocked the light, casting a shadow upon them all. Gibbs could see how solid she was – an older version of Carla – but more strong-willed.

Mary looked around at each man. Finally, she just shook her head, turned and went inside. The men looked at each other, surprised.

"Why's she so cold to you, Harm?" Todd whispered. "What'd you do to her?"

Harm Fox looked down, used the toe of his boot to move a stone along the ground.

"It goes back to her husband, Bonner Rising," he said. "Me and Bone – we was good friends. We fought together in the Paint Creek War."

Todd whistled.

"Bloody Paint Creek," someone said.

"Bone was just bustin' to go," Harm nodded. "Finally, we set out one morning. He told Mary we was going on a huntin' trip. We was there two days, at Mucklow Mine. The Baldwins had throwed all the families out, just like they've done in Sovereign. A bunch of us decided to camp up the road a piece. We was just standing there when two Baldwins rode through on a motorbike – both of them drunk as hell. Fool's courage. We just watched them ride on past. Didn't so much as fling a rock at 'em. But the second time, the man on back fired his pistol. He hit Bone – shot him just for being there. I watched him fall."

The others took it in.

"They catch who done it?" Gibbs asked.

"On the spot," Harm nodded. "Bill Barnes – lanky, he was. Nervy too. Bill ran up and kicked that motor right over, on its side. Back-seat fellow spilled off and lost his pistol. Then, all of us, we just turned mean. We beat both those men to butcher's meat."

"But Mary never saw her man again," Todd ventured.

Tildy's hand took hold of Carla's.

"No," said Harm. "We brung him back on the train. Carried him right up that trail here."

"That's right. You tell it." Mary stood in the doorway again, glaring at Harm. "Laid him out, right on my cabin floor, didn't you?"

Harm's back straightened as he turned to see his sister-in-law.

"Damned fools, the both of you," she said. Harm looked away from her, gazing into the past.

"Bonner deserves better than that," he said.

"And don't I?" she growled at him. "Don't I deserve better than what you've done to me, then and since?"

"He deserves better," Harm repeated. "Bonner loved you."

"Bonner tell you that, did he?" Mary cried. "Did he say 'Oh, Harm, I so love my family!' Tell me, Harm: Did he love me as much as he loved your goddamn union?"

Harm stayed quiet, his eyes straight ahead. Mary's voice rose, giving vent to the built-up anger of many years.

"Is that what you-all was fightin' for? Fightin' for me and my family? Out there in Paint Creek, fifty miles away?"

"We was –!" Harm began, but got no further.

"So what'd you bring me for it, Harm?" she cried. "How many times these past ten years did you, or any union man, come up here to put up hay? Or pick tobacco? Or shoe the horse? How many times did you come and do the things that Bonner did for me?"

"You been too angry," he said quietly.

"You're damned right," Mary hissed. "You took my husband and brought me back a breathing corpse. I look at you and all I see is Bonner Rising, bloodied on my cabin floor. And what did my Bonner say *to me* that night? Not, 'I love you, Mary,' or 'I am sorry, Mary' or even 'God will provide.' No, sir. Not one damned thing! He couldn't talk at all; your union took him from me. You, Harm Fox! You took Bone Rising from this life! And now, you've done the same for his little girl!"

In growing horror, Gibbs and the other men on the porch watched the argument, their eyes going from Mary to Harm and back again. Lowcoal was the first to react. "I can't take this," he said. Getting up, he stepped off the porch and wandered out into the dark. The only sound Gibbs heard was Harm's labored breathing, the rattle of coal dust embedded in his lungs. After a moment, the old man continued his fight with Mary.

"Bone wanted to go to Paint Creek," said Harm. "The brothers there were suffering. We needed to do something."

"He *was* doing something!" Mary screamed, turning on him. "He was mining coal! Bonner wasn't no kind of soldier! He wasn't any kind of fightin' man!"

"He was to me," Carla said, and all the men looked at her. "He was a good man, Mama. And brave."

Mary stared at her daughter, open-mouthed; saw the tears running down her cheeks. Too angry to be moved, however, Mary turned to the woodpile and quietly began stacking a row of kindling on her arm.

"So my husband was a brave man," she muttered to her daughter. "And your Sid. He was a brave man too. So what? Just look at where it landed them!"

Too shocked to speak, the miners looked away in all directions, shifting their positions. Somewhere in the dark, Nick resumed his dirge. Carla's eyes were liquid and bright. Mary stood in the light, her back straight.

"My family's done with helping union," she told them. "We've done our share – and more, besides. This time around, I ain't helping either side. Me and mine is neutral, you understand? You all can fight it, if you want. But you just leave us the hell out of it!"

Gibbs had been shaking his head, his anger growing. When he spoke, however, he was able to keep his voice calm. He sat, leaning forward on his bench, his elbows on his knees.

"It's easy enough for some folks to talk 'neutral'," he said to Mary. "You're out here, thinkin' you're safe from it. That you're protected, way up here.…"

"Gibbs. No," Todd interrupted, wanting to reach out and grab his brother's collar like when they were kids. But Gibbs kept talking, working to keep his voice even.

"You might think it's 'Live and let live,' but I'm sorry, ma'am. You just don't know how it is with us. You don't know what it's like for a man – or a young boy – to go down into that hole every day, forced to work, earning next to nothing, with one gun at your belly and another at your head!"

"Be quiet, Gibbs!" Todd warned. "This ain't the time-."

"Why not? Why not now?" Gibbs cried, and looked from Todd to Carla, then back to Mary.

"We're getting blamed for everything by everyone, and you're telling us to stay 'neutral'! I don't think I know what 'neutral' means!"

"He's right!" said Harm Fox, taking up the argument again. "There ain't no 'neutral' here, Mary! To them in Logan, being neutral is just the way they want it! They know it only means you're cowed!"

"I don't care!" Mary screamed back at them. "You men keep my family out of it!"

"It was Bone's family too," Harm said. "And you got no right. No right to treat his memory this way."

"And Sid-," Carla began, but stopped, unable to continue. Her tears flowed.

"You're damned right," Harm nodded with tears in his own voice. "Both of 'em.... Both of them. They were the best of us."

Breathing hard, he turned and found his cap. He fixed it on his head and strode off the porch, joining the darkness.

Mary eyed the others around the circle. She stood straight and defiant, her angular jaw clenched, one arm wrapped around the wood she carried. Not one of the men could meet her gaze. Snorting, she carried her load into the house. They heard the kindling clatter to the floor, but no one rose to help. Darko spat tobacco juice into the night. As Mary moved around inside, the men on the porch settled into an uneasy quiet. Gibbs leaned back, tucking his father's steel whistle back into his shirt.

Now, Carla stood and, wiping her eyes, walked across the lot. They watched her enter the barn, where Sid's body lay. Todd got up, unhooked a lantern from the post and followed her.

At the doorway to the barn, he stopped and looked inside. Carla stood before Sid's coffin, still propped on the corncrib. With the cool of evening, they'd removed the top for viewing. Carla looked with sadness on her husband's quiet high-boned face, lit by a single candle to one side. A common miner, he'd been tall and wiry; stoic and pugnacious. Full of fire. Todd came to her side.

"I'm sorry for my mother," Carla said.

"I'm sorry for Gibbs," he said, but Carla waved it off. She wondered that Todd would apologize for his brother, who'd been right in standing up to Mary.

"It's hard on all of us," said Todd. He looked around and found a nail in a crossbeam on which to hang the lantern. Returning, he stared at the body, recognized the suit jacket they'd fitted on Sid – his wedding suit, the faded shirt and tie. A scar crossed Sid's chin just above the high white collar. Todd would never forget the night of that injury. Sid had sucked down enough hootch to fill a train car. It was late and he was so bad off, he'd stumbled up the wrong porch steps, finding himself in Harm and Tildy's place. All of Sovereign's houses looked so much alike.

Todd imagined Sid standing in Harm's front room, swaying as he looked around, puzzled. Finally, he would have turned around – apologizing to no one as he lurched back out the door.

Somewhat less drunk, Todd had realized their mistake almost before he'd walked into the neighboring house. This one was Sid and Carla's. Todd knew exactly where he was, but decided not to let it bother him; decided he'd play out the adventure, just as Sid himself might have done.

Todd remembered his pounding heart, how he'd let it carry him through the front room toward the light in the back. Carla had been awake, waiting. Todd stood quietly in the doorway as Carla got out of bed. Was she aware of the way the lamp light showed through her shift? At that moment, she didn't seem to care.

"What's going on, Todd?" she'd asked him. Her voice was tired but unafraid.

Todd could hear Sid outside, tripping on his own bottom stair. That's when he cracked his chin. They heard Sid sniggering at himself, mindless of the blood. Too drunk to go any further, he curled up on his own front porch. Carla went to see. Lying on the raw planks, Sid laughed once, then quieted down and fell asleep. Carla put a blanket on him, then came back indoors. To Todd, who kept standing there. Todd had done nothing to help Sid. Or Carla. Now, in the barn, Todd remembered being frozen there, in Carla's house. Just then, it had been her house alone, and Todd didn't want to leave it. He didn't dare move, lest his dream end. Todd wasn't sure what he expected of her, what he expected of himself. He didn't dare hope, and yet....

"Go home, Todd," she'd told him that night, and Todd wondered whether he'd heard her right. Something in her voice. A new awareness perhaps. Of him. Something saved up for another time. Todd left without a word. They said nothing more about the incident, although Todd thought about it nearly every day.

"The candle's burning low," he said, staring at Sid's body. "It wants another."

Carla looked at him, wiping her face. She wore her long brown dress. Todd knew that dress. Now, he took her hand, pressing it. As Sid's lieutenant – his best friend – this was a right thing to do.

"There oughta be a cross," he went on. "A Bible stand...."

"No," said Carla, her eyes welling again.

"Oh," Todd answered, catching himself. "I'm sorry."

"Sid wasn't like you thought," she said. "Not at all."

"Yeah," he admitted, without knowing what she meant. He shifted, uncomfortable with the silence.

"He was sure mean to tangle with," he offered.

Carla smiled and shook her head, wondering whether anyone could ever know Sid the way she had.

"He loved working for the future," she told Todd. "He loved thinking about it – about what he was doing. He said it made him feel powerful. He thought he was safe from everything, that having all you men around him would protect him. And the sheriff's letter, just a little piece of paper...."

She sobbed, letting go of Todd's hand to catch the tears from her face. Todd stood and stared at the candle, his thoughts racing.

"He saved my life."

The voice behind them was sudden and unexpected. Todd turned to see Gibbs in the doorway.

"He pulled me out of the mine," Gibbs said and came over to them. He was still breathing hard, embittered by their argument with Mary.

"I didn't do enough to help him when he needed it."

Carla heard the plea in Gibbs' voice and was glad – relieved – to see Todd shake his head in disagreement.

"We warned him," he told Gibbs. "You remember."

"But we ran," Gibbs countered. "Would Sid have run, if it had been us?"

He stopped himself.

"I didn't have a gun," said Todd. "You neither."

Carla closed her eyes.

"What if you did?" she asked. "What then?"

Gibbs stared straight ahead.

"Then...Sid might have had a fighting chance."

"Or more people would've gotten hurt," Todd countered.

Carla listened to the two brothers. Both had been good friends in Sovereign. To her and to Sid. Carla trusted them both and, weary of all the fighting, she allowed herself to relax. Todd and Gibbs talked awhile, then stopped. They were listening to her.

"Sid's pistol was in my bag," she told them.

The two brothers were quiet, not comprehending.

"Sid gave it to me," she went on. "He could've had it at the court-house, if he'd wanted it. I stood there, right next to him. I held the bag open for him. I'm pretty sure he saw it. He pushed me away."

Sighing, Todd put his good hand around Carla's shoulder and she leaned into him. Reaching down, she took Gibbs' hand, on her other side. She took comfort in them both – in Todd's clear dedication to her; in the way Gibbs thought about things. His compassion. Carla went on with her confession.

"He pushed me away," she said again. "That's when they came at him. He shoved me aside so I wouldn't get hurt. Sid likely knew right then. He knew they were going to kill him."

After a while, Tildy came into the barn with Darko and Ben. Carla stood with her, sometimes talking, sometimes quiet, watching a frantic moth dodge in and out of the candle's flame. Finally, the wick drowned in its own wax, leaving only the light from the lantern, hanging from the beam. For a long time afterward, Carla continued to stand with Tildy and the rest in the almost-dark, lost in a labyrinth of her own thought about the future and the past; about people around her, and about silent, suited husk that had been Sid Mandt, their friend and firebrand.

Act II

We ask you to strictly comply with the terms of your contract,
especially that part pertaining to 'stoppage of work.'
Let future history certify that the mine workers of Logan County
did their work well and proved to the world their loyalty
and their devotion to their country.

Notice from Gov. Morgan, October 1921

Chapter 10

Mary shook the rope she used for reins and cursed Swift into motion. No one could assess her mood, her face hidden in her shawl of indigo, as dark and shapeless as her newly washed skirt. She wondered about the missing flags. Harm had done it. No doubt, just to be mean. Now he was too cowardly to show his face.

Todd, with his arm still strapped across his chest, walked with Gibbs behind the hearse. Behind them, their friends trailed, talking quietly among themselves.

"Lowcoal wants me to run for president of the local," Todd muttered.

Gibbs thought it a strange thing to say here, along the path to Sid's funeral. Even stranger was that Todd seemed to be asking his opinion.

"All the boys would be for it," Gibbs offered.

"But how does a man fill Sid's boots?" asked Todd. "I ain't exactly fit." He touched his wound, testing it for pain.

"Which of us is?" Gibbs countered. "Your shoulder will heal, though. Just give it time."

Gibbs considered their situation. So much had changed for him and Todd. In the space of a few weeks, they'd lost their father, their home and jobs. Now, they'd lost Sid who'd pulled them together and led them in the strike. Further, Sid had linked the men of Sovereign to other miners, working mines up and down the Big Coal River; he'd called them all his "brothers." How many of those men and their families were now on their way to Blair, Gibbs wondered. And how many would keep going, deciding to "cut and run?"

We have to stick together.

"You should be president of the local," said Gibbs. "I think Sid would want it."

Todd nodded, deep in thought.

Gibbs found himself staring at the wagon – at Carla's back. Her squared shoulders were so much like her mother's. The braided hair, pulled back. The tilt of her head.

He'd spent the night listening to the chirping of the crickets, the soft wheezes of Mary and Tildy, sharing Mary's space just beyond the wall. Below him, Carla lay on a pallet by her brother. He'd assumed she lay awake, as he did, and fought the temptation to look down the ladder at her. Instead, he pressed his face against the mattress, intoxicating himself with what he imagined to be her smell.

Now, as he followed the wagon with Todd, Gibbs' eyes lingered on her. As far as he could tell, however, Carla continued to stare straight ahead, not looking back. Had Gibbs glanced over to his side, he would have seen that his older brother was watching her too.

The burial party emerged from the woods, surprised to come out into the dreary day and see the lower pasture full of men and women, crowds of people who'd come up the mountain through the sad, steady drizzle. Mary set the brake and looked in amazement across the packed meadow, filled with worn umbrellas – as if they'd sprung from the rain-soaked pasture like a sudden infestation of field mushrooms.

Where had they come from? Men and women, negro and white and everything in between, standing in tight, alien groups – miners in wet worker's caps; the women in foreign-looking bonnets and shawls. Mary could see that more people were arriving all the time, impossible numbers of people helping each other, arm-in-arm, up the hillside. She disbelieved her eyes: hundreds of them, crossing the glistening grass, a steady, somber parade coming up from Blair. Then, she spotted Harm.

He stood near the grave, greeting some new arrivals. Bleary-eyed and short of breath, he welcomed them, shaking their hands like someone in charge. Above his head, she noticed, a pale pennant fluttered, a red one, tied to the tree branch. She put it all together: The throng of mourners had come all the way from their tent camp, having followed a trail of Mary's own flags. Harm and Lowcoal had taken them, used them overnight to blaze the trail.

Harm looked back at her, unrepentant. She imagined how he must have yanked the pennant lines from her wagon, cut the twine and, with Lowcoal's help, marked the entire length of the trail to Blair. At dawn, they roused the strikers, calling upon them to pull on their boots and "show yourselves for Sid Mandt and your union!"

"Bone Rising never got the send-off he deserved," Harm had said to Lowcoal more than once. "Let's not make the same slip twice."

Mary glanced sideways at Tildy, who beamed at her husband.

"Go stand with him, why don't you?"

But Tildy shook her head and reached into Mary's coat to fish out her hand.

"No, sister. I'm fine standing here with you."

Mary shut her eyes and kept them lowered, in a lock-jawed pretense of prayer.

The preacher moved forward, climbed the steps of the broken church where he turned and cleared his throat. Tall and sallow-faced, his neck craned through his parson's frock and faded macintosh. Framed by the stone archway of the fallen church, the man looked like a fragile figurine in a broken shrine. Behind him, Gibbs could see the piles of rubble. Somewhere underneath it, he imagined, lay the remains of a worm-eaten cross.

The preacher's voice, a startling baritone, rang out:

Our days are like the grass;
we flourish like flowers of the field.

Carla stared at Sid's coffin, damp and nailed tight against the weather. Nick reached up and took her hand, made a game of squeezing it. Glad for the distraction and tired of crying, Carla smiled down at him, squeezing back.

Then the wind passes over, and it's gone.
We know this place no more.
But mercy endures forever for those
who love god and righteousness.

The preacher raised his hand, silently begging heaven to forgive him for the misremembered testament. Aloud, he absolved the mass before him of a thousand pardonable sins and blessed the grave.

"May peace be yours this day," he said. "And may god's heavenly city be your home."

Gibbs watched the man shake some of the rain from his coat, before he turned and started down the hill for Blair. Gibbs listened, feeling the crowd's waiting for what must come next. No one wanted to be the first to speak, and Gibbs looked to Todd. Glancing around, the older Bryant took a deep breath, pulled his coat tighter around himself and stepped forward. "I guess I'd like to say something," he uttered.

Hair matted by the rain, Todd strode over to the chapel step, where the preacher had been. He looked across the crowd and spoke loudly, hoping no one would notice his shaking voice.

"My name's Todd Bryant! A lot of you knew my daddy, Truman Bryant. He died in the Sovereign mine, not long ago. That's how I got hurt."

Gibbs watched his brother, trying to imagine himself in his place. He could not.

"We all knew Sid – or should have known him. He was a brave man. Not afraid of much. I seen him angry. I seen him mean enough to whup a dozen of you fellows."

Men laughed and nodded as Todd continued.

"Several was afraid of Sid," he said. "Nobody wanted to tangle with him, not in a fair fight. We've all been scared. A man can't be any kind of miner without bein' afraid of what can happen to him. My daddy told me, if you ain't scared to go into the mine, you're either crazy or a fool!"

The laughter of the miners struck Todd's ear like a collective sigh of relief.

"We've all been scared of going to work all day and not coming back of a night. My father was afraid of not pulling enough coal, not having enough money to buy food for his family. Now I got hurt, and we're on strike, and a lot of us are afraid of losing our jobs altogether. But we've all come up as coal miners, and we stick together, no matter what!"

The rain fell, lightly drumming on Sid's coffin. Water dripped from the trees, down Todd's nose and eyebrows, across his cheeks. Stirred by his words, the crowd urged him on.

"We was even more afraid, some of us, to hear Sid start talkin' union. We thought we knew what that meant, and some of us said we'd never get this far! We'd all heard what the Baldwins done in the past. Now, they done the worst to Sid – because he organized us! We've gotten this far, and he was proud of that. We can all be proud of what we're doing here. But, it's come at a price."

"Uh-huh!" someone exclaimed from the crowd, and old men nodded, whispering shared memories to each other, willing to be stirred by Todd's words – which had been Sid's. These men were ready, and Todd knew it.

"Those deputies gunned down our friend – a good man, an honest man, and a leader of our union!" Todd cried. "They murdered him in cold blood, like a chained-up dog! Now, Logan's a place where hired killers can find work. Well, they're the ones who should be put out of their jobs, not us!"

The crowd roared. To Gibbs, their voices were like something coming up from underground.

"Now is the time for us to put our fears aside," said Todd. "Time to stop running away and stop being afraid of the mine guards and the bosses!"

The sound came up again, cheering him on.

"We were loyal to Sid Mandt while he organized this strike for us. Sid's gone now, but we still have to be loyal to the union. To each other. Our union is fighting for our jobs and for our lives! We cannot back down! We're the American Miners Union, and we have to win this strike!"

He looked at Gibbs, whose fist had shot into the air – along with hundreds more. Harm and Lowcoal were cheering wildly. Darko Dresser. Ben Tate. All their friends from Sovereign. Carla watched him, eyes wide, her cheeks glowing and wet with rain.

As ceremoniously as they could, the pallbearers arranged themselves around the puddling hole. They slid Sid's coffin across the steadied ropes and lowered it into the grave. More prayers were spoken and, soon, the thing was over. The crowds moved off. Todd found himself shaking a dozen hands.

A tall man came forward. Angular and better-dressed than most, he went to Carla and removed his broad slouch hat. He leaned forward, saying something to her privately. Carla nodded and thanked him, briefly clasping his hand. Then the man came to Todd, who'd been watching them.

"That was a fine speech, Todd," he said, and put his hat back on. Todd shook hands with Tom Kenner and introduced him to his brother and his friends. As the head of AMU District 12, headquartered in Meridian, Kenner oversaw half the union locals in the state. Now, the union leader eyed Todd from beneath his hat brim, reminding Todd of Sid. Kenner had a jutting chin and nose that seemed ready and able to plow his way into into any conversation. Or any fight.

Kenner, in fact, had been an organizer almost before he was old enough to work. He'd been raised in another Logan coal camp where he read every book he could get his hands on. One of his favorites, as a kid, was Lewis's *The Art of Lecturing*. Afternoons, he would take the precious book into a patch of woods where he'd stand on a tree stump, delivering his speeches to the wind.

At fourteen, Kenner began working in the mines. His father and the other miners said the boy had the "gift of gab," delivering talks that made them think about their condition. It wasn't long before Tom Kenner had a reputation and a nickname – "Young agitator."

The head of AMU District 12 pulled Todd away from the gravesite.

"You're the new president of your local?" he asked.

"But we ain't had the election yet," Todd began.

Kenner scrutinized him.

"The vice president takes the responsibilities of the president if the president cannot serve," he said, quoting from the union manual.

"Aside from that," he said, "that speech you just delivered tells me that you're more than ready. You're just the man we need."

The way he said it, Todd realized that Tom Kenner was not accustomed to hearing "No."

"Sid Mandt was my right hand in this strike," the union leader continued. "Now, it's you. I want you to take a trip with me. I have a car."

Todd looked at him.

"Where are we going?"

Kenner struck a match and lit a cigarette.

"To Meridian," he said, pulling in the smoke. "We've got a meeting with the governor."

Governor Ephriam Morgan was a high-stakes gambler. Used to weighing all the risks, he enjoyed the thrill of betting on his instinct and winning. Which he usually did. Walking down the corridor toward the meeting, his mind was working out what he might get out of Tom Kenner, of the American Miners Union, and what he'd put on the table in return.

He'd met with Kenner and with others of his kind before. Morgan's business friends had warned him, of course, not to get too cozy with the union. But such friends had more money than political sense. The risks were clear enough. The AMU was less-than-powerless in Logan and the other southern counties, but the miners' influence in the north was substantial. A candidate for any state office needed these northern precincts, and the union carried thousands of votes there. Morgan was happy to meet with union leaders and give them *assurances* – although he never actually came out and promised anything. "Promise," of course, was a loaded word to Morgan. One of many.

The governor held only nighttime meetings with high-risk friends like Kenner. Not that it made a difference. The coal operators and their agents had an uncanny ability to learn everything about everyone else's business even as they held their own cards close. But Morgan had to try, at least. Any man who can't keep secrets is gonna get trumped, every time.

"Good evening, gentlemen," the governor said, shaking hands with Kenner and his body guard, a young fellow with a broken arm. Kenner introduced him as a local leader in Logan County. Morgan made a mental note of the name: Todd Bryant.

"How'd that happen?" he asked, indicating Bryant's arm.

"Mining accident. I'm on the mend, though."

Morgan scrutinized him. The man was clearly inexperienced. Likely, he was intimidated by the office.

"Good," the governor nodded and took his seat, glancing at the sheet of paper Kenner had put there.

Morgan leaned over the thing, scrutinizing it through wire-framed glasses. He didn't pick it up. He didn't even touch it. He didn't have to. He knew exactly what was written there. A sour expression crushed his bulldog face.

"I was expecting something more realistic, Kenner," he said, sitting down at last. He put his fingers together, noting Bryant's growing discomfort.

"Governor," Kenner began, "our issues are plain and clear. Other states passed these protections long ago."

Morgan didn't appreciate the observation.

"Other states are closer to more markets," he said. "And other states have more resources. Ours has just one, and that is coal. In this market, your workers' *demands-.*"

Kenner knew the word was trouble.

"I beg your pardon, governor," he said. "They aren't demands."

"Then what the hell are they?" Morgan shot back. He peered at Kenner across his glasses, his hands on either side of the paper, still not touching it.

Todd leaned back a little, as if the governor blew fire. He recalled Kenner's instruction: Say nothing and "look as tough as steel."

Morgan moved the list aside and, remarkably, recited its points from memory, counting the items on his fingers.

"You want me to regulate safety in the mines! You want the state to check the weighing scales."

Kenner shifted forward in his chair as the governor continued. "You want me to meddle in food pricing at their stores, and tell the county sheriff whom he can and cannot hire!"

Morgan pushed the paper back across to Kenner, as the union leader leaned forward, putting his hands on the table.

"The company guards are out-of-control," he said. "On the sheriff's orders, they've taken more than seventy of our men – held in the Logan jail without any charges filed. That kind of power alone...."

But Morgan didn't budge, scowling at the union leader. Now, Todd found his tongue.

"Our men are angry, governor."

Morgan turned to him, one eyebrow raised.

"And why, exactly, are they angry, son?"

"The company's Baldwin guards killed Sid Mandt," Todd exhaled. "Sid was more than a union man to us. He was our friend-."

Morgan removed his glasses.

"I hear he shot first."

Todd hadn't expected this. His anger took over.

"That's a goddamned lie!"

He thought he heard Kenner groan. The governor rose, signaling the meeting was coming to an end.

"Maybe it isn't true – *this* time," Morgan snarled. "But, clearly, your men have not been shy with guns."

Todd sat back in his chair, remembering Gibbs.

"Those men in jail committed no crime, governor," Kenner said. "Nothing worse than talking union and striking for it."

"Crime enough for some," the governor responded. Todd could see Kenner growing angrier, as he was himself.

"Only in Logan County-" the union leader began, but Morgan raised his hand.

"Don't start making those speeches at me, Kenner," he warned. "I'm telling you to do yourselves a favor: Take this chance to learn something from an older fellow who knows a thing or two."

The governor walked away from the desk. His burly state officers glanced at him, ready and able to clean the office with these two union men.

Morgan thought a moment, and ordered them outside.

"We need some privacy."

Even after the guards closed the door behind them, the governor kept his voice low.

"I'll tell you, man-to-man, Kenner: One day, we'll all be rid of this private mine-guard system. It twists my knot, just like yours. Sooner or later, Gore and his Baldwin Agency will cross swords with someone with deeper pockets than theirs and they'll regret it. But you should also know – right now, at least – I can't appear to take sides on this. Not with all that's going on today."

Kenner shook his head.

"The numbers are in our favor. Most folks are in sympathy with our union workers – and our boys in jail. Sid Mandt was known in the coalfields. He was popular, all up and down the Big Coal River."

Irritated, the governor waved his hand.

"That doesn't matter," he said. "Too many people were afraid of him. Frankly, Kenner, too many of 'em are afraid of you. The newspapers will have my ass on a platter if I give you so much as a horse blanket. Just about anything I do for you – at least openly – is guaranteed to cost me the reelection."

Todd watched as Kenner moved to the edge of his seat.

"So what *can* you do for us?" he asked.

"Son, I'm about the best friend your organization's got," the governor said, pointing at them. "You may be right about some things on this list. But being right and a nickel will get you a five-cent cup of coffee. Clout is what you need. Political power. But I'm telling you, son: Putting a gun to my head isn't going to get it for you."

"The strike-" Kenner began.

"The strike is bad enough," Morgan countered. "But your men are out there, threatening to march in and shoot up the Logan County Jail!"

Todd stared, suddenly realizing what the governor was getting at: Sid's killing was already being portrayed as an attack on "law and order" in Logan County. An attack by hot-headed union "rebels." The American Mine Workers organization was already widely portrayed as a violent threat to law and order, both county and state.

"The strikers aren't that fully organized-," Kenner said cautiously. "And, we've done everything by the book. If anything, Sid Mandt would have been the one to talk reason to 'em. The only one, maybe."

Kenner glanced at Todd as the governor put his hand down on the desk.

"Well goddamnit, son, you have to get your radicals back in line! Because, I'm telling you, some of these others are gonna start talking to them behind your back. I know it, because I'm reading the speeches they've been making for the out-of-town newspapers. They're coming in here, calling for a 'miner's army.' You need to stop it – get your men to put their weapons down. It's one thing to strike. It's another to overrun the place, shooting off your mouths and firing guns."

"But, the Baldwins have-," Todd began.

Morgan took a step closer to him, lowered his voice to a growl.

"The Baldwins *run* elections in Logan County, my friend, and five other counties besides. I know it and you do too. Take 'em at the ballot box if you want to change anything. If you rise to their bait with guns, I'll be forced to intervene. Keep your guns out of it. Do what you have to, but you tell your men to hunker down and wait. Show me that, Kenner, and I'll launch a state investigation of your grievances."

"Sir," said Kenner. "We have to win this strike."

But the governor had already turned away.

"I won't be bullied, gentlemen," he said, striding to the door. "There's no better deal. Not from me."

Chapter 11

Breaking into the mercantile was Lowcoal's idea. He'd been in a line of men heading for the miners' camp, each one carrying a grain sack on his shoulders. Lowcoal looked up and immediately was drawn to the big stone building. Leaving the line, he leaned against a window pane and squinted past his cupped hand. Big as a mine ballroom, the store was defined by a row of empty display cases, running down its center. On both sides were long, wooden counters that stretched toward the back, fronting cascades of dusty shelves that reached almost as high as the tin-paneled ceiling.

"We could store things in a place like that," he told Todd later. "The flour and potatoes. They'll all go bad if you leave 'em outside."

When Todd came to get a look, the sun was coming through at a better angle, bouncing off the wooden display cases and copper cash register by the door. Todd rubbed his lower lip.

"Well," he said. "Let's go in and see."

That afternoon, Darko and Gibbs threw themselves against the paint-peeled door, bull-dozing a small barricade of chairs, letting Lowcoal squeeze through. Todd was last inside. Touching nothing, he walked the store aisles behind Darko, Harm and Ben Tate.

The others boosted their courage with whispered jokes, but Gibbs was in awe of the place. He went along one row of cases, running his hand across a marble countertop, touching the dark wood and staring at the floor-to-ceiling shelves along one wall. The other men walked as if wading through knee-deep water in the mine, each footfall drawing voices from the building's wooden bones. Years of dust had settled on every surface and seemed to seal the store's detritus to the floor. In the back, tossed-aside boxes and broken watch chains mingled with empty wrappers and racks of emblem pins, their contents strewn about. Gibbs imagined the people of long ago: men in vests, women in leg-of-mutton sleeves and lace collars at the throat, their gloved hands pulling coins from tiny purses.

"This'll clean up nice," said Darko, leaning over a black spittoon. Beside it was a pyramid of rusting cans, each marked "Tanner's Gunoil."

Gibbs and Lowcoal followed Todd up the creaking stairs to a broad hallway of open doors. He wandered into the front office, the largest one, dominated by a wooden desk, too big to be moved. They watched as he pulled open and inspected every drawer. Beneath the desk was a telephone, pulled off the wall. Awkwardly getting down on his knees, he tugged the thing into the open, lifted the receiver from its cradle and inspected the cloth-covered cord.

"There's the phone pole, right out front," he said.

"Ben Tate could wire it," Lowcoal offered. "He knows that kind of thing and we could sweet-talk the switchboard girl in Boone to make our calls."

Lowcoal walked over to the first of two windows and undid the latch. The pane opened easily toward him, but no light came through. The window had been shut tight with boards.

"Hold on," said Gibbs.

A line of rusty nail points lined the chipped white frame like a row of buttons. Gibbs braced himself and, rearing back, let go with one good kick. A plank loosened, opening a dusty beam of light.

Still kneeling behind the desk, Todd frowned and made as if to protest. But Lowcoal egged the younger Bryant on.

"You're winnin' it!" he said.

Setting his balance, Gibbs gave the planks a second, harder kick. Two boards sailed into the yellowing yard. Gibbs stepped back, startled by the western sunlight, streaming in. He could see out the window, at the hills stretching away into the distance, a band of undulating olive green beyond the railroad tracks. From the foot of the mountain on their left, the water of Blackberry Creek tumbled through a railroad culvert, then beneath the covered bridge. To the right, the creek's long meander curved around two sides of the camp. Within the great bend, the tent city spread away from them, a sea of canvases surrounding the big circus tent.

Nodding, Gibbs gave Lowcoal a turn at the barrier. Before long, the two of them had kicked and pried all the boards from both windows, littering the yard below with splintered slats.

"Well, ain't this nice!" grinned Harm, coming in with Ben Tate and Darko.

Together, the miners looked across the creek at the camp, at the people carrying loads up and down its makeshift streets. The ever-present children crashed through the woods, happier than Gibbs remembered any kids from Sovereign being. He saw the smoking stovepipes, smelled the scents of raw pine and cooking food, and was suddenly optimistic. Clearly, something good was happening here. The miners were building a place for themselves, not so modern as their homes at Sovereign, perhaps, but a place where they felt free, at least. A place where sweat and muscle brought visible results, and no one had to fear reprisals. At least for now.

"Something good is cooking," Harm smiled. "What do you boys say?"

"I'm for it," said Darko. The men filed out, leaving Gibbs and Todd alone.

Still on one knee behind the desk, Todd continued to think about bringing the telephone to life. He rubbed his bandaged arm, a sour look on his face. From the window, Gibbs watched their friends amble across the covered bridge, laughing with each other.

"This place could be the union office," he said. "It's damned-near perfect."

Todd pulled open a drawer, held up a sheet of stationery. Gibbs recognized the familiar curls of bold, blue script.

"It belongs to Sovereign Coal," Todd said.

Gibbs brushed some dust from the window sill.

"Well, they sure as hell aren't using it. Look at the state of the place. Just left to ruin."

"But we can't take it over," Todd frowned. "That would stoke 'em bad."

Gibbs lifted his eyes to the tent city beyond the bridge.

"Shit," he said. "They probably don't even know they own it."

By the end of the week, Todd had overcome his doubts about occupying the office. Downstairs, the strikers fell into the work of cleaning up the mercantile. For her part, Tildy took on the project as her own. She immediately sent Harm and Lowcoal to find a pump, steel buckets and a mop. Others were given the task of sweeping up dust and dirt. Able men and women eagerly cleaned years of rubbish from the counters, the floors and shelving. They wiped the cash register and burnished old brass lamp fixtures on the walls. Food and dry goods went down into the cellar, which was cool and dry. With a bit of humor, Lowcoal Petry placed a hand-lettered sign in the front window, renaming the place "Blair Union Mercantile."

Before long they were carrying the food sacks and supplies back from the big community tent – bags of flour and dried beans, canvases and blankets. The tents and cots were kept handy in the store, along with sacks of grain and flour, the "basic" stores from the union office, the district headquarters in Meridian. Tildy oversaw the process, penciling entries into an old company logbook.

"We need a way of keeping stock," she told Todd. "Gotta make sure everything's accounted for."

"Sure," he said. He figured that Kenner would welcome this. Tildy pushed on.

"How many people would you say are in the camp?" she asked.

Todd gazed at the ceiling.

"More than a thousand, I figure. Plus the families."

Tildy clicked her tongue, shaking her head.

"Does the union have a way to pull bread from dust and dew?"

Their first miracle arrived in the form of some other store-owners in Blair. Happy to see the old mercantile unshuttered, the group dropped by to welcome the strikers. Their delegation was led by the manager of a hardware store, who brought them some drygoods and a little cash.

"We'll do what we can for you," he told them. "As long as there ain't too much ruckus."

"But we want to help you," another said and, looking around, added, "Between you and me, the mines has damn-near killed this town!"

On the mountain, Carla had retreated into the work of her mother's home – scrubbing clothes, baking bread, and preserving food for the coming winter. She knew that she was trying to recover some sense of harmony and order after the nightmare of her husband's death. Despite her mother's harsh words before the funeral, Carla found comfort in working alongside her again. As she never had before, Carla had come to understand her mother's pain and knew that the work of the home-stead had been her solace. The daughter welcomed it, glad to be occupied by the familiar daily rhythms of her mother's home. She enjoyed steal-ing an hour or two each day for excursions in the woods. Nick clearly loved taking her to his hidden sinkhole cave, where Carla praised his stone shelf of ever-changing treasures – the line of rocks and pine cones and candle stubs he'd collected. Most days, she would leave him there, preferring to be alone. Then, brushing herself off, she drifted off toward the clearing where she and Sid first met.

He'd come upon her here on a Sunday and simply started talking – just as if he'd known her for a long time. Eventually, he asked where she'd come from and about her parents. Carla told him, which made her feel both older and younger than her years.

"You shouldn't be running around out here alone," he warned her.

"I can handle myself," Carla replied, and told him how she and her father had once killed a rattlesnake.

"I ain't no snake, if that's what you're thinking," Sid grinned at her.

Immediately she liked the amiable miner. When Sid asked it, she agreed to meet him the following week. Each time they met, she discovered some new element of his character – and, perhaps, some of her own. From the start, she understood how Sid's admiration for her went beyond his attention to what she could do for him – beyond the things men wanted that Mary had warned her about. Carla knew that Sid wanted her in that way too. But there was more to him. Carla remembered how his eyes flashed when he talked to her; how he made her think about all kinds of new possibilities. She came to count the days until the next Sunday afternoon, when she would see him again.

They walked together, Sid taking her through a stretch of woods to their favorite spot – the wooded mountainside overlooking Sovereign. Listening to him, Carla absorbed the view, fascinated by his explanations of the industrial work, most of which happened in the deep underground. All about going into the mine each day and getting coal loaded into the miniature train cars. From their perch in the woods, Carla watched the cars appear briefly on the landing outside the mine before disappearing into the steep umbilical of covered mine track. At the end of the line, Sid told her, was the tipple, where the coal was washed and separated by size, then dropped from the hoppers into the long steel train cars, waiting below.

The camp was relatively quiet on Sundays. Sid sat close to her, Carla thrilling to his strong arm around her, as they watched people move among the housing rows. Sid had picked out several of his friends and pretended to introduce her to them, telling stories about each one. Carla didn't remember seeing so many human beings in store-bought clothes before and marveled at the fact that this exciting man – tall, lean and handsome – seemed to know so many.

"I want to meet all your friends – for real," she told him.

"Not before we're married," Sid grinned and she kissed him, not for the first time.

How happy she'd been to step across a common threshold with this remarkable man. How easily she had accepted the work of the rented house in the modern industrial camp, how the factory-like surfaces of the kitchen came so clean, with its modern, enameled counters – all so foreign in comparison to her mother's place. Carla was kept busy, of course, keeping coal dust from the house – off the counters and kitchen table cloth, out of the bedsheets and the seams of her husband's coveralls.

As she sat alone in the woods, Carla recalled the ways Sid had found to surprise her. He brought home gifts of flowers he'd picked along the path to the mine, or colorful stones and black fossils from underground. He'd share stories he'd heard, picked up from other men. He'd tell them to her slowly at night, as he peeled away his dirty work clothes. With supper warming, she'd listened to him talk about his friends – increasingly, her friends too. Before the meal, they did the thing that Carla knew she'd miss the most – the nightly ritual of her husband's bath. The steel tub was longer and shallower than most, a design that allowed Sid to lean back, exposing himself. Carla closed her eyes to recall how happy he was to recline in his metal shell, his head resting against a kitchen chair. Trying to be gentle, Carla scrubbed every inch of him, gradually becoming practiced in working loose the coal and sweat, then preparing new water to rinse his chest. Here, Sid raised his arms above his head, his already-washed hands gripping the chair staves behind him. Carla could feel his eyes in their closing, his features melting, emptying of their hardness, as he bathed in the clear pleasure of her touch.

How brief the time had been, she thought. Gone to the place of dreams.

"It's awful cold to be wandering about," Mary said.

By now, Carla had learned to listen beyond her mother's tone and know that her scolding was half-hearted. They sat in the cabin kitchen, where the three of them shelled beans. Carla focused on her hands as they separated beans from shells, then dropped them into a pot.

"The air's good for us," she said. She glanced at Nick, giving him a half-smile, knowing how much he enjoyed his secret place.

"Plenty of air right here," said Mary. "And work enough."

"Yes," sighed Carla, picking up a new handful. "There's work enough anywhere."

Mary raised an eyebrow, watching her daughter toss another skin into the bucket. "I was thinkin' about making a run," she said.

Carla's eyebrows went up, her thoughts going to her friends, wondering what Todd and Gibbs were doing. And Tildy and Harm. What they might need?

Mary put down what she was doing to peer out the little front window, with its view into the yard.

"The hens have slowed their laying," she said. "And we got eggs enough. With all the canning we've done. Yet, still so many apples about."

Carla could see where her mother's talk was going. She broke another bean, as Mary talked to the window.

"Blair is full of vagrants, but more than a few of 'em's got scratch. I figure we can load up tonight, leave early and be down there by mid-day."

That evening, Carla and Nick stocked the wagon with a familiar exhilaration, recalling earlier times. Hoping to prolong their stay, Carla packed as much food as the bed would carry.

They rolled into town the following day. Sitting in front with Mary, Carla noted how much had changed in Blair in the time that they'd been gone. The nameless main street seemed to hum with a surprising vibrance. The covered bridge was constantly trafficked by strikers and their families, going to and from the booming tent city. Carla waved back to several people who greeted her as the wagon passed.

Mary parked right across the street from the busy "Union Mercantile." She dropped open the tailgate and tacked up her hand-lettered produce signs. Soon, Carla was helping her mother's customers, responding to their questions, measuring out their groceries and counting money. It felt good to be among people again, she thought, her eyes searching the street for more familiar faces. Finally, she spotted Todd, who waved as he came out of the store.

"Well, good morning!" he called, although it was past noon. His injured arm was still bound to his chest but he seemed less hindered by it than before. Carla smiled. Mary gave him a wary look.

"You got something against us selling here?" she asked.

Surprised, Todd's gaze went from mother to daughter and back again.

"Why, it's a free town," he grinned. "Are your prices fair?"

Mary's eyes narrowed.

"Who's to say?"

Todd scratched his head.

"Well, Tildy's inside, running the mercantile," he hazarded. "Why don't you come inside and talk? Maybe you can work together."

Mary shook her head.

"I always done it this-a-way," she said. "Too old to change."

"You ain't that old," said Todd, half-smiling, and Mary made a noise before turning away to rearrange her signs.

Todd caught Carla's eye.

"It's good to see you back."

She nodded, knowing he meant it.

"How's the arm?" she asked.

"Getting better," he said, and moved the shoulder to show her he was on the mend.

"The camp is really comin' together," he told her, unable to hide his enthusiasm. "Some of the men are building a bathhouse on the far end.

We meet in the circus tent and give everybody one hot meal a day. The women bring their kids and they sat down to organize a school, even the foreigners. One of 'em sits there with a baby on her lap, telling the rest what they need to do."

At this, Carla looked away. She scanned the huge campsite across the creek and Todd stopped talking.

"How are you doing?" he asked, moving slightly toward her.

"We're all right," said Carla. "Working hard. Putting everything up."

"We're busy here too," he said, but the words fell flat. He seemed eager to get back to the mercantile.

"Come around sometime," he said, and meant it. "Other folks want to see you too."

Carla smiled, promising she would.

Lounging on the corn and dried tobacco, Nick hummed his strange tune as he stared into his own fingers, drawing the occasional gawker from the busy street. Carla sat on a low crate in the shade, seeking out the faces of those she'd known in Sovereign, when she was suddenly reminded of her father. Although only a little girl when Bonner Rising died, she recalled the energy he carried into every project. Each time something went wrong – breaking a new plow shear or a piece of furniture – he frowned, and Carla could see his distress.

"Your mother won't like that," Bonner would say. But the daughter recognized this as a mere excuse. Her father had had his own standard, a level of perfection that only he could judge. He never left a job until it was done to his own satisfaction. If he could, he did a thing better than anyone had expected.

"I need to ask you something," Carla said, causing Mary to glance up at her.

"What?"

"You once said my father was a 'fool'. Do you really think that of him? Did you think it always?"

Mary eyed the street for her next customer. She said nothing for so long that the girl gave up believing she'd ever get an answer.

"It doesn't matter now," Mary said at last. But Carla couldn't tolerate any door staying closed to her.

"I want to know what kind of man he was to you," she persisted. "Was he ever angry? Was he *mean*?"

"No, he wasn't mean," Mary sighed. "But he wasn't shifty either."

Carla edged closer.

"What do you mean, 'shifty'?" she asked.

Mary turned her attention to the wagon bed. She reached down to rearrange some ears of corn in a crate.

"He worked hard enough. But there was so much that he didn't see. He missed enough things that sat there, right in front of his nose, no less than the things that lay out ahead. Or just around the bend.... He trusted the outside world too much."

Like Sid, thought Carla to herself.

Across the street, a group of men gathered before the mercantile. A few raised their arms, beckoning to a dark-haired girl who walked by. The girl, about fifteen, squared her shoulders and pulled a fiddle from a worn case. Carla watched with interest. Her conversation with Mary floated in the air between them like cottonwood silk.

The dark-haired girl on the sidewalk began to play her fiddle. Hearing it, Nick scrambled to the back of the wagon and watched in amazement, ready to jump out of his skin. The song the girl played was full of fun, from someplace wild and foreign.

Mary wordlessly helped a customer as Carla and Nick kept watching. The girl played and danced, her feet keeping time against the sidewalk boards. Carla marveled at the way her knees drew up, her boots coming down in time with those of the dancing men. She could almost feel the sidewalk shaking from across the street. As she watched, Carla knew she envied the girl, surrounded, as she was, by men who listened, laughed and slapped their denimed thighs. Nick continued to stare, openmouthed.

"We never danced like that, did we?" Carla smiled down at him.

"I ain't one for parlor tricks," Mary scowled. "There's plenty of work for us – but not enough for such as them, apparently."

When the first tune was done, one of the men reached out with a small plug of tobacco. Surprisingly, the teenaged girl accepted it. Tucking the knotted thing into her jaw, she launched into another song, wilder than the first.

"I'm gonna get some water for us," Carla announced. Mary nodded, fully focused on her trade.

Carla crossed the street. As soon as she stepped up onto the wooden sidewalk, she realized that her own feet were keeping time to the girl's music. The closer she came, the more the music astounded her, exciting the very air around the mercantile. The clapping men, all strangers, watched Carla go by. In passing, she noticed the rifles strapped to their backs.

Soldiers, all of them, she thought. *Dancing, singing, letting off steam before the fight.*

She raised her hand to them and smiled. She walked into the mercantile, not looking back. Tildy came around the counter to welcome her. Carla felt her aunt's warm embrace, and realized at once that she would not be returning to her mother's homestead.

News of the strike traveled to other towns around the east. People read about Sid's death in Cinncinati, Louisville, Pittsburgh, Baltimore and Washington, DC. The *New York Times* reported that he had tried to "get the drop" on the deputies, and they'd simply outdrawn him. The breathless story went on, however, to describe the miners' outrage at the killing of their hero and told about the arrests, without charges, of "about fifty strikers who'd witnessed the event."

"We're marching on the Logan jail!" one miner told the *Times*. "We're all goin'! One big union, for working people everywhere!"

In a short time, the mercantile became a place where people came for their most basic needs – donated canvases, cornmeal or new blankets from the union office in Meridian. A steady stream of volunteers kept the store shelves stocked with goods, carried in on trains operated by the sympathetic railroad workers. Carla slipped easily into Tildy's organization, often carrying or delivering goods across the creek, to women in their tents. On one such mission, Carla came across the bridge to find Todd, standing before a group of men, more than twenty leaders of the union's "local organizations" that made up the camp. Todd held a daily meeting with these "local" men, Carla knew. Curious, she stopped to listen.

"The strike pay is coming from our brothers at the state and national union," Todd was saying. "A dollar a week for each man may not seem like much to your people, but there's more than two thousand of us here now, and that's a lot of money. Kenner wants to encourage us to make it work as best we can."

Todd looked up from some papers he held. Seeing Carla, he smiled a little before continuing. Carla scanned the crowd before him and, for the first time, noticed her Uncle Harm with Lowcoal, Ben Tate and Gibbs, who glanced off in her direction from time to time. Todd shuffled notes in his hand.

"Donations are coming in every day," he said. "And the union is taking up collections for us in different places, mostly in the East. Early this morning, a truck came in with coffee, along with some big sacks of rice and flour and soap and there weren't enough men around to meet it. Tildy Fox is doin' all she can, but she's got her hands full. I want everyone to make sure she has all the help she needs – her and the other women, working there with her."

He looked again in Carla's direction before returning to the sheets in his hand.

"Now, about our pickets," he continued. "We've got groups of roving picketers, hitting eight mines during daylight hours, every day. If any of coal companies have transported in scab laborers to take our jobs, well, we don't know it. None of our brothers on the trains say they've brought any replacements in. Also, none of the Baldwins nor Sheriff Gore's deputies have shown up at any of our picket lines."

"They'd better not, neither," said one of the local leaders. "We'll knock that man on his ass."

The other men laughed, and Todd smiled a little before continuing.

"Things have been quiet up until now, but this could change on us at any moment," he said. "Kenner says we should be on guard at all times. He says we should do our best to avoid a fight. We have to raise a picket line when the scabs arrive, so they know exactly what they're doing, and decide to go back home – not take our jobs."

Gibbs raised his hand and spoke.

"Can't we just shoot the scabs, Todd?"

The men around him laughed. Todd's face took on a look of irritation. "No, Gibbs," he said. "Shooting or thumping the scabs ain't gonna get us our jobs and our houses back."

At this point, Todd glanced again in Carla's direction and she was suddenly reminded that she would probably never return to Sovereign, to the life she'd enjoyed with Sid. *Will I ever be somebody's wife again?* she wondered. *Will I ever be someone's mother?*

"Tom Kenner wants us all to remember why we're here," Todd continued. "We need all the companies of the Southern Coal Association to recognize the unity of their workers. That we will not compete against each other to go down into the hole for longer hours at lower pay! They have to see that we are all union men, saying the same thing – that we all want fair shake at every coal mine. Or there'll be no work. That's why we're on strike! They should know that we will return to our jobs, and gladly, when the companies can promise us fair pay for the coal we dig every day."

"Amen to that," said one of the local leaders.

"They have to promise to weigh the coal fairly and to pay us some kind of wage for the 'dead work' too," said Todd. "All the checking for gas and putting up ceiling props. Then, there's the most important thing: We have to be free to hold our union meetings, to talk among ourselves and organize during the evenings and the weekends without the Baldwin police coming in and thumping us for it!"

The men nodded their assent.

"Now Tom Kenner wants us to keep a sharp eye on those mining camps," said Todd. "And get as many of our men as we can out on those picket lines! But, I'm telling you, he's hearing some things in Meridian that he doesn't like. We have to keep this place under control – and you all know what I'm talking about."

His eyes locked on Gibbs, who spoke up again.

"Why don't you just let us train 'em, Todd?" he asked. The other leaders in the group grew quiet.

"We have so many men here now," Gibbs went on, "we are busting at the seams. Todd, these men are all set to start the biggest march on Logan you've ever seen. Let the Baldwins and Sheriff Gore try to stop us! Anything they do will be on them! Our boys are out here, ready to string those murdering Baldwins from the highest tree. All you and Kenner need to do is just give us the word!"

"You cannot be serious," said Todd. "Gore has more guns – and the law's on his side."

"The law," Gibbs sneered. "You mean 'Logan law.'"

Todd turned on his younger brother.

"Is yours any better?" he asked, losing his temper. "That's what you want, isn't it? To take the law into your own hands? I am telling you, Gibbs, we are letting things get too wild here. I know what the men are up to. I know you're out there with them, doing drills and target practice in the lower field. And you need to stop it, before somebody gets hurt."

Listening, Carla felt suddenly out-of-place. She started walking, but continued to hear their voices as she went.

"How can Kenner blame us for wanting to stay on the march?" Gibbs was saying. "The Baldwins were the ones who started shooting, and the sheriff stood by and watched! By god, Todd, how can you keep us here – after what they done to Sid? Can anybody blame us for wanting to defend ourselves?"

Todd stared at his younger brother. "All of us have to stick with the union," he said calmly. "It's the only thing we have. We have orders to stay on the pickets and try to convince the scabs from crossing the picket line. No picking up guns and marching off to Logan."

The next day, Gibbs was standing before the mercantile, eying a green-paneled truck as it came into town. Recognizing Ben Tate at the wheel, Gibbs watched the clattering machine round the corner around the mercantile. Together with Darko, Gibbs made a beeline through the building to the loading dock, in back. Emerging from the truck, Lowcoal and Ben Tate beckoned them down the steps. The men circled the parked vehicle. The motor ticked as it cooled as Lowcoal whispered in time, "We got 'em now. We got 'em now."

"Where'd you get the truck?" asked Darko.

Ben Tate slapped the side panel, where "Express Delivery Co." was written in artful, red-and-white letters.

"We found it," Ben winked. "Call it an early Christmas."

Lowcoal dropped the rear gate and jumped into the cargo box. The others stared inside, where more than a dozen long crates were stacked. On one side, a canvas tarp had been thrown over several irregular shapes. Ben and Lowcoal stooped to drag one of the wooden crates out to the tailgate. Gibbs glanced toward the mercantile.

"Let's get 'em inside," he said. "Down the back steps."

Going back and forth in pairs, the five men stacked almost twenty crates in the darkest corner of the basement. Darko and Ben hefted the four canvas-wrapped bundles and set them on the concrete floor.

Carla had been helping Tildy in the store when she noticed all the activity. She came down and stood at the bottom of the stairs. A strand of her hair had worked itself loose and fell across her face.

"What's this?" she asked.

Gibbs looked back at her, uncertain.

"Just storing stuff," he said curtly, then added: "You and Tildy don't want to know about it."

"There's nothing in this place we don't want to know," Carla shot back and boldly walked over to their stack of crates.

"You can't-" started Gibbs, but she turned and gave him a look that went right through him, daring him to keep secrets from her.

Gibbs frowned but didn't argue as they all circled around. Lowcoal pried open the first lid revealing ten Springfield rifles, lined up butt-to-barrel. Harm Fox whistled. Lowcoal turned to Gibbs.

"There's at least two hundred guns here," he breathed. "Ammunition too. And look at this."

He pulled away the tarp. At first Gibbs mistook it for a land-survey instrument, or a section of fat, grey-green pipe. It was the body of a Browning machine gun, and there were two of them.

"Goddamn!" he said.

Lowcoal uncovered the legs, and stretched them out on the concrete floor like metal spiders. Alongside, he laid a folded stack of belted cartridges. Gibbs glanced at Carla and wondered what she might be thinking.

"Here's the best of it," Lowcoal said.

He reached out, pulled a packing slip, a blue ink-stained invoice. Named as "Purchaser" was the Southern Coal Association. The SCA's "Recipient of Goods" was its comptroller, Sheriff Riley Gore.

"We took it right out from under their noses," Lowcoal explained.

"Todd won't like it," muttered Ben.

Gibbs studied Carla's face.

"Don't worry about Todd," he said. "He's too busy on that telephone to Kenner to worry about us."

"Just like Paint Creek," Harm Fox said, half to himself.

"What do you mean, Harm?" Lowcoal asked.

"I mean there might be hell to pay."

Gibbs turned to him. "This ain't the same as Paint Creek, Harmon. Not at all the same."

"How do you figure that?" the old man asked.

Gibbs' eyes flared wolfish.

"With all this?" he said, pointing to the weapons. "And more than two thousand men? I'd say the odds are better in our favor this time around, wouldn't you?"

Act II

Jock Moore told me that when President Harding was made
acquainted with the situation he said, "Why, Jock, they would not
murder men who were being held for trial, would they?"
"Mr. President, they have done so," Moore replied.
Jock also informed me that President Harding called Governor
E. F. Morgan...over long distance telephone and told
the governor that if any more men were shot or mistreated while
awaiting trial, he would hold him responsible for the acts.

– Fred Mooney, Secretary-Treasurer,
District 17 United Mine Workers of America, 1921

Chapter 12

Todd paced around the office, carefully exercising his arm, massaging
muscles long unused. He went to the window. Gibbs was looking out the
other one, to Todd's left, his foot propped against its frame. Thus, each
from his own window, the two brothers gaped at the field, a wide sea of
tents.

"There's more today," said Gibbs. "I figure we're getting close to
three thousand, now."

Todd returned his arm to its red-bandana sling. He had just reported
the new head count to Tom Kenner on the telephone, along with an account of strikers on picket lines at different mines. Kenner's instructions
to him were still fresh in Todd's mind as he waged what was becoming
a familiar fight with his younger brother.

"We are striking to get our jobs and houses back," Todd said. "We're
picketing eight different mines."

"While the Coal Association replaces us with scab workers at seven
others," Gibbs interrupted. "We're not doing enough."

"Tom Kenner is working in Meridian to get our jobs back. You and
your bunch want to do it by yourselves. You are not going to win without
the union."

"At least let the pickets carry guns!" Gibbs countered. "The coal
companies' power lies in their private guards. That's where we should

hit 'em! There's no chance for justice as long as the Baldwins are here, and there's only one way for us to get rid of them!"

"Our power is in the union!" Todd argued, shaking his head. "Kenner and the state organization will *not* support us if we're trying to blast our way into Logan County. We cannot start an all-out shooting war against the Baldwins!"

"It's already a war!" said Gibbs. "But we ain't exactly fightin' it. Even if we do get a work contract, we can't expect the company police to stick to it. We'll sign an agreement, then the Baldwins just take everything into their own hands, as usual! They're a power unto themselves."

Todd studied his brother's face, so much like their father's – the severe countenance, the solid jaw.

"We're not getting enough pickets out there to cover all the mines," Gibbs said. "And the companies would just as soon set their gun thugs loose on us as pay us more to bring us back to work! I say we meet their paid police, blow for blow! Fighting's the only thing they respect."

As he listened, Todd was surprised to recognize another voice. His brother sounded more than a little like Sid.

"We can't do this with guns, Gibbs. Not before we've tried everything else."

Gibbs' jaw went tight. Had Carla told Todd about the stolen Springfields? He'd seen the way Todd looked at her, the way he was with her. Gibbs was suddenly aware of a new reason to be jealous of his older brother.

Gibbs glanced over at Harm Fox, sitting watch by the door. The old man was leaning over, his elbows on his knees. He stared at his shoes. Listening, thinking.

"The Baldwins got two hundred thugs," Gibbs went on. "Each one of 'em's got a high-powered rifle and a lawman's badge. Every day, they seem to bring some new charge against one of ours. New officers filing their court papers, trying to pull us in – just like what they did to Sid. They aren't even signing their own names. They're a bunch of killers, handing out death warrants!"

Todd tried to keep himself calm. "We're sitting on a goddamned powder keg and you're out there, wanting to light it up."

Gibbs turned away from the window, laughing to himself.

"What's so damned funny?"

Gibbs turned and looked at him. "How could you forget what they told Sid? 'Come in peacefully. Leave your guns at home.' Todd, we should have made him take that pistol. We should've been his bodyguards, every one of us armed, just like them."

"You don't know what would've happened if we'd started shooting," said Todd.

"Well, I know what happens when we don't! Sid is dead and more'n seventy good union men are inside the Logan jail, hanging by their heels for all we know! You expect them to get justice from Riley Gore? What are you doin' for them, Todd? Nothin'!"

"Kenner says we lose everything as soon as the shooting starts."

"Screw Kenner," growled Gibbs. "We should arm ourselves and march on Logan – and you should be leading it."

"The hell you say," Todd returned.

"I do say it! Those men out there respect you a hell of a lot more than they do Tom Kenner! Get out in front and lead them!"

From the door, Harm Fox raised his head, showing interest. Todd looked from one to the other. "I can't even talk about this," he scowled.

Tired, Todd searched the desk for something that he might chew or smoke. His arm hung helplessly in the sling. To Gibbs, his older brother looked like a broken soldier.

"Think of it," he said, pointing to the field of tents beyond the window. "Every one of those men out there are itchin' to march. Think of all our brothers in that damned hell-hole of a jail, just waiting for us. Why won't you do something for them?"

"Gibbs, you just don't understand-"

"What don't I understand? Goddamn it, Todd, I've been living in your shadow all my life! Quit telling me what I 'don't understand'! *You* don't understand that your men are tired of just standing around, waiting for the company to give 'em their houses back and a little justice! It ain't happening for us, Todd! For most of us here, this is the first time we're actually standing up for ourselves! We've got enough men and guns here to blow the sheriff's doors wide open. And, we all know, those Baldwins will just run like crazy. For one thing, they can't shoot worth a damned! They're a bunch of slicked-down city boys a long way from home and no real stake in this fight! Todd, we can't quit now. If you tell us to quit, you're gonna see me – and all these good men walk off. They'll just lose all respect for you."

Todd clenched his fist. "Kenner's a good man, and he's been at this longer than you or me. I'd say he knows more than Harm here, even. By god, Gibbs, Kenner talks to the governor! And the governor is listening! Do you know how many years it took for the union to get this far? We can't just give that up."

Harm stood up. "Come on, Gibbs," he said. Gibbs stared at Todd, now working his arm again.

"Right," said Gibbs. He joined Harm at the door, then turned back to Todd. "If you can't lead us, then do us this favor: Just go back to the governor and tell him how much we appreciate all he's done. Tell him to come on down here with all his flags and promises. We'll stand up and cheer – just as soon as we're finished."

"Finished with what?" Todd asked, suspicious.

"Doing what we have to do."

"You can't shoot the union into Logan County!"

Gibbs looked at his brother as if he were a stranger. "Well, it's a damn sight better than watching you talk it to death."

The two men were silent going down the steps. Then, Harm stopped on the landing overlooking the mercantile. He turned and took Gibbs by the arm. "You know," he said quietly. "Todd is in something of a tight spot on this one." He pronounced it as a single word, *tightspot.*

Gibbs looked out across the busy store. Carla stood there, working the register and listening to a customer. Gibbs saw that she was giving the man her full attention – the way she did. Whatever that man needed, Gibbs thought, Carla Mandt would sort it out for him. She was just that way. *Nice,* he thought. She was nice to everyone.

Gibbs sighed, surprised to realize how hard he'd been breathing, as if he'd been in an all-out fight with Todd. "What kind of a tight spot?" he asked.

Harm studied the floorboards, scratching the back of his neck with a coal-stained hand as he searched for words. Gibbs leaned against the sturdy banister, his eyes on Carla.

"There're things that Todd can say to us," the older miner began. "And things he can't. He's up there in the union leadership, like you said. Now, that's a fine thing – in some places. But, in Logan, the law's on the other side."

"The Baldwins ain't exactly the law," Gibbs began.

"You're damned right," Harm nodded. "They'd just as soon piss on a rule book as read it." He paused a moment, trying to calm himself.

"There's not a day that I don't think about those men in jail," he said. "Not a day that I don't want to make the Baldwins pay for what they did to Bone and Sid. It can't go on this way. Gibbs, those assholes gotta learn, and we gotta teach 'em." He stopped to catch his breath.

"Back in '12, they arrested a bunch of us and put us in front of their own drum-head court. Gave us all secret trials, held in this one fellow's office. It got to be a regular thing: They'd find somebody on the street and drag us in there, two or three at a time. They told us: 'You boys done this and that…blab-blab-blab,' and they'd give us our sentences, right there on the spot."

"Where'd you hear this, Harm?"

The old miner looked at Gibbs, seeing he'd been distracted by something down in the store.

"Look at me, boy! I'm telling you, I was there! They arrested me just for standing on the street! Back in those days, I was still pretty damned mean – man enough that it took six of those sons-of-bitches just to pull me in! I did two weeks in jail, and it was hell to pay! Let me tell you, I feel for those poor boys in that jail now. But Todd has a point."

Men and women were filing into the mercantile. Carla was joined by Tildy. They stood together behind the register, laughing over something. Gibbs turned away, forcing himself to listen to Harm. "Todd says he wants us to sit tight. Are you sayin' the same thing – that we should just give up on our men in jail?"

Harm shook his head. "We can't march against them, not out in the open. Two thousand men with guns might seem like a powerful thing. But Todd's right. We march in there, and the companies just bring in more gunmen to come down on us."

Gibbs shifted uncomfortably. "Well, what do we do, Harm? You want us just to sit here like the governor wants?"

"Let Todd and Kenner deal with the governor," Harm said. "They got their lawyers and all. But, you and me, and some of these others, we should get back to work."

He gave the younger man a wily look and, here, Gibbs saw a new Harm Fox. Despite so many years of working with him every day, Gibbs had never really known his father's best friend. Harm was a man who'd been fighting a battle, one way or another, practically every day of his life. Standing before him was a soldier. A veteran of the Baldwin wars.

"It's all about our work, ain't it?" Harm said.

"About the mines," Gibbs nodded.

"Then, make sure they don't move no coal. If the Logan mines get up and running again, we've lost the game."

"I get you, Harm," Gibbs said, and clapped his old friend on the back, his mind working on a plan.

As they continued down the steps, Gibbs treated himself to another glance at the two laughing women behind the counter. Spotting him, Carla smiled. Startled, Gibbs almost missed a step, but managed to wave to her. She was Sid's widow, so he didn't care to think too much on it. At the same time Gibbs knew, or imagined, that other men must be coming into the store every day, just to see that smile.

Gaujot entered the jailblock, not bothering to turn on a light. He'd sent the regular deputies away, telling them to get themselves a drink. His guards had wasted no time in leaving, happy to abandon this place, always smelling of piss and fear.

"Let him sharpen his own goddamned edges," the men told each other across their pint jars at the speakeasy.

Gaujot entered the cell block, eager for the thrill of meeting his enemy up close. One or two of the newest prisoners rose from their bunks to see who it was. He considered opening their doors, introducing himself. But he moved on. Others, who'd been there longer, feigned apathy. They knew Gaujot; it was better not to watch, much less draw attention to oneself.

The big captain walked the center line, quietly seeking out his man. He looked for clues in each one's eyes, for body motion.

In moments like this, Pearl Gaujot loved being in his own skin. He felt surrounded by his enemy, like on a battlefield, as he imagined it – for he'd never been. Hostile forces all around; but all of them were cowardly and primitive, lacking discipline.

This keeps your edges sharp, he thought.

He stopped before the cell of a man whose name he knew.

"Wilson."

A burly machinist, Matthew Wilson roused himself and straightened. He'd been sleeping, using his folded jacket as a pillow. His once-blue work shirt was wrinkled, burnished dark with coal and oil. He'd been a lumber man before – a job that had knocked him around, some. His family and friends nicknamed him "Tick" although most had forgotten why.

Gaujot quietly hung his pistol out of reach, felt the heat rise inside him. Tick Wilson, union red, muttered something at him and flexed his hands.

"How's that?" Gaujot asked.

Every nerve in his arms and chest woke up, in anticipation of "trying out" Tick Wilson.

A few of the other prisoners started making noise – a rising chorus of protests that only served to egg Gaujot on. Taking a quiet breath, he opened Tick's cell door.

Wilson sprung at him. The move was clumsy, but he still succeeded in connecting, sending his fist tight into Gaujot's gut. Gaujot was only a little surprised. Still glad for the challenge, he pulled back his steel fist, and knocked Wilson between the eyes. The miner staggered back against his bunk, the cartilage broken at the base of his nose. He stayed there, unwilling to get up again.

Offended at this cowardice, Gaujot shook his head. He went to the bed, pulled Wilson up and used his massive fist again. Hard as knotted wood, it repeated its work, softening Tick Wilson's flesh like bread dough. Cries from the other prisoners grew louder, but Gaujot took it as someone cheering him on. He clawed at Wilson's bloody shirt. Soon, Wilson knelt before him – bare-chested, bruised and crying.

"What do you want from me!"

Gaujot smiled, puffed great amounts of air, bent and gripped him by the back of the belt. Like a bar bouncer, he lifted the prisoner, although the man wasn't small. Tick Wilson thrashed like some great fish, then froze. Gaujot's pearl-handled knife had appeared from nowhere, suddenly pressed against his crotch.

"Be still, you red," Gaujot whispered. "Don't wiggle, now."

Wilson emitted a pitiful moan as the tears crawled down his stubbled cheeks. Wordlessly, he surrendered to the nasty nuzzling of Gaujot's blade.

"Sir."

Gaujot turned and looked. A squirrelly jailer's son stood at the cell door. The boy watched him from beneath a mop of tossled hair.

"This came for you," he said, holding up an envelope.

Sheriff Riley Gore had one eye on the drink in his glass as he wrote another check from the Coal Association, this one for his hotel rooms. Leaning forward in his upholstered office chair, the sheriff rewarded himself with a sip of Canadian Club.

No one is blessed with contraband so fine, he thought. *A man gets a job and is proud to manage a company. My kingdom's built on a hundred businesses and black gold. My realm's the size of twenty Manhattans. And I'm the goddamned boss.*

Gore's rise to power in Logan had been rapid. He was twenty-four in 1899, the year George Waddill signed him as a bookkeeper for the Wolfpen Mining Company. In Gore, Waddill saw a young, sharp mind – a little smart, perhaps, but tough. Gore had told the businessman how he'd worked his way through college and Waddill liked that. In fact, Gore never finished school. He'd learned his trade by traveling the country, bilking investors with a series of phony land deals. Not long after landing in Logan, however, Riley Gore could see new potential.

"This coal industry is going places," Waddill assured him. "In twenty years, you won't recognize this town. We're gonna build it up to look as good as any Eastern city. We need smart men like you."

Waddill himself had been a brakeman – later, a surveyor – for the railroad. With the face and posture of a bulldog, he started making land deals. Young Riley Gore couldn't have asked for a better place to learn. Shuttling back and forth between the county courthouse and the offices of Wolfpen Coal, the young accountant easily came up with new tricks for luring new investors and acquiring property. Under Gore's sharp eye and hand, Wolfpen Coal became practiced at two important skills: Identifying elements of risk and getting rid of them.

In Logan, Gore learned genuine land management from more experienced – and wealthier – teachers. He learned which liabilities to hide and which assets to overplay in the stacks of figures between the company letterhead and the bottom line. If state officials asked for a meeting, Gore met with them alone. He learned to respond to their questions without giving anything away. Under his system, entire trains of coal could disappear, and the state authorities had little ability or incentive to disbelieve him. Those who were inclined to dig any further posed problems from time to time. But, as Gore knew, every man – even a government man – had his price. And his partner's pockets grew deeper every year.

By 1907, Wolfpen Mining had gobbled up several competitors and had changed its name to Sovereign Coal. Gore thought he'd reached the top, but, as Waddill told him, "This is just the beginning."

Together, they reached out to other coal operators. They co-founded the Southern Coal Association. Waddill agreed to serve as the first president. Riley Gore, his protege, was treasurer. In March 1911, Waddill came to Gore with an entirely new assignment. They'd just finished a dinner of potatoes and beefsteak, washed down with imported whiskey.

"The members of the association believe you can serve us better elsewhere," Waddill said.

Immediately, Gore wondered whether he's slipped up, somehow. Had someone found something out? Had he gotten too greedy?

"You want me to leave the association?" Gore asked.

"Not at all," Waddill smiled. "We want you to run for public office."

The following season, the coal association ushered Riley Gore into his first elected post, that of county tax assessor. There, he was able to guide new members of the association – all distinguished land attorneys – through the maze of Logan County title records and land surveys. He had but one goal: Each SCA company must save as much money in land taxes as to be worth the "price of admission" – the payment of association dues. Gore had proven himself to be up to this task. Waddill fell into the habit of calling the association "*our* union."

As county tax assessor, Gore got to know a lot of people, a good skill for getting elected. He developed a knack for finding men in their fields. He often had friendly talks, learning what a man needed to run his farm or conduct county business. He chatted with miners and their supervisors in the coal camps.

"I'm tough, but I won't lie to you," he told them. "You'll never wonder where you stand, not with me. And any man who supports me will always have a job in Logan County. I'll see to that!"

With such practice, Riley Gore soon learned how to handle crowds. As it turned out, he had a natural talent for politics. He made his patron proud.

"Our man Riley knows how to dance and how to dip!" Waddill boasted to his coal association friends. "That boy could sell steel-toe boots to copperheads."

After two years in office, however, it was time for Riley Gore's promotion. He was encouraged to hand the assessor's position over to a younger candidate – someone whom he could control. The next campaign would be more challenging, a bigger investment. As always, the risk was assessed beforehand and determined to be worth it. Gore would run for Logan sheriff, where his responsibilities included collecting taxes and enforcing the law – including labor contracts. The 1916 election gave Gore the largest majority of votes that had ever gone to any sheriff. Best of all, the whole campaign hadn't cost the coal association more than five thousand dollars.

Gore sipped his Canadian Club, recalling a story that had circulated among his deputies that first campaign. One had been given the task of signing-up new voters in a distant mining camp. The man stood in uniform before a group of foreign workers, and told them they could register to vote in Logan County if they passed the American loyalty test. After talking about the local election, the deputy decided to read these men some of the questions required for citizenship.

"Who's president of the United States?" he asked.

To a man, those rangly fellows yelled one answer: *By god, it's Riley Gore!*

Fighting down his laughter, the young deputy spent the rest of the afternoon signing up every fellow in the place to Gore's party.

Gore smiled to recall the story. And, after all, it was only fair. By voting his ticket of candidates, each of those men came out a winner: They would keep their jobs as loyal, productive citizens of Logan County. Loyalty and productive work counted for everything, from top to bottom. Gore was proud of the fact that Logan miners – his people – delivered more tonnages of coal than men of any other county or state, east to west. That was a fact. It spelled growth for everyone – for the companies, the organization, and for Logan Township.

Gore poured himself yet another congratulatory drink. George Waddill had delivered on his promise: In just a few years, Logan had been transformed from a poor backwater into a thriving city. He was sipping from the glass when he noticed Pearl Gaujot standing in his office doorway.

"By god, Pearl!" he said, putting down the whiskey. "For a big fellow, you sure got a way of slipping up on a man."

"We've got a problem," Gaujot said.

Gore frowned at the word *problem.* He didn't especially like dealing with difficult pieces of work this late at night. Pearl Gaujot was a solid officer – as loyal as they came. But he wasn't always savvy about solving problems on his own.

"It's important to take some initiative, Pearl. Sometimes you have to make your own call."

Gaujot handed him the note. "From a friend," he said.

Gore took the paper, and read it:

UNION CLOSE TO DEAL WITH GOV

The sheriff smiled in satisfaction, immediately forgiving his Baldwin captain. Gaujot's work as a spy, after all, was second to none. His agents were everywhere. He was worth his weight in scotch.

Gore nodded at the note. Pulling himself forward in his chair, he breathed deeply, giving himself time.

"We have to act on this," he said, at last. "Let folks know just where we stand."

He capped the bottle.

"Round up some of your best men. Wake that fellow Howell, over at the yard. We'll call up the Special."

Chapter 13

Nick rose on his elbows and cast a sleepy eye toward his mother, who stirred next to him in the wagon bed. Carefully the boy slipped out from under the canvas and over the side. Moving silently through the dark, he entered the wooded area near the creek and found a tree. He unfastened the rope that tied his pants and urinated. He was awake now. With his eyes and ears, he searched the woods beyond his fingers for nightbirds and other signs of life. Beyond the trees, the diving bats made their frantic trails against the roof of stars.

Retying his trousers, Nick wandered back onto the path. He crouched some distance from his mother's wagon, deciding whether to go back to bed or play. Even in the dark, he knew where all his friends were sleeping. He could easily pick out his sister's tent, his aunt and uncle's, and the two men with the silver toy. Nick liked being in the camp; had gotten used to the people and their sounds. There were also woods enough and he knew – or could easily guess – the paths that would take him back to his homeplace. And to his place, underground. In the clear stream, he'd found some new stones and he was eager to put them on his shelf.

Padding down the tent row, he peeked into his sister's tent. Hearing him, Carla woke immediately. She stared at his shape in the opening until Nick spoke a made-up word for her.

"Go back to mama, peanut," Carla sighed, and he withdrew.

The clay beneath his feet was cool, mildly insulated by the thinning thatch of grass. Out on the path, however, he heard something that drew his attention toward the town. He looked, standing in the center of the wide lane between the tents. The sound grew bigger.

By the railroad track, a miner named Paul Macey dozed on his watch, his chair tipped against a mail-bag post. Hearing the sound, Macey stirred. The familiar metal squall approached and Macey stood, turning to see its lights. He stretched and was preparing to wave at the engineer when, to his surprise, the window lights winked out. The train was a short one, not pulling any freight at all – and slow, Macey thought, as if carrying something much heavier than it was.

Frowning, Macey looked at the time and tried to puzzle all the ways this nighttime train was out-of-place. It had a single passenger car, black and private. Up top, he saw steel housing. Like a metal crow's nest. Finally, his eye picked out the shape of a man perched there.

"By god-" Macey said, and went for his rifle. Before he could touch it, though, a sniper's bullet snapped his head backward. The shot up--ended him, spattering blood against the post and his fallen chair.

Now, bullets poured from the train coach, spat from the rifles of fourteen men, crouched behind its steel-plated windows.

Nick stood, transfixed, as the engine pulled into position alongside the camp. The metal storm whipped the black air like the bats. And the noise began. Nick didn't think to be frightened until the tents started moving. Their taught white skins began to pop and shake, as if they were being slapped. From inside, men called out, then shouted to each other in different languages. A child woke and screamed. Then, the women.

Nick watched the camp come alive – all the tents around him dancing and bucking like ghosts in the frenzied night. He didn't move, even to raise his fingers.

Bending over his rifle, Pearl Gaujot settled into the rhythm of the battlefield: *Fire, eject, reload.* He thrilled to the assassin's game, sighting his weapon on a random tent's black mouth. *Fire. Eject.* He found another target, creeping along in the dark. *Fire. Eject. Reload.* He sneered at the shadows' futile dodges, watched them fall. *Fire. Eject.* Just like a machine.

From the other end of the armored train car, Mouseface Moler raised his head and grinned. Between them, twelve sharpshooters curved their bodies into their guns, a dozen knees pressed into seat leather, lined up like competitors at a carnival shooting gallery. Mouseface sighted his own rifle, hoping to nick another red, irritated that the light wasn't better in his favor.

Gibbs woke to the volume of noise. Two bullets had already pierced the tent he shared with Todd. Outside, a light flickered against the shimmering canvas wall, telling him something was on fire. Now, he could see Todd, lying under his cot.

Get down, Gibbs!

Immediately, Gibbs tumbled off his bed, crawled to the tent door and looked outside. People were running and stumbling everywhere, trying to get away from the deadly train. Seemingly unaware of the bullets, two men tried to pull a flaming canvas from its platform, working to free those inside. All around, the night air shimmered and screamed with flying metal. Men and women ran blindly with their children, desperate for any kind of cover.

Stay down! Stay down!

Run here!

Don't move!

Without thinking, Gibbs scrambled across the path to Carla's tent. He pulled open the flap and found her, crouched beside her pallet. Sid's gun was in her hand. Instinctively, Gibbs froze and showed her his empty hands. To his relief, she lowered the gun. The terror, however, was still in her eyes.

"Nick is out there!" she cried.

Turning, Gibbs scanned the chaotic scene. People scrambled in and out of tents. Nowhere seemed safe, grown men competing with each other for scant cover behind low tent platforms or piles of wood. Some had found their guns, although more than one hugged his rifle close – too afraid to use it. A young man got tangled in a clothesline of sheets and was riddled with bullets. Others tripped over tent stakes, knocking down poles. A second tent collapsed onto its burning stove, catching fire.

Then, Gibbs spotted Nick. The boy stood, as if mesmerized, in the middle of the path. His eyes were on the sky, oblivious to the cries and chaos and the bullets whizzing past. Gibbs bolted toward him, calling his name. By then, however, Nick had turned to see the source of another, more familiar voice – the howling of his mother. Having climbed down from the wagon bed, Mary was screaming.

"No-No-No!" she cried, taking no breath.

Gibbs ran harder. He could see motion in the windows of the train and was almost on Nick when the boy's arms stretched up. Gibbs' eyes widened to see Nick reaching high, as if he was taunting death, or bathing in the bullet-shattered air. Gibbs heard Mary's scream just as he closed the distance on Nick, who'd already fallen to his knees. Grabbing him, Gibbs brought the lithe, limp body down to the ground.

Tildy Fox burst from the tent she'd pitched with Harm. It had taken a beating, half caved-in like an old storm-shattered house. She went down on her knees by the sleeping campfire coals and hovered over what looked to Gibbs like a pile of clothes. Then, he recognized the mound as Harm. From where he lay, Gibbs couldn't see the blood spreading across Harm's white shirt but he didn't have to. Tildy looked up, clearly lost, her face a mask of grief.

"Oh, god, they've taken him! My Harm!"

Gibbs heard those words, over and over, as Tildy caressed and kissed her husband's face. Then, she rose. Gibbs was stunned to see Harm's old shotgun in her hand.

"Tildy! No!" he cried, but he kept his hold on Nick who did not move. Tildy couldn't hear him. Bent low and surprisingly fast, she was already running toward the train, her gun raised.

"Goddamn you! Goddamn your souls to hell!"

Tildy ran full-tilt toward the armored carriage and Gibbs watched her crouch down at the earthen berm among some other men, just below the lumbering metal giant. Gibbs turned his face away, heard Carla's screams join with Mary's.

Gaujot saw the charging woman. He tracked her in his rifle sight then changed his mind, smoothly ducking aside. He took deep breaths to calm himself, eying the plainclothes deputy in the next window, a man named Collins. Gaujot felt the time pass and, watching, let himself go cold. Collins had been tracking something else, not noticing the old woman and her antique. The shot came through his window, pounding into Collins' cheeks and eyes. The guard reeled back into the aisle, crying, "Oh god, oh god, I'm hit!"

Sneering, Gaujot jumped into action and grabbed the oil cloth he'd been using to clean his rifle. The other guards glanced over briefly before returning to the shooting spree. Gaujot used one hand to push the gun rag into Collins' buckshot face. His other hand slipped through his patient's pockets, tugging up a watch on a silver chain. As Collins moaned, Gaujot quietly tucked the watch into his own shirt for safe-keeping.

At the other end of the car, Mouseface Moler stood, panting heavily. He surveyed the line of trusted Baldwin agents. Most were still shooting, despite the fact that the train had now passed beyond the trees. Mouseface looked down the line, across the heads of the others. He saw his captain and grinned savagely, jabbing the air with his rifle, like a spear, as he bounced on his feet.

"By god, what a time that was!" he cried, eyes shining.

Unable to contain himself, he called out to Captain Gaujot, still kneeling in the aisle.

"What say we tell the engineer, chief! What say we have him back 'er up and give 'em another round!"

Gibbs watched the metal-clad mammoth move west through the trees and out of sight. Then, suddenly, someone was pulling at him. Moaning, Mary pushed him aside to get to Nick. As Gibbs rolled off the boy, she took him into her arms. Her throat would not work for nervous spasms, her words drowned as she crooned and rocked the boy's body in a tight embrace. Gibbs sat on the ground, open-mouthed, then turned about to see Todd before their tent, one hand fumbling at his sling. Across the way, Carla emerged, her face stricken and pale. Slowly, she approached her mother, who continuously rocked and crooned, gripping her motionless son.

Don't leave me. Don't leave me. Please. Don't leave.

"Oh, no," Carla cried, falling to her knees.

As if in answer to Mary's prayer, Nick's lean arm came up. Gently, the boy hugged and stroked his mother's back.

Senator: You knew the town was inhabited that night?
Deputy: Yes, sir; I could not help knowing it.
Senator: At the time the fusillade was going on?
Deputy: Yes, sir; I could see the flashes –....
Senator: You know reasonably that it was an inhabited town.
Now I want to ask, did you approve of the use of the machine
gun through an inhabited village?
Deputy: It was not a question that I could approve or disapprove.
I had nothing to do with the machine gun.

*Hearings before the U.S. Senate Subcommittee
of the Committee on Education and Labor.*

Chapter 14

Shaking their heads in disbelief, women wandered the bald footpaths, quietly reaching out to grasp each others' hands. Having carried away the bodies, weary men slouched between rows of collapsed tents, pulling bloodstained bedding from the remnants. They plucked at fallen canvases, muttering their intention to reset the poles, but their words were laden with so much doubt as to render them meaningless.

Two doctors, strangers to each other, set up a makeshift clinic in the left-hand wing of the mercantile. Both men had seen accidents in the mines; both had served in the European war. With five volunteer nurses, they worked through the night, sewing cuts and bullet-guttered flesh, salving scrapes and burns and pulling slugs. Acquainted with the mess and noise, they'd said almost nothing to each other for most of the night. At dawn, it was time to count the injured and the dead. The two physicians looked at each other, their eyes exchanging an unspoken message: *Nothing prepares a man for this.*

Todd Bryant and the local union leaders passed through the camp, earnestly trying to comfort the grieving men and women they'd come to know. The men stood before one tent and its wooden deck, now a pile of smoking charcoal. A stovepipe twisted upward from the mess like a black snake standing on its tail. Survivors whispered how the miner's wife had escaped the bullets by squeezing underneath the floorboards only to suffocate – she and her baby – when their canvas caught fire and fell.

Todd and the others moved toward another bullet-riddled tent, this one closer to the brook.

"Harm was a friend of mine," Todd said, and went to comfort Tildy.

She sat by the wreckage of their last home. Gibbs and Lowcoal worked sullenly nearby, putting up a new one. Tildy quietly accepted Todd's condolences, before he and the union leaders walked off, to meet in the Blair mercantile. Gibbs watched Todd slouching toward the bridge, bathed in the harsh early-morning light. The two brothers had barely looked at one another. Gibbs rubbed his eyes, wondering what next. From Blair Mountain he heard the sudden hammering of a distant woodpecker, and the beckoning calls of hawks. Swallowing his anger, Gibbs went back to helping Lowcoal replace Tildy's canvas.

Two days later, the new coffins leaned against the stone footing of an iron churchyard fence. As one, the big community fell into the ritual of mourning – a familiar practice, transcending the different stories and cultures borne by the striking thousands. Men in ragged boots knotted their calloused hands with those of their worried wives. Women embraced friends and strangers and stooped to comfort barefoot children too small to understand the darkness that had fallen over everything. Older children asked when they'd be able to go "home," forcing their parents into silence, unable to tell them that this brittle place, their vulnerable tent at Blair, was the only home they had.

Spread beyond the churchyard gate, the funeral crowd extended well into the street. The uneasy clergyman spoke of "God's peace," the phrases catching in his throat.

"These days are evil," he said. "But be not unwise! Be not drunk with the excess of wine; rather, let us speak to each other in the psalms!"

With that, he began singing a hymn and, somehow, was able to get countless mouths to shape the same familiar words.

Once stand-offish, the older residents of Blair now saw the attack of the Baldwin train as an attack on their own. At the funerals, townsmen stood shoulder-to-shoulder with the desperate miners. Young children stood on tiptoe, straining to see.

Standing with Carla by the churchyard fence, Tildy listened to the preacher, imagining his baritone as coming straight from Harm. As if her husband stood beside her, whispering.

This darkness is the work of one who hates
and he will call you 'fools.'

See to it that you are circumspect.
Do not walk as fools but upright, as wise people.
Recognize each other and go about in reverence.

Tildy counted the caskets again, stricken by the cruelty of it. And that one, just a baby. Her mind went back to the night of the accident at the Sovereign mine. She'd been embarrassed to mourn Truman Bryant while, at the same time, feeling grateful that Harm had not been with him.

He survived the mine for more 'n twenty years, she thought. *So many injuries. And the wounds that wouldn't ever close. You'll always be married to him, Tildy Fox. All the pain Harm suffered. It's all yours now.*

Tildy's gaze lingered over the other survivors of the shooting – people wearing care on their faces like sullen masks, their tired eyes having seen too much. The armored train had come like a flood, sweeping away so many souls from this place.

Now familiar faces filed past; women pressed themselves to her, speaking words she didn't understand. Tildy nodded, muttering senseless things, just to keep going. Hats removed, the men came to her, stammering coarse sympathies.

"...He never talked much, not about hisself...."

"...I never seen him riled...."

Sunk into her grief, the words meant little. She was startled only once, by something Mary said, at her side.

"I don't know which is worse: them that can't stop talkin' or them that don't know what to say."

Beneath the bright and turbulent sky, Tildy trailed her sister and Nick through town. Carla walked next to her, their arms locked tight. They passed the quiet mercantile and said nothing. Beneath the covered bridge, Tildy leaned into Carla but kept up the pace, their two heads bowed like nuns in contemplation. Mary gripped Nick's shoulder, keeping his body well within her sometimes-shadow. He fiddled with a new prize, tied on a cord around his neck: Gibbs had awarded him his father's whistle.

Just beyond the bridge, they stopped. Nick clutched the whistle, moved it slowly before his eyes. Carla watched, knowing the little trinket would end up in the cave, on his shelf of treasures. As if reading her mind, Nick glanced back at her – then toward some point high above her head. His attention was such a fleeting thing, she thought, always drawn to some arbitrary motion of the sky. Carla turned in time to see the sun slide behind another cloud. The clouds swam through heaven like lazy fish, she thought, and turned back to Nick.

Nothing much touches you, she whispered.

For several days, the three women secluded themselves in Tildy's tent. They saw visitors, a small tide of people from Sovereign passing through to give assurances. Saying little, Tildy received them. Once they were gone, however, she returned to her bed, hidden behind a blanket curtain they'd rigged for privacy. She showed little interest in anything beyond her canvas walls. She lay there all day. *Like an invalid,* Carla thought. *As if the train had killed her too.*

Once, in the evening, Carla went behind the curtain. Kneeling, she put her head down on the edge of her sleeping aunt's tick mattress, and took Tildy's aging hand into her own. Tildy squeezed Carla's fingers, but did not open her eyes.

Harm Fox had been with Tildy for more than twenty years, Carla thought. Not like herself and Sid, married for barely one. Her aunt and uncle had been so close, Carla had often thought of them as a single person. *TildyandHarm. HarmandTildy.* Even a strong woman couldn't stand up against too much grief, she thought, and worried that Harm's death would weaken Tildy, turn her into something less than what she'd been.

How would this fear and sadness invade the other tents around them? Carla imagined the contagion of mourning, of death, how it could infect the entire camp. In her mother's home, she'd always known the night as a time of peace. Now, all around her, the children would go to bed fearing bullets in the dark. Then, tired of being sad, Carla felt her anger rising, like Tildy's when she charged the train. She knew that the feeling would grow. More and more, it would be harder to control.

That night, Carla dreamt about the rock-faced giant again. He'd grabbed her, trying to push her down. Afraid and angry, she woke up, in a cold sweat. She sat up and listened. The only sounds she heard were the crickets and frogs and the tumbling creek. Nearby, her mother and brother slept, breathing softly. Tildy was silent behind her curtain.

Deciding she needed air, Carla pulled on her tan trousers, acquired from Sid. Fastening the belt, she walked outside. She walked quickly, charging against the cold air, and crossed the covered bridge to find herself standing before the mercantile.

The building loomed, dark and foreboding, but this only drew her closer. Climbing the stone steps, Carla circled around the overgrown courtyard and sat on a bench among the towering colonnades. Here, in the mercantile's hidden patch of wilderness, Carla took in the scent of rosemary and rotted fruit.

Then, from inside, she heard voices. Curious, she went to the broken back door, peeked through and saw a light coming from the stairwell. The sound came from the basement: Hard and serious, men's voices rose and faded. Carla crept down the steps. Crouching at the bottom, she could see seven of them, gathered around to talk. Gibbs Bryant stood at one end, his angular face just below the basement's only light bulb. Aside from him, there was Lowcoal and Darko Dresser, the foreigner. And Ben Tate, with three others. Carla knew their names, but little more: Dan Jakes, Vick Mattern and "Dix." She looked for Todd. He wasn't with them.

Quietly, she sat down on the steps and listened, her resolve growing. These men were no longer strangers to her, after all. Both in Blair and in Sovereign, she'd shared so much with them. Once again, her mother's house had become the fading dream. She was eager to hear what they were saying. The more she heard, the more excited she became.

"It's time we struck back," Gibbs began. "Teach these Baldwin thugs they're not going to run us over anymore. Todd's calling for a meeting of the entire camp tomorrow. We'll know then whether or not he's ready to take this organization where we want to go. Either way, I'd say we go on the march the next day after that."

"How many others do you think are with us Gibbs?" asked Darko.

"A good many," Gibbs answered. "Not many of the local leaders – they'll do what Todd tells 'em – but plenty of the rank-and-file. We won't go into Logan from the main road. The Baldwins and Gore's deputies have that covered. I'd rather hit them from the hills."

Hovering over a table, Gibbs moved his hand across a penciled map.

"We'll take as many men as we can on the march with us. We'll get them up to this point on the first day," he said and marked a spot on the ridge of Blair Mountain. "We'll all camp there for a day or two. From here, though, our little gang will split off from the march and raid the mining camp. We'll get there early, before dawn. The idea is to get in, hit the Baldwins and take out some rails – maybe even the whole the rail line going from the mine down to the coal separation plant. Then we get out again."

Carla leaned forward, trying to see where Gibbs' finger rested on the map. She imagined the route from the Blair ridgetop and knew each hill and valley in between.

"There's Sovereign," Gibbs continued. "I figure we come down on it from someplace above the mine mouth. If the Baldwins know what's good for 'em, they'll high-tail it out."

Lowcoal studied the map.

"Where do you think the Baldwins will be, Gibbs?"

"Maybe in the houses, but I'd say they'll be in the barn," said Gibbs, pointing to an octagon alongside a rough square, representing the big coal separation plant, the tipple.

"Riskier than picketing," Dan Jakes said.

"Might work," drawled Dix. Gibbs looked around at them.

"Running pickets is no good unless we can be there all the time – that's all the mines, everywhere," he said. "Plus, you're always out in the open. Sooner or later, the Baldwins are gonna shoot another bunch of us, send their low-rate workers in to take our jobs, and start moving coal again."

"So, we sneak into Sovereign first, and fix it so they can't even start," said Lowcoal. "We'll tear up the track, running from the mine down to the tipple. If we can do that, we've stopped the coal from moving down that line and into the train cars."

"I'd like to see a bunch of scabs up on that high scaffold, trying to re-lay the track," laughed Ben.

Darko was first to squint beyond the table's bell of light, and see Carla by the stairs. Ben followed his gaze and frowned, glancing around at the others. Gibbs was now pulling a thin pencil line across the map.

"One way or another, we'll be up there with the rest of them, on Blair Mountain. This group will get up early, do the job at Sovereign, and get back again in the afternoon, before anyone knows we've been gone. From here, on the mountain, we'll be going along this ridge, coming at it from the northwest...."

Carla moved out of the stairwell to see.

"You can't go that way," she interrupted.

"Christmas!" someone whispered and several of the men jumped, reaching for their guns.

Gibbs turned to her, staring. "What-?"

Ignoring their excitement, Carla went to the map and set her finger on Gibbs' pencil line.

"This way's cut by a long rock wall," she said. "It runs up all through here. There's no climbing it. It'd be crazy to try."

She talked and pointed to the map, telling them of the places she knew, of paths that none of them could know. They listened, their eyes darting from her to Gibbs.

"This way is best," she finished. "From the east. It's a harder road to find, but it ain't near as steep."

Gibbs watched her, keeping his mouth shut.

"How do you know so much about this?" he asked, finally.

Carla looked at him. She felt the heat rise to her face as she remembered the smell of moss on the cliff-side caves, the feel of Sid's fern-covered bed against her back. Lowcoal broke in.

"You can show us the best way can't you, Carla?" he asked.

She nodded.

"Wait a minute," Gibbs said sharply. "She can't be part of this. She shouldn't even know about it."

"The way you boys have been buzzing at the mercantile, it ain't too hard to guess," Carla told them. Then, straightening her back as her mother might, she looked at the men, saying, "It's easy enough to see what you're planning, and I'm going to be a part of it."

Gibbs frowned.

"I'm coming with you," she said, her eyes level with his. "It'll be dark, and you need someone to show you the way. After all they've done, I'm going. Don't try to stop me, Gibbs."

At a loss, Gibbs turned to the others, all open mouthed. Lowcoal spoke first.

"She's right," he said. "We don't know the hills. If there's anyone who should show us how to get there, she's the one."

"She's Sid's widow, Gibbs," nodded Darko earnestly.

Gibbs stared at Carla for a long moment. He searched her eyes for some frailty, but couldn't find it. The determination in her face was startling. Suddenly, it occurred to Gibbs that Carla Mandt was likely assessing his own resolve – just as he'd been appraising her. He took a quick breath, aware of the pace of his heart.

"We're still a union," he said. "We'll take a vote. Who's against Carla comin' along with us?"

Ben's hand went up with two others – Dan Jakes and Victor Mattern. Gibbs counted them.

"That's three against. Who's for it?"

Lowcoal raised his hand.

"What the hell," drawled Dix Mace as he put his hand in the air. Glancing around, Darko put his hand up too.

"Three in favor," said Gibbs.

"You didn't vote," said Lowcoal. "You break the tie."

Gibbs turned back toward Carla, his face calm. "How much have you told Todd – about the guns?" he asked.

"Nothing," said Carla, surprised at the question.

"Well, this is more important now than ever," he told her. "You have to keep this secret. Always."

Carla's eyes met his, then took in each man around the circle. "We have to do this," she said. "I'm in it with you. I won't tell anyone."

Tildy slept another day. On the far side of her blanket wall, Carla sat with Nick. She had been day-dreaming, watching the small movements of the tent door, when, suddenly, it was pulled aside. Sunlight streamed past Mary's skirt, briefly filling the space with a startling shade of blue. Nick rubbed his eyes.

"Visitor's comin'," Mary announced. "Todd Bryant."

Parting the tent flap, Carla saw Todd striding up the midway, then stopping to talk with another man. It had been days since she had seen him. She turned back, assessing the place.

"Probably comin' to collect some rent," Mary frowned.

Carla was about to protest when she heard Tildy stir. "How can you say such a thing?" she asked, her voice surprisingly clear.

Carla stopped putting seats in order, heard Tildy lifting herself to a sitting position on the cot.

"Where are my stockings?"

Carla went to help her.

"You know how miners are," Mary said tentatively. "To them, widows are bad luck."

Tildy cleared her throat. "I swear, Mary," she scolded. "That old tale ain't been told in years – and never by any of the Bryants."

"We ain't no good to them or their damned union," Mary persisted. She spoke the words to Carla as if she, and not Tildy, had raised the argument.

"They'll cast us out, just like Old Scratch."

Feeling her own anger rising, Carla stoked the stove, one eye on the tent door.

"Mother, please be quiet," she said, and the firmness of her own voice surprised even Tildy, who stood now. Her hair was uncombed and wild, but it didn't matter. Carla was relieved to see her up and around, the old spark returning. Shoving a new piece of kindling into the stove, she shut the little iron door with a loud ring.

Having slipped outside, Nick ran up to Todd. Reaching him, the boy took out his whistle and pressed it against the big miner's chest, no longer bandaged. Todd backed away.

"Hey, buddy! What's this?" Todd recognized his father's warning whistle, and briefly wondered how it had come to Nick. Taking the boy's hand, he called inside the tent. He had put off this visit for so long and was more than ready to see them – to see Carla. She came to the door, welcoming as always.

Todd went to Tildy first, and pressed her hand.

"I'm sorry I couldn't come by before," he said.

Mary nodded sullenly to him from the far corner.

Carla offered him a seat, but Todd waved it off. "There's lots going on," he said. "Not a day goes by without somebody bringing a problem that needs fixing. I talk to newsmen all the time.

"We miss you both at the mercantile," he added.

"Thank you, Todd," said Tildy.

He looked at Carla. The words came quickly.

"I just came to tell you," he said. "We're calling a meeting this afternoon, the whole camp. Some things need to be said about the other night and what's to be done about it. I'd like you to be there with everybody else."

Carla was curious, but said nothing. She nodded. With a few more words, Todd took his leave and ducked out of the tent. Outside, other men circulated among other families, spreading news about the meeting. Carla stepped out to where she could see into the neighboring canvas. Gibbs was inside rolling a bundle. From his movements, Carla could clearly see his irritation. Looking up at her, his features barely softened.

People packed their way into the big marquee tent, the erstwhile community center in the center of the camp. Carla wedged her way in with Tildy and saw Todd, standing on one of the dining tables in the center of the space. He held a megaphone, and watched the door and smiled a little, upon seeing the women enter. Behind them came Gibbs and his friends and the smile left Todd's face. Most of the men from Sovereign, including his own brother, were carrying guns. They filed in, taking their places in the back of the tent.

Carla gripped Tildy closer to her as Todd began to speak. Amplified by the long, brown megaphone, his voice rang out across the space and, Carla guessed, even to the crowd listening outside. Their voices stilled as Todd spoke.

"We've been dealt a bad blow," he said. "Word is going out about the raid on our camp. Tom Kenner, our union president, will be coming in here tomorrow with more news. He tells me, though, that the governor is sending some of his own people to find out about it."

Carla could see people in the crowd, muttering and shaking their heads. Behind her, on the ground at the edge of the tent, a long row of packed bags. Todd raised his voice.

"This is hard," he said. "I know what it's like to lose good people. My own friend, Harm Fox, was one of the best and we will miss him dearly – so were these others. But he and they died for our union and it's up to us to hold it together!"

"What are we gonna do, Todd?" yelled Lowcoal, sparking a small wave of noise from others.

"We are all angry about this!" Todd called, using the full power of the megaphone. "Justice will be served on the men who did this! Our union brothers in Meridian are working to make sure that happens!"

Carla was somewhat gratified, for Todd's sake, to hear responsive cheering, especially near the front. Others – including Lowcoal, Gibbs and their friends from Sovereign – retreated into silence.

"I know plenty of people are talking about leaving," Todd went on. "I don't blame you. You're scared and we're all angry. I'm angry too. But, I'm telling you, the union and the governor are gonna get the devils who did this! We will drag them into court – someplace far from Logan County, someplace where justice ain't for sale!"

"Let's go get 'em ourselves!"

Carla's breathing quickened. It was Gibbs who had shouted the words.

"We're all one union!" Todd yelled back. "We have one thing that we have to do, and that is *win this strike!* Our work is here – not picking up guns and storming the Logan County Jail! Every day we sit out is another day the companies don't mine coal. That hurts them plenty, and they know it! They might try to get scabs in the mines. They will try to bring men in here, past our picket lines, to get the coal trains moving again."

"Fight 'em where they live!" cried Gibbs. "Let's march on Logan and hang Riley Gore from a sour-apple tree!"

All around Carla, men shouted and raised their fists, many of them with guns in hand. Carla was tempted to join in the cheering herself. For his part, Todd swung the megaphone higher, making sure he could be heard above the din, which quieted with respect.

"We have to keep working together!" Todd insisted. "We couldn't get this far without our union and we have obligations to it! Union miners help each other. We support each other, especially in times like these! Right now, we have to win this strike, and we won't do that by marching off to a war in Logan! We have to stick together!"

"Let's stick together and march!" Gibbs cried. "They've attacked us twice now! An eye for an eye!"

"No!" Todd began, but Gibbs went on.

"You might want to take this lyin' down, Todd! Some of us want ours standing up!"

By this point, most of the men around Gibbs had begun cheering. Todd looked away, barely able to control himself. Seeing his frustration, Carla grew worried for him.

"I'm warning all of you!" Todd cried. "If you let some hot-heads talk you into doing something stupid, you're no better than a goddamned fool! And these fellows pushing us into an open fight against the Baldwins? They ain't your friends! And they ain't your brothers!"

He looked straight at Gibbs as he continued. "Tom Kenner, our union president, is coming here tomorrow!" he said. "Anyone that wants to pick up a gun and march into battle in Logan, go ahead! But I'm warning you: There'll be hell to pay for it!"

The meeting broke up soon after this. Todd stalked back to the mercantile office, where he'd begun spending his nights. Carla and Tildy returned to the tent they shared, where they found Mary packing.

"I've heard more of this talk – and seen more of its outcome – than I can stand," she said. "All of these men – and all of us – getting dragged into something that can only end in sadness."

"It doesn't have to end that way, Mama," Carla began, but Mary ignored her. "I must have been crazy to bring my boy down here," she muttered.

Carla stared, at a loss for words. Tildy stepped forward.

"I'm not going to try to stop you from leaving, sister, but I believe you are wrong. These union men are having a hard time of it, trying to figure out the right way to go. It's true, as you say. Things have ended in the worst way for your husband and, now, mine too. But Harm Fox never got dragged into anything against his will. He *joined* the union, Mary, because he *wanted* it. All these miners, up and down the Big Coal, they need this union. I am for it – and I will keep on working for it, even though Harm is dead. Because Harm Fox fought for it, and he deserved it. He fought hard and he paid the price for this union and for his brothers in the mines. It looks bad for all of them now – and I don't like to see them fight. But this ain't over yet. We ain't finished with it. Not by a long shot."

For support, Tildy had kept her hand on Carla's arm. Now, hearing her words, Carla took her aunt's hand in her own. In that hand, Carla felt the smoothness of the older woman's skin, and the strength of her grasp.

"Mary, you can think what you like," Tildy continued. "But I want you to know this much, at least: My husband died for something. And, as best we can, this girl and I are going to help these men work their problems out."

Mary's lips pressed themselves into a line. Her eyes took on a familiar chill. A long moment went by.

"Where's my boy?" she said at last. Turning away from them, she ducked through the open flap. Carla's spirits fell. "Pay Mama no mind," she told Tildy. "She'll make her peace, eventually."

She searched her aunt's eyes.

"Mary don't want peace," Tildy scowled. "Bonner worked so hard for her. She never did let up on that man."

Carla nodded and spoke in a low voice. "She can't forgive him for dying."

"I've thought that same thing," Tildy nodded. "She can't stop feeling sorry for herself."

"But what good is that?" asked Carla. "It was the mine guards that killed her husband. *That's* what oughta make her angry."

"She's afraid," said Tildy. "She's afraid for herself and for Nick. All the police threats and killing, up and down the valley. After so many years, it makes you more than afraid. It makes you angry. It makes you hate."

Suddenly, Mary was back with them. She went to her cot, where she closed the valise she'd been packing.

"We're leaving *your* place," Mary said to Tildy. "And we're goin' home to ours, where it's safe. If you had any sense, you'd come with me too."

Carla bristled at the idea of returning to her mother's homestead. The air stilled around them as Mary waited for her answer.

"Not me, Mama," said Carla coldly. "I'm sorry."

Tildy half-smiled and shook her head. "No, Mary," she said. "I mean to stay here and help, if I can."

Mary's face turned sullen. "It ain't safe," she warned.

"Nowhere's safe," Tildy responded. "But I cannot go. Honestly, Mary, I'd feel like I'd be leaving Harm behind."

"You could stay, Mama," Carla offered. "Maybe you and Nick are better off here."

"No," said Mary. "You go ahead and fight your battles. My place is my own."

Within the hour, Carla stood with Tildy in the shadow of the bridge, marveling at Mary's stubbornness as her wagon pulled away. The two women could see Nick in the back, humming into his closed hands. Carla didn't wave and it didn't matter. Neither Mary nor her quiet boy was looking back, as the wagon drifted over one last rut, lurching onto the sun-dappled highway.

The next day, Tom Kenner arrived at the miners' camp just in time to share the noontime meal with Todd and some of the others. Having driven the pitching roads all morning, the state president of the American Miners Union ate hungrily as he gave Todd the latest news. Todd and some of the other men watched wordlessly as the union official relayed what had been said at a meeting with the governor in Meridian the day before. One of the men at the table asked a question.

"I'll get to that," said Kenner. "I'll cover it when I talk to the men."

Kenner assessed the expectant looks of the miners up and down the table, and of the others, gathering around them. Examining their faces, the union leader became aware that he knew only a few of the rank-and-file miners gathered here, a fact that bothered him.

Finishing his plate of beans and cornbread, Kenner got up and stood in the clean-up line with all the rest. Everyone followed him outside, where more people waited.

"You here to call the charge?" one of the men asked, showing a wry smile.

Kenner grimaced, glancing at Todd. The young miner kept his head down with his hands deep in his pockets, saying nothing.

Walking out of the tent, Kenner was glad to see several hundred men waiting to hear him speak. He eyed the crowd for any sign of serious dissent. Several men shouldered weapons – bird guns and hunting rifles. One old fellow carried a relic pistol tucked into his pants. He wore an ill-fitting woolen Army shirt, heavy with decorations. How many of these brothers, Kenner wondered, had heard about the bounty on his head? Five-hundred dollars, it was said, would go to any man who gunned Tom Kenner down. Five-hundred dollars. Remarkable, the things that the Southern Coal Association's cash could buy – a politician, a mine guard, a union leader's life. What kind of accident might be arranged for him? Kenner didn't care to think about it. Little wonder that no union organizer was eager to work in this part of the state. He recalled one man, years ago, who'd sent him pages upon pages of solid information about the Logan Coalfield. Good reports, every one. Yet, they all ended the same way.

"Please get me *out of here,*" the man wrote. "If it was only the coal owners, I'd have no quarrel. But how can we work in a place where every policeman is a paid assassin?"

Ultimately, the fellow disappeared. Kenner liked to believe the man had abandoned his job and quietly moved to Cincinnati. He'd often thought about taking that route himself. He'd do it today, if he thought it would make any difference. No. Right was right. Kenner had no choice but to see this through. Besides, the Baldwin agency was powerful. With offices in seven major cities, the Baldwins could find a man in Ohio as easily as any other place. Far worse for any union man who stopped half-way – for those who showed fear. The Baldwins knew exactly where to push, which arms to twist – and just how hard. Anywhere Kenner went, a Baldwin agent was likely on each corner, at every stop. And times were rough, with no lack of recruits, all desperate men who, for the right amount of cash, would easily condemn every union leader as a "goddamned red," and do him in.

"Let's take this out into the open," Kenner said, walking among the tents toward a patch of cleared ground. Again, he noticed Todd's discomfort. Kenner was tempted to stop and ask what was the matter, but the crowd was gathering closer. This was just not the time. Kenner searched for someplace to stand. He moved toward the edge of the grass clearing, where someone had parked a truck. Good. He stepped onto the running board. Turning, he nodded at what seemed like familiar faces, scanning them for any hostiles. Still, he could not relax.

Now, as he looked over the crowd, Kenner realized just how big it was – one of the biggest he'd ever spoken to. The sun was coming out – the first sign of it in days. Kenner climbed up onto the hood of the truck. A mass of strikers pressed around him as he tipped back his hat. The men in front pushed backward, clearing him a little room.

Kenner smiled, starting to warm to his task. These men around him were his brothers, after all. By and large, they held their heads and chins high, as he did. Some grinned back at him. He could whip up enthusiasm as well as any other speaker. Better, even. But this crowd would not be easy.

Kenner took a deep breath, straightened and raised his hands for quiet. The crowd was more than a thousand strong.

"My name's Tom Kenner," he said. "I'm from the state office of the American Mine Workers Union. At our request, the governor has demanded a full account of the crime committed here last week."

Men nodded, grumbling.

"Newsmen are coming in here from New York and Baltimore. If you meet one, I want you to send him to me, if I'm around. Or to Todd Bryant, here."

"What good are newsmen?" somebody muttered. "Don't they all work for King Coal?"

Kenner shifted, straightened, aimed his words to the back of the crowd. "The American Miners Union supports this strike!" he said. "We are striking to demand union recognition, a fair weighing of the coal and a fair wage for support jobs underground! We're calling for an end to the deadly Baldwin system of hired thugs, the unfettered private police of Logan County!"

The miners cheered. Kenner spat, waiting for the noise to die down.

"Remember this, though," he called. "Our fight is with the owners of the Southern Coal Association! And with the Baldwins! We got no beef with the state governor! Nor with *genuine* law-enforcement in Logan!"

The crowd erupted in confusion. One man called out to him.

"How the hell do we know the difference! Sheriff Gore and the Baldwins is workin' hand-in-hand!"

Other voices echoed the thought.

"The only good Baldwin is in the grave – and Riley Gore can go with him!"

"Free our boys in jail!"

Kenner waited, looking down to check his footing.

"The American Miners Union backs this strike!" he yelled. "But we cannot support a march on the Logan Courthouse! We're not equipped to fight a war."

"The hell we ain't!" a man called, raising his gun. Others around him laughed.

"Get some balls, mister!" someone jeered and Kenner responded instantly, leaning forward and pointing a finger directly at the heckler, a gangly youth.

"You wanna try me out, son?" he thundered. The boy raised his hands, shaking his head.

"Now, we're all members of the same union!" Kenner yelled. "If you're not a member of the American Mineworkers, you don't belong here! And the rest of these boys will be glad to send your ass back to where you came from! Because *real* union men stick together! Boys, we need to stay put, right here in Blair. No march! No war! That kind of thing does us no good at all!"

To Todd's ear, the men in the crowd bellowed an even mix of praise and curses.

"What about our men in the Logan jail!?" someone yelled.

"Free the brothers in jail! We need our rights!"

"We *will* free them!" Kenner yelled. "The governor told me *personally* we'll be rid of the mine-guard system. And we will hold him to it! But we cannot fight a war! For now, we need you to rest easy and stay put in Blair! …That's all I got to say!"

There was more shouting, but Kenner ignored it as he climbed down from the truck. His speech had gone over as well as anyone might expect. He'd told the miners to stay away from Logan. With luck, they would stay put, and his words would be reported by the papers. No one could say he hadn't tried.

Todd helped him make his way toward the bridge, where his own car was parked.

"That was good enough," Kenner said, checking Todd's reaction. He was surprised to see the young man scowling.

"You call that 'good'?" asked Todd. It was the most he'd said all morning.

"I've been through worse," said Kenner, looking at him. "What are you saying?"

"These are your stragglers, the ones who didn't leave," said Todd. "Or couldn't. The rest of 'em is gone."

Kenner stopped and stared.

"What do you mean?"

"There was at least twice as many men here yesterday," said Todd. "Your hot-heads have already flown the coop."

"Gone where?" asked Kenner, fearing the answer.

"They're on the march," said Todd, miserably. "Headed up the mountain, hell-bound for Logan."

"Why the hell didn't you tell me before?" Kenner bellowed.

He didn't like losing his temper – especially at this new lieutenant, still so young. At the same time, Kenner never liked being played for a fool. He studied Todd's expression, wondering whether the boy had kept him in the dark on purpose. That train to Cincinnati was looking better all the time.

We should be winning, he thought bitterly. *Something always goes south.*

Walking past his car, Kenner crossed the covered bridge and plodded up the concrete steps into the mercantile. Todd followed. When they came to the office, Kenner immediately picked up the telephone.

Todd stood near the window, his back turned. He'd failed to tell the union leader about the militants going on the march that morning. But Kenner had arrived late and seemed in no mood to hear it. He'd been on the run, quickly relaying information from Meridian, giving Todd the feeling that the union leader had other, more important places to be.

In the office, Todd glanced around. Kenner was yelling at someone over the telephone. Would he mention Todd's mistake? Why hadn't Todd said something? He knew the answer: He didn't want to admit the truth: Many of the miners on Blair Mountain were his friends, men from his local. His own brother was likely among those who were leading the miners' assault. Todd had tried his best to keep them from going. In the end, however, he could do nothing to stop them. Several thousand men – and many women, besides – were now marching into the hills, bent on attacking the Logan Courthouse and free their friends in jail.

What hurt Todd most, however, was the fact that Carla had gone with them. This was something he didn't understand at all. She had always followed his advice. Todd tried not to think of her, risking her life. Risking everything, together with all the others. With Gibbs.

With Kenner speaking into the phone behind him, Todd stared out the window at the mountain and wondered how much worse things could get. Carla's betrayal had cut him far more deeply than he could have imagined. As he looked out across the dwindling tent city, he felt newly injured, an emptiness and heartache deeper and more frightening than any mine.

The political radical conducts the warfare of the savage,
who doesn't know fair play. Like the alien subversive, he is guided
by no rules or customs, but instead strikes his unsuspecting enemy in
the dark and from behind. The deliberate tactic of domestic enemies
during the Great War, for example, was to prevent the shipment
of vital supplies to the Allied forces. They sought this end by blowing
up ships, burning factories, and fomenting labor troubles.
It mattered not the slightest to them that, in this activity,
they destroyed the property of a people who were at peace with them.
This is the warfare of the savage radical.

Army Intelligence and Foreign Spies.
Tillman J. Munro, 1919.

Chapter 15

Colonel Stanley Ford checked his watch. Five minutes after nine. The
general was late, as usual, and Ford sighed, tempted to open the folder
in his lap. He wouldn't though, knowing he needed no more time to re-
view the material inside. Two days of research and interviews had prepared him well enough. He only hoped the general could be in a position
to listen to his briefing, and study the consequences. The situation was
infinitely more complex than anyone in Washington understood.

"I'm sure you'll apply your usual finesse, Colonel," the general had
told him. "Examine their devices and tell me what makes 'em tick."

Ford had smiled as if he'd never before heard the pun, a reference to
his first speciality: Explosives, gas detonators, acid-based fuses and clock
timers. It was as close to humor as Brigadier General Charles Mitchell
ever came.

After two years as his chief intelligence officer, Ford knew more
about General Mitchell than the man knew himself. The general was
"nuts" for every mission, real or theoretical. He enjoyed nothing more
than lecturing a subordinate on the details of forgotten battles as far back
as Thermopylae. Each problem Mitchell confronted was a nail, begging
for a good *whack* from his own "hammer" – the flying machines of the
brand-new unit he commanded: The Army Air Service.

Ford opened his watch and grimaced. The general was almost twenty minutes late. Ford had made plans for a ten-hour day, including a late meeting at the local airfield – one he was looking forward to. In his head, Ford began to rearrange the day's schedule – just as General Mitchell came through the door.

"Good morning, Colonel."

Ford stood quickly and snapped a smart salute.

"At ease," the general said, and pulled off his coat. He didn't apologize for being late.

"Tell me what we have."

Ford opened his file as Mitchell pulled a plague-green chair from the far side of another desk. Finding an ashtray, he lit a cigarette and nodded for the colonel to begin.

"Our meeting with Governor Morgan is set for one o'clock this afternoon," said Ford. "The Logan sheriff arrived yesterday, a day early. I think he likes coming here for R&R. Morgan canceled a prior appointment for him. They've already met."

"They got together alone?" the general asked, puzzled.

"Yes sir."

"The governor give you a briefing since?"

"Not yet," said Ford.

"That's tough."

The general frowned, examining Ford through his wire-rimmed spectacles.

"Just how many cages are we rattling down here, Colonel?" he asked.

"More than I can count, sir."

Ford proceeded quickly through the information he'd gathered during the past two days. Aside from daily news stories, he'd combed records of the state Mining and Minerals Office, and had two private interviews with good contacts, both Army veterans. The general absorbed the briefing, especially interested in Ford's descriptions of the Baldwin Agency, the union and its leaders, the affected mines and surrounding communities, all with detailed maps.

As he was talking, Ford became aware of a presence at the door. He stopped abruptly. The governor's gaunt-looking aide stood there. General Mitchell turned in his seat.

"What is it?"

Dressed in a worn suit, the clerkish man slipped into the room.

"Excuse me, sir," he said to Ford. "Governor Morgan would like to know if you want to have Sheriff Riley Gore join you this afternoon. That's the Logan County sheriff. He's in town today."

Mitchell looked at Ford, questioning. Ford took the hint.

"The general would like to know," he said, "what the *governor* would prefer."

Mitchell glared at the aide, who looked uncomfortable.

"I'm sure I cannot say, sir. Not for certain."

"What's your gut tell you?" asked Mitchell.

"I figure," the man answered, "that Governor Morgan would be gratified to meet with you and Sheriff Gore together."

Mitchell nodded.

"Then we'll be happy to oblige," said Ford, and closed the office door.

"So, the sheriff comes to the mountain," said Mitchell, flicking his cigarette ash into the ashtray. "Seeing us on our turf."

"I'm not so sure of that, sir," said Ford.

"You don't think Gore really wants to see us?"

"No, sir," said Ford. "I believe the sheriff of Logan County is very much at home here. The state governor's office is his turf."

Governor Ephriam Morgan was relieved to get Mitchell's request to meet with him a full hour before Riley Gore was expected to arrive. When the two military men appeared in his waiting room, he was there to greet them. Smiling, he showed them to seats around the great table. Then, Morgan turned to his aide.

"Please wait outside, Daniel," he said softly. "And tell us when Sheriff Gore gets here."

Ford looked at Mitchell, each noting the fact that the governor was excluding his own right-hand man. Seating himself, Morgan immediately leaned toward them. He addressed General Mitchell, whom he'd given a seat at the head of the table.

"I hope the president realizes how much trouble we're in," he said. "This strike – and, now, the miners' march has me up a goddamned tree. This game could go south at any moment. The coal market being what it is, the miners should be glad to have any kind of a job at all. But the southern coal owners are throwing more at them than anyone can take. Or should, if you want my real opinion."

Colonel Ford's eyebrows went up. The governor was leveling with them.

"The record supports what the governor is saying, General," Ford said. "The Logan workforce has not been stable, even under the best of circumstances. There is a lot of migration, both in and out."

"Now, don't get me wrong," the governor said. "We have good, solid people there in Logan. But I am grateful for the president's help. This conflict is more than we can sort out by ourselves."

He went on to describe the power held by local politicians in Logan and six other coal counties.

"But none of them holds the kind of clout Gore has," he said. "He's so tied-in with all the coal operators. They're as thick as thieves."

Ford nodded, having told Mitchell much the same thing that morning. He was glad to hear it coming from the governor.

"Their political organization is flawless," Morgan went on. "Come election day, the southern deputies become election managers. They load voters into company trucks and take them to the polls. When they get there, the guards watch each man as he fills out his ballot, making sure that miner votes the way his bosses want."

"But Logan is only one county," Mitchell said. The governor shook his head.

"You misunderstand me, general," he said. "I'm talking about all the counties held by the Southern Coal Association. That's virtually half the state – at least two-hundred-thousand miners all together. Can you imagine what it takes for me to challenge that kind of power?"

The governor assessed Ford and Mitchell, watching the light dawn on them.

"I don't mind playing the hand I'm dealt," he continued. "But I sure hope you men can appreciate my situation."

At that point, a knock came at the door. Morgan looked at them.

"The sheriff is here. It's a different game now."

Ford frowned. The time had gone too fast. The governor had given them an earful, a fascinating lesson in local politics – exactly that area in which General Mitchell was weakest.

Gore stood as straight as a solid infantryman. His great chest was thrown forward as he crossed the room to shake hands with Ford and Mitchell. There was not a speck of deference to his manner, and Ford noted that his starched white suit was cut to fit, the work of a fine tailor. Gore smiled as he hung his Homburg hat on the rack by the door. Standing at the table, the sheriff poured himself a glass of water. Each movement, Ford noted, was deliberate, the work of a showman. The sheriff reminded Ford of an officer he'd once known. Whenever he passed a mirror, the man couldn't resist checking the cut of his uniform, the alignment of his medals.

Gore took his place at the far end of the table, making sure that he was last to sit down.

"How're things at home, sheriff?" the governor asked casually. Ford noted a change in Morgan's accent. He'd suddenly acquired Gore's rural twang.

"I figure we'll win 'em this time again," Gore returned. "There'll be room to spare."

Gradually, Ford realized that the sheriff's subject was an upcoming election, the results of which he predicted as easily as tomorrow's weather. Ford glanced at Mitchell. They were excluded from this conversation, its local names, districts and precincts sounding like a foreign language.

"So, Riley," said Morgan at last. "Do you see a quick end to this strike?"

"Well, Epp, let me be clear."

And, here, Gore paused to shift, getting more comfortable in his chair. He took a drink of water then eased back and crossed his legs. Ford watched as the governor and Mitchell moved slightly toward the edges of their seats. The colonel could see it clearly: They were watching the performance of an accomplished showman.

"Governor," said Gore, his voice going soft. "There is no miners' strike in Logan County."

Ford felt the air go still.

The man's a master.

"What do you mean by that, Riley?" Morgan asked. Apparently, he was accustomed to Gore's practice of teasing an audience.

Gore played with a cufflink, admiring it.

"We're mining coal – and we have a loyal labor force," he said. "Those workers who've been *incited* to join the union are just a few rotten apples – unfortunate victims of a gang of ungrateful and violent malcontents. It's these outside agitators who have come in and led our loyal workers to break the law. But it won't last. The bad apples have done us the favor of weeding themselves out, and taking a bunch of lazy bastards with them. They've left their workplaces. Logan County can get along just fine without their kind."

The sheriff's performance was so impressive Ford was tempted to applaud. At the same time, he could see General Mitchell taking it all in, a confounded look upon his face. If their meeting was going to end well and on time, Ford thought, it was up to him to bring the curtain down.

"Excuse me, sheriff," he said. "But our information suggests that Logan's coal production has fallen behind by more than a million tons since the strike began."

Gore's smile lost some of its polish. His eyes narrowed.

On the scent, General Mitchell jumped in.

"Could it be, sheriff, that this fight in Logan County might be something bigger than you understand?"

For a fleeting moment, Gore looked as if he'd tasted something bitter. Then, the smile returned and he waved his hand.

"I don't question the colonel's word, general," he said. "But there's no telling where those figures came from. Much less whether they're accurate."

"The numbers were reported by the Southern Coal Association," Ford said smoothly, "an organization you serve as treasurer."

Governor Morgan watched Gore with the interest of a man being dealt a new hand in a game of rising stakes. Gore glanced at him, but his smile didn't break.

"Just as I thought," he said. "Those figures are quoted from the shippers' logs. You can't take the shippers' logs, not on their own. Other factors come into the mix, especially during a time of crisis, as we have now.... No offense, Colonel. But, unless you live where I do, these numbers are tough to nail down."

Ford felt himself warming to his task. He shifted in his chair, much as Gore had. Ford knew it wouldn't be long before his own speech took on some of the characteristics of Gore's. Sometimes other men noticed it; sometimes not. To Ford, the practice was involuntary, like a chameleon changing color. It was his way.

"That's just what we're after, sheriff," he said softly. "A clear picture. Late last week, for example. There was the shooting from a train."

Gore frowned to see Ford open his folder to a newspaper article, a piece clipped from the *Meridian Gazette.*

"A bad situation," the sheriff said. "Some security men got word that several in the miners' camp were drinking to excess. With my chief deputy along, the private force went to Blair to make arrests. Some of these strikers stupidly fired on the train. They injured one of the guards, who also was a deputy. Things could have gotten out of hand. I'm glad to report that the Baldwin agency men nipped everything in the bud."

Ford gave no indication that he'd heard the sheriff, and read aloud from the article.

"The shooting killed five people at the strikers' camp, including a woman and her infant son."

"And one of the Baldwin guards, almost," the sheriff growled, straightening in his chair. Then he stopped himself, as if remembering something. Ford watched him ease back, coiling himself into the upholstery.

I've just poked a snake.

"My chief deputy took some detectives to the miners' camp at Blair to make arrests," Gore said slowly. "The train was ambushed, and these men don't back down from any provocation. Ever. It just isn't in their training. I do not blame the Baldwin guards for firing back at their attackers. I blame the union man, who hides behind a woman's skirts."

Ford was quiet, his fingers folded.

"It was an unfortunate time and place to make arrests," he said.

Gore looked impatient, tempted to stand. Again, he sighed and regained control over himself.

"I don't think you two gentlemen truly appreciate the kind of enemy that Governor Morgan and I are up against," he said. "These radicals have no respect for law and order. They won't sit still for your appeasement. Believe me, I know. The union sends its best trained agitators – foreigners, many of them, with experience in Russia. They come in, pretending to look for work, but they're really here, just to make trouble. I recognize the type. I can name most of them for you. They think they are operating in secret. But, my boys have files on just about every one of them. They come with one thing on their minds: To rile-up our loyal workers. If he's not on his guard, even a good man is apt to fall under the agitator's spell. Innocent men are his bread and butter. He will draw them in and train them to do anything – even kill an officer of the law. This is their mission now."

The sheriff spoke with a growing enthusiasm, a force that almost pulled him from his chair. Mitchell and the governor listened, spellbound, a fact that Ford noted.

"I'm telling you, General," Gore continued. "These radicals are poisoning our nation's well. If you and the president allow it to continue, they will crawl up from their slimy pits, and they will take control. The good coal operators of Logan County have come to me, crying for help. And I'm glad to help – me and my men."

Morgan cleared his throat.

"You believe the situation to be this bad, Riley?"

"I do," said Gore.

Ford broke in.

"If it's so bad, Sheriff, why aren't you joining the governor in his request for federal support?"

Gore sat back in his chair, his eyes losing a little of their fire.

"Because I've got the very best detectives in my force," he said. "We don't need anyone's help to adjust this strike – this small disruption."

"But, Riley-" the governor began. Gore interrupted him with a glance.

"Governor, you can trust me and my men to handle this," he said smoothly. "A little time is all I need to show you – and to show these gentlemen, as well as our president – just what my trusted men in Logan County can do."

Ford said nothing. He assessed the sheriff, now sitting easily in his chair. His white suit, thought Ford, gives him the look of a Southern plantation owner. Mitchell took his turn to speak.

"Sheriff Gore," he said. "Colonel Ford and I have been ordered to come here and remind you and Governor Morgan that the United States government has a substantial interest at stake in your labor 'disruption.' The federal government purchases a significant amount of coal."

Sheriff Gore seemed to search his memory.

"The Norfolk shipyards-," he said.

"That's the least of it," Mitchell responded. He picked up the briefing paper that Ford had given him that morning. Glancing at it, he found his place. Then, Ford noted with appreciation, the general stood up. All eyes were turned to him.

"The U.S. Army uses two Shay engines and one hundred-fifty train cars to transport thirty-thousand tons of bituminous coal from the Logan field. That's a weekly supply. Some twenty-five percent, more than seven thousand tons, is stored for use by different units of the US Army."

Ford folded his hands on the table, his eyes closed. He pretended to absorb the list of figures, but could have recited them himself. He took simple enjoyment in the sound of hearing his data delivered aloud, much as a composer might enjoy a performance of his work. General Mitchell paused, looking up from his paper.

"As we have shown," he said, "coal supplies have been curtailed since the Logan strike began. Unfortunately, this is fuel on which the federal government depends. I'm here to tell you, gentlemen, that the U.S. Army is neither willing nor prepared to draw upon its valuable coal reserves. If your strike continues, we could be forced to impound coal from a municipality, from Washington, Baltimore or Philadelphia. The president has no desire to face this kind of situation."

Here, the general paused, checking Gore for some reaction. The sheriff frowned, listening with interest. Mitchell spoke plainly, making sure he was understood.

"Mister Gore," he said, emphasizing the civilian title. "Our armed forces require this coal. Aside from all the machinery it drives, winter is coming. There are risks that continuation of this strike would put the United States government into a position that it simply cannot afford."

Ford sat quietly, his fingertips together before his face.

"In other words, Sheriff," Mitchell continued, "your workers' rebellion poses a serious threat to the security of our fighting force and, therefore, to the security of our nation."

"The White House is watching everything we do," Mitchell continued. "My orders are to determine whether you gentlemen are doing everything in your power to insure the uninterrupted flow of coal to our military, both here and overseas."

Now Ford handed the governor a printed sheet. Taking it, Morgan nodded and passed it across to Gore. The sheriff scrutinized the flier with the look of a man getting bad news. Mitchell pressed his point.

"I hope, sheriff, that you can understand: The colonel and I are absolutely committed to carrying out our mission here. We bring this to you from the highest levels of government. I'm not here to negotiate. I'm here to inform you what you can expect, once I receive the order to intervene."

Gore looked up again, his face registering genuine surprise. Mitchell opened another sheaf of papers. He addressed Morgan, his voice taking on a legal tone.

"Governor, these are general procedures for the operation. Such procedures may involve – but will not be limited to – direct engagement with residents of your state who resist enforcement of the federal order. The order will insist that all private forces that are engaged in conflict – or preparation thereof, for whatever cause – must stand down. All combatants must yield to federal command, all private weapons to be handed over to federal officers. We will then assess and define the need for military intervention and the terms of engagement for our troops."

Gore leaned back in his chair. He seemed to be chewing on something as he stroked his chin, scrutinizing the two military men. He turned to Morgan.

"It seems, governor, that these men are already set for a fight. Do our people – yours and mine – have any say in this? I'd like to know, Epp: How does this sit with you?"

Before Morgan could answer, however, Mitchell moved in. He closed the space between himself and the seated sheriff, hovering over him.

"Sheriff Gore," he said. "Governor Morgan has already officially asked the president to intervene. And the president is prepared to grant it. That is why the colonel and I are here. When I speak to you, in other words, I am speaking not only for myself and the United States Army, but for the president of the United States."

Gore kept his eyes on Governor Morgan, but curtly nodded his understanding.

"Colonel Ford intends to go to Logan, where he will deliver the president's warning to the combatants," General Mitchell continued. "At the same time, I am ordering him to meet with all sides toward the possibility of a negotiated solution. Under these conditions, you will be given time to share more of your ideas with him about the deployment of your forces to 'adjust' the conflict, as you put it. Frankly, sir, this is not that time. Upon receipt of this order, in fact, I rather think you should be eager to keep your own deputies – as well as the private Baldwin Agency guards – well away from any potential areas of conflict. Am I making myself clear?"

Ford always enjoyed seeing the general speak candidly. It reminded him of the reason he enjoyed serving under him. Here was a powerful man who bluntly spoke the truth. Gore, however, seemed unrattled by the speech.

"I see," he said and, from the way he said it, the colonel knew that the local sheriff would yield as little ground as he could.

"Good," said Mitchell. "I'm done, Governor."

Gore straightened in his chair.

"I can see, gentlemen, that I will not be able to dissuade you from carrying out whatever plans you have," he said. "May I ask you, then, to tell me and the governor what kind of 'intervention' we are discussing? I believe we deserve to know."

"Fair enough," Mitchell nodded. "Naturally, our goal is to make every effort to get the miners to withdraw from the battlefield and return to their jobs. If, however, conditions on the ground seem to require intervention, I am prepared to inform the president. Upon my counsel, he will give the order. Within two hours of sending that order, our aircraft – a full squadron – will be there, right overhead."

He pointed. Gore was almost tempted to look up at the ceiling of the governor's office.

"These are state-of-the-art machines, and they're loaded for bear," Mitchell said. "Each aircraft carries up to five-hundred pounds of explosives. Their crews are well-practiced in flying repeated bombing missions. The initial sorties will 'soften' any armed entrenchment. Once the planes are finished, however, the ground attack will be mounted by our infantry."

Gore nodded. "General, I know your enemy pretty well," he said smoothly. "These men are used to hiding underground. The coal-mining reds can tuck themselves into any gutter or gully, tunneling down into the earth, like rats. What good are your machines against such vermin?"

"We have heavy artillery," said Mitchell, as if reciting from a field guide. "For an enemy who is deeply entrenched, as you describe, we'd drop gas."

Gore's eyes shone with a gleam that forced the governor to look away, shifting his attention to Ford. Seeing that the colonel was taking in everything, the governor took a deep breath and turned to Gore.

"Riley, I hope you understand our position here."

The sheriff tucked in his chin, as if in deep consideration of all that he'd been told. "There's been a lot said here today," he sighed. "General, Colonel: You have to do what you have to do. Well, so do I. Until the president gives that order, I figure I am still in charge of Logan County."

Again, Ford was surprised at Sheriff Gore's audacity. The man was now ending the meeting on his own terms. Each of the others waited to see how the governor would finish. But Gore continued, having already shanghai'd the meeting.

"I do believe we have a good foundation – one of mutual understanding and trust," the sheriff said. "I will do all I can to make your task an easy one."

Mitchell stood. He diplomatically shook Gore's hand as he issued his final message.

"Sheriff, we have shared these plans today, assuming your full cooperation from the start. I must discourage you and your men from acting further on your own, without consulting me or Colonel Ford."

Morgan leaned forward, boldly putting his hand on Gore's arm.

"I might add, Riley," he said, "that I have talked with the president about this. Each of us shares some degree of risk here. You. Me. *All* of us. All our reputations are on the table. If we are not successful...."

Riley Gore looked at Ephriam Morgan, and knew exactly what the governor was trying to say.

If we aren't successful, each of us can kiss it all goodbye.

An ice cream wagon was the only platform available.
Gov. Cornwell mounted this and, with Mr. Keeney beside him,
began to speak. Silence fell upon the miners.
The Governor begged them to disband.
He told them that they did not know what tragedy their
action might lead to. He said that if they would go home
he would cause an investigation to be made of
conditions in Logan County, and if women and children were
being killed there, he would see that it was stopped.
The Governor produced an effect. As he stepped down, a trapper
boy (whipped) his pistol (out) over the Governor's head and, with a
whoop, shot into the air. Instantly, a thousand guns spit fire and
bullets into the darkness. Keeney turned upon the trapper boy.
"Put up your gun, you fool," he said. The trapper boy answered:
"Can't a fellow salute the Governor?"...

Winthrop Lane, *Civil War in West Virginia.*

Chapter 16

Within an hour of leaving Tildy and Carla at the miners' camp, Mary's wagon had clattered across three familiar stone-filled gullies that interrupted the road. Now she and Nick were approaching a fourth. She watched the brown and sun-dappled trail – trying to forget her troubles, as she always did, by thinking of fruit trees and the jars of apple sauce and condiments she'd put up. Soon, Swift would be taking them uphill, high into the mountainous woods, to her log-walled home.

"We'll have us a good supper," she promised Nick, seated at her side. The boy watched his fingers, fluttering before the road. Beyond, in the distance, he saw men and a truck.

Eventually, Mary saw them too – three men smoking cigarettes, loitering around a campfire. Her face wrinkled at the stink of petroleum and she realized the three had used it to start their fire, built more out of boredom than from any need. The three men carried guns.

Four others stood on the far side of the road. At first Mary thought they all had weapons too. But, no. They were long-handled tools. Two of the men had shovels; the third, a bare-chested man with shining skin, leaned against an iron digging bar.

"Road overseer's clearin' brush," Mary muttered, as much to herself as Nick. But she knew better.

The four workers waited on the other side of the wide trench, from which they'd just pulled the drainage stones. The resulting gully was wide and deep – enough so as to stop any sort of wheeled truck or buggy, including Mary's.

Swift halted before the edge of the trench. His ears played back, anticipating his master's voice. The three smoking Baldwins stared dully at Mary's odd-looking wagon, too small for freight but bigger than a truck-farm bed. And at her, frowning and wild-haired in her brown hunting jacket.

"Why're you men tearing up this road?" she called, putting aside her reins. She was unused to any barrier in her path and was easily tempted to impatience – but these days were strange, each one becoming stranger than the last.

The lead man flicked his cigarette into the fire. He moved forward easily, crossing a one-plank bridge that spanned the new gap. His face was narrow, severe and topped by a rippled haircut that Mary could see had been oiled in town. He wore the uniform of a sheriff's deputy, a Sam Browne belt passing over his shoulder to cross the vertical row of buttons of his jacket. As he drew close, Mary saw that the man's left eye was stuck in place, independent of the right. She briefly wondered how such a one could carry a gun, and decided he'd be dangerous in a fight, regardless of which side he fought on.

"Mornin', ma'am," the man touched the brim of his peaked policeman's hat. "You got business in Logan?"

Mary stared at the unnerving eye.

"I'm going up the mountain," she said. "The left-hand fork."

The officer's good eye looked off.

"Sorry, ma'am. That road is closed."

"The hell you say. That road takes me home."

Clearly surprised by her strong talk, the man corrected his flawed gaze on Mary.

"I'm sorry, ma'am," he said again. "Sheriff says no one goes that way. Your mountain's full of unionists."

"Well, I'll be damned," Mary said, her voice betraying nothing. She unfolded her arms, and saw the futility of argument.

"We'll turn about, then," she said, picking up the rope.

The back road was steeper, she thought, and she would need more time. But they'd still get home.

The officer shook his head.

"No ma'am," he said. "I can't let you go back, either. Not to Blair, and not up the mountain. Not without a written pass."

Mary studied his face.

"What's your name, son? Are you a Damron?"

"No ma'am."

"One of Murphy Damron's kids," she said again. "Up by Shaver's Fork?"

"No, ma'am. It's Reed."

Mary frowned.

"Well, you got the Damron nose."

Over by the truck, the other guards laughed.

"Hell, I'll be a damned 'Ron,' if the lady wants!"

Reed's jaw went tight.

"You're tellin' me," said Mary quietly, "that I need permission from the Logan sheriff to ride up to my own place?"

Reed stepped forward, put his hands on the buckboard. Mary felt Nick edging closer to her. Her mind busied itself, reckoning the wasted time in lost chickens and rotted fruit. Reed's misaligned eyes went owlish.

"It's for your own safety," he said. Mary noted how he'd left out the *ma'am* this time. She knew the tone, the look. She said nothing as Reed turned and waved a smooth hand at the crew. The workmen went to the tree and produced a row of heavy planks, which they dropped unceremoniously into place, bridging the new gap for her rig.

"Come on," Reed said to her. "We'll take you over into town."

Mary's mind turned on the situation. Suddenly, she felt tired to the bone. Tired of men, their power and the violence that enforced it. She looked at the three gunmen and knew she was afraid – afraid for herself and Nick – as she had every reason to be. Gazing at the stranger standing before her, Mary realized that he was likely just as scared as she was, although this was no comfort. When a man is frightened, he becomes unpredictable – sometimes dangerously so. Especially a policeman.

Mary sighed as she stared at Reed and – nodding to him, saying nothing more – guided her wagon toward his makeshift bridge. Swift balked some before stepping skittishly across the boards. Reed climbed into the truck. Its engine snapped into life, startling the horse and causing Nick to turn and stare.

Mary looked past the horse's rump, down the road to Logan. Twisted in his seat, Nick's eyes were bright, filled with excitement over the rattling automobile. Mary could hear the boy's low monotone, exactly matching the hum of the truck motor. She touched the knotted blue handkerchief that nested in her pocket, tied full of coins. This trip might cost her plenty, she told herself, but her safety – Nick's safety – was worth any price.

We'll make it home, she assured him in her thoughts. *Soon, I promise, we'll have this whole thing done, behind us.*

The following day, as Tom Kenner climbed onto the hood of the truck to speak to the miners in Blair, Gibbs, Carla, and the men of Sovereign were slogging along the winding path up the side of the mountain, some miles and at least two more ridges east of Logan.

To dispel his own nervousness, Lowcoal had been joking around with his friends. He walked backward as he taunted Dix Mace, who puffed beneath the weight of the heavy machine gun.

"Come on, give it to me, brother!" the small, stocky miner goaded. "It can't be that hard."

Behind them, more than a thousand backs were bent into the hill, the men of Sovereign and hundreds more besides, all of them eager to "get their licks in" against the hated Baldwin police. The group had marched off from Blair sometime before dawn – and well before Kenner's arrival. They labored up the hill, taking bites of stiff bread as they went. About fifty women brought up the rear, carrying the field kitchens and followed by packs of dogs.

Toward the front of the procession, Lowcoal had been walking backward, goading a tired but tolerant Dix. Then the smaller man turned around – just in time to run nose-on against a sudden flicker of red, hanging from a tree.

"Goddamn!" cried Lowcoal and flailed in surprise, almost falling down. Dix laughed out loud.

Regaining his balance, Lowcoal gazed up at the red muslin leaf, fluttering in faint breeze, and immediately recognized it as one of the pennants he'd tied with Harm Fox several weeks before. The miner stared, momentarily overwhelmed by the memory of that night, on the eve of Sid's funeral, when the two men had performed their small act of rebellion against Mary. Gibbs came up and, seeing the flag, clapped Lowcoal on the shoulder.

"We're doing what Harm would have wanted," he said, and Lowcoal turned to look at him.

"Goddamn," he returned. "I sure hope so."

As she moved up the hill behind Gibbs, Carla shifted the weight of her horseshoe pack. On the trail behind her, she could hear the sounds of the strikers' army and continued to be amazed at the number of men deciding to join them. She couldn't help but hear her mother's voice in her head: *They ain't no kind of soldiers.*

We might be, Carla answered to herself. *We just might.*

Climbing the hill, she pressed her hands against her khaki-covered thighs to give herself momentum. Her high-topped boots were a size too big, but they struck the ground with determination. Her pants were cinched with a woven strap and Carla took comfort in the knowledge that much of what she wore – the boots, the pants and shirt – had once belonged to Sid.

They marched in long strides past red oaks and sycamores. Carla watched Gibbs' pack sway in time to his pace as he moved in and out of the filtered sunlight on the trail. Carla felt a twinge of pride as she walked behind him, near the front of the march to Logan. They would find the Baldwins and make them pay for their brutal crimes – for Sid's death and her Uncle Harm and even for the death of Carla's father, in a more distant place and time. Together, this miner's army would strike some kind of blow for justice, she thought. A blow the Baldwins and Sheriff Gore would likely never forget.

Miles away, at Sovereign, Luther Simms lay on his bunk. He weighed the cards in his hand as he watched some of the other men around him, measuring their moods.

It's a wonder what a man gets used to, he thought, his eyes moving slowly around big community space the miners had called "the barn."

E freddo, muttered Bartolo, on the bed across from Simms' own.

"What's that?" Simms asked. He laid a card on the arm-length board that spanned the space between their cots.

"I'm cold," said Bartolo. "Like iced meat."

"Don't say 'meat'," Simms warned, glancing around. "These men are so hungry, you'll get us both thumped for it."

Back and forth, the two men lay their quiet cards on the dirty plywood. All around them, a hundred-twenty other beds were filled with "finks," as the guards called the replacement workers. Simms didn't mind the name too much – it was only a little better than "scab," in his mind but, in any case, he'd been called far worse.

It's a wonder what a man gets used to, thought Simms, as he waited for Bartolo's next play.

Like Simms, most of the men on the cots had arrived at the camp three days before, transported on the cars from Philadelphia. He still carried the torn paper a dark-suited man had pushed into his hand:

WORKERS BEING HIRED. * GOOD MONEY
* GOOD WORK * NO STRIKES.

The first two items proved to be true enough, but the second pair were bald-faced lies.

Simms shook his head at the thought of it, wanted to kick himself for having been drawn into this – for having believed the low-life devils at the train yard.

"Where are these jobs?" he'd asked them.

"Someplace where you get paid two sawbucks a day, just for showing up," one suit told him. "And the train ticket's free."

Simms had doubted it, but the dream always won out. Not many of the men around him, black or white, had seen a paying job in weeks. He signed the papers and followed the rest into the train car, every one of them feeling like a rich man with hope and a free knot of bread in his hand. Simms settled on a seat beside the Italian, who offered his hand and name. Bartolo Bonati.

"Pleased to know you," Simms nodded.

Simms could see that Bartolo might be a good one to have around in a pinch. Bigger than Simms, his boxcar arms hung slack in his work jacket, marked by pinhole burns from countless hobo fires.

On the first day, Simms and Bartolo watched Pennsylvania's industrial yards creep past, giving way to the unfamiliar countryside and wide, rolling farms. The men dozed to the sound of the thumping carriage and woke to see the bobbing lines of wires on phone poles against the sky. By dusk, the mountains came, their steep slopes looming.

In the middle of the night, the train was sidelined. The mine guards came on board, pulled everyone from the comfort of their coaches and unceremoniously hustled them outside. Here, new guards, with guns, herded the men into straw-strewn boxcars whose metal-studded doors were slammed and locked. Tired and surrounded by the mountains – dark and unnervingly silent – the finks remained subdued, none of them uttering a word of protest.

Simms suspected the truth, that they were being used to break a strike someplace. On the first night after they'd arrived in Sovereign, his suspicions were confirmed. From the surrounding mountains came the sound of someone hooting, as rocks came whistling down to slam against the barn roof. Many of the finks had thought it was gunfire, but Simms knew better. Outside, their guards fed the illusion, firing blindly into the amphitheater of black woods at the report of every stone.

Their first few days were defined by a strange and arbitrary regimen. Most of the finks slept in their clothes, certain that anyone – a guard or one of their own – was likely to rob them blind while they slept. Only the toughest man could afford to sleep in his socks and leave his shoes unwatched.

In the morning, five or ten Baldwins stormed noisily into the barn. Like bulls into the fighting ring, they charged down the bed rows, mindlessly clubbing cot rails or the bottoms of finks' feet.

"Praise god, transports!" cried one, whose southern twang set Simms' teeth on edge. "Rise and thank heaven for a new day of work!"

The tired finks cleared their beds away for breakfast. For tables, they set up sawhorses, bridged with long and dirty planks. A stove had been fired for porridge, boiled to just-this-side-of-burning. The cook was called "Goose" Watson, a name the finks had learned not to use to his face. It was said that Goose had either been a fink who'd risen up; or a mine guard who'd taken a fall from grace.

Simms watched as the finks filed toward Goose, who seemed to challenge each one from his spot behind the serving boards. Goose ladled gray breakfast into each pan while another man doled out bread, sliced as thin as a wish. The men slouched by, scratching their vermin-infested clothes, eyeing the guards (and each other) like caged tigers. As he passed, Simms listened to Goose, trying to chat up a young Baldwin who leaned against the wall.

"Good in town last night?"

"Pancakes all day, poon-tail all night," the other man drawled, his eyes elsewhere.

Simms moved forward. Goose dragged his spoon through the sludge, landing smaller and smaller portions on each plate. Simms considered saying something but moved on, having seen a small pistol weighing down the pocket of the cook's dirty white apron. *No wonder,* Simms thought, as he moved to a table and found a seat. Hearing a grumble from one of the others, Simms could sense a collective anger – bottled-up, but just barely. He imagined the harshness of all their lives, a thousand other grievances, both larger and smaller than the lousy food.

The men ate greedily. Many had nothing but their hands to scoop the mealy porridge into their working jaws. Simms used his dish to squash a beetle crawling on the food-splattered board. He didn't frown or shake his head. Such things only drew attention to oneself, and a man knows better.

The things that we get used to, he thought.

After breakfast and a fast, cold washup, the finks would be herded from the barn and up the hill into the mine. Simms and Bartolo had both mined coal before. They carried two old kerosene lamps and busted tools that had been given to them by the guards. For a while, they had tried to teach some of the others, so they wouldn't get hurt. This didn't even last a day, though, before Simms realized the truth: None of their overseers gave a damn how much coal, if any, got pulled out of the mine.

Every day after that, two or three guards posted a halfhearted watch while the finks put on their show of going "down the hole." None of them ventured farther than twenty poles into the mine, however. Down at the barn, the rest of the guards stacked their weapons against a wall to play cards and dice. After dusk, they picked up their guns and herded the finks back into the barn, queuing them up for a meal of cabbage and potatoes.

Watching Bartolo across his cards, Simms ran a hand across his close-cropped head. He was growing tired – not just physically but by the constant sense of powerlessness – of waiting – that seemed to fill this place. *This is no better than slavery days,* he thought, knowing they were being played by the guards and their employers. The coal owners could afford to wait out the strike. Up in the hills, the workers would get desperate.

Simms hated to think that he'd been drawn into the wrong side of another man's fight. How long could he stand it? Another week? A month? No. Not a month. At least his card-playing was getting better, he thought. He beat Bartolo about two out of three games.

"This ain't no kind of work," the Italian whispered during one evening game, on their cots.

"You got that right," Simms nodded, and took the trick.

Their card-playing had become little more than an excuse to keep their heads down, talking. At night, they would sleep in shifts, five hours each, alternating posts on watch, guarding their things. The deal saved them a dime each day, paid to the guards for the rented blanket.

This night had been relatively peaceful. No rocks had whistled down from the hills. Simms slept well enough until Bartolo roused him after midnight, ready for his turn. Simms sat up in time to see an officer enter the barn, apparently for the change of shift. He was a new man, one Simms had never seen before, a surly giant with a crooked face. Simms watched as one of the regular guards approached the fellow, handing him a rifle. Simms' cot was close enough to hear them talk.

"This gun jams," the young guard said.

Gaujot inspected the weapon, saw that it had been fired.

"What'd you shoot at?"

"Nothing," said the first, shrugging.

Gaujot nodded. He went to the door and opened it.

Simms blinked to see a new group of guards walk in – twice the usual number. Each one carried a high-powered rifle under his arm. One tried to hide a riot gun beneath his fraying coat. Simms wondered why the guards were dressed so shabby. Their worn-out jackets made them look nearly as bad-off as the finks themselves.

"Wake up, Bartolo," he whispered. "There's something going on."

Act II

THREE CARS OF RELIEF COAL ARRIVE
Situation 'Acute'

BALTIMORE, Md. (September 28, 1921) – Baltimore's coal situation assumed a slightly dimmer outlook today with the release of just one car of coal to Proctor Rail this morning. Another car went to Chesapeake Water and Light this afternoon. The Engineering School has released one of two cars it had to the railway agent and local coal distributor, J. C. Babbitt.

The Chesapeake Water and Light Company has called N. B. Kessock, the railway superintendent of transportation, asking him to request permission of the fuel committee to divert more coal cars to the Water and Light Company.

Despite the slight relief today, Mayor Broening said this afternoon that the situation is still acute. He said that, in the face of the untimely coal strike, colder weather could create public inconvenience for some time. Indeed, the telephones in coal dealers' offices are rung incessantly by customers who either have very little coal or who have run out completely.

Judge Hollis Collins, the eastside fuel distributor, spent yesterday in conference with the City Fuel Committee, then made a visit to the railway offices to plead for at least one more coal-bearing car for the city from the strike area, some 200 miles from here.

The railway and the coal authorities said striking coal miners were being encouraged to return to work with inducements of a Thanksgiving Dinner, to be given by the philanthropic Southern Coal Association whose members are seeking donations for it.

– *Baltimore Globe* Sept. 28, 1921

Chapter 17

Nick Rising had never seen such a place in his life. He could hardly keep from making noises as his eyes, wide and furtive, tried to take in all the wonders of the room: The broad wall of wooden boxes behind the long front desk, itself almost as wide as his mother's house. There was a staircase that narrowed at the top, all carpeted in blue and, nearby, an iron-and-brass cage that carried a man up into the ceiling. The furniture floated on the carpet – standup ashtrays beside brown upholstered chairs and tables and lamps. Nick gripped his mother's hand, trying to determine in which direction he would run, if he had to. He kept his eyes on the floor, on the vast expanse of blue weave that covered everything. The pattern pulled his eye across the room, into the boundless tangle of white curves, tumbling across each other on the azure sky. Through his fingers, Nick searched and found the pattern – then, new patterns and yet again, seeing something that was both uniform and wild. Pulled by Mary, Nick placed each foot carefully against the white grid of waves, lest he fall in.

Mary noted all the people in the lobby. Fresh from carriages and cabs, men and women pushed their way through the hissing revolving door. Professional men wore wide lapels and five-dollar shoes and were often followed by stiff-collared secretaries. Or smiling wives. Or escorts. With a sudden discomfort, Mary noticed how many people were staring at her as they passed. She was briefly tempted to smooth her hair, but didn't. They could take her as she was. So what if her dress wasn't new? It was the blue one – the best of the two she had – and it had only been washed three days ago. Nick fiddled with his rope-tied pants, beaten and worn.

The sheriff's deputy, Reed, waited for the clerk behind the desk to notice them. Thin and ravenlike, the man was standing on a raised platform, a long boxlike runner that enabled him to look down on anyone standing across from him. Otherwise, Mary thought, he didn't figure to be much taller than Nick. Attending to Reed, the clerk leaned over, putting his elbows on the desk, casting a critical look on Mary and her boy.

"Sheriff ain't there," said the clerk. "Likely at the courthouse."

"Is it worth waiting?" asked Reed. Mary could see that he didn't care to stay.

"Your choice," the man shrugged and, with well-faked benevolence, moved away to help a guest.

Mary eyed the suited lobby men, carrying their newspapers. Others leaned against the pillars, smoking machine-made cigarettes, importantly killing time. In one corner, three dark-clad Baldwins studied the rest. They talked quietly together, smirking at everything, pretending not to draw attention to themselves. *Like men anywhere,* Mary thought, and was thinking this when Gore walked in.

He breezed past her, not looking right or left as he strode across the room, somehow staying within a knot of mine guards, all dressed in matching black suits.

"It won't happen," the sheriff was saying to one man walking alongside him – a big fellow with a fighter's face. "They want to have it all their own way."

Two men had been waiting in twin arm chairs for the sheriff. Seeing him, they sprang up to introduce themselves. They wore identical lapel pins, although what they signified, Mary couldn't see. They caught up with Gore on the wide steps, smiling and selling something.

Mary looked down at herself again, at her threadbare blue dress and oversized hunting jacket. She began to lose hope. Riley Gore was more likely to toss her out on her ear than give her what she asked, she thought.

Although the sheriff hadn't seen her, the man with him – the fighter – glanced at Mary and her son several times, his eyes locking onto hers as he touched his tie with one stony hand. Gore stopped at the stairs, where he greeted the businessmen. His main guard, however, turned and approached Mary and Reed.

She was struck by the appearance of the man. Nothing about his face was even. A pale scar lifted one eyebrow, throwing everything below it out-of-line. His ears were large, the right one cut, as if bitten. Beneath his crooked nose, swollen at the bridge, a crease on one corner of his mouth gave the effect of a permanent snarl. A face to set dogs barking, Mary thought. The eyes of a rattlesnake on edge. Next to her, she heard Reed suck in some air before speaking.

"Cap'n Gaujot. This lady would like to see the sheriff."

Gaujot studied her, then the boy. He looked back at Reed, waiting.

"She came to where we closed the road to Blair," the deputy continued. "She says she lives up on the mountain."

Gaujot's face contorted into a frown.

"Name?" he asked.

"Sheriff knows me," Mary said. "I want to talk to him."

It wasn't courage that made Mary address him as she did. It was the only way of speaking that she knew.

"Can I go now, sir?" Reed asked, the truck key rattling in his hand.

The captain nodded. Without another word, the deputy turned and pushed through the lobby door.

"I asked your name," Gaujot reminded her, his voice high and smooth.

"Mary Rising," she said. Something in Gaujot's cold, dark eye signaled recognition.

"You carrying a weapon, Mary Rising?" he asked. "Any gun or knife?"

Mary had never met a policemen as hard-barked as this one. Words came out of him like meat from a steel grinder.

"No," she said.

Nodding, the hulking deputy went to the staircase, and whispered to Gore who looked past the two suited men. Spotting her, the sheriff stopped short and smiled. Mary gripped Nick's hand a little tighter. The boy continued to stare downward, awed by something on the lobby floor.

After a few quick words to the two men, Gore shook their hands and they moved away. Straightening, the sheriff's smile widened as he motioned Mary to join him at the stairs. Still holding Nick's hand, she crossed the distance, fighting the sense that she was being given an audience before the king.

"By god, it's been some time," Gore said, stepping down to take her hand. Mary looked at him, unsure of how to begin. She couldn't remember feeling so out of her element and, by some instinct, pulled Nick closer to her.

"Good morning," was all she said.

Holding his mother's hand, Nick's eyes focused on the man in white, his glittering badge and the gun inside his blinding jacket. Gore glanced down at him, his smile fading only a little.

"What can I do for you?" he asked, searching Mary's face.

"Deputies blocked the road to our homeplace," she said. "That's what I come for."

Gore frowned, looked puzzled.

"Let's talk," he said. "Come on up with me. Captain?"

Suddenly, the massive guard was at Mary's side, a touch too close. Nick looked up, now distracted by the giant. Sheriff Gore put a smooth hand on the boy's shoulder.

"Captain," he said again, pulling two nickels from his pocket. "I think this young man wants a sweet roll."

The sheriff handed the coins to Gaujot.

"Get him what he wants."

Mary looked down, not bothering to search Nick's eyes, but squeezed his hand.

"Go on," she said.

Boldly, she put her hand on Gaujot's forearm, massive and taught as steel cable. He looked back at her in surprise, but Mary spoke directly into his face.

"The boy's dumb," she warned him. "He'll listen to you, if you talk slow enough. But he won't talk back at you. Don't take offense on him."

Nick took Gaujot's battered hand. For a moment, he stood between his mother and the guard, all of them holding hands like some strange family. Then Mary pried hers away.

"Go on," said the sheriff, smiling at Gaujot's look. "The kid don't bite. ...Or does he?"

"He'll do what you tell him," Mary said, and then, to Nick: "This here's a friend. Go with him. I won't be long."

Gore ushered her up the staircase, but Mary looked back one time. As she watched, Gaujot accepted her boy's hand and straightened, as if daring anyone to challenge him. Turning back, Mary climbed the stairs behind Gore. She placed one hand on the bannister and shuddered to notice, once more, her permanent scars and the dirt around her nails. How rough the hand looked against the smooth, dark grain of the wooden railing.

Suddenly, she was aware of Gore, and the fact that he'd been talking.

"...that these are desperate times ... Your mountain just ain't safe...."

The sheriff paused to greet a pair of deputies coming down the stairs. One smiled bashfully, showing a mouth full of broken teeth. Gore stopped to ask them questions, and the two men nodded. Their eyes tried to stay focused on Gore, glancing uneasily at Mary once or twice. When he was done with them, they touched their caps and continued down the stairs.

In a quiet third-floor hallway, Gore produced a ring of keys. Mary imagined the locks they opened – doors to rooms or iron boxes, she imagined. Or vaults at the bank.

"I have some connections here," Gore smiled, finding the right key. Mary didn't follow him into the room.

"Come on," he said. "I won't bite either."

Grimmacing, she went in.

The luxury of the place almost made her forget about Riley Gore. Sunlight streamed in from the window, illuminating the big double bed. Just a few steps away, a white porcelain sink rested in a wrought-iron stand. Mary went over to it and turned one of the dark brass fixtures, shaped like a sparrow's wing. Water splashed into the basin on its own. She stuck one of her hands beneath it, then pulled it slowly away. No amount of water could make her clean enough for this place, she thought.

"Every room's got one of these?" she asked, looking over at Gore.

"Just about," Gore said.

Mary shook her head, trying to reckon the time and money it must have taken someone to make this room. She reached out to smooth the dark wood of the bureau, stroked a marble tabletop and the sofa's Foxton stripe. Gore continued to keep his distance, moving in her opposite orbit. His pockets chimed with his important keys and change.

Mary crossed behind the sofa, pushed the weighty fabric with a gray thumb. What would it be like to have water come without having to work it up from the ground every day? How would the rust-colored carpet feel to her son's naked feet? These thoughts embarrassed, then angered her.

"It's something, huh?" Gore prompted.

"Yep," she said, without looking at him. Gore stood in a corner, quietly appraising her as Mary turned and examined the inside of a tall wardrobe.

"Bathroom's right here," Gore mentioned. "Water there runs hot and cold."

She stopped staring at some wooden moulding and turned to him.

"What're you showing me all this for?" she asked. "I came for a letter from you, sayin' we can go back home."

Gore looked down.

"I can't do that," he said. "Things being as they are…. There's no kind of safety on that mountain now. I can't even tell you."

"I'm safe enough," Mary countered. "This fight don't touch us. We ain't in it."

She stared past him, knowing she didn't believe her own words.

"How's that pretty girl of yours?" Gore asked quietly.

Mary looked at him and swallowed hard. She had tried to prepare herself for the question, but the same answer never came up twice.

"I never could control that one," she said at last. "She left my house a long time ago. She ain't comin' back to me."

The sheriff's eyebrows went up, but he nodded.

"Children need a man's influence," he stopped himself. "From the right man, that is."

"Children need their own homeplace," Mary countered. "And so do I."

She'd said it. Her chin went up, her eyes fierce as she assessed Gore's response.

"I know," he said, raising his hands. "I don't always like the way things stand. And I have promises to keep."

Mary felt her shoulders relax.

"But, I'm telling you god's honest truth," he continued. "This is no time to be on that mountain. For your safety, and your boy's, I want you here in Logan. We'll call it a natural disaster for you, so the county can pay your expense, including board. We'll take care of you – you and him both. You won't have to worry about it."

"Stay here?" Mary asked, surprised. "How can I? The animals are out. A farm don't just set there, without care."

Gore studied her.

"It won't be that long," he said. "But I could still send up a squad of men, to take a look."

"No," Mary said sharply. "No call for that."

Gore turned and paced to a table with an electric lamp. He touched the marble top.

"Well, then, you can stay here, for now. It ain't a bad place, as places go. We can get whatever you might want or need. If it's payin' work you want, I know the manager. Tony Veltri's his name. A real nice fellow."

Mary set her jaw, knowing that her thinking was the last thing that Sheriff Riley Gore wanted to hear.

"I can't fix no water pipes," she managed sullenly.

"Nothing so hard as that," Gore smiled. "Veltri needs cleaning done. Maybe some kitchen work."

Mary folded her arms, trying to imagine the work of this big-city hotel. Was this bad luck? Or something else? There'd been a note in Gore's voice – something that instantly set Mary on edge – when he'd warned her about the danger. Now, here he was, offering his help.

"How do I know my homeplace is gonna be all right?" she asked.

"Well," said Gore, eyeing her. "If I knew the miners weren't going that far south, I wouldn't worry so much."

"I don't know anything about that," she told him, and Gore shrugged. He would not push the point.

"My offer stands," he said, moving toward the door. "The room is yours, if you want it."

"This room," said Mary, focusing on him. "Together with my boy."

"Sure," Gore said. "Honestly, I don't figure it'll be for long. The strike will run its course. They always do."

Mary flinched, but his words seemed well-meant. He'd included Nick, which she took as a good sign. She looked around the room, seeing only the work. Five floors of rooms. Her mind reeled with the number of bed sheets, towels, toilets and tiled floors. What would Nick do while she was working? He could not stay in such a place, not for very long, she thought. And city people can be cruel.... Mary knew she had to find a way to get him home.

"Nick stays with me," she said again.

"Why, sure," said Gore. "You'll both have complete freedom. You can come and go as you wish."

He reached into his pocket, unfixed one of the keys.

"Here," he said, holding it up before her. "You keep this. Don't lose it. It's the only one I got. You're a guest of Logan County."

Gore smiled, letting the thing dangle between his two thick fingers. Mary's mind stayed locked on the sheriff's promise of "freedom" although she sensed that his understanding of the word was very different from her own. Mary stared at the key he offered, its brass token marked with the room's number, swinging like an oversized coin. Reluctantly, she accepted the key, thinking she would have to make the best of it. Besides, as Reed had clearly said: She really had no choice.

"You'll like it here," Gore grinned. "I'll make arrangements at the desk. You can talk with Veltri when you like. Just let me know."

They went back out into the hall. Moving back toward the stairs, the sheriff took her arm in his meaty hand.

"And, if you need something – anything at all," he said. "My own room's just upstairs."

Chapter 18

In a winding line, two and three abreast, the miners struck their way up the woodland path. Burdened by their packs, bedding, tools and guns, they neared the crest of the mountain, the sound of their gear keeping syncopated time with their rasping lungs.

Gibbs propped his loaded pack against a sycamore to watch men pass. Since early that morning, at the bottom of the hill, he'd been listening to the sounds of the march, so similar to what he'd heard every working day since he was fourteen: the ring of equipment; men talking and laughing as they prepared for ten hours of digging coal. Here, however, the sound of men's boots was more sustained along the miles of trail, and it wasn't shovels but rifles and ammunition boxes that knocked against their canteens. Gibbs squinted down the line, reckoning their number at more than fifteen hundred men. He was surprised at the effect of their call to action: A real miners' infantry.

At last, he thought. *We're out here, doing something.*

But was it the right thing? In this moment, he had his doubts. Pressured by their men, several of the local leaders had broken with Todd and come on the march.

"Picketing the mines ain't enough," one man told him. "We have to hit them just the way they've done us!"

Now, in the afternoon, the front of the line was crossing the wooded ridgetop, their goal for the day. Gibbs barely noticed the change but for a new ache in his legs: They were going downhill again. He slowed and blinked as they came out of the woods, into a high hillside meadow. The sudden afternoon sun spilled down on them, just as if they were coming up from underground. Gibbs and his friends dropped their packs into the grass. They lay down and set aside their guns and breathed heavily in mindless fatigue. They were unconditioned for this kind of legwork, crossing long distances above-ground.

"Goddamn, I ain't never done so much walkin' in my life," Lowcoal said, but no one answered, everyone's thoughts being on the surrounding mountains and his own fatigue.

As more men filtered out of the trees behind them, the miners listened to the quiet changes of autumn wind and bird calls. Almost as one, they became aware of the view across the valley, startlingly beautiful. Darko smiled at the view, almost identical to a field he'd known as a boy, a hillside overlooking the Drava River. Inhaling, the Croatian recalled the slopes of his native Osijek, the smell of syrup from Valpovo, where the town's only factory made five-hundred tons of sugar every day. In his almost-dream, Darko saw old friends who, even now, might be tossing heavy sacks onto the same boats, preparing to pilot down the Drava, toward the Danube.

It's good to rest, he sighed in his own language and no one disagreed.

Emerging from the woods behind them, Carla came over and squatted down near Gibbs. Immediately he sensed her impatience, her eagerness to keep going, and realized she wasn't as tired as any of the men.

"It's time for a break," he muttered, so only she would hear.

Carla looked at the nearest miners: At Darko with this eyes closed and Lowcoal, lying against his rucksack, too tired to take it off. Nodding, she slid out of her pack – a simple bedroll bound horse-shoe style. She settled next to Gibbs who leaned back into the grass.

"You could out-walk any of us here," Gibbs muttered. "But we can dig more coal."

"I know," said Carla, mindful of men's pride.

"This is sort of where you came from," he said.

Carla looked around, measuring the landscape.

"Our place is farther south," she said, and then: "*Mama's* place, I mean."

"We'll keep clear of it," Gibbs told her. "No need to bring more of this on her and Nick."

Behind them, a seemingly endless line of strikers continued to spill out from the woods. Like ants, they migrated north along the bald mountain ridge, seeking new spots to drop their loads. Finding good places, they spread their canvases, blankets and mackintoshes on the ground. Carla looked across the valley, to the next ridgeline, a quarter of a mile off. She could pick out landmarks, spotting them through the rolling cover of green.

"That way's toward Logan?" Gibbs ventured.

Carla looked up and pointed farther right.

"See that darker line, running through the trees? That's the cut of the road."

Gibbs squinted at the uneven line of woods, leading west. Carla pointed to a more distant hill, on the left.

"That's Sovereign," she said. "Over there."

Gibbs followed her eyes to a thickening curl of smoke. It rose from the hills, interrupting the multicolored dusk, a dark column rising into the battered sky.

"Damn," he said, causing some of the others to turn toward him. Darko stopped humming a foreign song and looked to the horizon.

"Goddamn," he said and, one by one, the men recognized the smoke. Slow anger spread among them like a creeping flame.

"The bastards," Lowcoal growled. "They've opened up the mine."

None of the other local leaders had given any order for the miners' army to "dig in." Yet, all across the ridgetop, the digging-in began. First a few, then more men started hacking at the ground. By that afternoon, at least two hundred canvases had been poled and pegged, forming a ragged defensive line. By early evening, the miners' picks and shovels had pitted Blair Ridge with an uneven line of foxholes and good-sized trenches. The miners' infantry – ten units, each with more than a hundred men – seemed here to stay, entrenched. From the woods behind them came the sound of the women who'd joined the march, who set up new kitchens, their cookfires smelling of bacon grease and burning pine.

On the left-hand flank, Gibbs and his group of friends from Sovereign dug a wider ditch than most, a single square pit with space enough to sleep a dozen men. Mounding the dirt along the downhill side, they pitched their poles at an angle; a big tarp hanging low, across the front. From this roomy dugout, they had a shaded view across the valley to the opposite hill, less than a mile away.

Some distance up the hill, Gibbs and Lowcoal helped Carla raise her own canvas, a private button-down pup tent, rifle-height. They used Darko's hunting knife, to harvest oat-grass for her bed. Between the two shelters, the men rolled up wide logs for sitting on and cleared a pit for their campfire. After the meal of bread and potatoes, the small band of Sovereign strikers circled around Gibbs, who opened the subject of their plans for the raid.

"Things are changing up on us," he told them. "The company's brought in scabs. They're likely living in our places and have taken our jobs."

Around the ring, Carla saw a dozen faces harden with anger.

"We'll get a couple of hours' sleep," said Gibbs. "Then we slip out of here quietly. It's better if nobody else knows what we're doing, even our closest friends. We don't want anybody blabbing everywhere about it."

The others nodded, knowing the risks.

"Carla will get us through the woods," Gibbs went on. "We'll come into Sovereign on the side where the mine is – and the coal plant."

He turned to Carla. "You stay back and wait for us high on the mountain, away from the shooting," he said. "We'll need you to call us together when we're coming out of there."

"No," said Carla. "I'm going in with you. I'll go crazy sitting up there, not knowing what's going on."

She shoved her hands deep in her pockets and Gibbs frowned, aware of his heart beating. Dan Jakes put out a bony hand. "How about she helps me with the Browning, Gibbs?" he said. "She can feed me the ammunition belts."

"All right," Gibbs nodded, relenting. "You both will be up in the woods with the machine gun, up beyond the coal tipple plant. Keep firing at the Baldwins, down in the community center. Keep up your fire, so they don't even think of coming out. That will free us to tear up track in the mine."

Turning back, he laid out the plan for the others.

"We probably won't be able to get much farther than the mine mouth," he said. "But if we can pull up some of that rail track – and some of the outside rails, on the scaffold that goes down into the tipple. If we can do that, I figure we can keep those scabs from mining coal for a good, long while. Maybe scare some Baldwins into going back to New Jersey, besides."

"What about the scabs?" said Lowcoal. "Do you think they'll come after us?"

"Maybe," Gibbs admitted. "Any man with a gun is fair game. But we'll have the drop on them. The thing we have to do is to get in and out of there fast. Use the Browning to keep Baldwins and the rest of them inside. Just keep at it, Jakes. The rest of us will be in the mine, doing what we can in there."

Gibbs looked around at them. "I don't care who it is. If a man comes out, firing his gun at us, he's fair game," he said. "Just like any Baldwin thug who's fool enough to come outside. We have to show them we've had enough."

The sun eased downward. Across the hillside, other groups gathered around their campfires, talking and, sometimes, singing. The small band from Sovereign sat together quietly, several of them smoking cigarettes. Gibbs sat with Carla, watching the last of the sun dip down behind the rolling blue hills, leaving waves of red in the sky. Having lived his whole life in a valley, Gibbs couldn't remember ever seeing the dusk like this.

He asked himself whether Carla had learned to take it all for granted, seeing these mountains and their wonders every single day.

Carla lay against the log, taking in the smoldering horizon. In the dimming light, she could see gentle waves of grass coming up from the field below them. Beyond it, a flank of poplars, oaks and maples, fronted by a dark snarl of rhododendron. She listened to Gibbs, talking to Mattern and Jakes. "After this," he said, "they'll pick up and take more notice of us. We're gonna give them a taste of their own justice."

"It's about more than that," Carla said, surprising herself.

"What?" Gibbs asked, turning to her.

Immediately, she took comfort in the question, Gibbs' tone telling her that he was relaxed and prepared to listen.

"A new beginning," she said, looking at him. "To get a better start on things."

"I was thinking the same thing," said Gibbs, looking down. "Years ago, my father first came to Sovereign and thought that it was a fine place. He kept telling us, 'All these houses each one with its own water!' He'd never seen anything like it. He used to tell Todd and me, we were living like kings."

"Things sure change, don't they?" laughed Mattern.

"We can't hardly get food enough for what they pay us now," Jakes added. "Try to complain about it, and the Baldwins will throw your ass out of there."

"And if you can't help mine coal," said Carla, "there's nothing there for you there at all. The company owns everything in sight – and all the people too."

Gibbs nodded. "A man comes to want more from life than indoor plumbing," he smiled, and they all remained quiet for a time, listening to the sound of the encroaching night.

"It felt good, though, to be building something for ourselves in Blair," Gibbs continued. "I almost forgot what it's like to live in a place where people can trust each other. Where you don't have to worry about someone ratting you out to the thugs or the boss."

"Where you ain't afraid all the time," Carla nodded and, listening to him, she realized that Gibbs Bryant was a different man from the one she'd known in Sovereign.

"That's why we're fighting," she offered. "At least, that's why I'm here."

The nearest ridgeline had become a single dark band that climbed and fell in gentle waves. Lit from behind by the sun, now almost gone, the other, more distant hills lay across each other like undulating bodies in repose. In the fading light, each line of mounds had turned a different shade – purple, orange, blue – all the colors of a healing bruise.

Without thinking, Gibbs reached over and briefly pressed Carla's hand.

"We'll be all right," he said. Carla exhaled, surprised at this act of comfort from him.

"We should get some shut-eye," said Gibbs, raising his voice so all could hear. "We've got a lot in front of us."

Carla rose to say goodnight. The rest of the men chorused their goodnights back to her, some of them raising their hands.

Later, she looked out from her tent. She could still see their fire, along with scores of others, illuminating the dark hillside. Hundreds of canvases and dugouts extended across the ridge, running more than a mile. Carla marveled at the ways that large numbers of men could change a place – and how fast.

Gibbs bedded down in his blanket between Dix and Darko, his mind turning. Finally, he fell asleep, surrounded by the sounds of their breathing.

As he slept, the dark trench around him became the familiar city of tunnels in the Sovereign mine. He wandered down one passage until its walls and floors became wet, then liquid. The mine became one thing – neither stone, nor air, nor water – and Gibbs felt himself sinking into it, into the rock. Before long, he was swimming through the mine, both along the tunnels and through the rock walls. With strong strokes, he passed through the coal and the empty passages, through stone and air. Seeing a point in the darkness below him, he swam eagerly toward it. His arms pulled him through the liquid stone as he dove deep into the mine. Rising again, he broke through dark surface of a slate floor, gasping for air.

"Hey, it's time!" a sentry whispered hoarsely down at them, and Gibbs was suddenly awake. He remembered where he was. The plan.

Close by, Darko grumbled something that Gibbs took to be a European curse. Lowcoal crawled along the line of men, eagerly shaking their ankles.

"Come on, boys," he said. "Let's go."

Dix cursed in his Southern drawl. Vick Mattern, unwound himself from his blanket, waking Ben and Dan Jakes.

"Goddamn, that night was short."

As he pulled his kit together, Dix glanced over at Darko who sat up, scratching chigger bites on his arms. A wet chill that had come up the valley. Lowcoal now combed the trench with an electric torch.

"Damn, Low!" hissed Ben, covering his eyes. "Careful where you point that thing!"

"Can't find my bullet box," Lowcoal said. "You seen it?"

"By god," frowned Ben. "It's been diggin' in my side all night"

Quietly, they unpacked themselves from their trench, breaking into the cold night. Gibbs smiled as he climbed up and stood, brushing grass seedlings from his arms and hair. He directed himself up the hill, wanting to be the one to wake Carla.

As he approached her tent, however, he saw that she was already up – already dressed in the pants and heavy jacket of the day before. She rubbed her arms against the cold. Gibbs waved to her, noting the rifle strapped to her back. In the dark, she looked like any of his friends, any of the men.

"Morning," he whispered, and she faced him. "You hungry?"

"A little," Carla admitted. "I'm ready, though."

Gibbs went up the hill, to the woods where he did his business. In a few minutes, they all stood together on the grass, quietly passing around two canteens to wash down fists of bread, torn from a single loaf. Carla had tied her hair into two tight braids and tucked them beneath the old fisherman's cap. Gibbs recognized the cap as her Uncle Harm's and it occurred to him that wearing a man's clothes only made Carla Rising Mandt more appealing to him. Startled by the thought, he turned to the others. "All set?" he whispered. Everyone nodded, their eyes on him and Carla.

They walked slowly through the grass to where two sentries stood watch. Gibbs confirmed the password, passed the evening before among leaders of the big march: *I come creepin'.*

"Don't none of you forget it, comin' back the other way," one of the watchman whispered to them. His words came whistling through gapped teeth. "I'd hate to shoot ye just for not knowin' it," the man said.

They marched the rest of the way down the field, breaking through the brush to enter the thickening woods. Carla led the way with Gibbs keeping pace behind. He was blind to everything but her back as they moved together, deeper into the viney dark. It was difficult for the men to stay quiet, every footfall seeming to bring a sound, igniting a dozen kinds of mute panic among them. Only Carla seemed to walk in silence, Gibbs thought and struggled to follow her example.

Behind Gibbs came Lowcoal and Ben. Then Dix and Vick Mattern, who hummed a low, aimless tune before letting it go. Dan Jakes carried the machine-gun legs, draped across his back like some giant spider. Every so often, he turned to check on Darko, bringing up the rear with the Browning gun itself, riding heavily on his shoulder.

Carla leaned into the wooded dark, her eyes picking out the most distant obstacles. She never veered from the narrowest trails – paths Gibbs couldn't even see. He would have liked to walk alongside her, but didn't want to break her concentration.

"Damned pricker weeds," came Lowcoal's voice behind him, and Gibbs stopped to help. They moved ahead more carefully, though at a steady pace, past hill bends and detours. At one point, Gibbs thought he'd lost sight of Carla, then spotted the slanted line of the rifle on her back as she moved farther up the invisible trail.

They came through a pocket of warm air. Gibbs felt the weight of forested mountains, looming overhead like pillared walls on either side, reminding him of the first time he'd gone underground. Instinctively, he stopped to listen. The wooded valley walls echoed with a strange chorus – the calls of distant owls, accented by some nearer bobwhite. Gibbs recalled stories his mother told them, of forest ghosts and "haints." Now, he felt like one himself.

"What are you laughing at?" Carla asked, suddenly next to him.

"Nothin'," Gibbs said and almost lost his balance.

"We're gettin' close," she warned. "Be as quiet as you can."

Her feral eyes held his for a moment in the dark before she turned back up the hill. Gibbs whispered back to Lowcoal.

"Be as quiet as we can."

"Quiet"…."Quiet"…."Quiet." The message traveled back.

A new path took them up the slope, their ragged warrior line, moving up the ferny hillside path. Scrambling past knotted trees and stone mono-liths, they came out onto an old abandoned road. On a whispered word from Carla, Gibbs signaled to the rest that they should hunker down and wait. Darko brought up the rear and, with a great sigh, set down the machine gun. Setting aside their rifles, the rest of them lay out along the scrabble road, like a pack of dogs in summer.

"Glad I don't have to do this ever' day," panted Jakes, staring at the machine gun's tripod. Ben pulled a dried-up vine from the gunworks and they passed around canteens.

Gibbs squinted down the wide path where they rested. Long unused, it had dwindled to a narrow cart road, choked with weed trees. Gibbs could see, though, that it had once been heavily traveled, long ago. His fingers traced two thick rills, four feet apart – parallel cuts carved deep into the slate by a century of iron-rimmed wagon wheels.

Carla removed Harm's cap, then tipped back her head to see pools of stars among the high clouds.

"Rain's coming later," she said. "Might be in our favor."

She looked over at Gibbs, her face pale in the night and Gibbs allowed himself to openly admire her young woman's features in the dim light; and he told himself he wanted to remember forever whatever he could of this, to see past the fear and doubt that each of them shared, and absorb the wonderment of Carla's eyes – perhaps to grasp something of her remarkable courage, which all the men admired. And, either from anxiety for what they were now doing or out of some other selfishness, Gibbs leaned over and spoke so only Carla could hear.

"I'm sorry for being against your coming," he said. "I'd thought maybe you were giving up our plans to Todd."

Carla frowned, and shot him a sidelong glance.

"I told you I wouldn't," she said.

"Yeah," said Gibbs, smiling a little. "I know. I'm sorry I doubted you, that's all. And I'm truly glad you're here."

"Let's get through it, then," Carla nodded, fighting the temptation to look away from him.

Gibbs' heart beat faster for these words. He turned to the others, waving them closer.

"This is the high road," he whispered. "If we get separated, we can regroup right here. But we have to make this quick. We get in, tear up some mine track and let 'em know we're here. Then, let's get out of there, and fast."

He allowed himself another look at Carla, at the rifle she carried on her back, just like the rest. "Remember to keep your head low," he said.

Nervously, they all checked their guns and ammunition another time before setting off, crossing over the high rim. Climbing down the other side, Carla became aware of an unfamiliar rumble, like the sound of a thunderstorm.

"Come on," Gibbs whispered. "Come on."

Together, the band came part-way down the hill, making no sound. They hid behind the trunk of a fallen poplar whose old, scraggly roots rose ten feet overhead. A gap in the trees gave Carla a clear view of the mining camp. Here lay Sovereign, the place she'd briefly known as "home" with Sid and she inhaled familiar machine air that came up at them from below, along with an unseasonable heat. Around her, the men stared into the gap, disbelieving.

"What've they done?" Lowcoal whispered, but no one answered, each of them absorbed by the new industrial glare, killing any trace of the moonlight.

Carla could see the swale of Wolfpen Creek, now lit by a line of arc lamps mounted on wooden poles, illuminating the two main buildings of the camp – the community building and the three-story tipple where the men had separated the coal, by size, to be dumped into train cars for different uses, different destinations. Both of the big buildings and some of Sovereign's houses, besides, were now bathed in the sterile blue glow of artificial light, an eerie sight that made Carla feel exposed, with no-where to hide.

In the indifferent light, she could see a line of new fencing, ten feet high, that now defined the perimeter of their former village. In fact, the whole camp had been encircled in long, tights strands of barbed wire, a barrier that surrounded all of Sovereign, and Carla could see no break in it.

She could see her own vacant house, where she'd lived with Sid, and she imagined the front door left open, blowing back and forth in any small wind. Field mice would creep in, with weed trees pushing up through the floor. *A vacant house falls apart so fast,* she thought, her eyes drifting to all the other empty houses alongside her own. At this point, Carla Rising knew she'd likely never return to Sovereign and live there.

"Christ," breathed Dix. "It's a god-damned fort."

"More like a prison," whispered Gibbs, aware of how the unnatural light caused the hair on the back of his neck to rise – that, and the roaring sound that came from the upper branch of Wolfpen Creek.

"Look," said Darko, pointing toward the noise. "They're burning coke again."

It was true. Fifty roaring ovens lined that part of creek, a line of shining limestone hives stretching off to their left. Long defunct, their coke-making fires now blasted red hot, almost white – glowing like a chain of orange ingots, reflected in the water. The collective flames from the ovens made the otherwise black creek seem to have caught fire, a jagged bolt of red, extending away, up the hollow from the camp. To Gibbs' eye, the scene was as if a crack had opened in the earth, with molten rock bubbling up from someplace deeper than any mine.

"Why'd they fire up the glory holes?" Lowcoal asked and Gibbs' jaw went tight. "Just to show us that they can," he said. "To prove they can do anything. Any damned thing they want."

Chapter 19

"Keep your palms open, like this. The bolt slams back and forth. It moves fast and hard."

Jakes had begun instructing Carla across the machine gun. Gibbs saw her dark outline as she listened and, pausing, nodded to her shadow before turning to follow the others down the trail. He imagined her watching him, and fought the urge to turn around one more time.

"...Don't get your hands too close to the chamber. You don't want to get your fingers caught in it."

Gibbs continued down the hill, toward one towering post with an arc lamp on it, throwing harsh shadows across the no-man's land of grass. The six of them crouched behind a small hemlock. Beyond the tree and the pale hillside, the mine mouth opened. Waiting for them, Gibbs thought as he eyed the familiar black, lopsided door. Just like any day of work.

Our daddies dug this mine since we was small. Now, we're breaking in like bandits.

Eager to move, Gibbs turned to his friends – Lowcoal, Ben, Darko, Mattern and Dix.

"Who's got the cutters?"

They made a four-foot hole in the fence, then crabbed their way through the high grass. Gibbs gripped his rifle in both hands, feeling naked in the cold, industrial light. Halfway across the meadow, they hid in the meager shadow of an upturned coal car, its detached wheels lying nearby, in the rust-flaked grass. Watching past the stumped axels, the raiders had a view of the entire bowl of valley. Around the hill, they could see some of their old houses, three rows deep. High on their left loomed the mine. Gibbs' eyes scanned the scaffold that towered over his head, bridging the gap between the mine and the coal-separation plant at the foot of the hill. This rail bridge had been crossed by countless buggies filled with coal, down into the tipple building, the separation plant, where it fell through screens and was sorted by size, falling further into the big steel train cars. This place, Gibbs thought – this big wooden tipple plant before him, and the covered rail umbilical cord stretching out from it to the mine landing overhead – this was where the coal they dug under-

ground stopped being natural rock and started down the rail path to being someone else's power. Every day, when the place was working,
scores of buggies were winched down from the mine into the tipple at
the bottom of the hill. Beside the tipple, to the left, was the barn where
Gibbs had spent so many Saturday nights, dancing with his own mother,
alive and happy. And there, through another door, in front, their meager
commissary.

Beyond the lower houses, Gibbs could see the company's new fence.
It ran up the hill, right through the backyard family gardens, now a field
of weeds. Along the other creek branch, the line of glowing coke ovens
was watched by three tenders. Gibbs discounted them, unlikely to hear
anything above the roar of the ovens or see beyond their glare.

*My father helped build this mine. Even some of the houses. Never
had a time-clock; was never paid for his time, just the tonnages he could
blow and throw. He went back to the days when Sovereign Coal didn't
even pay a genuine U.S. dollar, handing out scrip instead.... The Baldwins are strangers here, not us. They don't know half of what we've
done. Or what we can do.*

"Dix, you stay," Gibbs whispered. "The rest of us will go in."

"You think any guards are hidin' in the mine?" asked Mattern.

"No," said Gibbs, not knowing.

Lowcoal fidgeted. "I'll find out," he said.

They watched as he crept up to the mine entrance, then disappeared
inside. They did not breathe as they eyed the hints of Low's flashlight,
leaking out the front.

It wasn't long before all five men were inside the mine, a different
place than they'd known before. Gibbs' breath went shallow as he scanned
the scattered mess of sawed-off timbers and trash on the rippled slate
floor. The unnatural blue light made the entire wreck of his former workplace seem as if it had been the victim of some merciless attack.

"Lookie here," Darko whispered.

Two empty coal cars were parked some distance from the mine mouth.
Lowcoal pointed his torchlight into one bucket. Gibbs spotted something there, reached in and turned it over in his hands: a old miner's
leather cap and headlamp. Twisting open the brass container, Gibbs found
it full of carbonite.

"Guess they been doin' something," he shrugged.

"A lot of sitting around," said Darko. A listless sheet of newsprint
blew across the floor.

Mattern shoved one of the empty carts and it rolled with a noise that
made them all jump.

"Shit! Those assholes. They left the cars unmoored!"

Then, the five of them crouched on the open landing before the mine mouth, looking down on the community center and tipple. Beside them ran the tram rail, reaching backward, miles into the mine. And forward, into the wooden cowling, over the scaffolding that crossed the steep gap, down into the tipple. Gibbs looked right and raised his hand, greeting Dix on the hillside, in the shadow of the upturned buggy.

Get ready.

Then Gibbs stretched himself out on the slate landing alongside the others. To their left, by the distant creek, a few coke tenders moved listlessly, trying to stay clear of the plumes of ash and smoke spewing from their ovens. Dirty clouds from the furnaces crossed the creek and doused the first tar-paper houses. Lowcoal lay next to Gibbs, and sighted down his rifle.

"This blood-suck place," he said. "All lit up, just like a jail cell. And just as foul."

"Start 'er off, Low," Gibbs whispered, gratified by the iron in his own voice. "Take care of them lamps first."

At last. At last, we're doing something.

The cracks from Lowcoal's rifle came satisfyingly fast, like a declaration echoing from one hilltop to the next. Lamp glass and sparks showered down onto the pavement around the poles. Gibbs smiled and wished that Sid might be there to see it. Suddenly, a fifth light behind the tipple snapped out, all on its own.

"They know we're here," Darko whispered. The five men flattened themselves against the landing and gripped their gun stocks.

Up on the hill, among the trees, Carla and Jakes saw the last light go out, and felt the night wash in. Once her eyes got used to the dark, Carla could see past the fallen tree, past the lattice of the tram bridge to the tipple, clear to Sovereign's barn, where new light now spilled out onto the pavement.

"Something's up," said Jakes, and he swung the Browning. Sighting along its barrel, his finger went to the trigger.

"Here they come," he said, becoming anxious, and Carla's breathing quickened.

Black outlines moved before the open door of the barn. Carla clasped her hands together to keep them from shaking. Voices came up to them from below.

"Come on!" "Get out!" "Up the hill!"

"Be ready," breathed Jakes. "They're gonna charge the mine."

Obeying, Carla lifted the belted ammunition as she watched the scene below them.

"Wait," she said. "Something's not right."

A dark line of men had emerged.

"They're coming!" Jakes whispered, his panic rising.

"Wait!" Carla said again. "They ain't Baldwins!"

Jakes frowned.

"What?"

"Look at 'em," Carla pleaded.

Jakes cursed the truth of it. The shapes in the well-lit door trudged out slowly, their heads hung low. He spat into the brush.

"Just a bunch of goddamn scabs," he said. "Assholes are marchin' up to the mine, think they're gonna break our strike."

He took aim with the Browning.

"Jakes, no!" Carla whispered. "You can't! Not like this!"

Without thinking, she grabbed her own rifle and climbed out from behind the tree.

"Hey! Wait!"

But she was already down the hillside. Reaching the fence she called out to Gibbs.

"Don't shoot!" she yelled. "They ain't Baldwins and they ain't armed! Hold your fire!"

"By god," cried Lowcoal. "What the hell's she doin'?"

Gibbs scooted forward to see Carla's shape at the fence. From behind the wreck, Dix was calling, "Goddamnit, girl! Get down!"

They all looked back down the hill, to the men around the barn. They'd stopped their march and stood there, frozen, the truth dawning on them. Then, near the front of the line, one of the scabs threw up his hands and screamed out, into the alien dark.

"By god, don't shoot! Please! Lord, have mercy!"

A single shot was fired. To Gibbs, the man seemed to bend double, backward, before he fell. The rest of the scabs went in all directions, fleeing the gunfire that suddenly seemed to come from everywhere in the camp. With a sudden horror, Gibbs realized that there could be only one genuine target for the Baldwins.

No! No!

Wide-eyed, he turned to see Carla. She had slipped through the fence and was running down the hill.

Staying low, Carla kept herself from danger, putting the tall scaffold stairwell between herself and the mining camp. The Baldwins continued to fire blindly at the hilltop where she'd been. Dix was taking the worst of it, but he was safe behind his mine car. At least for now. Carla made it to the stairwell. Here, she stopped and looked inside – up toward the top. From there, she thought, a person might crawl into the covered track. From there, inside the cowling, she might climb up and reach the mine – as long as there were no Baldwins behind her, in the tipple. Cautiously, she entered the tower and climbed the stairs.

"Goddamn," Gibbs said. "Carla's at the tipple."

"Scaly Baldwins," said Mattern, watching the chaos around the barn. "They put the scabs out for us, like bait."

"Don't fire yet," said Gibbs.

"Why not?" Ben cried. "Those bastards are here to take our jobs...."

"Hold your fire, Ben!" cried Gibbs, his eyes on the tipple. "Carla's down there."

On the hillside, Jakes clicked the safety on the Browning. He couldn't shoot anywhere down the hill, not being sure where Carla was. And now, of course, he knew she had been right: They couldn't justify killing other working men, even the scabs. Jakes grabbed his own rifle and, leaving the machine gun behind, headed down toward the fence.

Suddenly, more Baldwins came out of hiding. They lay on the lower house porches and in the upper windows of the commissary. As one, they fired their rifles up the hill. Like repeated claps of lightning, the bullets cracked against mountain and the mine. The raiders pulled back from the landing.

"By God, it's like they been layin' for us!" cried Ben. "It's a god-damned trap!"

Pressed to the slate, Gibbs kept his eyes locked on the stair tower. He had to figure out where Carla was, and get her someplace safe.

When the first fink fell, Luther Simms submitted to his instinct. He went belly-down to the ground and crawled straight for the darkest place, a ditch at the base of the big coal tipple.

"Simms," he told himself, "you're in a fix, and that's a fact."

"Who you talkin' to?" said a nearby voice. Simms smiled, glad to realize that Bartolo had followed him. The Italian stared through the dark, eyes wide.

"In a fix," breathed Simms. "You know what that means?"

"Means we inna fix," Bartolo blinked.

"You got that right," Simms said. He'd spotted the guards near the commissary and others near the shacks where some of them slept. They weren't in the tipple yet, but Simms knew they'd be there soon, perhaps drawing the miners' fire their way.

"Goddamned thugs," Simms continued. "Sonsofbitches want us in another war."

His eyes scanned the hillside, where too many finks lay, frozen in fear. He recalled a terrible fight, years before, when he felt the same desperate desire to dig a hole and burrow deep. That time, it had been the ruins of a Belgian town, going up in flames. His unit had been trading fire with the enemy – another lost company, like his own, detached from its command. An isolated battle in which there was nothing to do but keep scoring kills on the pitiful other side. Simms lived five days and nights of killing across that ruined town, while its remaining villagers – hungry women, children, and old men – cowered in tight stone basements. Now the numbness of that battle returned to him. The sense of futility. The only difference here was the woman's voice, calling.

Don't shoot! it said. As if she might stop it.

In the stairwell, Carla wondered what had carried her so far. Moments ago, she'd been safe in the dark, watching Gibbs go to the mine. Like seeing him off to work, she'd thought. Lowcoal, Darko.... All of them so eager to get back down into the hole. To push out the Baldwins, so they thought.

Carla watched from the top window of the stair house, trying to see through the chaos. The guards shot blindly at the hillside. How long before they came here, to the tipple? And, taking it, how long before they found her, inside the stair tower? It would be just a matter of time. She had one escape: Up the rail umbilical to the mine, inside the wooden housing, to the mine landing. She could make it, she thought.

Then, from her perch in the stair tower window, Carla noticed a movement in the tipple, low and to her right. A Baldwin guard peered over a window sill. She froze as the pig-faced man spotted two scabs below, crawling along the building's stone foundation. With cold deliberation, the guard leaned over to aim his weapon down at them. Reflexively, Carla raised her rifle, aimed, and pulled the trigger. The man's head and shoulders pitched forward. He fell from the window, landing in the grass with a sickening thump, not far from the two startled scabs. Carla watched as one of them, a black man, moved like a cat and scrambled out to grab the dead guard's rifle. In a panic, she took aim.

"Point that up here and you're a dead man!" she called.

"You got no trouble with us!" said Simms.

Carla heard the voice, considering it.

"Get up here, then," she said, knowing it sounded something like a dare, but couldn't fix it.

By the community center, a Baldwin guard scrambled over a sand-bag wall, which landed them in a machine-gun nest. He grabbed a canvas tarp and pulled it away. Briefly catching the tarp on the long barrel of the Browning gun beneath it, the man quickly moved into position, taking control of the gun. He pulled and released the cocking handle twice, releasing the first cartridge from the ammunition belt and sending it into the machine. The man took aim at the union attackers, up in the mine, and fired. A series of shots tore through the air and hit the field around Dix, hiding behind the abandoned coal car. Dix had been unsure of where to aim his rifle and turned to see Jakes, running toward him from the fence. Jakes had almost made it to the safety of the coal car, when the barrage of bullets came. Hit by more than one, Jakes fell near Dix, who watched in horror as his friend died, in clear pain.

The storm of machine-gun fire from the Baldwins then spread to the mine. The first rounds shattered stone above the entry. Hit by stinging shards of slate, Gibbs, Lowcoal, Darko, Mattern and Ben turtled down against the floor.

As he crouched there, Gibbs heard the thudding of the machine gun and the hammer of bullets against the stone, accented by the ongoing roar of the coke ovens beyond Wolfpen Creek. The shooting had come at them so suddenly, Gibbs thought. Shielded by the unarmed scabs, the Baldwins commanded the situation, firing up at Gibbs and his friends from positions in the miners' own homes. Gibbs fumed to think of the thugs getting the upper hand; that he and the men were being forced to cower in their workplace. Further, the thought that Carla might be in danger sent him into near fury. He had to figure out a way to regain control, to get themselves out.

Gibbs had flattened himself down on the cold floor, when his right hand closed around something hard and familiar. He pulled it before his face: The old miner's hat and lamp he'd found....

"Ben!" he cried. "Reach me your canteen!"

Struggling to overcome his shaking, Gibbs opened the brass canister and poured the water in. He tightened the threaded chamber and swirled it around, praying for a good reaction. Next to him, Lowcoal appeared. Having seen what Gibbs was doing, Lowcoal struck a match and waved the flame before the steel armature. The acetylene candle sputtered to life. Gibbs put the mirrored lamp on his head.

"You runnin'?" Lowcoal asked.

"No," said Gibbs. "Gonna try somethin'. Keep 'em off. If the Baldwins get in here.... Take the others to our section. We can meet up in the stables."

"Good a place to die as any," Lowcoal muttered, but Gibbs had already disappeared.

Ben called over to Low.

"The big gun has stopped! Let's get back out there."

"Dead men if we don't," said Mattern and moved forward to fire haphazard shots, high and wide.

"You got another gun?" Simms asked when they came up.

Carla looked at him, not understanding.

"For my buddy," he explained. "It would help get us out of this."

"Why would I have two?" Carla asked. "Make do!"

Taking her rifle, she entered the long wooden tunnel that housed the rail line that ran from the tipple up to the landing at the mine. After listening for any movement in the tunnel, Carla crouched back in the stairwell, keeping her rifle trained on the tipple opening, where more guards might appear.

"'Make do with the one,' the lady said," Simms shrugged at Bartolo. The Italian nodded, grimacing as he kept watch on the building adjacent to their stair tower, to where the first mine guard had fallen. Simms glanced back at the girl, their rescuing angel, admiring the no-nonsense way she handled herself. He knew the guards wouldn't be appearing anytime soon, deterred by the screams of a second man she'd winged while Simms and Bartolo had climbed the stairs. The guard's moaning seemed to make no impression on her. Deadly serious beneath the brim of her fisherman's cap, the girl eyed the tipple entry like a hawk.

Simms scanned the field from the stairwell window. He could see the guards' positions – and their strategy. Their gunfire would keep the poor sons-of-bitches in the mine pinned-down. Then, they'd give it everything they had, send more goons charging up the hill, fill the mine with fire and lead, then kill anyone left inside. Simms could sense, but not yet see, the earliest sign of dawn bleeding through the high trees. The light would favor the guards.

Suddenly, the machine gun rattled into new life, sending another barrage up the mine. Simms was relieved. The guards hadn't yet noticed the woman and him, in the tower.

"Goddamn," he muttered and took aim. He never thought he'd be doing this again.

Hold steady.

He looked down the rifle site, drawing a careful bead, then cursed again as he exhaled to fire the shot. His sniper's bullet spun across the distance and struck the Baldwin gunner in the chest. The man slumped across the steaming gunworks as if seeking something he'd lost, down by his shoes.

"Porco dio," Bartolo whispered.

As quickly as he could, Simms reloaded and fired again, hitting two more guards. The rest ran for cover, unsure of where the shots were coming from. Simms decided to take the advantage. He'd try to correct the thing he could never fix in Belgium.

"Hey, you finks!" he called down. "Best get out of here!"

In the mine, Ben moved forward, raising his head.

"Who's that?"

"Dunno," said Lowcoal.

"Go on, finks!" Simms yelled again. This time, the men moved off the field, most heading back into the barn. A good number of them didn't stop there, however. Forming a small mob, they bolted through the front gate and down the road. The Baldwins no longer cared. They could now locate their enemy, and took aim.

Gibbs couldn't move fast enough. Battle sounds chased him down the tunnel, cracking like buckling beams. Breathing hard, he reached the cave-in site. Planting one foot on the edge of the half-buried mine car, he hoisted himself up and through the hole. All sound from the surface stopped and he was through, on the other side. At the bottom of the rubble pile, he listened, assuring himself that the battle hadn't ended; that the mine hadn't been taken by the Baldwins. No. There was the muffled thud of the machine gun. He breathed deep. The air was wet and stale.

Please. Let there be no gas.

Gaujot burned with anger. His men had taken an unexpected pounding. He counted at least four lost already and most of the replacement workers had flown. Standing beneath the barn eaves, the chief deputy stared up at the mine, furious at having given ground. He had not reckoned on the man in the stair tower by the tipple. Gaujot turned, his eyes locating the sharpshooter. It was time to put things right.

With surprising speed, Gaujot scrambled to the machine-gun nest. Two of his men helped him throw extra sandbags, raising the front wall. He pushed aside the dead man's body. Under his breath, he sang.

"Tell me, little gypsy, what's my destiny?
I will cross your palm with silver, then, please try to see...."

Taking his seat behind the blood-soaked gun, Gaujot took aim at the assassin in the stair tower and immediately let go with a new cannonade of fire. The tower's oak-lathe walls popped and splintered. Furious, Gaujot swung the barrel to the right and strafed the covered track, stretching up toward the mine. Suddenly, he stopped firing. In the pre-dawn light, Gaujot could see that six of his own men were moving along the mountainside, sneaking along the work path. These men, Gaujot knew, would get the drop on the bastards inside the mine.

"That's it!" he growled. "Move in on them! Move in!"

To ready his own assault, he re-cocked the machine gun and took careful aim.

Seeing that the Baldwins' attention had been drawn to the tower, Darko and Ben crawled forward from the mine. Deeper inside, Lowcoal got an idea. "Mattern!" he called. "Help me with one of these buggies!"

The two men shouldered the first coal car and, grunting, rolled it out of the mine. They knew to keep the buggy between them and the guns below. They hadn't figured on the Baldwins coming up the narrow trail, however. Lowcoal was dangerously exposed.

Two dark-suited guards led the new attack. Heavy and clean-shaven, the front guard raised his weapon. Seeing it, Lowcoal dropped to the ground just before a copper-jacketed bullet slammed into the car, missing him by inches. "They're out here!" he yelled to the men in the mine, and scrambled beneath the coal car.

Vick Mattern wasn't as lucky. Not hearing Lowcoal's warning, he poked his head out from behind the steel buggy. The second gunman fired, and Mattern's jacket shoulder bloomed in bloody cotton. Mattern fell into the open, giving the Baldwins their target. Their shots pushed him backward, off the hillside. His body landed on a pile of slate below.

Lowcoal crunched himself behind the car's steel wheel. Crying in frustration, he overcame his fear to pull his rifle to himself and use it. It was only by some miracle that he was able to aim the thing and pull the trigger. The closest gunman fell, landing hatless on the path.

The diminutive miner scrambled backward as the second man, crouching, fired his pistol. The bullet skittered wide but Lowcoal knew that he would not be able to dodge another one. He looked out from behind his narrow buggy wheel. Seeing the gunman behind the pistol, Lowcoal recognized the terror in it, surprised to realize how much that man's face must have mirrored his own.

The shot came, but not from the Baldwin side. The man dropped his weapon and fell to the ground, blood flowing from his front. Writhing, his fingers tore at the grass. A third Baldwin fell before he could take a shot, allowing Lowcoal time to scoot back behind the coal car. There, he watched as the rest of the attacking force turned tail, back down the hill. Now Lowcoal could see why: A tall negro with a rifle was helping another man out of the wooden tram tunnel to join Low behind the coal car. *Two scabs.*

Coming up behind them, however, was Carla – keeping her rifle aimed down the chute.

"Watch out, Low!" she cried. "They're coming up behind us!"

Lowcoal understood. "Let's go! Let's go!" he called, waving her out.

Meanwhile, Gaujot's machine gun returned to life, sending a volley of blows against the mine car. It was no use, however. Staying well hidden behind it, the two scabs, Carla and Low were able to push it back into the mine. Darko briefly clasped Lowcoal's shoulder, in welcome.

They kept pushing the car into the back of the tunnel. There, they found Gibbs, kneeling over a slab of slate.

"Goddamn, where have you been?" Lowcoal asked.

"Brought us something," said Gibbs. Lowcoal's eyes went wide.

One by one, Gibbs carefully laid the sticks of dynamite on the stone. "By god!" said Darko.

Gibbs looked up at them briefly, exchanging a quiet glance with Carla. He said nothing, staying focused on the task before him.

Having pulled back from the landing, Ben Tate had been watching from inside the mine. Finally, too angry to contain himself, he squared off against Simms and Bartolo.

"We got us a couple of scabs here!" he snarled. "You fellows come to take our jobs?"

Simms had been silent all week and was tired of it. He faced Ben and tried to keep his temper.

"The man promised work," he growled. "Nobody told us about a strike."

"Let 'em be, Ben!" Lowcoal interrupted. "They saved my life out there."

"Mine too," said Carla. She watched the Italian scab, who had squatted down beside Gibbs and rolled up his sleeves. Recognizing the powder burns on the man's hairless arms, Gibbs smiled. "You're a blaster," he said.

Nodding, the Italian scab squinted at the miner's cache: Eighteen sawdust-colored tubes, their stiff red fuses, folded and aligned. Gibbs had retrieved the dynamite that Sid had left in Truman's room, weeks before.

Bartolo nodded, admiring the sticks, laid out like new candles at a shrine. "Is that all you have?" he asked.

"That's all there was," Gibbs confided.

Bartolo raised his head, eying the tipple. "How heavy this buggy?" he asked. "You know?"

"Less than a ton," Gibbs reported.

"She might work," the Italian said.

Bartolo directed the packing of both mine cars, measuring each fuse line to give its car enough time to run, unmoored, down the covered rail line into the tipple.

"It better work," Gibbs said to Bartolo as the Italian pinched the twisted fuse lines, showing Gibbs where to make the cuts. After fraying the ends of the cords, Bartolo climbed into the first bucket and secured the sticks of dynamite with pieces of slate. He asked for a fire.

"We need some help here," yelled Gibbs, and Ben came back.

They pulled the cars some thirty feet behind the point where gunfire from below made it dangerous. Ben, Gibbs, Lowcoal and Simms circled around the first buggy. Experience was on their side. Their jaws were set as the Italian struck a match.

"Fire in the hole," said Lowcoal, readying himself.

The fuse sizzled to life. Bartolo jumped from the bucket.

"Go! Go!" cried Gibbs and the four men pushed at the car.

To Gibbs, the heavy wheels seemed slow to gain momentum. He pushed harder, fearing for their lives.

"Send 'er home!"

Giving the car one last push, the men reached the mine opening, then dropped to the ground as one. The car glided across the landing, hit by a half dozen bullets from Gaujot's machine gun. For one heart-stopping moment, Gibbs thought the car would stop before reaching the edge of the open landing. He held his breath and took Carla's hand as the car rolled further, disappearing into the big wooden chute.

"Again!" cried Bartolo.

He had already packed the dynamite into the second car and was lighting another match.

The fuse was shorter this time. Its sulfurous smell gave a fearful metal taste to the air. Bartolo almost stumbled as he jumped from the car. The men pushed harder, more practiced and more eager to be rid of it.

"Get down! Get down!" Gibbs shouted as the tramcar sailed off. Lying flat, Gibbs whispered a prayer into the mountain.

The Baldwins in the tipple heard the brief rumbling from the rails, then the startling crack of a flimsy gate. Three men at the window saw the car come into the big room. They swung their guns around, but were too surprised to shoot at it. The car stumbled and tipped, then slid across the floor, crashing sideways against a beam.

"What the hell...," said one guard, then saw the fuse and the smoke. "Run! Get out!"

He and the other two had gotten partway down the stairs when the explosion came.

Lowcoal cried, "By god!" and the blast climbed up and beat them, blowing dirt and board fragments into the mine.

Gaujot turned just in time to see two tipple walls blown outward. Everything in the powerful wind that followed became his enemy.

"Get down!" the captain raged at everyone around him. Ignoring his own advice, however, he stayed at the Vickers and continued firing at the mine. The redneck miners didn't deserve such good fortune. He would make them pay.

The explosion rocked the building. Two guards were tossed by the interior stairs, bucking like a bull beneath their feet. The building seemed to rise then fall, as if the mountain had kicked it over. Somehow all three men made it to the bottom of the stairs. Desperate, they scrambled frantically for the door as the second car rolled into the tipple and blew.

The new concussion took more uprights, tearing the structure open. The barn and all the houses shook, the second blast pushing a new storm of dust and broken planks across the camp. Over the heads of the Baldwins, the wooden building groaned like the chorus of a ship's timbers, yielding to the power of the wind and sea.

Gibbs raised his head in time to see the tipple's upper floors lean over. Something in him mourned, but the feeling was soon pushed aside by relief. The building tilted like a great toppled oak, falling toward the barn.

Gibbs pushed the others toward the mine mouth. It was time to run. "Come on! Come on!"

The three-story coal plant tipped over. The great structure crashed straight through the walls of the community center, tearing into the angled beams of the barn's roof. Inside, the splintered wood and shingles rained down on a group of Baldwin guards, whose guns had been trained on a slightly greater number of finks, too desperate or scared to run. As the upper floors of the building tipped toward him, Gaujot abandoned his machine gun. The weapon was soon battered by the ruins of the structure that had buried it.

Carla had thought she'd go crazy from the noise and dust and the shock of the explosives. Now Gibbs had her hand, pulling her toward the fence. Lowcoal blew past them on the field, then was on the other side of the hole they'd cut. There was Dix, waving them through. Behind them came Simms and Bartolo then Ben. Darko was last.

"Come on!" yelled Lowcoal, but Darko had stopped to check Jakes' body for any sign of life.

Looking through the clouds of coal dust, Gaujot assessed the ruined tipple, now piled into the Sovereign barn. The wooden beams had buried his sandbag nest, making the machine gun useless. Leaning against one of the walls, however, was his rifle. Grabbing it, Gaujot turned toward the hill. The tipple and a broad section of the rail bridge were now gone, giving him an unobstructed view of the hillside and the fence. He could see the miners escaping into the woods. Using a sandbag to brace his arm, Gaujot aimed the gun.

Lowcoal heard the crack. He turned to look, just in time to see Darko getting up, having stumbled. His rise was awkward, though, and Lowcoal paused.

"Come on, Dark!" he yelled again. Darko seemed slow to get his feet under him. He made it partway to the fence, but fell again. Lowcoal went to his friend, then saw the wound. Darko was bleeding from his stomach.

"Oh, no...."

Lowcoal tried to close the gash. The blood only came faster. Darko lay on his back, staring up, blood dribbling from his mouth. Slowly, his eyes lost their focus, going still. There was a rattling sigh, and Darko Dresser was gone.

Another bullet whizzed through the grass nearby and suddenly Dix was there, at Lowcoal's side.

"Come on, buddy! They'll get us too!" Dix yelled, as he worked to pull Lowcoal away.

"No," cried Lowcoal. "No! We can't!"

Dix practically had to wrestle his friend through the fence. Lowcoal fought Dix's heavy arm, his mouth moving of its own accord, like a child's shapeless cry. Over and over, he repeated the dead Croatian's name.

Act III

Clinker: *A Mass of Fused or Molten Ash.* An accumulation
of clinkers in a boiler furnace is one of the most annoying things
in power-plant operation, and is the cause of many shut-downs....
The thick, heavy clinkers adhere to the grate and can be readily
pulled out. The thin clinkers often run all over the grates...and are
about the consistency of molten iron.... Some coals will, at the end of
three or four hours, make such troublesome clinkers that the fire
grates must be thoroughly cleaned in order to keep up steam.

Coal Manual, 1921. p 62–64

Chapter 20

As he drove down the hill toward Logan, Mouseface tried to hum a
hymn he knew from childhood. Then he stopped, deciding he was fool-
ing himself. He touched the mound of coins in his pocket, looking forward to spend them on a drink or a girl. He'd hand a portion over to the
captain, of course, and replay the whole act for him.

"These men were taken from us," he'd told the frightened finks.
"Done-in by union radicals! Come on, boys! Pay up something for their
funerals...."

The stunned workers had thrown their nickels in, almost five dollars'
worth.

Mouseface guided the truck through the empty streets of Logan, up
a rise and over a new steel bridge. He drove with the window rolled
down, needing the air. When the gears stopped grinding, he could hear
the sounds of the rushing creek below. The smell of fish entrails came up
from the wet rocks where someone had just cleaned his catch.

The truck came down the well-graded road and, at the bottom,
stopped before a chain-link fence. Mouseface jumped out, slipped a key
into the lock and drove on through. The rubber tires slid against the
hardpack, strewn with cinders and scorched metal.

Opening the truck door, Mouseface was comforted by the familiar
rumble of the big machinery. He crossed the lot, following the moonlit
rails to the big double-doors, where he found a carrier. Minutes later, he'd

rolled the three canvas-wrapped cadavers off the truck, and pushed them on the cart.

An operator stood near the grate door. Mouseface waved to him. The man turned away and disappeared. Mouseface sighed in relief. He didn't want to talk to anyone; didn't want them in his business. He parked the carrier and took the iron pole in hand. With some experience, he wrestled the door open and pulled out the wide grate. He was struck by the hellish blast of heat, hot enough to singe hair from his arms at five paces; hot enough to boil glass. Quickly, he pushed the bodies onto the big metal lattice. He felt like an engineer as he fixed the iron bar back against the coal grate and shoved it in. The rack with the bodies slammed back into the furnace and Mouseface closed the metal door, flipping the latch.

"Ashes to ashes," he muttered to himself. He fought down the familiar sense of nausea before he returned the iron rod to its place. He'd feel better once he got outside….

The furnace turned everything to ash and grit – fried wallets and hair, toasted ribs and belt buckles. The bodies of these finks became nothing but fragments of buttons, shoe grommets, manacles and cindered bone. In time, the ash and cinders would be removed from the furnace, spread on the parking lot outside. This was how Logan consumed its enemies, erasing every memory.

The power plant cleaned everyone of responsibility. Mouseface felt his culpability – nothing so strong as guilt – dissipate like smoke and flyash going up through the chimneys, mixing into the sweltering air.

Tony Veltri looked up from his desk. Although his face was expectant and polite, nothing in his broad features told Mary that he gave two cents for anything that she had to say. The more she studied him, in fact, the more Mary decided that this man, Veltri, had the eyes of a billy goat, blind to everything but his own food.

"It's about the work," she told him. "I'm here to work."

Veltri's smile faded. His jaw moved to accommodate his tongue, going after some memory in his teeth.

"My boy and me can't get home," Mary explained. "We're kindly stuck here. Sheriff said you'd sign us on to do some work, you know? We want to earn some honest cash…. On account of –. …We've been drummers, see?"

Never had she spoken so many words that sounded so foolish to her own ear. Nick gripped her hand as Veltri smoothed his thinning hair. Mary found herself shifting positions just to meet the man's eyes. At last, he spoke in a voice so ragged and full of smoke, it sounded like a machine wanting oil.

"Your name's Mary, right?"

She suppressed a sigh and nodded.

"It's nice to see you, Mary."

Veltri searched among the papers on his desk.

"I'm not sure how much I can do for you."

"Don't you have work that needs doing?"

Veltri's goat eyes returned her stare.

"What did the sheriff tell ye?"

"Is he the boss here too?"

Veltri's smile, such as it was, picked up a little resolution.

"He don't exactly own the place. But everybody gets along better if we treat him so. What kind of work did the sheriff say?"

One of his eyebrows went up.

"Well, I don't know," said Mary, fighting the urge to leave.

"I suppose I could cook," she offered. "Or clean. Some of these hallways, the rooms...."

Glancing at Nick, Veltri pushed his chair out from his desk.

"Let's walk a bit," he wheezed.

Together, the three of them rode the iron elevator up to the third floor. Strolling the red-carpeted passageway, Veltri pointed through the open doors of rooms, but said nothing. Women in starched white uniforms – identical caps and aprons – carried stacks of pressed laundry. None of them looked at Mary as she walked past, although one or two cast furtive glances at Nick, who walked behind. Two women swept the hallway carpet, pushing mechanical sweepers back and forth. Mary stared at the modern devices, yellow-lettered mahogany boxes with rollers filling them magically with dirt. Veltrie looped his arm under Mary's.

"Sheriff's top men sleep on this floor," he said importantly. "You can't ask for a safer place."

As if I had a choice, she thought.

He led them down the hall, nodding at another crew of cleaning girls, their eyes darting after them.

"Hotel's pretty full now, what with all the excitement. The girls clean the rooms on alternating floors, so everything gets done every couple of days. You just move up the line, to the one that isn't being done by someone else."

Mary realized then that Veltri was giving her a job.

"Do you have set hours?" she asked. "Where do they get their cleaning things?"

Veltri shrugged.

"I don't know that. Just ask one of these others."

Gratified despite herself, she gripped Nick's hand a little tighter. Yet, to her, this place still seemed as foreign as France.

"What about money?" she asked.

"Money," said Veltri, his eyes threatening to glaze over again. "How about five dollars a week?"

Mary took an involuntary breath.

"Five dollars?"

"Well," he said, looking at her, "it's just a trial period."

She wondered whether to believe it. Five dollars every week. And for doing less, in her mind, than what she'd done on her own homestead.

"That's the policy," said Veltri. "Talk to the sheriff, if it don't set with you."

"What about you? Don't I report to you?" she asked.

Veltri studied the ceiling. He was quiet so long Mary wondered whether he'd forgotten her.

"I just want to make things clear," she prompted. Veltri looked at her.

"That won't get you too far. Not here. You superstitious?"

Mary looked at him blankly.

"You want to get along with Sheriff Gore," he said. "If you don't, well. That's bad luck."

Gaujot carried a cooling cup of coffee down the fourth-floor hallway, stopped and knocked on the door of the sheriff's suite. Riley Gore appeared and took the cup from him. Gaujot followed him into the room. Unshaven and in his stocking feet, the sheriff looked as if he'd spent the night in his clothes, not sleeping. Gaujot closed the door behind him. Gore looked at his watch.

"Goddamn…. It's later than I thought."

He found his flask and quietly poured bourbon into his coffee. The deputy winced. The sheriff was due to appear downstairs but Gaujot knew better than to rush him. He watched Gore go to the mirror, where he ran his hand through waxy hair and cursed.

"Where's my collar and tie?"

The desired clothing lay on a chair. Gaujot plucked it up. "Folks saw the newspaper," he prompted. "Volunteers are waiting downstairs."

Gore gave him a hard look. His red eyes flared, no longer tired. "We got a crowd?"

Gaujot nodded once. "The trucks are ready too."

Gore stood before the mirror, and fiddled with the buttons on his collar. His mouth was set in a permanent frown.

"Our enemies are all around us, Pearl," he said. "Blood will be spilled today."

"Yes sir."

Gore finished dressing while Gaujot looked out the window. Men were arriving at the hotel. The pharmacist came out of his store and called to the barber, who had also closed up shop. Both men shouldered rifles. Every conversation on the street, Gaujot knew, would be about the strike and the sheriff's challenge in that morning's paper: "You're either a defender of Logan County or you're on the other side."

The sheriff came up next to Gaujot and clapped him roughly on the shoulder.

"Go on, Pearl," he said. "Go line 'em up for me."

The lobby smelled of gun oil and buzzed with talk. Like iron filings to a magnet, the black-suited Baldwins moved toward Captain Gaujot as soon as he appeared. The place had almost filled up, a sea of men in hunting clothes and broad-brimmed hats.

Good, thought Gaujot, knowing how the sheriff loved a crowd. The Baldwin captain talked briefly to his men, assigning each to a door.

Far from the stairway, the Logan Ladies' Auxiliary had commandeered a large alcove table. They staked out their own encampment, fussing over plates of sandwiches and pie. Some of the younger ones tried to shoo the men away, but the crowd grew too much for them. The ranking Baldwins, hungry and ill-tempered, led the way for others to follow. The women watched and pouted as the horde of volunteers, many decked out in military gear, wolfed down entire sandwiches or wrapped them in waxed paper to take away.

Gaujot circulated among the crowd, tapping ten of his nobles to stand along the lobby steps. The sheriff's black-suited guard took their places, each man's stance carrying an implied warning: "Don't try me."

Satisfied, Gaujot was leaning against the big lobby desk when the cheering started. Gore came down in the elevator, its iron cage descending slowly down from the hotel heights. The car landed by the wide carpeted stairs, gentle as a cloud from heaven. Now, the cheering spread across the room.

Gore stepped out into the lobby, smiling and waving, shaking hands on his way to the staircase. Gaujot scanned the crowd, sometimes glancing up at the sheriff.

Behind his phalanx of nobles, Gore took his position and began, as he often did, by staring at his shoes, gathering his wits. Looking up, he rocked on his heels, his hands folded behind his back, waiting for his audience to settle down. Finally, he gave a little cough into the back of his hand and, as if it had been given an order from the deity, the crowd fell instantly quiet.

"In the Bible, there's the story of a rich man!" Gore bellowed. "This man had his garden of olive trees! But one tree bore no fruit."

He paused, climbing to a higher step.

"The rich man told his gardener, 'Now you go ahead: Cut down that tree!' The gardener did it. He cut it down."

Gore looked at their expectant faces and smiled at them.

"We all know what it takes to make ends meet," he said. "You and me, we've all worked hard! Workin' for this American way of life, so dear to us!"

He put his fist against his chest, pronouncing the word 'American' slowly, in a way that made his listeners taste it, like sugar on their tongues.

"Through our hard work, we've achieved a way of life that's second to none. This is a place of miracles! Buildings, inventions and machines, made by the smartest minds this great country can produce! Over there, however – on the other side of that mountain – we have a different breed of dog!"

Pearl Gaujot surveyed the crowd. He recognized the signs. People began to give themselves up to the sheriff's influence, letting his words move them.

"Those lazy union reds are barking at our heels! They're massing at our borders! The union red has but one aim: to tear down our good industry and government! Just look at how they live! In tents, like savages!"

The audience gave a collective growl, a mass of upright gun barrels and nodding hats.

"That redneck union miner wants to put his own hands at the levers of democracy! Does he appreciate all the blessings bestowed by his employers? Does he love the industrial power of our nation? Is he loyal to it?"

"No!" shouted a single voice in the audience, causing some to laugh uncomfortably. Gore, however, rewarded the man who spoke, pointing to him.

"You're right, my friend! No! He isn't loyal to us! I'll tell you what the redneck miner loves; I'll tell you where his loyalty lies – to mother Russia and her communist dominion!"

The audience hissed. Gore stood back and mopped his brow.

"These men, our enemies, don't read or love the Bible! They work to undermine all that's sacred! I, your sheriff, have given the union miner every chance to redeem himself. I have tried to talk reason with him. I've tried to warn him. But did he listen?"

"No!" cried several male voices.

"No, sir! They crept like bandits on the helpless town of Sovereign, where our brave and loyal men continue to work! I'm telling you the truth: A foreign power swept down on us last night. They killed three innocent laborers and five good deputies, as well! Held men hostage and blew up the mine! Is that the way a loyal worker thanks his employer for an honest job?"

"No!" the lobby answered, its trust growing.

"The foreign union miner has just spit in our eye! It's no secret anymore, what he wants from you. He'll come and steal your property, blow up your workplace! All across these United States, the union worker wants to bring this nation down. He wants to put us all under the thumb of communist rule!"

The sheriff pointed at people in the crowd as he shouted, giving life to each word. Row by row, men and women caught the fever and began to sway, yielding themselves up to him. By the end of the speech, Gaujot noted, the crowd was moving like a single animal with four hundred eyes and fists. When the sheriff stopped pacing, he slowly raised his hands. The crowd quieted, tamed. He bent in close and purred his secret loud enough for all to hear.

"Who will stand up with me against these hounds of hell? Our state government won't do it. The one in Washington will not. It's up to you and me. You and me, we're in the middle of it. Surrounded and besieged!"

We're here for you, sheriff!

We are! We're for you, sheriff! We'll take 'em on! Send 'em all to hell!

The room howled for blood. Gore swayed as if intoxicated by the power of it. He climbed another step and called out to the back of the room. Gaujot watched, astounded.

"Come with with me, then, to the mountain! That's our garden! It's your garden they're moving onto! You want our garden to be a place for slack-jawed union laziness – trampled by union men who will not work, tending trees that won't produce?"

Hell, no!

"Then get up there and cut 'em down! That union red cannot hide from you! Get every god-damned foreign radical you can find and cut him down! Cut him down! Every damned one of 'em, I say! Clean them out, and cut them down!"

Chapter 21

As she woke, the ache she felt made Carla wonder what she'd done to herself the day before. She'd been dreaming. Something that had taken her far away. Slowly the memories returned. Of the battle. Of the march back through the fog and coming down the mountain.... Carla cocooned herself tighter in her cotton quilt, holding one corner of it in her mouth, a sleeping tussock moth.

Tildy talked and moved around the stove. Then, seeing her niece was awake, brought her several slices of bread wrapped in newsprint.

"It came out so good last evening," her aunt was saying, "I had to save some for you."

She offered the slices with a steaming cup of coffee. Sitting up, Carla took it. Tildy watched, grateful that Carla had returned to Blair. She had come back alone. What the girl had been through, she could only guess. And Tildy would not pry.

Carla nursed the hot coffee with both hands as the older woman talked. The work was slowing at the mercantile. Food and supplies weren't coming in as fast. The weather had turned gray.

"Lord, I hope it don't snow," Tildy said.

Carla stared into her coffee.

"What will come of it?" she asked, but her aunt didn't seem to hear.

"I got an idea," said Tildy, turning toward the tent door. "Let's you and me clean out that garden, over in the courtyard of the mercantile. Someone else can mind the store today."

Carla set down the coffee, pulled her arms back into her blanket and curled her legs into the cotton. Before, she had felt small and insignificant. Now, something different....

"I got one other thing I need to do, Aunt Tildy," she said.

She had to find Todd.

"Take some time with me first," Tildy persisted. "That garden needs cleaning out for planting in spring."

Carla looked at her.

"It doesn't belong to us. We don't even know if we'll be here then."

"It needs cleaning out, and this is the time," Tildy persisted. "Come on. Get yourself dressed."

In the courtyard garden between the colonnades, they worked in silence, pulling vines and weeds. As Tildy spaded swaths of sedge grass, Carla attacked the ground, her hands rediscovering their skill. She worked across the morning, freeing remnants of hydrangea from invading thistle around a redbud tree. She pulled away the tangled grapevine tendrils whose dark lobed leaves already were edged in gold. She found two small pumpkins ready for harvest and twisted one from the vine, setting it on the steps. Touching the stem's tiny spines made her recall the work of her childhood.

From the street, the sounds of Blair drifted up to them. Voices rose and fell. Two men fought. A mother hushed her crying child. Resting on the flagstones, Tildy heard it all.

"Listen to 'em," she smiled. "That's life, too. The street is so close, yet so different from this pretty garden."

"Not so pretty," Carla said. "Not yet, anyway...."

She worked with enthusiasm, digging among several currant bushes, their branches hung with a few remnants of the fruit, dried black and hard as pebbles. She saw more of them hidden in the sedge and imagined the bushes as they'd been in spring, their branches dripping with clusters of red beads, sour to the taste.

"You can almost see how nice it was," said Carla. "You think someone will come to plant it in the spring?"

Tildy studied her hands, hard with work yet fragile with age.

"I don't know," she said.

Finally tired, Carla leaned against the maple, pulled her knees close to her. She followed Tildy's gaze to one corner, taking satisfaction in the pile of wilting weeds, stacked near the cistern. New voices drifted up to them from the sidewalk. Two women tried the door and, finding it locked, continued down the street. Carla frowned. Her mind suddenly returned to the battle.

"Aunt Tildy?"

"Yes, child?"

"Did Uncle Harm regret the things he'd done at Paint Creek?"

Tildy considered her niece, sensing what lay behind her question.

"What do you mean?"

Carla looked away.

"There was an man and his wife who lived south of us," she said. "They bought our apples, eggs and such. He was old and sick and his wife complained to Mama of how he'd wake her up at night. Crying in his sleep, she said. Explained to us how he'd been at Sharpsburg, and I thought she meant some big town, like he'd been to Meridian. But no, the woman said he was sick in his head – always crying about the war.

"It got worse. Before long, the old man was begging Jesus for forgiveness, even when he was awake. Kept telling his wife how sorry he was for all the killing he'd seen and done."

Tildy nodded, knowing. Carla found a twig and used it to trace lines along the stone.

"Mama must have liked them a lot, because she carved a little cross for him. Made it out of briarwood and cat willow. It was a pretty thing – red and brown, with a rough figure hanging on it. ....I remember asking for one too. But she told me to hush. I didn't need it the way he did, she said.

"She never made another like it. No time, I guess. But she must have really liked those people...."

"Mary never made anything that wasn't good," smiled Tildy. She reached out to stroke her niece's cheek. Carla looked at her, a new sharpness in her eyes.

"Was Uncle Harm ever sorry for the things he'd done? For those men at Paint Creek?"

A robin landed on the exposed earth. It began a high-headed search for overturned grubs, making sudden jabs at the soil. Carla examined her aunt's face, the lines around her mouth and eyes, now closed. Tildy slowly inhaled the scent of dirt and wilting weeds and sighed.

"I don't guess Harm ever got a chance to feel that way. Mostly, he stayed angry at what they'd done. Like most of 'em around here, I guess. He wasn't finished fighting yet."

"Now, that don't mean that he liked it," she went on. "Harm wanted to build something better. But they just wouldn't leave him alone. He was strong, my Harmon. Strong for your daddy and for Sid. And for me.... He so wanted that union. He just knew it would make things better for us – keep bread on the table, shoes on our feet. He had to fight. Every so often, the men – and all of us. Every so often, we have to fight. But that's not the only thing we do. It's not all that Harm Fox was...."

She shook her head, letting new tears come.

"I know, Aunt Tildy," Carla said. "Uncle Harm was so much more than that."

Tildy smiled and stroked the stones. She closed her eyes to the cooling breeze, then opened them to see the robin, which had flown. Her head came down to rest on Carla's shoulder and the girl took her aunt into her arms and held her there. Tildy's mouth twisted in silent lament for the ones they'd lost.

Holding her aunt, Carla steeled herself against the pain. She'd known other such times, when the question of what's 'right' and 'wrong' got tangled up together. Somewhere, she thought, the angels slept side-by-side with their opposites, the good and bad, both coming from the same fragile root. There had been misery enough already, but Carla knew it was not yet over.

As she held her aunt, the young woman uttered a silent plea that she might never have to revisit the battlefield. Or, if she did, that she might be able to keep her soul intact, free of remorse, as Harm Fox likely did. Not like so many veterans of long-ago wars who, at the end of their lives, regretted the past and begged forgiveness from the empty air.

Chapter 22

Colonel Stanley Ford strode across the field, feeling the weight of the two leather satchels he carried. He stopped briefly on his way to the wooden shop. Breathing the chilly air, he stood and admired the long, shining bodies of seven airplanes, a row of Martin bombers just in from Langley. Now resting on the makeshift airfield in Meridian, these seven war hawks comprised half the squadron the general had ordered, the rest to come in two days' time.

Ford placed his satchels on a bench by the shop, a shed attached to the makeshift hangar, a converted warehouse. The colonel walked toward the nearest plane, where the armorers loaded guns and bomb racks.

These seven birds were more advanced than anything used in the European war. The new Martin could reach a hundred miles an hour and fly four hundred miles without refueling. As Ford came close, he knew from the luster on their olive-colored skins that the planes had been scrubbed that morning. Mitchell's orders were to keep them shining for the spectators who inevitably came to gawk. People of all kinds lined the fences, no matter how distant, to get a first-hand look at the Army's newest weapons.

Ford waved to a crewman who stood in the cockpit. The man was checking the forward gun. At the front of the plane was the great aluminum shroud, an inverted prow concealing a powerful arsenal. From under the dark cowling its crew could drop (with remarkable accuracy) two-thousand pounds of bombs. A dozen of these dark-green missiles lay on the grass before the plane like giant darts, their tail vanes sticking up.

The munitioners worked in sober silence – no joking, no easy laughter. Most of them were men whom Ford had trained. They were self-assured and knew the risks, unrattled by the fact that their instructor stood by, watching. Two men rubbed their hands together, preparing to lift one of the heavier olive-green bombs. The weapon went smoothly into the fuselage. Everyone breathed easily.

Going down the line, Ford watched two others loading another plane. They finished wiring in ten 100-pound demolition bombs, designed to destroy buildings. Anti-personnel gas and fragmentation weapons were being lifted into the next machine. The colonel grimaced, scanning the arsenal on the ground – enough to wipe out five brigades of militants. Finally, there would be one last piece of ordnance, an experimental bomb that the Army had designated for testing. Known only to Mitchell and Ford, it remained in the hangar, under lock and key.

Ford approached the plane, returned the salute of Captain Harold Steck, then shook his hand. The two stood together in silence, watching the munitioners at work. After a moment, Ford tugged the sleeve of Steck's flight jacket. "Come on."

Stanley Ford was grateful to be out, away from the cramped, wooden offices of the state Capitol. He wasn't a pilot himself, but always leapt at every chance to fly, relishing the view of any landscape from the air. Harry Steck was usually the man to take him there. Steck always knew the mission, as well as all the maps. With Steck piloting, Ford would be able to work without distraction, thousands of feet above the ground.

The two men walked toward the squadron's temporary hangar where Steck had parked a five-year-old DH-9 he called "Old Betsy." Behind the nose propeller, Betsy's face was flat, like an upright washboard. She lacked the sleek cowling of the darker Martins on the field and – Steck had to admit it – she was a lesser craft than the rest. But Old Betsy remained a sturdy machine, and Steck's favorite. She was well-matched to Ford's needs.

"You get much shut-eye last night?" Ford asked, glancing at the pilot as they walked.

"Enough."

Deep wrinkles in Steck's jacket confirmed for Ford that Steck had likely slept under his plane, a wartime habit.

With a wry smile, Steck ran a hand across his close-cropped hair. Of some Mediterranean background, he'd been raised in Ohio, trained at the Wright School. Before that, he'd worked an auto assembly line, where he'd risen to become a top mechanic. He wasn't big, but he was strong – strong enough to lift an engine block off the ground. In the air, he could wrangle his aircraft through all the elements: wind, rain or the pull of gravity.

Ford returned to the bench, where his satchels lay. Behind it, under a grimy window, someone had installed a narrow board, an arbitrary shelf, holding up a line of cracked clay pots with dead geraniums.

Steck nodded toward the shed as he wiped his hands with a rag. A windsock moved lightly against an old telegraph pole.

"Wind looks good," he said. "And Betsy's set to go."

They suited up: jackets, scarves, helmets and flight goggles. A ground crewman clapped a ladder against the plane's fuselage. Steck climbed up, pausing to spank Old Betsy's shell for luck.

"Maintaining her is something of a headache," he said. "But she does all right. You got your ammo?"

"Yup," Ford patted his satchels. "Two thousand rounds."

He hefted the bags onto his shoulders, asked Steck for anything as ballast. Steck searched the cockpit. "Here," he said. "I just took these off the fuses."

He tossed down two heavy iron cups. Ford picked one up and examined it: the screw-on iron cap for a 100-pound cooper bomb. "You're joking," he said. "We're flying armed?"

Steck grinned down at him. "Nah," he said. "Just the forward gun…. Those're surplus."

"Very funny, Captain." Ford placed the weights in his satchels and checked a pocket to make sure he had his pencil and notebook. He climbed the ladder, settling into the rear gunner's seat, directly behind Steck. Old Betsy had him sitting facing the rear, back-to-back with the pilot, allowing Ford to take notes while talking with Steck over his shoulder. Ford noticed that the rear Lewis gun had been removed, perhaps for his own convenience. He buckled himself in as a crewman pulled the ladder away.

"I'm just short of a hundred hours in this bus," Steck smiled, patting the fuselage. "Old Betsy and me, we're getting to know each other pretty well."

Ford tested his straps, twisted around to hear Steck and the ground crew exchange the familiar litany.

"Switches off…gas in…throttle down…air line in…contact…Swing prop!"

The crewman stepped forward and gave the propeller a mighty heave. The engine exploded into life. Steck taxied out, approached the runway with a practiced zig-zag, enabling him to see around the plane's high, tilted nose.

They barreled down the field. Sitting backward in the plane, Ford felt the unchecked wind blowing against his leather helmet. He thrilled to the sense of being under way, loving the throb of the airplane's engine, the sense of power. To Ford, flying was simply the most remarkable thing a human being could do.

Looking to his left, he watched the field drop away. As the plane banked east, Steck adjusted the carburetor, smoothing the engine's heavy knock. The capital city, Meridian, moved to the left, its streets and gray buildings rotating below. Finally, they banked again. Within minutes, the town had fallen away from sight, and they were headed into a sky of brilliant blue.

Betsy leveled out, and they were soon flying over a dense carpet of trees, interrupted by few man-made roads or buildings. Ford rarely got to see such wilderness. The boundless view of rolling green hills and shadowed valleys was broken only by the occasional ridgetop bald or tiny thread of road or stream. It was the middle of fall, so the mountains were tinged with hints of rust within the undulating green. Ford could see the various shades, from the fern-colored fields to the dark-lime color of the deeper hollows. In some places the landscape was darker, marked by black creeks or basins. Before too long, Ford knew, the autumn hills would be bright with reds, oranges and yellows – a range of multicolored trees.

He eyed various features of the landscape, taking note of things he'd never see on any map. On the way south, he gave Steck orders to tilt this way or that, revealing the geographic oscillations, ridge upon ridge – waves of land, as if from some ancient geologic storm.

"Hold on sir," the pilot called. "I have to run a test!"

Steck signaled toward a monolithic outcropping of stone, a grey cliff rising from the forest. Ford closed his eyes, imagining the veteran pilot's feet at the pedals, his hand altering the stick's tilt. Bounced and buffeted by invisible, changing currents, the bomber banked toward the rock face. Ford was conscious of his own intake of breath. His hand felt its way into his clothing. He loosened his belt.

Then, without warning, Steck pulled the trigger of the Vickers gun. Ford jumped as the pilot fired some twenty rounds. Chunks of quartz flew off the cliff face, sending a rain of stones into the greenery below.

"What in hell-?"

"I had to test the forward gun!" Steck called. "Standard procedure!"

Ford nodded, a little angry with himself for being spooked – and for doubting his captain.

"Right!" he said, and turned back around.

They flew south. Below them, the miraculous landscape continued to roll by. Topography and terrain were always factors. No intelligence officer wants to miss anything, risking a wrong conclusion. Below them, the mountain vegetation was interrupted only by the narrowest roads. Ford thought of Europe, recalled the hours of parsing such beautiful scenery into tactical missions and air assaults. Working quietly for the British, he'd mapped scores of targets in Germany – steel works, refineries, harbors and railyards, even metallurgical mines. All subsequently wiped out.

Ford heaved a sigh, knowing it could not be heard over the engine's drone. Today, he was assessing a very different enemy – a domestic one. Of course, the Army was giving the militants fair warning, and Ford hoped they knew enough to heed to it. General Mitchell was not a man to hesitate, even eager to prove the might of his Air Service. Orders were orders. Steck signaled him.

"We're coming in on your targets! Best get ready!"

Signaling back, Ford bent down and ferreted through one satchel. Rising, he held the first sheaf of papers in his hand and looked out of the cockpit.

His first view of the camp at Blair surprised him. The field was covered with standard Army-issue tents. In well-ordered rows, the canvases numbered in the hundreds, many more than Ford had expected. Still others were scattered on outlying sites, on fields across the creek. The number of strikers living there must be huge, Ford thought, although he didn't see too many men in camp. The whole thing looked like a training exercise at Langley.

On his order, Steck took the plane low enough to get a better look. Ford saw the upturned faces of skinny kids, playing in the creek; women glancing up with open mouths as they hung laundry. The kids ran, chasing the plane's shadow on the ground. Ford made a note: "Camp at the town of Blair: Mostly women and children. Few men."

He tapped Steck on the shoulder.

"Go through again, as low as you can," he said. "Then, we'll hit the town."

Steck nodded and pulled up. Banking east, he dipped again, tracing the line of the railroad for a hundred yards. Ford readied the contents of one satchel as the aircraft came in low, directly over the camp. He opened the case, tossing a handful of notices from the cockpit. Like oversized confetti, the white sheets scattered in the bomber's wake. Ford looked behind, watched the handouts flutter down across the field of tents, some landing in the creek and trees. He took more handfuls, letting them fall evenly as the plane passed over the mercantile building, then the town. Steck leaned back, half-turning.

"You want to go through again?"

"No," said Ford. "Take us up to the battle line."

Steck pointed the plane southwest. He knew the area well, having flown a similar sortie two days before. When the time came, Captain Harry Steck and Old Betsy would likely escort the entire squadron. Fourteen planes. Ford hoped it wouldn't come to that.

The DH-9 banked south again, then started its thumping upward rise.

Ford fought to suppress the familiar sickness as the biplane bounced on the mountain crosswinds, like climbing invisible steps. He craned his neck, eager for a first glimpse of the miners' mountain camp, somewhere near the top of the next ridge.

They found it higher and farther than Ford had imagined. Two other things surprised him: First was the sheer number of men he could see on the mountainside. He did a quick assessment of their battle line. Three miles, with far more men than he'd known. What was worse, true to Gore's prediction, the militant miners had dug initial trenches. Ford could even see a log bunker or two. Judging from the smoke rising from the woods, the miners had more than one kitchen there, perhaps even supply depots. Colonel Ford could not escape the ominous conclusion: The miners' army was much bigger and better organized than he had thought. He began to feel a begrudging admiration for them.

"Hey!" called Steck. "Where'd they come from?"

Ford looked to where the pilot was pointing: On the next ridgetop, across the valley, new units were digging in. Trucks were parked across the mountain balds, their drivers lounging in them. Scores of others, however, were busy digging trenches of their own. Having seen the appeal in yesterday's paper, Ford realized what he was seeing: Sheriff Gore's volunteer force. Its numbers didn't match those of the miners. From what Ford had heard of Gore's resources, however, he knew that any fight with these men would likely be a bloody one.

"You didn't notice this the other day?" Ford asked.

"No, sir!" Steck called back. "They weren't there then!"

"Fly the length of each line," Ford ordered. "We'll drop notices on both sides. Then, bring me back around, so I can get some kind of count."

They dropped leaflets as they flew along the lines, starting with the miners. Ford glanced at their fortifications, a ragged line of men, sitting lying and standing; men of all colors and types. Some of them raised guns and cheered the plane as it passed overhead. Ford let the leaflets go quickly, eager to return for a better view of the miners' construction work – the trenches, lean-tos and log bunkers.

The camp on the other side of the valley was leaner, but clearly full of fire. Under the instruction of the Baldwins, the Logan volunteers were building more disciplined lines. Ford imagined a relatively narrow chain of command, and made note of it. After releasing the last of the leaflets, he took a final look. One group of dark-suited men stood around three trucks, gazing up at the plane. They used their hands to shield the sun from their eyes.

"A little higher, Captain," Ford ordered. "Once more, over the tree cover in the middle. Then we'll head home."

The colonel opened another notebook before tossing the weighted satchel to his feet. The plane ran up the central valley, flying north. Ford did his best to see both battle lines. He jotted down positions, identifying what weapons he could while noting the reinforced log structures on both sides. By the time he were done, the intelligence officer had a good sense of each side's likely tactics and strategy – as well as the Army's. ...*If it comes to that.*

Ford did his troop-strength calculations. Looking at the numbers he'd written into his log, and almost dropped his pencil. On the miners' side, he had reckoned a force of "7,000 to 9,000 men." Logan's defenders were something less. The two camps faced each other in a tense stand-off. Both sides were quiet now, but Ford had no illusions: This scene had all the makings of an impending war.

All it needs, he thought, *is one, small spark. Then, the whole thing blows sky-high.*

Ford was sketching a diagram of the battlefield when the DH-9 jumped. He turned his head toward Steck.

"Damn, soldier! Hold it steady!"

"We're under fire, sir!"

Only then did Ford become aware of a barrage of bullets, hammering the fuselage. First there were just few metalic *pings;* then many. The sound was unmistakable, like someone throwing nails against the hull.

"Get us out of here!" he called.

"Yes, sir!"

Steck pulled the nose up sharply and did a semi-roll. Ford gripped his book and dropped the pencil. It sailed out of the cockpit. Ford closed his eyes, suddenly realizing that Steck's war instinct was taking over. He sent the plane into a gunner's dive, apparently planning an assault on the miners' line. Ford was horrified to see the captain's hand on the Vickers gun, swinging it into position.

"No!" the colonel cried. "Do not meet the enemy!"

"We're under fire, sir!" Steck yelled.

"I said, 'do not engage'! Captain, that's my order! For pete's sake, Steck, get us out of here!"

Steck nodded, pulling his hand away from the gun. The plane leveled and pointed back toward Meridian.

But it was too late. Ford watched the black smoke pouring from the fuselage. There was a foul smell of diesel fuel. His spirits sank fast.

"We're hit bad!" yelled Steck. "She's leaking fuel!"

"Bring us down slow!" Ford commanded.

With a sickening feeling, he looked at the rolling landscape below. They had little hope of finding any landing field in such rough terrain.

The engine bumped and sputtered. Steck reset the choke, adjusted the flow of gas into the engine.

"Hold tight, sir! This won't come easy...."

A knot formed in Ford's stomach as Steck opened the throttle, pushed the engine hard. Ford searched for any kind of landing field but saw only a great, unbroken wave of hills, so much less benign than before. All of Steck's concentration was focused on Old Betsy's motor, as he fought to keep the machine aloft. Ford twisted around in his seat, looking everywhere he could.

"Down there!" he called. "The river!"

Steck looked and nodded. With effort, he banked the plane toward the dark ribbon Ford had spotted, a river bordered by a long cornfield. The engine belched as they wound through the hills. A new cloud of black smoke poured from the fuselage.

Damn, damn, damn!

Steck went for broke, opened the throttle wide, banked left. The plane bucked and bounced beneath them. They were quickly losing altitude. Old Betsy's wings finally evened out and Ford could see: They were over the river now.

Thank you. Thank you.

Steck closed the throttle, shutting the engine down, continued his fight to level the wings. Smoke blew through the cockpit, choking both men. Suddenly, Ford thought of his father, going to his machine shop in Pennsylvania. His mother, in the kitchen....

Now he heard the wind rush past. Time seemed to stop, the seconds moving with agonizing slowness. The river came up quickly – much too fast. Ford suddenly imagined the worst death possible: Strapped in Old Betsy's broken fuselage, upside-down in the water. He tried to turn his head to see where they were headed. Giving up, he closed his eyes.

The bomber glided down without power, veering toward the right-hand river bank, to the adjacent cornfield, to the east.

"Hang on!" Steck yelled.

Then the pilot unstrapped the flare pistol from the side of the cockpit and handed the gun to Ford.

"Use this!" he said. "Fire it now!"

Ford grimaced, knowing the chance of being seen or rescued was slim. Still, he gripped the flare gun, pointed high, behind the plane, and fired. They were within fifty feet of the ground. Ford felt the heat of the gun against his palm. He tossed it overboard and braced himself for the crash.

Old Betsy raced in at fifty miles an hour, her axels cutting across the rows of drying cornstalks. The wheels hit, bouncing against the ground before rising again, then knocking into a wooden fence. Ford felt the shock of the collision, certain that the landing gear was wrecked. Old Betsy struck down again in the next field, harder this time. The plane began to crumble. No match for the newly plowed earth, its left wheel tore away from the frame, then the right. The bomber's axel snapped, the struts separated. The wings twisted and caved. What was left of the bi-plane fish-tailed, almost tipping over, then came to a sudden, lurching stop.

Ford sat in stunned silence. He listened to the dried corn rustle, the hot engine's loud sigh. Then, surprisingly, a songbird whistled from across the river. Water rushed through a hand-made dam of rocks. Behind him, Steck heaved a great, glad curse. Ford closed his eyes and said a word of thanks. He breathed, checking himself for injury. Finding none, he began taking huge gasps of air, not wanting to be sick. His hands fumbled at the harness, eager to be free of the plane.

Steck tilted his head back and laughed out loud.

"Do you believe this?" he cried. "I just clocked a hundred hours in her!"

Ford shook his head, clambered out, bent over the muddy ground and regurgitated the contents of his stomach. Standing, he glanced up at the plane, felt a pocket for his notebook.

"Did you see which side got us?" Ford asked.

"Nope," said Steck. "Did you?"

"Not exactly," the colonel said. "But I've sure got my suspicions."

Together, he and Steck surveyed the damage. Steck examined the bullet holes, asking what kind of "redneck blunderbuss" had brought down his favorite plane. Ford's pulse quickened as he thought of the necessity of getting "back on the horse" – back into the air with a squadron. He looked at the plane, trying to shake off the thought of how close they'd come to death.

"We gotta admit it," he told Steck. "There's a hell of a lot of those red-neck miners out there, and they're not screwing around."

Steck turned from his examination of Old Betsy and scrutinized the colonel. "Nothing we can't handle," he said.

Ford nodded, knowing he would follow orders. In fact, he was eager to get back to the work that waited for him, at his temporary desk in Meridian. There, he would get busy, writing the report that General

Mitchell was hungry to see. Colonel Ford would file the report, mapping out a strategy, the military solution. The Air Service crews were trained and ready to apply their skill with these new weapons, designed for overwhelming any enemy from the air. He would estimate the number of bombing runs, up and down the battle line to clear the miners from their nests. They would send five regiments of infantrymen, enough to occupy the region, starting with the town of Blair. Ford would estimate damage. The casualties will be high, he thought, but certainly no worse than allowing both sides to continue a prolonged conflict. Better to end it fast. All this would go into his assessment.

Too bad, thought Ford, shaking his head. He understood Sheriff Gore's organization, and knew exactly what the striking miners were up against. He recalled their numbers on the field, how quickly they'd moved, how they manned their lines. *They're tough,* he thought, with some admiration. *And with a noble cause.* The worst kind of enemy.

As he walked with Captain Steck, following the river to the next town, Ford considered his next assignment, the mission's next phase. They had one more chance to bring the two sides together for a peaceful settlement of the conflict, and Stanley Ford decided he would do his best to make that happen, just as the general had ordered.

Ford noted the time. He would mark the small days and hours until the president's deadline. The countdown to intervention had begun. Yet, as the Army's chief federal officer on the ground. Colonel Stanley Ford would do what he could to avoid conflict and bring both sides together. He wanted this for the miners, and hoped for a negotiated settlement. In the end, however, he was a military man, and his orders would be clear: He would mobilize the entire flying force of the U.S. Army against the combatants, if they didn't heed the president's command to stand down – a command he'd just delivered to some 15,000 very angry men.

...Sheriff Riley Gore assured his listeners that the militants
on Logan's eastern border "do not represent
true working men of Logan County."
"The great majority of our men are strong and
one-hundred-percent loyal," the sheriff said. "They are grateful
for the bounty bestowed upon them!"
"These others are weak," he said, "They are manipulated by
foreign elements. Some of them come from Europe and Russia,
the birthplace of their socialist ideas...."

– The Logan Herald, October 15, 1921.

Chapter 23

Simms and Bartolo sat in the dugout, playing their ritual of cards.
Simms leaned into the game. His long limbs were spread like the legs of
a grand-dad spider. His elbows rested on his knees and framed his hand,
which was not a good one. They waited for Lowcoal to play a card, then
Dix. There was no pot, as none of the four owned much of anything that
he didn't already share.

During their first full day on the front, the Sovereign raiders had
slept. They lay awake most of that first night, listening to the sounds of
over-revved truck motors. Gibbs got up one time to see lights moving
across the valley, creeping down from the woods, onto the distant ridge.
He sensed the defense line of strikers, wide awake in their holes. All
along the miner's line, men watched the barren dark. The enemy's
shouted commands couldn't be understood, the words drowned-out by
someone yelling curses from the miners' side. One time, as Gibbs listened, a striker screamed something and fired a single shot across the
valley. It had no effect.

"Goddamn waste of ammunition," Lowcoal muttered. "They're
likely out of our range besides."

The next morning, they rose to the startling scene across the gap: The
Logan volunteers had been hard at work on their fortifications. A constant string of trucks still snaked along a series of now-visible trenches

and log walls, broken only by an occasional bunker, made of strong concrete.

The ragged cards went down, but Gibbs wasn't following the game. They were at war – or they would be soon – against a stronghold that put the miners' dirt-and-canvas shelters to shame. And he missed Carla, felt as if a part of himself had gone with her.

Where is she now? he wondered, knowing the answer. What would Todd think of all this now?

"Your play, Dix," said Simms. Dix waved him off, needing more time. In a corner, Ben muttered his desire for a cigarette. Lowcoal nibbled a dry biscuit, sometimes getting up from the game to view the Logan line. It taunted him.

"Bet they got a Thompson in ever' goddamned hole," he said.

"Screw that," Dix objected. "Them Baldwins is just a bunch of Jersey corner boys. Heads the size of baseballs and twice as thick, they cannot shoot worth a damn."

But no one was convinced.

One by one, the cards went down. Gibbs began to hate the waiting. Aside from the ominous silence in the air, the deaths of Mattern, Jakes and Darko weighed upon them all.

Harder still were the stories other men were telling about the raid, tales of masked unionists who'd killed twenty Baldwins at Sovereign; that they'd burned the entire settlement to the ground; that no one on the other side – guard or scab – had been left alive.

The raiders knew better to speak of it themselves, even to their friends. They stayed in their dugout, playing cards, frightened about the consequences of their own legend and grateful to be alive. Outside, the strikers – hungry for heros, even anonymous ones – continued to snatch up any piece of news to inflate. Yet none of their stories, Gibbs noted, were about the woman among them who fought at least as bravely as any man.

"She didn't say anything to you, did she, Gibbs?"

"Nope."

"Damn," Lowcoal said, and lay down his hand. "Seems like she just pulled her things and went back down-," he said, and stopped himself, having almost said, "…to Todd."

Gibbs shrugged, not wanting to give himself away. But Lowcoal wasn't fooled, eyeing him from across the trench. "You don't think she'll talk, do you?" he asked.

Gibbs glared back at him.

"What do you think?"

"No," Low admitted, looking away. "I'm sure not."

Gibbs closed his eyes, missing Carla, trying to be sure that she would be back. *At least she's safe,* he thought, and played the scene over in his mind.

In getting away from the battlefield, Carla had outrun the men. Gibbs had tried to keep pace, but lost sight of her in the woods and fog. Finally, he stopped and waited for the others to catch up. No one had said anything. All were eager – desperate – to get back to camp. They'd left the Browning behind, along with their own dead.

They found her again in the woods, just below the miners' line. Breathing hard, Carla sat beneath a chestnut tree. She'd set aside her pack and gun.

"I don't feel good," she said.

"None of us do," said Gibbs, trying to put down his fear for her, his frustration at having her leave. He waved the other men on and they continued up the wooded hillside, shouting the password – *I come creepin! Patrol returning!* – through the trees, heading toward their mountain camp.

"I wish you hadn't run," Gibbs said. "We need to stick together."

Carla looked out, into the woods. They heard the others, shouting their greetings to the sentries.

"You're right," she said, and looked Gibbs in the eye. "But I need to get back to Blair."

"To Todd," he said. "Or what?"

"Yeah," she said, still looking at him. "Todd should be here," she said. "It's not right, him not being here with us."

Grimacing, Gibbs put his hand out to her, helping her up. Standing, Carla ferreted into her pack and he was startled when her hand came out with Sid's pistol. In one motion, she tipped open the chamber and let the shells fall out. The bullets drummed the ground like metal seeds. She held the gun out to him, as if in surrender.

"Take it," she said.

"Ain't no good without the bullets," he told her, trying to smile. Carla picked up the shells and dropped them into his hand, mixed with a little dirt.

Gibbs took the gun, felt the iron of it along with the weight of her leaving. He wanted to argue, tried to summon the will to order her to stay. Instead, he'd become tongue-tied. He said nothing. She left him there. Gibbs watched Carla's long strides carry her toward the strikers' line, knowing she would not stop. There was no way to stop her, he decided, no words he knew. She'd left both guns behind.

The steady cards went down. Gibbs, his eyes still closed, was deep in his own thoughts. He was tempted to accuse himself of cowardice, not ordering Carla to stay. Through the long hours in the trench, however, he'd grown tired of thinking about it, knowing only that he wanted her back.

Hell, he told himself, *the woman's allowed to have her own business.* And her business wasn't his. ...Or was it? Carla had insisted on coming with them. Since then, Gibbs figured, her fate had gotten pretty well tangled with his own. And, for that matter, with the fates of all the men around them – everyone.

Carla must know what she's doing, he thought. Gibbs trusted her to know it. He did trust her – as a friend, and more. So he sat as the other men played cards and waited for more fighting. Gibbs' eyes were closed as he rationalized: Carla Rising Mandt would share her thoughts with him, if and when she was ready. She would not betray him or anyone else here. And, even if she did...well...maybe he'd have to accept that too.

Gradually, Gibbs realized that his friends had been talking about him.

"He's readyin' hisself to get back into it," Dix had drawled. "Can't wait to get back there and do it all over again."

"Me too, by god," Lowcoal was saying, but without emotion. "What are we waitin' for?"

"Let's catch our breath first," said Gibbs, making them laugh. "Let somebody else have a turn."

Simms smiled as he gathered up the cards. Dix held out his hand. "My deal."

Outside, the smell of burning pine and bacon drifted in from across the divide.

"Them other sons of bitches is eating good," said Ben. "Don't it just figure."

Then a new noise came.

"Sounds like a bee in here someplace," Dix said.

Simms rose, pocketing the cards.

"No," he said. "That's a motor...."

Even from a distance, the thing seemed huge. A great eagle with a double set of wings. Soon the plane was overhead, dipping along the miners' line, and hundreds of men had stood up to see. Forgetting their guns, they watched open-mouthed as the plane came in low. By the time the handbills fluttered down – small half-sheets dancing in light breeze – the machine was halfway across the valley. Men scrambled to snatch the papers as if they were notes from home.

"'By Order of the President'...." Lowcoal started.

Simms quickly read the news, which sunk in like a stain.

"Don't this beat all," he said.

"The Army's taking the other side?" Ben asked.

"Ain't it always like that?" said Dix, crumpling a flier in his hand. "What do they want us to do?"

"Put down our guns and get on home," said Simms, reading.

Lowcoal laughed. "Buddy, if we *had* a home, don't you think we'd go back to it?"

"Right here's home enough for me," said Dix.

"Wonder what'll they do, if we don't wanna move?" Gibbs mused.

"I'll tell you what they do," said Simms, and everyone looked at him.

"A couple of thousand soldiers will come marching down that hill behind us. And their guns will be fixed with bayonets. If they don't kill you, they'll push you across the valley – right into the arms of your mine guards, over there...."

"Some choice," said Lowcoal.

"And we got a whole week to think about it," said Dix, shaking his head.

The airplane made its final pass, dropping more leaflets on the Logan camp. The miners watched, surprised at how fast the novelty of the big flying machine had worn off. As they watched, they heard gunfire from the other side.

"I don't believe it," said Simms. "They're firing at the Army's aeroplane!"

"Damn," said Lowcoal, as the plane flew off. "Baldwin sons of bitches have no respect for anything at all."

Swift was uneasy as Mary brushed his coat, his eyes darting. Nick shoveled cracked oats into his trough.

"It won't be long," Mary calmed him. "Not much longer, now."

But she didn't know. The guns had started up that morning; like the irregular pounding of steel hammers or a great, thudding engine that would not stop.

She gripped Nick's hand as they crossed the street, passing sidewalk loiterers, many of whom now looked familiar to her. A regular flow of day-jobbers was coming into town, fallen men, trying to scrape together any kind of life. They leaned against the front wall of the hotel, as if holding it up. Their hats pitched at defiant angles, they smoked begged and salvaged cigarettes and waited for any kind of work to come.

A big group was now gathered around the trucks. These were the professionals, the hired guns, constantly surrounded by younger ones who admired them for their weapons. Nick tugged at Mary's hand. She could hear the drone in his chest, mimicking the truck's idle.

"No," she said. "We don't have time."

Unable to resist, however, the boy broke loose from her and ran.

"No!" cried Mary, causing men to turn and look.

She pushed her way after him through the crowd of patriots. She lost him briefly before seeing him, smiling from the truckbed. Mary was terrified that the machine might pull away, carrying him off.

"Boy, you get down from there!" she cried. A farmer's kid looked at Nick and laughed. A sharp-nosed Baldwin blew smoke from a cigarette and put his hand around Mary's shoulder. He was a big man, older.

"They's just havin' fun," he drawled. And, then, to Nick.

"You all ready to fight the reds, ain't you, son?"

"No!" said Mary. "He's too damned young!"

"Well, he looks ready to go!" grinned the Baldwin.

Mary pushed away his arm. She glared up at the farmer's boy. "That's my son. Give him back to me."

Everything grew suddenly quiet. Mary wondered what she'd said, then turned to see that Sheriff Gore was standing at her side.

"Come on down here, boy" said Gore. He motioned to the others and Nick was lifted down. He took his mother's hand.

"There's a good fellow," the sheriff said. "A young defender."

Surrounded by uncertain smiles, Mary leaned down to whisper in Nick's ear. "Get inside. Wait for me upstairs."

Nick ran off. Gore's face took on a look of mock penitence.

"No harm in it," he offered. "Boys need their fun."

The rest had turned away, the thing forgotten. Mary headed toward the hotel. Gore followed. Catching up, he took her arm as if to help her step up to the curb. Mary wheeled on him, forcing her voice into a self-possession she did not feel.

"That boy's never mined no coal," she said. "He's hardly been off our land. *He's not in this, you understand?"*

Gore's eyes narrowed.

"That may be," he said. "But you should trust me better."

She stared back at him, locking his eyes on hers.

"Then do as much for me," she said, "and help me keep what's mine."

Chapter 24

The tent city was eerily silent as Carla passed through it. A few skinny, mud-streaked kids ran along the rows, pretending to hunt down "Bald-wings" with their sticks. Women sat in quiet watch over the smallest children or helped scratch lunch together. Most of their men had joined the militants on Blair Mountain.

In the town, Carla saw more newcomers, men in unmuddied clothes walking alongside women wearing catalog hats. Oblivious to the strikers and their fight, the strollers stopped to consider chalkboard signs promoting hot dogs, coffee, leather goods, five-cent beer and guns.

Tourists, Carla thought without kindness for the curiosity-seekers who'd come to see the "workers war" first-hand. The younger ones, all would-be fighters, loitered at the edge of town, discussing the union. The loudest of them boldly declared themselves to be "socialists," clearly working up their nerve. Carla could see the way they looked at the rumbling mountain, their glances filled with fear and longing. She stood and listened. The gunfire was ever-present now, rolling down from the twin ridgetops like distant thunder.

She found Todd upstairs in the mercantile, in a big room down the hall from his office. He stood alone in the chamber, a space big enough for a bank of desks, all of them shoved to one side. Room for a dance, Carla thought. Or a boxing match.

The floor was littered with remnants of countless surveys – two stiff wooden tripods and a dozen long crates, all broken open. The boxes had held geological core samples, long striated poles of rock, cut and lifted from the earth. These stone cores were scattered about the floor – granite tubes of various broken lengths, the width of Carla's fist. Looking at them, she imagined hillsides up and down the Big Coal River, all pocked and riddled with drill-holes.

Todd stood by a dusty cabinet. A pegboard lay on it, with dowel rods sticking up in even rows. Each rod had hash marks on it, noting depths – 200, 250, 300 feet. Criss-crossing lines of black string went from one rod to another at each mark. Todd was staring at the wooden thing as Carla came into the room.

"What's this?" she asked, side-stepping any greeting. He looked at her with sad eyes.

"An engineer's model of a coal mine," he explained. "The strings are tunnels. The spaces between them are rooms of coal. It's how they take the measure of a mine, in tons of ore."

Carla stared at the thing, appraising it.

Todd watched. Under his gaze, she felt like a stranger.

"You cut your hair," he said and Carla's hand went up, automatically touching a place above her ear.

"Tildy did it," she said, and almost smiled at the memory – how the two women had laughed together over Carla's girlish braids as they hit the floor. Tildy had been squinting into the tiny photo of the magazine, made Carla's bangs go straight across her forehead, just above her eyes.

"We have to talk," said Carla.

"So, talk," said Todd, unable to look at her. He pretended to survey the room, lost in thought. Carla followed his gaze and realized he had been moving the desks and stacking empty crates along one wall. Working alone, she thought.

"What's this gonna be?" she asked.

"Another office. For the boss."

It took her a moment to realize, he'd meant Kenner.

"We need to build the organization here," Todd said. He used his foot to shove a stone core sample. The tube-shaped thing rolled like a cannon ball on a ship's deck. Carla listened to the urgent sound of the battle. They were losing time.

"How can Kenner think of setting up a new office with everything that's going on?" she asked.

"I'm not sure I should tell you that," said Todd, looking at her for the first time. "You want to tell me about Sovereign?"

She stared at him, surprised that he'd been the one to bring it up.

"I was there," she admitted, and Todd's face took on a look of disbelief.

"By god, Carla...."

"...and I'm glad of it," she said.

"How could you?"

"How could you not?" she went on. "You should have been there, Todd."

"You don't know what you're saying."

"You don't see what the Baldwins are doing to us. Sovereign looks like a prison camp! The Baldwin police were using our houses, our homes, while all the scabs were there, living like slaves."

Frowning, Todd shook his head.

"That's what you say. Others see it different. Take a look at this."

He opened a newspaper on the cabinet, dated that morning. Reading the bold headline, Carla scowled.

Unionist Bombers Blow Up Mine
And Shoot Up Sovereign,
Kill Three Workers!

"Our side didn't shoot any scabs," she said.

"Even if I believed you, it wouldn't make any difference," Todd said. "You do a thing like this, and you let Gore and the newspapers say whatever the hell they want! And what they say sticks. To you and all the rest of us!"

"You should have been with us," Carla said again. She read more of the story, then looked up at him. "The Baldwins set up those men. Set up the whole thing, maybe. And the scabs weren't even armed."

Todd took the newspaper. "Who else was with you?" he asked. "Was Gibbs in on it?"

Carla said nothing.

"Of course it was Gibbs," said Todd. "He couldn't wait, could he?"

Todd paced the room.

"This is just great," he said. "Kenner's trying to negotiate a deal for us, and my brother's out there, sparking up a goddamn war! Gibbs wanted a fight and now he's got one. Well, I hope he's ready for it, because now the U.S. Army's on its way."

Carla fell silent. She'd seen a copy of the warning flier that morning.

"What's the union saying about it, Todd?" she asked.

"What? About the soldiers?"

"When they come," she said. "What's Kenner say we ought to do?"

Todd rubbed his forehead, irritated.

"Well, you won't have to worry about that," he said. "Not if Gibbs and the rest of them put down their guns and come back down here with us."

Carla stared at him in disbelief.

"So we should cut and run? Let the Baldwins stay here and come after us until they hunt us all down?"

Todd glared at her. "It ain't about the Baldwins anymore! Or even about Kenner and the union! This is the president of the United States! Do you think Gibbs and the rest of 'em can stand up to the United States Army? Well, that's just crazy! They have to back down!"

"You're quitting," said Carla, disbelieving.

"I'm not quitting!" Todd fired back. "If anything, you're quitting! You quit the day you walked out of here and went with Gibbs! I don't know what you think you're doing up on that mountain, Carla – but you sure ain't fighting for the union!"

"We're the only ones who're fightin' at all," she returned.

Todd wheeled on her.

"Kenner told you not to go! And Kenner is the union – not Gibbs!"

He loomed over her, but Carla didn't flinch. She glared back at him with her dark eyes. Gradually, Todd came back to himself. He turned away from her.

"I told you not to go," he said.

Carla heard the pain in his voice, his sense of betrayal. She inhaled, fighting to overcome the storm of of emotions between them.

"After they killed Sid," she said, "I couldn't stop thinking about it. Up at mama's place, I worried about everybody here. About Aunt Tildy and Uncle Harm. And Gibbs and you. I worried about you, Todd. I was so glad that you had taken Sid's place, that you were leading it."

Todd looked at the floor, his heart in his throat.

"So, I came back here. And I was so happy to be back with every-body, trying to build something here in Blair. It felt good, like I was facing up to things. Not running away to mama's. Then, they got Uncle Harm, and here was Tildy, going through the same thing I went through. And it all came back on me. All the pain and anger. ...Don't you feel it, Todd? Everything the companies and the police have taken from us?"

Todd was silent, not looking at her. Carla pressed on.

"We *had* to go up that mountain," she told him. "We had to go to Sovereign, and I am proud of it, Todd! You should see what they did at that place. To your own homeplace...."

Carla's eyes leveled on his.

"If we don't fight them," she said, "they'll just hand our houses over to yet another bunch, like those poor men we found up there the other day. And when that blows up, there'll be another group after that, and another. To the company, we're nothing but a bunch of gypsies – all of us, men, women and kids – moving in and out of a place with never a chance of owning it. Some of these men, your friends, have spent their lives going from one place to the next. They move in and go to work, treated like so much muscle and bone, bought and sold like some ma-chine. You wanna know why your brother's up there, fighting them? That's the reason."

Todd opened his mouth, but no words came.

"So what are you and Kenner doing?" Carla continued. "Are you giving up on Gibbs and them? On your own brother?"

Todd picked up the newspaper.

"I haven't given up on anyone," he said. "If anything, you've given up on me. I wanted things to work for us. I wanted things to get back to normal. Just doing a good day's work and getting decent pay for it. I thought you and me, maybe we could have had that together."

Carla stared at him.

"You really think we can go back to that?" she asked.

Her tone was so soft that Todd mistook it for something else. From her voice, he took a note of hope.

"Carla, I'd dig coal at Sovereign or any other place for you. Hell, I'd work for next to nothing if I knew you were behind me."

As he said this, Carla turned away.

"What else could there be?" Todd finished.

What else? Carla could only begin to know. In Blair, she'd been caught up in the excitement of building something new. How many other places could be like that, she wondered. Where else did people work together, help each other out like this? To support each other, not just at one thing, but everything? Carla saw a wilderness of untried paths, leading to places where people made decisions together and had real control of their lives. In Sovereign, she'd only seen its opposite. The company camp had everything built around coal, a single product and just one boss. Life there could never be the same for her. With Todd or anybody else.

If I knew you were behind me, Todd had told her. The words rang in her ears. He wanted her *behind* him, in Sovereign. How different he was from Gibbs, who had helped her to lead.

Carla turned, looked at Todd and shook her head. Upon seeing this, he knew he'd been wasting his breath. He could see it in Carla's eyes: He'd completely lost her – to Gibbs and his futile cause. Todd let the sadness wash over him. Worse, he felt humiliated. In trying to recover, he retreated and turned cold. As if, inside him, some switch was thrown.

"All right," Todd said, his voice with a new edge to it. "But there's this other thing."

He pointed to the newspaper, to a photograph on a different part of the page.

"What's this?" Carla asked.

The photo showed Sheriff Gore beaming at a group of men, all armed. Among them, on a truck, was Carla's brother, Nick. Mary was at Gore's side. Carla couldn't believe what she was seeing.

"This can't be right." She looked up at Todd, hoping that he might explain it to her. Todd's face hardened.

"What do you think it is?" she asked him.

Todd stared at the wood-and-string engineer's model on the cabinet, one finger tracing the edge of its base.

"What do you think it is, Todd?" Carla repeated.

Todd softened a little. "OK," he began. "No one else needs to know about it."

Carla backed away from him.

"What do you mean?" she scoffed. "That's my mother's picture in the Logan newspaper! How could people not see it?"

Todd scratched his head. "Well, we don't have to think it's how it looks," he started.

"How does it look?" Carla challenged him. "That my mother's in it with the sheriff? That she's a Judas for Gore? And we can just ignore that? You think you can protect her from that, somehow?"

"That's not it," said Todd.

"Well, what is it then?" Carla cried. "Maybe it's Nick! Is he a spy too? Or do you think it's me?"

She stopped suddenly.

"Oh, god."

Todd was silent. In fact, Kenner had shown him the photo that morning and raised the same question. Kenner wanted to know whether Carla might have goaded Gibbs into his action on the mountain, bringing internal conflict to the union. Todd had defended his brother and Carla, assuring Kenner that they were "not the kind." Todd couldn't bring himself, however, to tell any of this to Carla, whose anger was growing by the minute.

"I'm up there, in the union," Todd told her. "Kenner says...."

But Carla didn't want to hear it.

"Kenner says you can protect me from this? That's what you're saying, isn't it? Well, to hell with that, Todd Bryant!"

"No," Todd began. "Don't be like that."

Carla's mind was racing. She searched Todd's face for some evidence of the friend she'd known. There was no trace, no bit of solace there. She saw only his own confusion and his fear, sparked by Mary's picture in the newspaper. With sudden fury, Carla tore the news sheet from Todd's grasp and ripped it into pieces. The shreds flew from her hand, landing among the engineer's cylindrical stone samples around their feet.

"Goddammit, Todd," she cried. "What the hell are you trying to do here?!"

"I'm standing up for you!" he shouted. "I'm defending you – in spite of what you and Gibbs have done! And your mother! I'm trying to keep things safe!"

"Safe!?" cried Carla. "Safe from what? From the Baldwins? Or from Kenner? Sure, Todd, it seems real safe here in Blair right now! Not a soul around! Wake up, Todd! You're 'safe' because nobody is here! The fight has picked up and gone someplace else! Look at yourself! You're all alone here! You think you're doing what is 'right'? While all the real union men are up there fighting the Baldwins on Blair Mountain! They're doing what they have to do!"

Stung by Carla's words, Todd simply stared at her, his sense of betrayal deepening.

"You should stay right here," he said, keeping his voice cold and even. "This is the only place where you'll be all right."

"Safe," Carla sneered. "Well you can take your 'safety' and go to hell!"

Angrily, she swept her arm across the cabinet top, sending the stick-and-string mine model crashing to the floor. Todd struggled for words, fearing that Kenner would hear the noise. His eyes darted toward the door.

"Be quiet," he told her, desperate to protect her from herself. "Please, just stay here. Lay low for a while."

"Yo, Todd!"

Now, Tom Kenner was coming up the stairs. Todd went to the door.

"I'll be right with you!" he called and, glancing at Carla, paused in the doorway. He watched, sending a smile into the hallway, as Kenner appeared, coming up the steps with an unseen guest in tow. Todd closed the door, and turned back to Carla.

"I have to go," he said to her back. Carla faced the window, fuming as she looked up at the thundering mountains. She was breathing heavily.

"You should stay here," Todd said again, hoping to calm her down. "Stay and wait for me. Keep quiet. I'll only be an hour or so. Don't talk to anybody – not even to Tildy. The way things are, you can't trust anyone."

Carla couldn't believe her ears. She had wanted to report to Todd – and even Kenner, if he'd asked – about the men on the mountain, how they might be reconciled with the union leadership again. How everyone might trust each other once again.

But Todd didn't wait. Afraid he'd already said too much, he left Carla in the room, and closed the door. She could hear Todd's receding footsteps, as he went briskly down the hall. She heard his knock on the office door and Kenner's call for him to come in.

Carla stood in the dusty room, her breath coming in gasps.

He wants me to wait, he says. And not to trust anyone.

Her mind made up, Carla opened the door and headed down the stairs.

Inside the office, Todd shook Kenner's hand. Smiling, the union leader introduced him to their guest. The tall man stood with his back to them, quietly gazing out the window. Almost by instinct, he'd made a quick count of the tents in the colony. Stanley Ford turned as Kenner spoke his name.

"Colonel Ford," said Kenner. "I'd like you to meet my right-hand-man, Todd Bryant. He'll be going with us."

Todd was struck by Ford's sharp brown uniform, the barrage of decorations on his chest. Then, Kenner's words sunk in.

"Where are we going?" Todd asked, trying to sound casual about it.

Kenner gave him a half smile.

"We're finally getting what we wanted," he said. "The colonel is taking us to Logan. Tomorrow, we'll be sitting down for direct talks with the coal operators – negotiating an end to the strike through the U.S. Army."

Chapter 25

Mary watched Nick moving from one end of the tub to another, earnestly making waves. He stopped for a moment, sometimes patting the water's surface to see the reflective ripples lap against the white ceramic shore. Glancing at Mary, the boy poked his finger into the dry spigot.

"No," Mary said. "It's bed-time now."

As Nick toweled himself, Mary glanced at the cuts and bruises on his limbs, marks whose causes had been long forgotten. The marks were from the land and matched her own knees and shins, scarred and battered from scrambling over rocks and through briers in countless searches for the horse or hens.

Having seen Nick off to bed, Mary closed the door and bathed herself but didn't linger there. She begrudgingly admired the conveniences of this city bath with its seemingly endless flow of hot water into the tub, and no later need to carry it outside. When it was over, though, Mary could only think of how much time she'd wasted, waiting on water that served no other purpose but to wash. Almost everything on her homestead – the iron woodstove, the steel tub and the water – served some kind of "double duty," and she missed her own.

Standing by the door, clean and dressed again, Mary watched her boy sleep. Crossing her arms, she massaged the taught muscles of her biceps, hard as pine. No number of hot baths in that cold, tiled room would make her stop missing the warmth of her own oak floors, her iron stove and skillets; even the nights of wind that wheedled through the chinking, worrying the candle flame. Mary closed her eyes, almost smelling the sweet-william and cinnamon rose, hanging from a kitchen beam, or the great shanks of tobacco drying in the barn. Such memories were only made more vivid by this sterile hotel room and its surrounding city.

I've got to get us home, she thought, assuring herself that she would not have to endure this place much longer. She was here for just one purpose, she knew. She had to see it through.

Standing by the door, Mary calmed herself, satisfied that Nick, tired from all the day's excitements, slept easily. She was confident that, if he woke, he'd know just where to go. Like a migrating bird, the boy could follow any path Mary showed him, and he would find her. He'd already learned the hotel's carpeted passages just like his deerpaths, criss-crossing through the woods. Mary quietly watched her sleeping boy, and waited for the gentle knock.

Gaujot knew things. He knew the location of the steel box, the books where Gore kept his actual numbers. Gaujot even knew the real name of the sheriff's distant bootlegger and just about every drop-off point the local men used. Now, the Baldwin captain carried the key to Gore's basement hideaway, where his most prized treasure was stored.

"Two bottles, Pearl, just to start."

Gaujot slipped through the hotel like a ghost. Gripping the key in one hand, he carried an empty flour sack in the other. He glanced up and down the hallway before starting down the basement steps. Unlocking the hidden room, he switched on the light. Ten cases were stacked in the corner. Gaujot pulled two bottles from one, hesitated, then pulled another one for himself. A bit of security. The sheriff would not notice. Gaujot was something of an expert in managing the dependencies of his demanding client.

Gaujot had been raised to serve. His uncle had taught him more about "respect" than any boy should learn. Gaujot remembered the time before that, helping his young mother before she died. Every day at breakfast, she dined on a single soft-boiled egg, which Pearl dutifully brought her in the same chipped china cup. At the end, when she'd become very sick, Pearl would have to feed her, lifting every spoonful of egg, sometimes spilling the white translucence on her chin. Pearl often glanced back in horror, terrified of the uncle, fuming in the corner, waiting for the boy's next error.

At night, the man gave his sister whiskey, calling it "medicine" he'd bought by pawning her things, piece by piece. Pearl's mother accepted it from him without comment, drinking it down, staring at the man with once-pretty eyes. The drink sometimes made her talkative. Once, when the uncle had left the room, Pearl worked up the courage to ask about his father.

A sailor, his mother had said, one eye drooping. *I wanted a daughter, but I made do.*

She'd named her baby "Pearl" to spite the father, then dressed the son in lace and soft black shoes. The uncle had arrived like an avenging angel to set things straight. Under his brutal hand, Gaujot grew up with hatred, never forgot a single beating and made a pledge to get even some day. Years later, the old sadist begged for forgiveness as he died. His body was never found.

Returning to Gore's rooms, Gaujot laid the bottles carefully on the bed. The sheriff, in his shirtsleeves, sat in his chair, scowling at a stack of papers he'd brought from the courthouse. On top of the pile, Gaujot could see two of them. One was the flyer from the battlefield.

By order of the president....

The other was the newest memo from the man Gaujot had posted at the telephone office in Boone, listening to most of the union's long-distance conversations:

KENNER LOSING CONTROL OF HIS MEN....

Sheriff Gore stared at both sheets, fingering the note. "Have the boys carry the conference table out," he ordered.

Gaujot nodded and checked his new pocket watch. The spindly hands showed almost five.

"You'll want to know how it went today," Gaujot prompted, feeling some urgency.

The situation on the mountain had blown into a full-scale war. Gaujot had been up and down the line that day, touching base with his top men. Most of them were getting antsy, several asking, 'What comes next?' There'd been a few casualties, mostly self-inflicted. But, the Army's leaflet had changed things for the men. And the deadline was only days away.

Gaujot wanted to report everything to Gore and get solid orders, before that evening's party. Once the sheriff started into the bourbon, getting orders from him would be useless.

Gaujot hazarded a quick report on the day's mobilization. How two hundred Baldwin regulars had managed to move several thousand volunteers across Hunters Ridge. How the Baldwin agents had ferried arms and ammunition up four back roads, feeding a loose, two-mile line of men and trenches.

"That's good, that's good," the sheriff nodded, but glared down at the flyer. "By order of the president," he muttered.

Gaujot coughed. "I've got a question, sir," he said.

One of Gore's bushy eyebrows went up as he raised his glass. "What is it?"

"If we don't want the Army coming in, why not just beat 'em to it?"

Gore lowered the glass again, eying his captain. Gaujot plunged forward.

"We've got better guns than them. More than enough. Why don't we just take them? Push them back down that mountain and across the countryside?"

Gore put the glass down with irritation.

"You don't play poker, do you Pearl?"

Gaujot recognized the tone. He fought to control his breathing.

"No, sir," he said quietly.

Gore's eyes narrowed.

"No, you don't."

The sheriff began gathering up the maps and papers from the table.

"You don't gamble. You don't drink and, as far as I've heard, you don't play with the girls. By god, you're a goddamned farmer. What *do* you do?"

Gaujot knew better than to respond. He kept his eyes on Gore as the sheriff stood, now fumbling the papers into a cardboard folder. When his hand knocked the glass, sloshing whiskey on the blotter, the storm broke.

"You think you control this thing, do you, sweetmeat?" Gore ranted. "You wanna end it? Well, think again! I've done the goddamned numbers! As much as it's costing us, this strike costs those union assholes more! Oh, they have their friends, Pearl. But not enough to count beyond a year! I've already seen to that!"

Gaujot winced at the repeated use of his first name. His confusion grew, crowding his ability to speak. He considered grabbing the sheriff by the throat, just to make him stop talking.

"You want to string it out," Gaujot said slowly. Gore glared at him.

"You're goddamned right I do! Let the union pay its own tired layabouts! We'll just bring in more! From Mississippi or Poland or wherever. The market's filled with men who'll work – all them that know the value of a yankee dollar!"

Gore turned and slid his arms into his jacket. He straightened, checking his reflection in the mirror.

"No, Pearl," he continued. "We'll poke 'em, just to agitate 'em. Then, you watch what happens. The federals'll come in with their aeroplanes and try to stop our strike. Maybe they will stop it. Maybe they won't. But, tell me, Pearl: Why do you think they even want to try?"

Gaujot looked into the sheriff's face, flushed with anger. The mine guard stayed quiet, hearing the echo, the slurred words.

Gore waited for Gaujot to respond, then moved closer to him. The sheriff's hand gripped his deputy's tree-bough forearm and leaned in close, whispering the answer to his own question.

"The Army. The president," he hissed. *"They're the same as you and me. They just want their cut."*

Then, the sheriff backed away, filled with his own sense of the game.

"If the Army breaks the strike, the president gets to be a hero," he said. "Then what happens? Our coal operators decide, 'Well, maybe Uncle Sam ain't so bad after all.' They start paying federal taxes. Before you know it, they don't need our professional service. Can you imagine, Pearl? Defending the mines from the reds with a bunch of farm boys on a lousy public deputy's pay? Where would that leave us?"

Gaujot said nothing. Gore pointed his finger at him, answering his own question again.

"Out. In. The. Cold." Nodding slowly, the sheriff backed away, still pointing. "The Army, the president…. They're all the same: *They're after your slice of pie!"*

Gore returned to the mirror, where he smoothed his jacket. Exhaling, Gaujot quietly went to the bed to retrieve the bottles. He placed them in the cabinet and turned around. Now, the sheriff had picked up the file of maps and papers.

"Take these to the courthouse," Gore said. "Then, pull us some phonograph records for tonight. Take care of things. You know what-all we need."

Gaujot took the stack of county files, noticing Mary Rising's name on the top one. Inside the file, Gaujot knew, there would be a map. Tucking the files under one arm, the Baldwin captain breathed again. He stood back and smoothed the front of his own shirt with a rocky hand.

"And on the mountain?" he asked. "What do you want, there?"

Gore looked up at him. Gaujot waited. He wasn't about to assume anything. Not anymore.

"I'll tell you what I want," said Gore, leveling his gaze. "I want every red-neck miner on that mountain so full of piss 'n' vinegar, he'll fire at every goddamned tin-hat he sees. Then, I'll have two birds for supper."

Gaujot nodded once before lowering his eyes to the files in his hand. He turned and left the room, shaking with anger.

In the downstairs hallway, Rose did a little twirl, showing off her evening dress for Mary. It was a thing of red and pink, a startling complement to her own dark hair, worn long. The light material revealed much of her shoulders, then feathered down her front showing more skin and chest than Mary had ever seen in public.

"Hmm," she frowned as Rose turned again.

Rose stopped then to look at her new friend. She fought the temptation to laugh out loud.

"Mary," she said. "We aren't going there to clean!"

Having nothing else, Mary had simply tied a clean work apron overtop her own blue dress and work shirt.

"Please, dear," said Rose. "You may not want to have any fun tonight. But at least start out on the right leg."

As Rose guided her toward the closet, Mary pondered what she knew about this young, modern woman. The two of them had chatted as they worked together that afternoon, Rose doing most of the talking. She knew all the ropes at the hotel and kept no secrets. She'd told Mary about "getting into trouble" in Columbus, of how her stay in Logan had been a "gift of time." The promise of a secretary's job "fell through, of course." She found the hotel and Veltri, who gave her the job cleaning rooms. Soon, she was following the other girls' example, cultivating friendships among selected Baldwin guards.

"The best ones know how to treat a girl," she said. "They'll take you out to dinner, buy you drinks and cigarettes."

She said that many of the top men had been policemen once.

"Maybe good; maybe bad. I don't know," said Rose. "But what's done is done. They all want to be detectives now. It's a booming trade, you know? Plenty of 'em already moved up, out of here. Gotten jobs in the big city."

Standing before the closet, she found a cigarette and lit it.

"They're all trained when they leave Logan, but they forget how to write," she said. "Well, that's all right with me. Most of them aren't worth remembering, anyhow."

For her part, Rose planned on staying in town "just another year or two."

"By then, I'll have enough cash saved up to go back home and start fresh."

Rose's room was smaller than Mary's, but her closet was full of clothes. She picked out a blouse for her new friend. Mary said no, she wouldn't, but Rose insisted. Resigned, the older woman pulled off the apron and exchanged her faded workshirt for the blouse. When she looked in the mirror, Mary almost didn't recognize herself, so great was the effect of a simple, machine-made blouse.

"There, now. You see?" Rose cooed. "Makes that skirt of yours look like a million bucks. Go on, wear it. Tell 'em all you got it in the new Woolworth catalog."

Giggling like a schoolgirl, Rose led Mary to the door.

"After all," she purred, "they *love* to hear you lie."

"I never could do that," Mary said, half to herself, and Rose laughed.

Two more girls strolled up behind them. Mary knew their names, Emma and Gladys. Both wore long sequined jackets – Gladys in purple, Emma in green.

"How do we look?" Emma asked.

"Like a million bucks," Mary ventured, and the girls screamed with pleasure.

They were still laughing when they reached Gore's rooms. Mary followed, entering last. It was a place of fine tables with marble tops, upholstered chairs and chaise lounges, all smelling of cigar smoke. Mary imagined all the deals that must have been made in this place, beneath the uncompromising glow of the electric light. In one corner stood a beautiful credenza, made of the finest wood, polished and glistening. It drew *oohs* and *aahs* from the girls.

"And the phonograph!" cried Rose, begging Gore to put a record on. The sheriff nodded and Gaujot performed the task, his hand gently lowering the needle, yielding the familiar hiss and crackle of the music. Standing next to the sofa, Gore smiled down at his principal guest. Mary studied the man – over sixty, by the look of him, and heavy in a way that told her he'd once been burly. A worker's hands and face, she noted, with eyes that took everything in without revealing much.

Five or six Baldwin officers stood in an awkward cluster near the window. They smoked their cigarettes, looking from their boss to the girls, as if trying to put together the pieces of some puzzle. From the phonograph came the tinny notes of a smooth crooner's song. To Mary, the voice was surprising – hollow and distant. Rose smiled, pushing the girls toward the deputies.

"Let's go bust up that dog pack," she whispered.

Mary held back, but watched with interest as the sheriff approached her.

"You look nice," he said.

Taking her arm, he guided her to the sofa, where he introduced her to George Waddill. Mary shook the coal man's meaty hand. Gore was saying something about his friend being a "former brakeman for the railroad."

"That was a long time ago," Waddill laughed and examined Mary with his sharp eyes.

Now, Gore drew her to the liquor cabinet, where he poured drinks.

"It's working out all right, you staying here," he said.

Mary looked at him and knew it was not a question, but nodded anyway. Gore handed her tumblers of amber liquid, directing her to distribute them to his guests. The scene and the role she played reminded her of the work she'd done years before, at the boarding house in Blair. There, she had been told to look the other way when guests passed around a single jar of liquor, delivered by a man who came to entertain. He'd played popular songs on the upright in the sitting room, where the house guests sang together and, sometimes, danced.

Mary nursed her own glass into the night, refusing Gore's repeated offer to refill it. Outside, the autumn dark took over. Here, in the warm suite, the laughter grew, fed by music and games largely propelled by Rose. The girls wheedled dances from the guards, who began to laugh like boys. In the corner by the phonograph, Pearl Gaujot waited, cleaning his fingernails and changing records. Now and then, he glanced up to see the sheriff and Waddill, talking together on the couch. No one came near him.

In time, Rose went over and knelt at Waddill's feet. She chatted with the coal boss, occasionally sipping bourbon from her glass, one hand placed beside his knee. It was getting late. Mary could see the girls form their arrangements, pairing themselves with the guards. Waddill insisted that Rose sit next to him and she edged in close, smiling like a cat.

At Gore's request, Mary made more trips around the room with the tray. New tumblers of bourbon went into eager hands. She kept serving into the night.

"No limit on George," the sheriff whispered. "Get him what he wants."

Gore told her how he'd warned his men against showing any sign of "low character," even off-duty. A loose tie or shirttail could wreck a reputation.

"Loose tongues," he said pointedly. "They are the worst."

He directed everything.

"That one may have another," he told her. "But not those other two."

The phonograph scratched and warbled. Mary listened to the music, to the hollow voices singing their strange promises, conjuring other cities and distant places she could not imagine.

A favorite tune carried excitement. The women paraded onto the carpet, drawing their policeman partners into some fumbling semblance of dance. Rose seemed happy, flirting with George Waddill. Tomorrow, Mary thought, she and Rose would be cleaning water marks from the tables, sweeping ashes from the scuffed-up carpet.

Perhaps, she thought, her need to stay in Logan would end soon.

After tonight, she might be able to take Nick home. She glanced at Gore who watched everything. He delighted in owning the suite and everyone in it.

Later Gore and Waddill lit cigars. Mary went to the window and opened it, drawing a blast of crisp, fresh-smelling air. Then, like a thunderstorm in the east, came the sound of the battle – the repeated hammering of the guns. The war. The miners' war. Mary fought the fear that gripped her heart, and tried not to think about her sister and daughter, out there. In the war. *Each one makes his own decisions,* she thought. *Or hers.* She and Nick were safe, protected. Others would have to take care of themselves. Suddenly, Gore's big captain, Gaujot, stood next to her.

"Not here," he said, pulling Mary away. "Let's close these curtains."

Mary looked down, surprised to see the whiskey glass in her hand. She knew that it was hers, but could not recall having filled it. She drank, leaving the window to Gaujot. The room's red edges softened. The lightbulb, she noticed, had been cut off in favor of the gas lamps. Rose chose a waltz for the phonograph. Turning, she held out her hands.

"Dance with me?"

Half-smiling, Mary accepted her invitation. She'd never danced at the boarding house in Blair.

Mary moved slowly, holding the girl who was almost young enough to be her daughter. Together they swayed in the dim light. The dark wood-paneled room circled around them, as if she and Rose were riding a slow carrousel. The other girls circled with their sullen men, seemingly made of wood. All of them, Mary thought, all were trying to find their way home. As Mary held her new friend, the room circled around them, and Mary thought of her own homeplace. Unlike these others, her warm cabin waited for her, just on the other side of these parlor walls, beyond the city and its politics and war.

So much is possible if you just close your eyes.

Leaning over the couch, Gore whispered something to Waddill. The coal executive nodded serenely. The sheriff signaled to Gaujot, standing by the phonograph. Like a ghost, the chief deputy slipped through the room and, one by one, each Baldwin officer took a woman by the arm, said goodnight and disappeared. Mary continued her dance with Rose, pretending not to notice. She faced the door as Emma was leaving. Mary watched as the girl's pretty sequined robe wrapped itself around the brass doorknob, threatening to tear. Emma's giggling head of curls briefly reappeared while she unhooked it. She waved happily at them and went. But not before Mary caught the look of resignation on the girl's face, sad as dusk.

Rose stopped dancing and, turning from her partner, curled a finger at Waddill. She brought him to his feet. Not knowing what else to do, Mary began clearing glasses. She was setting them on a tray when Gore came to her.

"Where'd the party go?" he asked.

Mary looked at him.

"Here and there," she replied, without emotion.

It was past midnight. Remarkably, Gore poured himself another drink and, without asking, poured one for her. Mary took it, beyond caring. Nick was asleep, she knew. By what right should she be tired? she wondered. Had she done so much that day? She'd had a bath. And drank. For Gore. For this. The whiskey and the rest of it would rob her of the night, she knew, and maybe take something of tomorrow too, cleansing the memory of all that had gone wrong.

But, afterward, she thought. *Later, I'll have a place to go.*

Holding the glass tightly, she watched Rose's dance with Waddill. The young girl removed her shoes and brazenly let one strap of her dress slip from her shoulder. Mary imagined how the game would go, how the pretty frock would slip away.... Now, Gore's hand, soft and gentle, touched her arm and she looked at him.

"We have business to conduct," he said, and Mary knew it to be true.

He walked her down the empty hall, stopped before the door of another room, on the same floor as her own. Mary stepped inside. Gore closed the door behind them, turned the key, and tossed it on the nightstand. He didn't switch on the light. The street lamps from outside shined through the curtained window.

The sheriff walked to the side of the room and pulled an upholstered chair to a new position beside the bed.

"Sit down," he ordered.

Mary sat. Like an obedient school child, she folded her hands in her lap. She faced the bed, eyed it, looking forward to sleep. But not yet. Gore circled, saying nothing. Finally, Mary spoke, reminding him.

"It's about my place," she said.

"More dangerous now than ever," Gore soothed. "The enemy is near."

Don't I know it.

Gore touched her shoulder.

"Relax," he said. "None of it'll last. All this could be settled, come morning."

He stood behind her now. She felt his hands, a weight on her shoulders.

"You know you're better off here, don't you," he said. Again, Mary recognized the lack of question in the sheriff's voice. She closed her eyes, wanting to get up, to hit, to run. She knew she wouldn't. She had come this far. There was nothing else but to finish it.

Gore's thumbs dug into her shoulders and Mary wondered how this could feel good to him or anyone. Outside, she heard the guns and her fear of the war returned.

"We're better off on the mountain," she muttered. "My boy and me."

"I know," Gore sighed, his hands moving down to work the muscles in her arms.

"That's one pretty piece of land," he said.

His right hand touched her neck; the left wandered down her spine. The drinking had made him clumsy, Mary's fear rose. Now, Gore bent over, murmuring something in her ear.

"My friend, George Waddill. He'd jump to get his hands on that pretty piece of land."

Mary's eyes were closed. Her own voice surprised her. It rang like steel.

"He can't have it. I want that thing – the thing you said. It's mine."

Gore paused a moment before he grew bolder. Soon, his hands found their way down Mary's front, found the buttons to her borrowed blouse. Mary turned in the chair, and searched for Gore's eyes in the dark. She was desperate to make herself clear.

"I worked that land most of twenty years," she said, and Gore smiled, glad for the response.

"I know," he said, feigning sympathy. "I know, that's true," and he leaned over, putting his face close to hers, to where Mary could almost taste the smell of his whiskey and his smoke.

"But remember, girl," he whispered. "You would not be there, were it not for me."

Mary closed her eyes again and stayed quiet as Gore's arm moved boldly across her chest, drawing her back into the chair. Her blouse was now open, Gore's left hand at the front of her simple, *mono* chemise.

"I know," Mary exhaled and grasped the arm, suppressing her urge to fight. *This is the only way,* she thought, as Gore's hands moved with greater urgency. Breathing heavily, Mary put down her anger, letting her own hands hang limp beside her.

"You're safe with me," Gore soothed. "Here, you're safe."

He unbuttoned the rest of the blouse.

"You paid almost nothing for that place," he whispered hoarsely.

"Yes," Mary admitted. She sat for it, keeping her eyes closed.

"Such a small price," Gore breathed. "Such a small price to pay for so nice a thing."

His hands lifted the chemise. It moved across her skin. Mary listened to the rhythm of his breathing, imagined the twists and hollows of her home, Gore's "nice thing," her plot of land, the giant's ear. Protected. In her mind, Mary returned to her homestead, wondering whether she'd put up enough food for winter. Her thoughts blocked out the sound of the sheriff's voice.

Small price. Such a small price.

Gore came around the chair. His mouth touched hers. Mary tasted the bourbon, returned his kiss and filled her mind with thoughts of home.

"I felt sorry for you," he told her, his hands drawing up her skirts. "I did you that favor, all those years ago."

Mary walked in her distant orchard, full of fruit and birdsong.

It had been ten summers. Mary had just lost her husband to a cause she couldn't share – and never would. Then, Gore appeared at her weathered gate. Dressed in his fine white suit, he stood there, putting marks on a piece of paper in his hand. A map. Mary came out, and the stranger asked whether "her man" was there. He smiled at her, so young and friendly. A politician, he said, seeking votes for sheriff. He looked familiar. Then Mary remembered him. He'd been a regular guest at the boarding house. Each time, a different girl.

Gore hadn't recognized her, though. Mary watched him play the politician. Assessor, sheriff – it was all the same to her. Carla was off someplace, gathering chestnuts, and Mary had plenty of other work to do. Still, she talked to the visitor, the assessor, setting him straight about Bonner. Gore was "deeply sorry" for her loss.

"But, honestly, ma'am, you could use some help," he said.

He sat down on the porch, taking time – his own and hers – to explain things. He spoke slowly. He used big words, but was patient with her questions. Mary offered him cider, which made Gore laugh. He called her "smart, politically."

The man knew how to dance, she thought. And how to dip.

"This property sits near the county line," he said. "It don't appear on any roles – not in Logan, nor Boone or even in Meridian. You're here on speculation."

She had no title to the land, he said. No legal right to it.

"You're squatting here," he told her. "On unmapped land. It's in a gap, between counties. You're in limbo, so to speak. Strictly speaking, I should order up a survey."

Mary hadn't realized; never suspected. She could easily believe it, though. Bonner had staked out the property before they met. He'd already built on it. No. He wouldn't be bothered to get the deed.

Damn that man. That goddamned fool. So much like Daddy, who never owned a thing.

Angry, Mary had cried openly. Gore came over and sat down beside her, his arm going easily around her shoulder.

"Now, now," he comforted. "Things don't have to be that bad."

Quietly, he explained how she might get relief.

"You can still get clear title – an open claim."

"What's that?" Mary asked, wiping tears from her eyes.

"Farm the land ten years, starting now," he advised. "I'll work it for you in Logan. I'll keep you hidden from the surveys. I got the power to do that for you."

He would just go back to town, he said. And better that he not come back again. There'd be no survey, no questions. He'd protect her from all that. The land would stay hidden, off the books. Riley Gore would make sure that no one else would come around, seeking taxes or anything else from her…. He'd protect her from all that. His smile was full of teeth. A good man, she thought. Confident and powerful. She thanked him, offered him her vote. Food, tobacco. Eggs. Whatever he needed.

To his credit, he hadn't laughed at her, just reached out and boldly touched her hand.

"No, thank you, ma'am," he smiled. "I don't have much taste for eggs…."

Then, of course, she knew.

"Such a small price to pay," he said, "for such a fine little piece of land."

For a long time afterward, Mary couldn't even recall his name. Once, she'd caught a glimpse of him in Logan. She didn't go near him, fearing he'd want more. Or, worse, that he'd forgotten their deal. She had to trust him, though. He was her only hope. Mary had counted the years from that day, believing she had a friend, a protector in the Logan Courthouse. Certainly, he must have kept his promise. No one had come asking. He'd done this much, at least.

Now, in Gore's hotel room, Mary would repeat her favor. It didn't matter. Not now. Gore would get his small relief and Mary would have her peace of mind. She sat back in the upholstered chair, eyes closed, felt his still-familiar touch, his hands closing around her breasts.

"I did what I promised," he said. "Kept your pretty land hidden. Good to my word all these years."

His mouth worked at her. Mary willed her hands to touch him, just to hold his interest. Her hands went to the back of his head. His hair was thick and oiled.

"I want the rest," she whispered. "That last part. The title."

"I will," Gore promised. "I'll do you right."

He pulled her up from the chair and kissed her. His hands came around, worked down her skirt and undergarments. Her skin and flesh muffled his pleas and promises, the work of his busy teeth and tongue.

You'll have it all, free and clear. I promise.

Breathing heavily, Gore stood her up, naked, and kicked the fallen clothes away. He undid his belt, seeking her out with his other hand, his open palm and fingers. Mary inhaled, still hearing his promises.

"You're grateful, aren't you?" Gore breathed, leaning into her.

Yes.

Her voice sounded as far as the mountain, where she could hear the guns.

What of the boy? What of the house? How many jars on the shelf? How many days 'til Spring?

Gore's shirt was open, showing his broad chest and stomach. He guided her across the back of the upholstered chair and Mary grabbed the armrests. She felt his hand return, its rise and drop, pushing into her, low and high....

Bent across the chair, she told herself the whiskey had been water from the creek; that the crooner had sung bird songs. The mountain smelled of rain and overripe apples, thumping against the ground with the syncopated rhythm of the distant guns. She felt Gore move inside her, his hands touching her breasts and backside. Mary grunted, stared at her own hands, white-knuckled on the chair.

"You're grateful, aren't you, for all I've done?" he panted, his voice thickened.

"Yes," she recited. "Yes, I am."

They love to hear you lie.

"What'd you say?" Gore repeated. "I want to hear it."

"Grateful to you," Mary gasped. "Thank you."

Such a small price.

"More," he pushed into her harder. Mary chafed against the chair back. "Say it. Say it."

Somewhere in her mind, she counted jars in a basement larder – more jars than she could ever remember having there. A wealth of food....

"Thank you," Mary intoned, her words taking on the rhythm of his pounding, like the guns on Hunters Ridge. "Thank you...Thank you.... Thank you...."

Gore thrust into her, working himself up. Finally, with one last push, he completed his groaning indulgence. Mary collapsed onto the bed, buried her face in the pillow. There, she wandered again in the darkness of her private place, counting jars and listening to the distant thunder of apples. Gore sat down in the chair. He was out of breath, his eyes unfocused.

"You'll have the title in the morning," he said flatly, as she dressed. "You'll own the land, free and clear."

Mary nodded without looking at him. She closed the door quietly behind her, careful not to catch her skirt. The task was done. After years of uncertainty, she would finally own her place: The rustic house and pole barn, her husband's grave, all free and clear.

Quickening her pace, Mary found her room key. Seeing Nick, still asleep, a new sadness welled up inside her. Small, unreasoning sounds came up from her throat. She prepared another bath, this one hotter than before. She wanted to be clean, as clean as she had been once. She felt as if she'd been away so long. But it was all for the good. For herself, for Carla and Nick.

I have it now. I own it. Free and clear.

Immediately, the tears began to fall. Aside from her children and, once upon a time, a man, that little piece of land she now owned was the only thing Mary Rising had ever really loved.

The Mixture of Oxygen and Nitrogen Gases
The two gases of the atmosphere...supply the means of carrying
out the great system of nature. The mixture of these gases is everywhere and always alike – yes, on the mountain top and in the plain,
in England, in America, in Africa, or New Zealand – ever the same....
What an all-comprehensive, intelligent Mind it shows, to cause one
simple principle...to produce so many important beneficial effects!
What dreadful havoc would be produced in the whole system if such
substances as oxygen were not nicely balanced and proportioned!

Conversation on Mines. W. Hopton, 1893.

Chapter 26

From the back seat of the touring car, Todd watched Captain Steck at
the wheel. Sitting straight as a sounding pole, Steck navigated the vehicle
past the biggest ruts. He adjusted the dashboard throttle, pushed pedals
on the floor, played the sedan like a pump organ. Under the experienced
driver's command, the car found the least-broken path, its rock-hard
rubber tires popping stones. Todd tried to imagine the work of the motor
that pulled them down the road, making the scenery blow past at a thrilling twenty-three miles per hour.

"By god," he said, looking over at Kenner. "I could get to like this."

Kenner had been staring out the window, mesmerized by the rise and
fall of the excavated road bank. Torn away, his dark eyes drilled into
Todd.

"Don't forget where you are."

Todd looked down at his own hands, his wrists extending from the
sleeves of his worn jacket. He considered his fingernails which had
never been clean as long as this. How they shined against the pattern on
the seat cover, a thin red-and-black stripe, a weave that suddenly reminded him of the rough kitchen curtains his mother had made of burlap
sacks, each one stenciled with: "Provincetown Peanuts, Hand-Picked,
Suffolk, Virginia."

He wished his mother – or his father, for that matter – could see him now, riding with the union's chief negotiator, being driven to a meeting by a soldier in uniform.

Would Sid have ever gotten so far? he wondered.

He wished he could have told Carla where he was headed, but she had disappeared.... And, besides, Kenner trusted no one. Not even Sid's wife.

Not Sid's wife, Todd remembered, biting his lip. *Sid's widow.*

Now Colonel Ford turned around in his seat. He'd been friendly enough, but Todd couldn't help but think that the colonel had been talking down to them.

"Chilly this morning!" he called, making himself heard above the motor's racket.

"Sure it is," Kenner answered, his face managing something like a smile. Ford turned his attention back to the road. Kenner leaned over to him.

"You know," he said. "Baltimore isn't too keen on us coming here. They don't think much will come of it."

Todd frowned. "Why are we going, then?"

Kenner shrugged. "If the man wants to talk, our job is to listen – to weigh what he's telling us," he said. "Remember, though, Todd: You have to keep quiet. If you want to talk, talk to me. You got it?"

Todd nodded. He was grateful to be invited to the table. Plenty of other union men probably ranked higher and were better qualified.

"Why'd you bring me, Tom?"

Kenner looked surprised at the question.

"They asked for you," he said.

Todd was perplexed.

"It's no secret about your brother. They figure you're connected to our people on the mountain."

"Is that what you think?" Todd asked.

"It doesn't much matter what I think," Kenner shrugged. "Our best bet is for you to roll with it and stay quiet. I'm the only one authorized to speak for us."

Todd nodded, still puzzling it out.

"What's the matter, son?" Ford said, turning in his seat. "Don't you trust your Uncle Sam?"

Todd said nothing.

"We'll have you back in Blair this evening," the colonel assured him. "I don't want to build up too much expectation. Not for the first meeting. Just sit down and clarify things. Get the issues on the table."

Kenner looked at Ford and decided to take the bait. "Union recognition has always been number-one with us," he said. "But, more and more, it's the company police. We have to get the Baldwins out of the coalfields. Good people won't stay in any town that's run by vigilantes."

Ford nodded. "What about your side?"

"What do you mean?" asked Kenner.

The colonel looked down the road, his eyes on the rolling scenery. "Are the union men on Blair Mountain prepared to put down their guns?"

Ford turned to see their reaction.

"This thing has boiled up from a long, long time ago, Colonel," Kenner said. "Those men didn't wake up this morning and decide to fight. If the other side gives us some incentive, though, we'll have our boys stand down."

Or we'll do our best, thought Todd.

"Fair enough," said Ford. "But, let me tell you, as a military man. As big as it may be, your force on the mountain stands little chance of winning anything. If they keep up this fight, you might just as well order them all into the cemetery."

Todd froze, unable to respond. Ford's words summoned images of Gibbs and the Sovereign miners being gunned down by advancing troops. What had Kenner told Ford already? Todd was suddenly frightened.

Kenner, however, took clear offense at the colonel's words. The tall union leader leaned forward and spoke directly into Ford's ear.

"A miner knows the grave well enough, Colonel. One way or another, we all end up underground."

Steck pulled up at the curb before the Logan Courthouse. Todd forced himself to open the door. Immediately, he heard the crack of rifles to the east. The battle had started up again. From the mercantile, it had sounded closer. But here, in Logan, the sound carried a harder note, the smell of fear and burned powder.

Todd quickly scanned the grounds. A letter carrier was coming down the steps. He greeted a pair of workman in coveralls, going the other way. On the street, a woman talked to the drivers of a milk-delivery wagon. A little girl was at her side, looking away. Several gunmen loitered before the hotel, but none of them seemed to notice the car and its four passengers. Todd exhaled.

He kept close to Kenner who was eager to move up the steps, to get inside the building. Upon reaching the first landing, however, Todd stopped cold. On this spot, the concrete was a shade lighter, newly scrubbed. Here was the place where Sid had died. As Todd stared, the landing colors began to trick his eye, like something pushing up....

Kenner turned and saw Todd, frozen where he stood.

"You coming?"

Todd looked up at him, then followed. When he'd caught up, Kenner clapped him good-naturedly around the shoulder.

"Come on," he said. "Let's try to talk some sense in here."

A uniformed deputy showed the four men through the building, taking them downstairs to a small, plain room. He turned a wall switch and the lamp came on – a lone bulb covered by an industrial tin shade. The room was empty of air and furniture, except for the large table surrounded by eight flat-bottomed banker's chairs. Its sickly yellow walls made the room seem more like a workshop than a meeting place. There was just one window, high and lonely, shut tight and out-of-reach.

The deputy stood in the doorway.

"Sheriff'll be in directly," he said, then left, closing the door behind him. For a moment, there was no sound. Colonel Ford looked around.

"Not too fancy," he remarked and seated himself at one end of the table.

"I've seen better jail cells," Kenner commented and pulled a chair for himself, next to the colonel.

They waited as the quiet minutes passed. Todd grew uncomfortable in the silence and breathed deeply to stay calm, as he would in the mine. Finally Ford's driver, Steck, spoke up.

"Sir," he said. "You want me go see what's keeping them?"

"Thanks, Captain," Ford nodded.

Steck went to the door, turned the knob and was startled to find a large plainclothes deputy standing there, facing him. Wearing a black suit, the man was big enough to fill the door frame. Todd recognized him at once: Gore's chief Baldwin guard, Captain Gaujot.

Steck straightened, expecting some message from the officer. Gaujot just stared, however, as if sizing him up. At last, the big deputy spoke.

"Sheriff's on his way," he said, and turned. Steck found a wooden wedge and propped the door open. The four men sat and waited.

Another ten minutes passed before Sheriff Gore appeared. Smiling at Ford, he breezed in, followed by Gaujot. Behind them came a well-dressed George Waddill. The aging coal executive lumbered into the room, saying nothing, barely nodding to the others. He took his seat beside the head of the table, which was left for Gore. The sheriff shook hands with the two men. Todd watched as Gore and Kenner held each other's grip for a long moment, their knuckles going pale. The sheriff smiled amicably, addressing Ford.

"I want to thank you, Colonel, for bringing me together with this man. I've always been eager to meet Mr. Kenner here.

He released his grip.

"And this one, too," he said, nodding to Todd.

They took their seats.

As if signaled, Gaujot crossed the room, his eyes resting briefly on Todd. The mine guard closed the door, positioning himself beside it, on watch. The sheriff nodded his approval and began.

"You've all met Mr. Waddill, founder and vice president of Sovereign Coal. He joins us today, however, as secretary of the Southern Coal Association. We're lucky to have him here on such short notice. He's a good Logan businessman, although his current home lies in Baltimore."

George Waddill stared at Kenner. He had not spoken, nor shaken any hands.

"Thank you again, Colonel Ford," Gore continued, "for coming all the way from Virginia. I know this hasn't been an easy trip for you."

Ford caught the jab about their crash. He exchanged a look with Steck, then got to his feet. It was a movement so sudden, it took everyone by surprise.

"Thank you, Sheriff Gore," he said. "I'd also like to thank everyone for coming, and begin by expressing the hope, held by many, that we can all come to terms."

Ford looked at each man, in turn. He had no intention of letting this meeting get out of his control.

"We're here for one purpose," he said. "To end the conflict that has grown from the labor strike of the past few weeks. And the hostilities now taking place at Blair."

"Colonel Ford," said Kenner. "I'd like to interrupt to ask whether the deputy is armed."

They looked to Gaujot.

"My man is an officer of the law," said Gore. "And this is the county courthouse."

"Nonetheless, sheriff," Kenner said. "We came here in good faith, without guns. It seems reasonable to ask the same of the sheriff and his man."

"Sounds fair enough," said Ford. "Sheriff?"

At a signal from Gore, the big deputy opened his jacket.

"No gun," he said.

Kenner frowned. He scratched his throat, doubt written on his face. Finally, he nodded. Ford continued.

"With authorization from Washington, it is my mission – and my personal hope – that Mr. Kenner, leader of the workers' union, and Mr. Waddill will discuss the situation. The goal is to see the way clear for arbitration and reconciliation of their differences."

Todd stared at Gore, who'd begun listening with his eyes closed. As Ford went on, the Logan sheriff grew more agitated. Finally, he interrupted.

"Colonel, I appreciate all you're trying to do here. But, I have to point out that we are putting our friend Mr. Waddill here in a difficult situation."

"What situation is that, Sheriff?" Ford asked.

"For Mr. Waddill, a private citizen, to be discussing matters with union representatives is to risk arrest."

Ford blinked.

"Are you suggesting, Sheriff, that you or your men would arrest Mr. Waddill, the leader of a coal company, just for talking to these union men?"

"I do not make the laws of Logan County, Colonel," said Gore. "But I do enforce them."

Todd glanced up at Gaujot who continued to watch him from the door.

"Well, Sheriff," Ford continued, "I suppose you and I must assure Mr. Waddill – and the union men, as well – that their trust in you is well-grounded. We have all come here under common faith and agreement among your office, the state governor's office and the United States Army. Again, Sheriff, I cannot overstate the importance of this conversation, lest the U.S. Army be compelled to intervene – with force, if necessary – to end this conflict."

There was a moment of silence. Then, Kenner spoke up.

"I have a question about that," he said. "Are you saying the Army will defend coal production in Logan County, condoning the companies' use of transported, captive labor here?"

Ford looked uncomfortable.

"We're not there yet, Mr. Kenner," he said. "Further, as I understand it, this is not among the matters that are central to the miners' strike. One of your key issues, I believe, is the unusual employment of private company guards as Logan County deputies."

Gore spoke up. "Colonel, this is not an 'unusual' practice. It's been a common one here for some time. Many other counties see this as an efficient, money-saving means of maintaining law and order. These men are well-trained to defend our local laws and enforce our injunctions. The union, on the other hand, continues to use outside forces to fight us any way they can. They've lost every case they bring into court. Every time! Logan, quite simply, has laws against union organizing if a company forbids it. And these laws have been upheld by no less a body than the U.S. Supreme Court. So, it is all *their* activities, that of the union reds, that must be illegal. Not the acts of Logan's private law-enforcement officers who are merely doing their jobs – defending themselves and private property."

Kenner could contain himself no longer.

"No law allows you to hold a man twelve weeks on a mere injunction," he said. "You cannot hold our men in jail without bringing charges against them."

"No one tells me what I can and cannot do," Gore seethed, pointing a finger at the union organizer. "Especially you. And not in my county. There is just one thing I want to hear from you: That your murderous band is disarming and leaving my county for good and all!"

"I take it, sheriff," Ford broke in, "that you're not prepared to release the prisoners in the Logan jail who, after so many weeks, still have no charges filed against them?"

Gore settled back into his chair. "We're holding no one in jail without charges," he said. "Such prisoners do not exist."

"That's a good one," Kenner snorted. "They don't exist...."

Gore gazed at him, smiling.

"We're charging them now."

The room was silent. Ford leaned forward.

"Sheriff, may I ask what charges you are filing against these men?"

The sheriff counted, touching a finger for each one.

"Conspiring to spread an illegal doctrine. Criminal conspiracy against the state. Associating with an illegal labor organization."

"Conspiring to organize slave labor," Kenner scoffed.

Gore suddenly slammed his palm against the table, making Todd jump. "You're out of line!" he thundered. "Scheming to force men in a free market into joining your gang of foreign criminals!"

Seeing his window closing, Kenner directed his appeal to George Waddill. "Mr. Waddill, you're a wealthy man," he said. "But this does not give you the right to rule over your workers, day and night – nor own them, heart and soul! You'd fight too, if you were forced to live under constant watch by these Baldwin thugs! They'll bust up any meeting of men, even funerals and church."

"These are radical ideas!" Gore broke in. "Your radicalism has no place in Logan County!"

"I wasn't finished!" Kenner said, and stood, trying to get through to Waddill.

Gaujot jumped into action, practically leaping around the table. The big man's movement was so fast, no one saw how he produced the knife. In no time, Gaujot had one arm around Kenner's chest, the blade at his neck.

Todd watched, terrified, as Kenner raised his hands.

"I'm not armed!" he cried.

Colonel Ford and Steck froze.

"Sheriff Gore!" said Ford. "I insist you call your man down!"

Gaujot did not move, but called to his men in the hallway.

"Guards!"

Three black-uniformed deputies came through the door, their pistols trained on Kenner and Todd.

"You saw it, Colonel," said Gore, standing. "Mr. Kenner's outburst betrays these men for what they are. This is merely the vanguard of their assassin force, coming to invade Logan County and kill our loyal workers and law-enforcement officers! You may not have what it takes to deal with them authoritatively. Well, *I do.*"

Captain Steck touched his holstered sidearm. Gaujot saw it. "Don't!" he cried. Instantly, one of the guards swung his handgun around and trained it on the Army captain.

Gore drew a sheaf of papers from his jacket and slapped it on the table. "These are warrants for the arrests of these two men."

Ford looked at the sheriff, his face cold as stone.

"No," Todd protested. "I never did anything!"

"I knew it," Kenner shouted. "Didn't we tell you, Colonel?"

"These are the charges," the sheriff said, calmly pushing the papers across the table. "Signed by the judge this morning."

Ford picked up the warrants and read them, frowning. "I don't believe this," he said.

"Conspiracy. Fraud. Larceny… And *treason,* Sheriff?"

Gore nodded.

"Treason against law and order of a sovereign state. The law doesn't allow radicals to intimidate my workers and policemen, Colonel."

At that, Tom Kenner could not contain himself.

"I've been thrown out my own house!" he yelled. "I've seen women and children tossed into the winter snow! Were they criminals? Were they 'radicals'? Only you would call them that!"

Todd watched wide-eyed, terrified of what Kenner might bring down upon them both.

"I was just a kid when a mine guard thumped me for the first time! I'd made your black list when I was just fourteen! You sent my name around! My photograph! By the time I was twenty, my own friends were afraid to talk to me! You call me *radical?* Well, who made me a radical, Sheriff? You did!"

Gore seemed to sink into himself, coiled like a viper. His voice came as a bellow, pulled up from someplace deep inside.

"Lock him up. Throw 'em both in jail."

Gaujot and the guards took Kenner and Todd, pulling their arms behind their backs. Todd felt the handcuffs tighten on his wrists as the guards pulled him through the door.

"Do something, Colonel!" Kenner cried. "Didn't we have a deal?!"

Ford stepped forward.

"Sheriff Gore!" he said. "These two union leaders came to talk in good faith!"

The sheriff wheeled around on him. "That's utter shit!" he cried.

Ford found himself staring into Gore's bloodshot eyes. Hands clenched, the sheriff sputtered, his mouth just under Ford's chin. "Union leaders, my ass! Look around, man! Do you see anybody *following* these two? No! Not one man here in Logan is stupid enough to take their side!" Gore wiped his mouth, examining Ford with a look of clear disgust.

"*Leaders.* These men lead the scum of the earth, and I'll fight any son-of-a-bitch who tells me I have to talk to them! You're free to stick around, Colonel. Watch me while I hang these reds for treason!"

Ford went cold as Gore turned away. "Sheriff," he growled. "I'm warning you."

"No, sir!" Gore shouted, turning again. "I'm warning you! These men are wanted by the law. And here in Logan County, I'm the law!"

Todd was too astounded to struggle, wanted to reach out and help Kenner, being dragged down the hallway before him. The union leader was bound and screaming.

"No one called us radicals in 1915, when we were digging coal for the war! You should have heard the promises made to us back then, Colonel! Are you there, Colonel?!"

Todd looked back, seeing only Captain Steck, alone in the hallway. The captain's mouth was open as he watched the two union men being half-carried toward the big steel door of the jail. Suddenly, the door was slammed behind them. Todd felt the vibration of the steel, reminding him of the big ventilation doors, whose closing meant that he was alone in the mine.

Captain Harry Steck turned back to the room, where Colonel Ford continued to confront the sheriff. Gaujot loomed behind them.

"Don't you interfere with my arrests!" the sheriff cried. "By god, if nothing else, I know the law! And yours don't count for nothin' here!"

Gore went to the end of the table, rejoining George Waddill. The coal executive was mopping his forehead with a handkerchief. The sheriff put a comforting hand on his friend's shoulder.

"Damnit, George, I'm sorry. So sorry you had to see this."

"Sheriff," said Ford angrily. "On behalf of the US Army, I protest these arrests."

Gore took Waddill by the arm and left the room. They turned down the hall, in the opposite direction from the jail.

"Sheriff," said Ford, keeping pace with them. "I hold you personally responsible for anything that happens to those men!"

Gore strode quickly, ignoring Ford. He appeared to be deep in conversation with Waddill, who lumbered down the hallway. Watching them, Ford was suddenly surprised to realize that Gore wasn't actually saying anything to the coal executive. Instead, the sheriff pantomimed talk, making a show of speaking. Aside from his own silence, Waddill didn't make any attempt at trying to hear Gore. The coal executive's eyes were more closed than open as the two men moved toward the door.

Ford stopped, baffled at the performance. It was as if Gore had been acting on a stage before an audience: The sheriff walked, making gestures, but only issued muttered words – words that made no sense.

Ford stood in place. He felt his breath return, as if he'd just lost a fistfight.

"Orders, sir?"

Steck stood behind him. Ford turned to the captain, his eyes burning fire.

"Get me to a goddamned telephone," he said.

Chapter 27

High, wispy clouds lingered over the mountain, lit by a blurred moon. Wide awake, Gibbs Bryant sat with his back against the wall of the trench, crowded with sleeping men. His head tilted up, he'd been watching the moon skirt quietly along the edge of the canvas. The temperature had dropped. A fog had formed in the lower woods.

Gibbs closed his eyes, unsettled by the quiet. This was a brief period of peace, sure to be followed by another round of fighting. Gibbs wrapped himself tighter in his wool blanket, awake but exhausted by the previous day's battle, and the others before it. For three days, he and his friends had been on the miles-long firing line, never wandering far from their own trench. Tired and dirty, they stayed rooted here, bent into their guns as they had once bent their backs over shovels in the mine. Terrified by the bullets coming at them in screaming swarms, the miners tried to give the enemy as much as they got. Still, Gibbs worried that too many of their weapons were poor, lacking the power to inflict much damage, or to hold the other side at bay.

The miners still carried a passion for their cause, and hated the Baldwins for all they'd done. But the reality of war had crippled them. Few could get used to the angry firefights that flared up unexpectedly, then ended just as suddenly, launching another long and tedious hour of waiting.

"What are we doing here?" asked Ben. "I thought we were marching to Logan!"

"We were," said Gibbs. "Now Logan's come to us."

Gibbs knew of four strikers who'd been killed. A Boone slate-picker had accidentally put a bullet in his own flank. His screaming so unnerved everyone, they decided to move the doctors' tent farther back from the line. There, deep in the woods, they'd found another casualty, an Irish miner hanging from a tree.

"He suffered a bad fright," Lowcoal told them. "Scared of the soldiers. That's what someone said."

"He ain't the only one," Dix replied tentatively. "A lot of 'em is runnin' off. Just strikin' out for the woods."

"Renegades," scowled Ben. "I say we declare 'open season' on 'em."

Bartolo and Simms glanced up from their unending game of cards.

"That's too hard, Ben," Dix put in. "I swear, sometimes you are a hard man."

But Ben wasn't having it. "We have to fend for ourselves. And our union brothers."

"Settle down, Ben," Gibbs said. "We have to stick together."

He knew, though, that there was no real resolution to it. Numbed by the battle, they all had grown unsure of the direction things were taking. Gibbs had never felt so tired.

We have too few men like Sid, he thought. *And enemies on all sides.*

Minutes of relief stretched into hours of boredom, giving them too much time to think – or not to think, like now. Two memorial services had offered Gibbs a strange respite. Remembering how Todd had stirred the crowd at Sid's funeral, men came to Gibbs and asked him to say some words. Gibbs stood beside the quickly covered graves and summoned what he could. An ongoing state of mourning, he felt, was now shared by everyone. Before leaving, he traded news with the pallbearers, strangers to each other.

"Thirty women hiked up from Blair today with food."

"Mines are still closed at Slago Creek, Diamond and Hewlett."

"A track scaffold collapsed in Sharples. Young 'bolt weevils' gnawed out the screws!"

"Some 'crows' done pecked out the glass insulators on the 'lectric poles at Bamford. Baldwins got no more lights there now."

Gibbs took comfort in such breaks, rare moments when he could feel something other than being trapped; when it seemed safe to breathe again.

We're less like soldiers than fighting dogs, he thought. *Chained and barking, bred to bite. Kicked and angry, always chained.*

The night had only made him more uneasy. He'd spent hours under the blanket, broken by one watch. He wondered whether stretching his legs on the open hillside was worth the risk of a random bullet. He knew they'd have to do something. Frustrated at the days-long stand-off, the men were getting antsy. Gibbs decided he would organize a new patrol at dawn. At intervals, in groups of three or more, men would venture into the valley, the no-man's-land separating the two armies. These patrols served to assure miners along the line that the forces from Logan were keeping to themselves. Gibbs didn't mind his own excursions into the woods. It relieved the monotony of the trenches, for a time at least, and allowed him to think of Carla.

Gibbs watched the moon and waited. Sooner or later, he knew, there'd be a new volley of gunfire. It might continue without pause, all day. Two days ago, the battle went long into the night. Gibbs could see the flashes of guns along the Baldwins' side, followed by the sound of their bullets, buzzing overhead like crazed insects. He didn't know what kind of inspiration or madness kept him on that parapet, always firing back. He felt an intimacy with death, always expecting a bullet to come in low enough to hit him with a loud and bloody slap. *Final as a rockfall in the mine*, he thought.

Mary hadn't expected to make another deal in Logan. The rabble outside the courthouse had gotten to her, though.

Almost every evening since Todd Bryant and the other one arrived, a crowd of men had gathered below the high line of barred windows. Loafers, she thought, people who'd never done anything for anyone but themselves. They came at five o'clock each evening to bang on their iron pipes and kitchen pans. From her room, she could hear them chanting.

Hang the reds! Hang the reds! Hang the reds!

It riled her, knowing it was Todd Bryant they wanted – or pretended to want. She tried to imagine the boy in his cell, listening to that racket. For all that he was, he did not deserve this, she thought. Mary decided to go to Gore again, this time on Todd's behalf. She didn't expect much, and said so.

"This boy had fallen into something over his head," she told Gore. "It's not his fault."

Surprisingly, the sheriff seemed ready to agree, assessing Todd as a "second dog," unlikely to grow into anything dangerous.

"I'm doing this for you," he said. "But he'd better leave the state. Tell him this: If my men ever find him in Logan again, I can only guess what they will do. And I will not care."

A uniformed deputy delivered Todd to Mary behind the jail. Todd looked frightened, not knowing what was happening, much less trusting it. The nighttime air seemed to make him dizzy. He had a furtive look about him, Mary thought, as if he'd aged. She put her hand on Todd's shoulder as she spoke to Nick.

"You know this friend, don't you?" she encouraged. "Take him home. Use the old road. You know the one."

Nick knew the path better than anyone, and took Todd's hand. As he did it, Mary knew, it was as much from her boy's desire to comfort the big miner as from any childish fear of his own.

"Can't you come with us?" Todd asked, his eyes darting.

Mary frowned. "Stay with Nick," she warned. "He'll steer you clear of the fighting, but keep an eye out for him. If you run into anybody, you should know the Baldwins' password: It's Amen."

"Can't you come too?" Todd asked again, his voice pleading.

"No," she said. "I got one last thing I have to do."

She hugged her son, feeling Nick's broad hand as it patted her back. Mary almost laughed through her tears, she had such faith in him.

"Boy, you are a puzzlement," she said, stroking his cheek. "And twice the man as most."

Then, turning away, she retreated into the shadows and, rounding the great stone corner of the courthouse, ducked out of sight. Nick turned and, pulling Todd's hand, headed off across the lawn. They struck out quickly for the darkened streets.

From the stairwell to the jailer's basement office, Gaujot and Mouse-face watched them go. Gaujot's finger played along the edge of the county map that Gore had given him to put away – the one with Mary Rising's name on it.

The two Baldwin agents watched quietly as the shadows of Todd and Nick crossed a distant street, slinking past the lamps and dead electric signs of Logan. Gaujot smiled, imagining the miner's fear, cultivated during several days in the Logan jailhouse. Gaujot imagined how the tortured Todd would cringe at any sound, eager to get past each darkened window, every little barber shop and hardware store. However exhausted, the desperate young red would not slow down, Gaujot knew, until he'd come to the house that he'd be seeking, deep within the eastern woods.

"Army Air Service crews tested the device in July 1921.
AAC discovered that the bomb was capable of burning a hole through
a ship's deck of four-inch steel. The device had been tested by
Air Service pilots using the new Norden bombsight. Under the test
conditions, Gen. Mitchell reports that his aviators were able to score
"hits" 30 per cent of the time. The General is asking Command
for permission to test the device further, perhaps in a remote site
not too distant from the base at Langley."

Internal Department Memo (Classified), October 15, 1921

Chapter 28

Gibbs' rifle lay beside him, cold and unused. He watched the sky for the oncoming dawn, when the air would become hot with new gunfire.

A single shot sounded, like the sudden intake of breath. Another accident, Gibbs thought. Or some drunken fool, in love with the sound of his own gun. The clouds marched overhead, and Gibbs felt the passing of another moment of relative peace. Exhaling loudly, he considered the possibility of sleep.

Instead, he gathered the courage to move. Still wrapped in his blanket, he rose and climbed the moonlit hillside. Reaching the upper woods, he found a tree and relieved himself. He stared at the moon and admired the smooth motion of the wispy clouds, indifferent to the armies facing each other from two sides of the valley. Tildy had once told him about a gypsy drummer who read men's fortunes in the stars. The fellow scrutinized the sky, consulting his peculiar maps. Gibbs smiled: Like listening for earth's secrets in the black of the mine, he thought. He stared into the dark night. What could these stars tell him now?

Maybe we should go back to Blair. Find her. Get right with Todd....

Pulling his blanket tighter, he turned downhill again. His thinking sharpened in the cold as he crouched before Carla's small, slackened tent. With a twist and a good tug, he tightened the ropes and crawled inside.

The breeze was coming up from the woods below. Gibbs sighed and, pulling himself deep into the tent, burrowed within his big wool blanket.

His feet were wet and cold, but he would not take off his boots, fearing the stink and chill. He dozed, warming the canvas-scented air with his own breath.

He missed Carla. Once again, he tried to understand her motivations for returning to Blair – for Todd, he guessed. Gibbs told himself it was better so – that she might escape. Better that she'd gotten away from this whole mess, maybe even run from Blair. He imagined her, getting on a train headed out-of-state, as far away as possible. He'd wanted to march to Logan, to free their friends. Now, he could only feel trapped.

How easily the men on Blair had accepted their wet trench; the daily tirades the two sides fed each other. The flying bullets, the constant fight.

Gibbs looked down the long battle line and saw a single army, many of its soldiers being veterans of similar rebellions someplace else. Here were Italians, Bohemians and Poles, collectively calling upon their experience of strikes against faraway despots – Gibbs had heard some of them discussed. In such moments, their own battle took on new life, connected with countless others, never aging.

"Sometimes you win, sometimes you lose," an Irishman told him. "But the struggle doesn't stop."

Gibbs covered his face with the blanket, shifted on the cold and brittle grass, then drifted back to sleep. A new dream came. It carried him away from the fear of gunfire, far from soldiers and their bayonets.

He found himself in a desert, surrounded by rolling hills of sand. A familiar brown-eyed girl came to him and handed him a shovel. She told him his job was to scoop sand onto a dam that would hold water in their garden. Gibbs didn't question this. Working together with the girl, he began piling sand against the embankment. Then, the water came – he didn't know from where – and the little garden plot was suddenly filled with flowering bushes. Rows of corn and red-currant trees came from nowhere. The dam held. Water lilies glided across the shimmering pool. Gibbs took new interest in his work – and in his helper. Smiling, he pulled her close.

Now, another man appeared. Against Gibbs' protest, the other man took both the shovel and the girl. Gibbs watched, powerless, as water began trickling through a hole in their dam. He worked alone to stop it, piling handful after handful of new sand against the mound. He couldn't move fast enough. More water came, widening the gap. Uprooted bushes and lilies began drifting through the breach. The garden was soon sucked dry, returning to the desert that it had been.

On his hands and knees, Gibbs continued to scoop wet sand, now digging for something he'd lost. It was useless. He woke, feeling tired and alone. Rolling over, he draped an arm across his face. He waited for the dream to fade, grateful for the warming grass against his back.

"Hey," she said.

Carla's eyes searched for his as she knelt over him.

"You're in my tent," she whispered.

Gibbs exhaled, forgetting the dream, forgetting the war and everything. All his thinking was pushed aside by this rare elation, a joy that enveloped him, reaching deep. Then he understood Carla's words, and moved to accommodate her – trying to pull himself out and return her place to her. He'd do anything for this girl.

"No, stupid," she said, touching his shoulder. "Just scoot over. Make room."

She left her bound-up horseshoe pack outside. Gibbs pulled himself free of the blanket, and opened it to her. Carla moved against him, tucking herself in. Gibbs put his arms around her to keep them both warm. Together, they shared a long moment, protected from the cold and dark by their nest of wool and heavy clothing. As Gibbs lay there, holding her, he was bathed in his own sense of exhilaration, the rightness of this small moment.

"I'm so damned glad to see you," he whispered, surprised not only at how easily the words came to him, but how much they raised his spirit.

Carla smiled and moved against him. After spending the night with Tildy, she'd hiked all the way from Blair that morning. Just for this, she decided. She floated in Gibbs' embrace, as if she could fly above the feuding miners and mercenaries, above the smells of wood smoke and gun grease. As if Gibbs Bryant carried her right off that fearful hillside war toward the thinning moon.

Just one moment more, she thought. Here, inside the tent, everything else could wait. Here, they could stay in a world to themselves. Carla didn't need to talk, didn't need to hear anything. Not from anyone, not even Gibbs. Not yet. He moved now and, before she knew it, he was kissing her.

Carla let it happen, welcomed it. She gave herself the time to taste Gibbs' mouth; to enjoy that taste and the temptation to go on, and even to encourage it.

But this was not the time. It would be light soon. Already, their friends and comrades around them were stirring. Carla broke the kiss and, still holding Gibbs, buried her face in his chest.

"Blair seems to be closing down," she told him. "There's no more meetings, no more meals. They've stopped holding school. Every train that comes, people are afraid of Baldwins being on it. Or soldiers. Nobody comes out to meet the cars anymore, not unless they're leaving. Tildy mostly keeps to the mercantile, but the shelves are bare."

She waited, letting Gibbs consider the news before continuing.

"Todd went away with Kenner and a man from the Army," she said. "Nobody knows where they went or why. They been gone for days."

Gibbs shifted. He closed his eyes, allowing his weariness to return.

"We've been shooting back and forth across this valley since you left," he told her. "We don't seem to have much effect. And I don't know how we ever could. They've got us stuck here. Can't go forward and we can't back down."

Carla saw the truth of it. Walking up the mountain in the night, she'd seen the trees, their leaves turning color. Even if the strikers and their families survived this battle, winter's freeze would be as bad as bayonets. She imagined a town of misaligned tents and hungry families. She could see the children, their faces drawn and thin, competing for position around already-crowded cookstoves.

"People in Blair want to pick up and move," she said. "But nobody knows where to go. Todd and Kenner had talked about another camp in Boone. But a lot folks just want out."

"That's just it," said Gibbs. "Most people have never been anywhere else. There's nowhere left to run. For us here, there's nothing left to do but to fight. Maybe bust through...."

Carla squirmed. "Todd says we should give up our guns and walk away."

"Same old story," muttered Gibbs.

As he held her in his arms, however, Gibbs wished only that he might make this moment last forever. It was a while before he spoke again.

"We gotta do something," he said. "The soldiers are coming. It won't be safe much longer, either here or for people in Blair."

He looked out of the tent, wondering. Another gun sounded in the distance, like a lightning crack.

"We need to go down and make sure the woods are clear," he said absently. Carla looked at him.

"We could go to Mary's" she said.

"What?"

"My mother's house."

"She wouldn't welcome us," said Gibbs.

Carla untangled herself from his arms and rested on her elbows.

"Mama's not there. She took Nick to Logan. I figure she was afraid." She stopped, not mentioning her fight with Todd.

"But the house might not be empty," Gibbs argued. "The Baldwins."

"No," she said. "It's too far south. And it's hidden. Barely a road leading to it."

Carla examined Gibbs' features through the dark.

"I need to go and see," she said.

Gibbs heard the familiar determination in her voice, saw it in the shadow of her brow.

"Well, if you're going, I'm going with you," he said. "I'm staying close."

He took in her face, her dark eyes. "If you die," he said, "I'd want to die too."

His words rang inside her like a bell. Leaning forward, Carla kissed him again. And, with this kiss, all of yesterday's assaults disappeared. Even the path of the coming day seemed to gain some resolution for them both.

Across the black hillside, men crawled up from their holes, peering tentatively through the early-morning haze. At the edge of the Sovereign trench, Dix's face appeared. Seeing Gibbs and Carla together in her tent, the Southerner grinned. Gibbs called down to him.

"Get ready, Dix!" he said. "We're going on patrol."

Now, six men and Carla passed again beneath the great red beech tree, still black against the predawn sky. Once again, they were venturing into the dark and quiet valley, the steep-walled frontier with Logan.

Despite his nervousness, Gibbs was relieved to be moving at last. After days of feeling trapped in the trench, he smiled to realize that he was back in the woods with friends – with Lowcoal, Dix and Ben, now joined by Bartolo and Simms – all of them following Carla once again. Although fearful, Gibbs was carried forward by the thought of returning to her homeplace, of seeing everything through her eyes.

She knows so much about the mountain, he thought. *She knows the rocks and paths, the quiet of the forest – so different from the stillness of the mine.*

Carla climbed up the hollow, making no sound. The deeper into the woods they went, the more she welcomed the return of her connection with the men – their sense of friendship, their common work and fight.

The raiders reached the bottom of the valley and found the far slope rising steep before them. They moved south, up the cut, keeping the Baldwin line to their right. High above, Gibbs knew, the Logan volunteers watched and listened in their dugouts. Like stalked deer, he and the others moved slowly, freezing at each snapped twig.

The green, indifferent divide was like a labyrinth – rough country puzzled with undulating saddles and unexpected rocks. Gibbs rarely saw the same thing twice, recognized no landmarks. Worse, the shadowed wood seemed to change according to each new breeze, causing tricks of light through the canopy. Fearing the worst, he unstrapped his rifle from his back. Behind him, he could hear incidental sounds from the men, terrified of waking the enemy guns, up the mountain to their right.

From somewhere, far away, voices called and the first gunshots came. Scores of missiles chirped through the trees. Then the shooting became general.

The seven raiders fell to the ground, cowering from the whine of bullets, crazed and shrill. From somewhere high on the mountain, a machine gun opened. Magnified by the valley, the weapon's rattle seemed to be all around them, an unceasing hammer coming from all directions. Overhead, metal shards tore into the forest and smacked against the wood. Fighting to overcome his fear, Gibbs looked up and realized....

"They're too far off!" he said. "Come on! Get up!"

It was true. The bullets continued to whistle through, shattering leaves and bark – but much too high to be of any danger to them. Gibbs got up, seeing how the dense forest shielded them from the firestorm. The others rose, cautiously brushing themselves off. Gibbs started off again, going at a faster clip through the squall of twigs and debris that rained down around them.

Following the creek, the group scrambled up the valley, getting away from the gunfire as fast as they could. In time, they climbed with confidence, the sounds of the war receding. Now, with Gibbs in the lead, they climbed another half hour before arriving at the top of the hill. From here, they made their way along a lefthand branch. They slowed their pace, the battle at a safe distance behind them. New sunlight beamed down through the trees as they walked.

At last, they came out onto a familiar field. Gibbs was glad to recognize the broad, grassy basin. At the top, he knew, they would find two stones, the graves of Bonner Rising and Sid Mandt.

Outside the little cemetery, the men lay down their guns and packs. Carla went to the church ruin, where she bent down among shaded patches of ironweed, black-eyed susan and emerald clumps of dill. When she returned, she carried two bunches of wildflowers. Gibbs met her at the rusted iron fence, holding open the gate. Their eyes met. For a time, Carla considered him from beneath her mannish bangs and smiled.

Lowcoal stared at Sid's grave.

"It all looks different."

Carla knelt down beside it.

"Just grown over some."

She set the flowers and wished for a small jar to keep them fresh. Gibbs stood by the fence, listening to the call of bluejays, playing counterpoint against the distant rifle fire.

"It's peaceable here," said Dix. Lowcoal nodded in agreement.

"You want to rest a while?" asked Gibbs. "Carla wants to check out her mother's place."

"We can set up watch here," said Lowcoal. "You just holler if you need us."

"Bring us back some lunch," grinned Ben, and Carla said she would.

The two of them set off. Crossing over the wooded hill, they continued down the trail on the other side, through the maze of twisting hillocks obscured by sycamores. Watchful and unsure, Carla felt as if a hundred years had gone since she – or anyone – had been here.

They came to the berry patch, where inky spatters of birds now marred the leaves. Carla pointed out a four-headed knot of hens huddled deep among the briers. The apple grove was littered with browned fruit. Here, she stopped and raised her hand. Gibbs stood ready, his eyes sweeping the gray grove. An apple fell and struck his elbow. When he looked up, he was startled to see Nick, grinning down from a high fork in the tree.

"Come here, you!" Carla scolded softly and welcomed her brother into her arms. Gibbs tossled Nick's hair as the boy pulled the steel whistle from his shirt and, turning away, wiggled it before his eyes.

"Well, now," smiled Gibbs, flattered. "You still got the toy I gave you."

Immediately, Nick pulled them both toward the cabin. Gibbs and Carla followed, skirting several piles of bloody feathers in the yard. A figure lay on the porch. It seemed to be a shapeless pile of clothes at first, but then uncurled itself from sleep like a waking child.

Todd sat before them on the porch. His hair went in all directions, his face scarred by what Gibbs recognized as stone fragments – as if he'd been caught too close to a mine blast. Waking, Todd rubbed his eyes.

"By god, what's happened?" Carla asked. "Where have you been?"

Todd stared up at her. "To hell and back."

Stowing their rifles and packs by the door, Gibbs found a lamp and lit it. Carla sat at the table, holding Todd's hands in sympathy. To remove the chill from the air, Gibbs went to the kindling box and picked wood for a fire. Every once in a while, he glanced up, waiting for his brother to speak. Todd was still, watching as Gibbs carefully lit the fire. Carla rose and climbed the stair, coming down again with her own quilt.

"Put this around you," she said to Todd, "until the place warms up."

Todd accepted the blanket, stood and wrapped himself in it before sitting down again.

Curious and uneasy, Gibbs eyed the man huddled in the white quilt, trying to reconcile this version of his brother with the one who had stood up to their father in the mine.

"Todd," he said at last. "What's going on?"

Slowly, Todd told them what he could about the failed negotiations. He would not talk about the rest, about lying on the damp hard-pack floor of the basement room, alive with vermin. Or about the scars on his face, caused by Gaujot's gunplay in a tiny, stone-walled cell. As he struggled to describe his arrest, two days before, Todd seemed lost.

"I really thought we could do it. I thought Kenner could convince them…. What's gonna happen now, Gibbs? We trusted them. All of them. The Army. The government…."

Carla took his hand again.

"Todd," she said. "You're safe here. Slow down and think. What do you want to do?"

He looked from her to Gibbs, his eyes red and tired.

"They got so much power over us," he said. "They'll hammer on a man until he can't hold out no more…. I cannot stay here, they told me so. They'll kill me if I don't leave the state."

Gibbs stood behind Carla, listening to Todd. The more he heard, the more he felt his old anger returning.

"Todd, you cannot run. To most of 'em here, you're in the leadership. You *are* the union. And, now, they got Kenner in jail."

Todd shook his head.

"I don't even know if he's still alive."

Gibbs clenched his jaw.

"If you just run – if we run – then the whole damned thing falls apart."

Todd chafed at the thought. He looked toward the door, considering.

"It's not what Sid died for," Carla said softly. "Or Harm."

Todd shifted in the chair.

"How're the men inclined?" he asked.

Gibbs joined them at the table. "Honestly?" he said. "They're antsy. Ready to bolt, one way or another, but no one to tell them where."

"Everybody's tired," said Carla, sadly. "They're ready to end it."

"Not all of them," countered Gibbs. "Some would still like to march over that mountain and kill them all."

Carla's silence, however, told him otherwise. He thought of his friends, back at Sid's grave, weary from so many days of fighting. He sighed.

"What would Kenner do, Todd? Would he run? Or fight? You know him better than most."

Todd stared out the window, remembering Kenner's fury as the guards dragged them off to jail. And, then, his earlier words on the way to Logan. *If the man wants to talk, our job is to listen.*

"I don't know," said Todd. "But, honestly Gibbs, we should get our people out of here before the Army comes. Some might call it runnin' scared. But at least we live to fight another day."

Gibbs looked at his brother, thinking about the words. The way Todd had said *our people.* To Gibbs, this alone lightened the gloom. He nodded.

"Where can we go?" asked Carla.

"There's two new strike camps going up in Boone," said Todd. "Kenner arranged it. Word came in from Meridian as we left for Logan. People in Blair should know by now."

"Let's go down then, and find out," shrugged Gibbs.

"First, we have to eat," said Carla, getting up. She began taking stock of the kitchen, her mind constructing a quick, midday meal for them and the others in the field. She fatted both of Mary's skillets and placed them on the edge of the stove to warm. Then, turning, she found a basket in the corner and headed for the door.

"I'm going through the garden," she said, and left.

Todd said nothing, fighting the sense that much of the light in the room had just left with her. He turned to Gibbs, unable to look his brother in the eye.

"I don't know if I can hold up through this, bo."

Draping the blanket around his shoulders, he stood and went to the small front window. From there, he watched Carla in the garden. They'd been through so much together. He'd tried to win her, wanted to believe she loved him – or that she might have. He stared at nothing, struggling with some demon he couldn't name. Not only had success escaped him; he'd forgotten what it was.

"Our choices just go bad," he said. "You put your faith in something. You think it's safe, and right and good. But it rarely is. It's never like you think."

Gibbs didn't know how to respond. He was suddenly reminded of their father's last hours in the mine – and wondered how alone the old man must have felt in the end.

"Gibbs," said Todd. "Do you think you could go back and tell the men to put down their guns? Order them off the mountain? On your own, I mean?"

Gibbs frowned. "Hell," he said. "You know, they don't follow anyone at any one time."

Todd smiled, nodding once.

"You have to come with us, brother," Gibbs continued. "We'll both go. We'll tell them together."

Todd nodded again as Gibbs turned toward the door, intending to see whether Carla needed help. The door opened before he got there and Carla stood in it, facing him, her eyes wide.

"We're all going back," Gibbs told her.

But Carla shook her head.

Oh, God, he thought. *She's changed her mind.*

But that wasn't it. Carla came forward and was followed by Mouse-face Moler, who held a rifle to her back. Behind them came Pearl Gaujot, his pistol trained on Gibbs, then Todd. The giant mine guard looked around the cabin as he closed the door and leaned against it.

"Now, isn't this something," Gaujot said.

For, behold! Jehovah comes forth…to punish inhabitants of
the earth for their iniquities. And the earth shall disclose her blood.
And no longer shall she cover her slain ones.

Isaiah 26:21

Chapter 29

Mouseface moved quickly to secure their weapons, two rifles by the
door and a heavy pistol he found in a bag. The place stank of wood and
dirt and Mouseface's long nose wrinkled. Everything here was a likely
home for maggots and buzzing flies.

"What do I do with these?" he asked, showing Gaujot the captured
weapons.

"Stash 'em in the barn," the captain whispered. "We'll take 'em when
we leave."

Mouseface did as he was told, then returned. He stood in the doorway, straight and noble in his black suit. He stared at Gaujot in open
admiration, proud of the fact that his captain had picked him to get the
drop on the fleeing reds. It was a thing for the books: The two of them,
arresting the remnants of Sid Mandt's insurrectionist band in its secret
mountain hideaway – to which the savvy Gaujot even had a map.

Mandt's wife was seated at the table. Mouseface searched her eyes
for recognition, saw the familiar look of paralyzing fear, a thing he knew
that soured reason.

Pointing his pistol, Gaujot went to Todd, who'd let the white quilt
fall to the floor.

"Stand up, scum."

Mouseface smiled to see the big union leader stand obediently before
his captain. If the man had stood up straight, he could almost be eye-to-
eye with Gaujot, but no one was any real match for the captain.

"Kneel down," Gaujot said. Immediately, Todd was on his knees.

"You want some more of what you got in jail, scum?" asked Gaujot,
Taking in a breath, Todd spoke to the floor, his voice barely audible.

"We're ordering our men back to Blair," he said. "You've won. Now, let us go."

Gaujot's left fist caught Todd behind the ear. The miner folded, going down onto the floor.

"You're not my mother, red!" the Baldwin captain spat.

"We're all backing down!" said Gibbs. "We're doing what you want!"

Gaujot glared at him. "How do you know what *I* want?"

As Todd returned to his knees before him, Gaujot's brow buckled into a frown. He turned to Carla, assessing. "Poor little gypsy," he said. "What a mess you made."

Then, leaning forward, he whispered into her ear.

"Your boys, here. They're both my pigeons, now. You and me. We'll make them sing."

Carla's face took on a look of stone. Mouseface straightened, more proud of his uniform than ever. How smart the captain was! The reds would always be outmatched by the Baldwin detectives, an investigative force at the top of its class.

Gaujot leaned closer into Carla. "We've got a dance to finish," he told her. "But, first, you're gonna hear a little music."

He turned and leveled his gun at Gibbs. "Tie this one up," he said.

Mouseface holstered his handgun and drew a leather strap. Soon, Gibbs' hands were bound to the staves of the chair behind him. Gibbs stared straight ahead, feeling his anger rise. Mouseface tested his strapped wrists. Gaujot led Carla to the door.

"Take her to the shed," he ordered, opening the door. "Touch her and I'll cut you good."

Terrified, Todd watched them leave. Still on his knees, he watched as Gaujot loomed over him, his pistol holstered. The Baldwin captain put a hand on Todd's chin, the stone fingers turning his face high. Gaujot squeezed the jaw to force it open and, without warning, produced his pearl-handled knife, its point landing in Todd's open mouth. Gaujot hovered over him, his grip tightening. The cold blade pressed against Todd's tongue, allowing Todd to taste his own blood, mixed with the smell of oiled leather.

"It's all in my hands, scum," Gaujot told him. "Your brother's life. The girl's. And yours. The only way to get through this is to accept it all. That's the way things are for you, and always will be. You stay right on this spot and do not move. Or, I promise, it will go bad for you. And I mean for all of you."

Gaujot assessed Todd's eyes and nodded, satisfied. The eyes always told him exactly what he needed to know.

"Good man," he said, and pulled away.

Blood returned to Todd's jaw. He glanced at Gibbs. Bound to the chair, his brother stared straight ahead. Gaujot turned to him.

"Time for justice, little red," he said. "I owe you something."

He slid around Gibbs' chair and waved the knife at Todd like a circus trainer holding his cat at bay. Todd looked away, forced himself to search the cabin – past the stove to the shelves of jars. Then opposite, to the window where he saw Nick Rising, looking through the glass.

Todd started, his right foot moving forward. Gaujot's knife went straight to Gibbs' throat.

"Don't move, I said!"

Todd stared back at the wall, trying to overcome his fear. Gaujot spoke to Gibbs.

"Did you think I forgot what you did to me?"

"Scaly bastard," Gibbs croaked.

Gaujot smiled. "You want to know the truth? If he'd lived, Sid Mandt would've been my pigeon too."

"That's a goddamned lie!" screamed Gibbs.

"Every man has his price," Gaujot shrugged. He knew it didn't matter what they thought. Doubt crawled among the reds like maggots on a corpse. In the end, their courage always failed. He smiled, squatting down to work. Prying open Gibbs' palm, he made the first two cuts.

"This hand struck an officer of the law," he said, slicing the skin and meat. Gibbs' flesh opened beneath the knife. Again and again.

"You'll never ball this fist again, son...."

Gibbs felt the knife blade and took in great amounts of air, trying not to cry out loud. Blood welled from his opened fingers and puddled on the floor planks. Still kneeling by the kitchen table, Todd watched, but was paralyzed with fear. Filled with self-revulsion, he stayed on the floor, unable to help his brother.

Gaujot repeated his work on the other hand. Gibbs puffed like a bull at slaughter as the mine guard listened to the voice in his head.

"Behold, I am against thee, you who are most arrogant.... The earth shall disclose her blood, no longer covering her slain ones...."

The passages absorbed him as Pearl Gaujot focused on the torture. He delivered each cut as the passages came into his head, sounding with a familiar cadence; the echos of the punishments he'd gotten for being something no one wanted: a male stranger, no longer fit for his mother's Victorian *tableaux vivants*.

"You'll think twice before you raise that fist at me!" he said.

Gibbs burned with anger, becoming dizzy with his own powerlessness. Cursing, he was afraid of already having lost everything. He wished the Baldwin captain dead.

Gaujot stood and assessed his grisly work. Then, he moved toward Todd, pointing the bloody knife to the quilt on the floor.

"Give me that," he said.

Todd obediently bent and picked up the blanket, handing it to Gaujot. With long strokes, the Baldwin agent cleaned his blade on it, slicing broad smears of blood across the white.

"That's all you get," he said, and tossed the quilt to Todd. "Be grateful."

He turned to Gibbs. "Make sure you behave yourself," he said, and opened the door, filling the room with a sudden gray light.

"You boys sit tight," Gaujot said, as he was leaving. "This won't take long."

As fast as he could, Todd went to the kitchen, found a knife and used it to cut Gibbs' cords. He let the knife fall to the floor and, taking up the quilt, quickly pressed it into his brother's bleeding palms.

"Come on, Gibbs. Take it."

Released, Gibbs went down on his knees, bringing his ruined hands before his eyes.

Mouseface Moler slouched back toward the cabin, souring as he watched the captain take the girl back into the barn. He became agitated, imagining what Gaujot would do with her. When he entered the cabin, he was immediately repelled by the mess on the floor. He leveled his rifle at the brothers, side-by-side on their knees like two women in church. The smaller one pressed his hands and face into a blood-stained bandage and Mouseface could only imagine what had happened. He backed away from them, not wanting to stain his shoes. He'd just as soon kill both of the lazy bastards on the spot. But the captain had told him no.

Gaujot removed his gun and holster, tucking them into a crossbeam, far from the girl's reach. He could practically smell her fear as she cowered in the corner of the horse's stall. Smiling, he grabbed her by the hair to pull her out, into the open.

Carla scratched and kicked at the Baldwin agent as he pulled her across the hay-strewn floor. Gaujot was reminded of a callgirl he'd had in New Jersey. As he was getting her ready, the girl had told him how much she loved his singing. In a shaking voice, she'd said how his voice soothed her, that it had the power to pacify any girl. Gaujot had known she was lying, that she would say anything to keep him from losing his patience. Still, he sang to her and pretended to take a somewhat lighter hand. Just as he did with Carla.

Tell me, little gypsy, what's my destiny?
I'll cross your palm with silver, if you want to see....

Setting his jaw, Gaujot applied the blade, cutting away the young woman's clothes. Her knitted brown sweater spread open, revealing a man's work shirt. This came away too, then the light chemise.

Carla sobbed, fighting angrily to keep her clothes. Blindly, she struck the brutal giant with her fists. Gaujot cooed as he took a clump of her shortened hair in his fist and pulled her head back. Carla writhed on the floor. Another flick of Gaujot's knife broke the strap that fixed her pants. How did they ever think to win? he asked himself. Why hold back from him?

He pinned her down, drawing involuntary cries of frustration. He grew excited.

"Goddamn you!" Carla cried, and Gaujot's breathing quickened.

She kept fighting. Releasing her hair, Gaujot allowed his knotted fist to deal several sharp punches to her softest parts. The girl fought still harder, a crazed cat. Gaujot grew impatient. Surrendering to his anger, he let the knife slip. Gasping, Carla felt the cut in her side, saw the blood and screamed. Responding to the sound, twenty swifts took sudden flight from underneath the barn eaves. Below them, Nick Rising sensed that this was the time to raise his voice. He pulled Gibbs' whistle from around his neck and blew. He put his heart into it, hoping his mother in Logan would hear. He bolted across the lot, running into the brush. He did not stop blowing. The alarm followed him into the woods, and did not fade.

Believing the reds had come, Mouseface wheeled toward the window. He was certain that they were surrounding the cabin. Todd saw his chance. He grabbed a black skillet from the stove and, in two strides, took his swing. With a sound like a splitting poplar log, the skillet caught the weaselly mine guard mightily in the temple. The blow jolted him sideways. Mouseface's eyes went wide, the inside of his head exploding with pain. Trying to command his shattered reflexes, the deputy raised his rifle. But Todd had already grabbed the gun, turning the barrel aside. Mouseface pulled the trigger, surprising them both. The wayward shot blew a hole through the cabin chinking, just beside the door.

At this point, Gibbs sprang up from the floor and knocked both men down. The three of them wrestled before the doorway, Mouseface on his back, still fighting to keep his senses. Gibbs scrambled over him, two ends of the bloody blanket wrapped around his weeping hands. This he forced the cloth down, covering the mine guard's open mouth. Todd tried to gain control of the rifle. With four hands fighting for it, the gun moved slowly up the mine guard's chest.

Mouseface Moler fought them. He tried to twist away from Gibbs, whose quilt garrote was now mashed down against his nose and mouth. The mine guard kept hold of the rifle but this, too, was futile. Todd forced the gun upward until, with agonizing slowness, he had it pressed down against Moler's throat. Now, the guard's hands flailed grotesquely, grabbing for Gibbs' face, his arms and, finally, a nearby table leg. Two black buttons popped on his jacket. Mouseface's tortured mind told him he could no longer defend the honor of his soiled uniform.

Gibbs' eyes went wide as he saw behind the broken buttons of Mouseface's open jacket. Strapped to the policeman's chest, apparently forgotten, was a holstered pistol.

"Goddamn, Todd! Watch it!"

Todd brought up his knees, putting his entire weight on the dying man, crushing his larynx with the warm gun barrel. Mouseface kicked at the floor one time before the life went out of him.

The Bryants pulled themselves away, mortified at their triumph. Gibbs unwound the blanket from his mangled hands and threw it over the mine guard's face, spattered with globs of bacon grease. Making small painful sounds in his throat, Todd pushed the rifle aside. He leaned back against a cabin post and closed his eyes, trying to catch his breath. Just then, Gibbs heard the sound of a heavy footfall on the porch.

"Gaujot's there!" he whispered.

It was no use. Todd lay against the pillar, in full view of anyone coming through the door. His head was turned away, as if sleeping – taking refuge inside a waking dream.

"Todd! Get over here!" Gibbs whispered. He crabbed backward to a spot beside the door, panicked lest Gaujot burst in. "Todd!"

But Todd remained silent, his eyes and mind closed to the outside world.

As Gibbs reached the wall, his hand brushed the iron skillet. As best he could, he used his mutilated hands to pick it up, knowing the thing would be the most desperate of weapons against a man like Gaujot. Trapping the skillet between his injured palms, Gibbs positioned himself beside the doorway. Suddenly, his eyes were drawn to a patch of sunlight on the cabin floor. The sun was shining through the mud chinking, through the new hole left by Mouseface's gun. Gibbs watched in fear, just as the sunlit spot winked out.

Gibbs froze, knowing someone would be peering through the hole from the other side. Slowly, he raised the skillet. It was slick with blood, and Gibbs was afraid it might slip from his hand. He held his breath, eyes darting.

Now a new and frightening sound came to his ear. Under the bloody blanket on the floor, Mouseface's corpse convulsed, as if the dead man was deciding to return to life. From the body came a horrible rasp, rising from someplace deep inside. The sound made Gibbs want to scream in terror. He glanced at his brother, still leaning against the post. Todd's face remained averted, oblivious to the movement of the policeman's body, just nearby. Gripping the skillet, Gibbs slowed his breathing and returned his eyes to the hole in the chinking and the door. He prayed that Todd would not draw attention to himself.

The leaf of sunlight briefly returned. Gibbs took in a slow breath. Just as his father had taught him to listen to the mine, Gibbs listened past the small sounds of the cabin, for any hint of movement on the porch. In complete silence, Gibbs watched, frozen to his spot, as a rifle barrel come sliding through the hole in the cabin wall. Like a snake, the gun barrel moved quickly, homing-in on Mouseface's blanket-covered body. The barrel stopped. Its forward brass grain steadied on its target. Gibbs listened, taking aim with the skillet. He listened harder, believing he could hear the shooter's moment; the small intake of breath, the beginning of its slow release. Now, with all his might, Gibbs brought the skillet down.

Like a blacksmith's hammer, the edge of the iron pan slammed into Gaujot's gun barrel, a split second before the mine guard fired his shot. In the rifle's damaged barrel, the blast from the shell reversed direction. Bits of gunbolt and wooden stock shot backward into Gaujot's bullish neck. Panicked, the Baldwin captain dropped the treacherous weapon and fell backward, tumbling off the porch. In agony, Gaujot cursed and writhed on the open ground before the cabin, convulsing the very air around him with his pain and anger.

Without thinking, Gibbs went to Mouseface's body and, despite his own mauled hands, was able to wrench the dead man's pistol from its holster. He went to the cabin door and stopped a moment, listening again to confirm that the Baldwin guard wasn't waiting for him on the other side. Hearing the screaming in the yard, Gibbs pulled open the door and came out onto the porch. Gaujot had tumbled through Mary's fence, but was now standing, breathing heavily. Gibbs raised the gun, seeing that the big officer was already bleeding from his neck. Gaujot screamed in rage at the miner, as Gibbs tried to steady the gun with his mangled hands. The gun shook from his effort to squeeze the trigger. But before Gibbs could fire it, his enemy turned and fled into the woods. The gun went off. In frustration and utter pain, Gibbs let the weapon fall into the dirt. He knew the shot had gone wide, its sound now echoing through the trees, mixing with the cries of distant birds, a chorus of vexed crows.

Caspar Anthony – inside, hit by a runaway coal car,
died November 10; John Kelmel – inside,
coal blast shot a nail through his arm, lockjaw set in,
died May 6; Paul Lucinski – inside,
killed in gas explosion, July 12; Furman Sockel –
inside, back broke in a top rockfall....

Pennsylvania Mine Fatality Report, 1921

Chapter 30

Gaujot stumbled through the woods, determined to get back to his men
on Hunters Ridge. From there, he would get a car and drive himself to
Logan where he'd find a doctor. First, though, he had to get through this
goddamned forest. He stumbled through curtains of sapling trees. They
slapped his jacket, blackened with a bloody sheen.

Suddenly, the trail abandoned him. Now Gaujot was crashing through
a tangled crop of mountain laurel that took him smack-up against a granite wall. He stood gasping before the rock, surprised to be so confined,
so far from anything familiar. He went forward, guided by the base of
the stone cliff, following it.

The rock wall sloped into the dense spoonwood. A lingering fog enveloped him and Gaujot knew then that he was lost. Cursing the endless
forest, he stumbled onward, finally coming onto an old wagon road.
Unused for years, its ancient ruts were choked with wild ash and sassa-
fras. Weakened by his wounds, he lay down, his back against a tree.

With agonizing pain, Gaujot pulled off his jacket. He considered
tearing it into strips to bind the seeping gash in his neck, but he did not
care to move. Instead, he stared into the woods, his neck wound burning.
How he despised the stillness of this place, the damp air and looming
trees. Groaning with pain, he seethed to think how the stupid rednecks
had almost gotten the best of him. But he would make it back to Logan.
He would heal, return and kill them. For now, though, he had to bind his
cuts.

The noise was faint at first, but Gaujot recognized it: The sound of men's boots coming up the road. Quickly, he rolled onto his stomach, then scooted backward, away from the path. He found a clutch of rhododendron at the edge of a pit. He scurried into it and hid within the bushes, his legs extended down into the trough.

With his hand clamped to his neck, Gaujot fought to stay conscious as he squinted through the brush and fog. At last, the patrol came into view. Its leader was a tall man. He wore a flannel hat which made him look like some kind of mountain shepherd, Gaujot thought. The man also had a long red beard that splashed across his shirt like Gaujot's own bloodstain. The Baldwin guard waited as the man raised his hand, signaling the others behind him to stop. The shepherd's gaze went down the road and, following it, Gaujot was surprised to see a second unit coming the other way.

With his rifle in the crook of his arm, the bearded leader walked with purpose toward the new group of men. He raised his hand in recognition to the leader of the second unit, a stocky fellow with a thick mustache. The two men nodded to each other, shaking hands.

"At ease, boys. Ten-minute break!"

"Take your ease, fellows!" the shepherd called back to his own. Several of the men collapsed to the ground, grateful for the rest. Gaujot scanned their faces, recognizing no one.

At the tail-end of the first unit, however, were five men who might have known him. Lowcoal, Ben, Simms, Bartolo, and Dix sat down and chatted with their new comrades, men from Hewlitt, being led by the red-bearded union man, named Dial. Patrolling south of the battle's flank, Dial's men had come upon the Sovereign miners in the meadow below Sid's grave. The amiable Lowcoal had agreed to accompany their patrol "down the road a piece." Ben, Simms and Bartolo went with him, leaving Dix behind to wait for Gibbs and Carla.

Dial sat down with the leader of the other unit, their backs to the tangled rhododendron where Gaujot hid.

"You boys seen much this mornin'?" Dial asked.

The stocky man strode toward the bushes to relieve himself.

"Just some of our own," he called back. "Been marching in circles, seems like."

Gaujot ducked deeper into his pit as more men wandered off the road.

"How long you been out?" Dial asked.

The other searched the fogged-in treetops for the sky. The mist seemed to be lifting, but not fast. Fastening his pants, he returned to his red-bearded companion.

"Started early," he said. "Just after the morning prayer."

"Prayer?" Dial asked, looking at him.

The stocky one looked at the ground.

"I know you look familiar to me," Dial said. "I'm of a mind to call you 'Bennett'."

"Something like that," the other admitted. "We should trade the password, I suppose."

Dial became distracted by something down the trail. "Go ahead and give it," he said.

"I asked you first."

Dial hesitated. Shrugging, he decided to say the words, just as his counterpart relented. Each enemy then spoke his own code. Alpha and omega; the chorus and its tragic coda.

"I come a-creeping."   *"Amen."*

The men closest to the two dull-witted leaders were the first to be aware of the mistake. Then, the terrifying realization moved up and down the road like a deadly wind.

Afterward, Ben would say he had "known" before it happened. He'd edged off to one side, pulling Simms and Lowcoal. Ben would be the first to have his rifle up. He fired a bullet into the stocky leader's chest and continued to fire, killing several that day, he was sure.

Men scrambled away from each other, raising their guns in panic and firing without discrimination. Shots hit their marks; friends and enemies alike dropped to the ground. Up and down the road, Logan's defenders and the union men clawed off in various directions, desperate to find refuge from the melee.

Gaujot watched the chaos, his heart pumping new pain into his neck. His eyes blurred over, trying to see through the smoke of the sudden battlefield. He had stopped trying to distinguish one side from the other. The two contingents atomized, almost a hundred terrified soldiers, running this way and that. Deep in the bushes, Gaujot's courage faltered. He was already trembling when he heard a strange note from somewhere low, behind him. He turned and looked down into the trench in which he hid.

Near his feet, he saw a face, as pale as death. It seemed familiar to him, at first. Like looking in the mirror. His own face, long ago. But this thing was more white. To Gaujot's horror, it climbed toward him – reaching up at him from underground. Like death's agent, the white-haired demon's eyes shone, its wide mouth speaking words that Gaujot couldn't understand. A sound like moaning, but the notes coming strangled and choked, as if from his own breathing wound. The monotone rose in volume, a guttural drone, a hymn of death that rose above the shooting and chorus of dying men, all around him. The white-haired devil came closer. It had full hold of Gaujot's ankle. The Baldwin chief screamed as he slipped. The thing had begun to pull him down, into the dark pit.

Gaujot drew his pearl-handled knife and jammed it into the ground above him, a desperate means to keep himself from being dragged in farther. Kicking free, and in horrific pain, he crawled up from his hiding place and backed away from the hole. He no longer saw the face, but he kept screaming in fear and fury. He stood upright, crying at the chaos of the war, the hated woods and fog.

Gaujot's screams caught the attention of men around him. Terrified, a wounded deputy – a glass-eyed guard named Reed – saw the hideous giant looming over him, a raging beast drenched in its own blood. Reed fired his gun. The monster spun about and fell back into the hole. In the end, Gaujot was terrified to find himself, head down in the demon's pit. He could see a line of flames on a stone shelf – a row of candles. The Baldwin captain died trying to get a glimpse of the world beyond his own feet, trying to see the crack of blue, just appearing beyond the canopy of treetops and clearing mist.

Nick scrambled out of Gaujot's way, avoiding the giant's fall into his cave. He had done his best to rescue him, remembering Gaujot as the big man with whom he'd once shared a sweet roll. He'd tried to pull him to safety, and even called out warnings. Nick continued to watch from within the bushes, hoping that the dying man could, at least, enjoy his treasures.

When, at last, the guns had stilled and all the rest lay quiet, Nick clambered out of the bushes. Swift and invisible, he ran through the dense woods straight to his mother's home, just as if she'd called him.

Carla gently cleansed Gibbs' palms and fingers in the chilly spring. He winced as the water flowed across the cuts, sending his blood into the ground. He gritted his teeth while she closed the worst of his gashes, suturing them with a needle and white thread. She dressed the wounds in boiled scraps of muslin, soaked in kerosene. Gibbs' hands felt like two throbbing mallets.

"Keep 'em raised up," Carla told him. "That'll help 'em heal."

Nick reappeared. Behind him came Lowcoal, Ben and Simms. They carried the body of Bartolo Bonati, who had fallen in the battle.

Together, the miners and Carla began the repairs to Mary's farm. In the cabin, they cleaned blood from the floor and fixed the chinking.

Todd, Lowcoal and Ben laid Mouseface's body in the upper woods, in a shallow tomb surrounded by a thicket of Christmas ferns. When it was done, they turned their backs and listened to the scattered sounds of battle.

"They're tiring of it," Lowcoal said.

Todd nodded, saying nothing.

They asked where they might dig Bartolo's grave and Carla didn't hesitate.

"In the cemetery, near Sid," she said.

Gibbs and Todd carried a stone from the ruined church. In tears, Simms dug his friend's grave, getting help from Ben. The miners and Carla held a muted service. At the end of it, Gibbs stood before the graves and sang Oh Death again with such feeling that none of their eyes stayed dry. Behind them, the gunfire on Blair Mountain rumbled on.

By evening, the guns had quieted, some. Once again, the comrades of Sovereign found themselves sitting together in the nighttime stillness of Mary's porch. Gibbs tried to work his mind loose from his throbbing hands, only somewhat soothed after he'd downed a half a jar of Mary's moonshine-laden tonic. Aside from the pain, he suffered from his memory of Gaujot's torture and the fear of not being able to work. Carla sat by his side. They were together now and Gibbs closed his eyes, listening to Nick, humming through the whistle. No one thought to tell him no.

Nearby, Todd had been watching the march of high, nighttime clouds. Moving slowly, they gradually overtook the sky, obscuring the constellations. "Rain's coming," he said.

Dix looked. "Yeah," he agreed. "But not yet."

They woke early the next morning. After a breakfast of potatoes and eggs, the Sovereign miners moved down the trail with their gear – except for their guns which they wrapped in oil cloth and stashed in a common trench near Sid's grave. They started off again, now with Todd in the lead. Carla hoped for Mary's quick return. She stayed back with Gibbs and Nick to give it an extra day.

"We'll see you soon," Todd called as he went.

Two more days stood between them and the U.S. Army's deadline.

Carla had given Mary's bed to Gibbs. She'd fixed cotton slings around his wrists, looping them across the carved posts of Bonner Rising's hand-hewn bedframe. Gibbs dozed through the afternoon. Waking from time to time, he admired the heavy hand-adzed beams supporting the roof, the horsehair-daub walls, like ripples on a white lake. Dim sunlight had pushed through the trees. Filtered by the window pane, it cast a shadow play of boughs and leaves, dancing on the wall. With his arms hung high, Gibbs watched the images move like a magic-lantern show, layers of shadow branches slipping across each other in the listless wind. Closing his eyes, he smelled the fragrant odors of sage and rosemary hanging in the kitchen, and listened to the chorus of evening birds.

That night, Gibbs became troubled by the strangeness of the place. Haunted by his memories of the war and Gaujot's torture, he startled at any new noise. He was suddenly awake, reacting to the far-off stutter of a machine-gun before realizing that the sound was actually close-at-hand – chimney swifts fluttering their wings beneath the cabin eaves.

Carla heard Gibbs call out. He had unhooked himself from the bed-posts and, half-asleep, tried to bring his sutured hands beneath his head. He woke to blinding pain. She came to him, dressed in her mother's long cotton shift. She worked almost an hour, gently salving his hands and re-wrapping them in new muslin.

"Keep them high, like I showed you," she scolded, as she retied the slings. "You'll be awake awhile, yet. Keep them like this as long as you are able."

She was his angel. He could do nothing else but love her and wished he had a better way to show it.

"There's so little I can do for you," he said.

But Carla shook her head. "More than you know."

She looked at him, trying to decipher him, quietly making the unavoidable comparisons to her husband. Sid had been outgoing and rough, where Gibbs was quieter, more reserved. Both had fought hard for their cause – the success of which was still in doubt. No one could be sure, from here, what shape the union might take, or whether it would come at all. No one could be sure if all the work and sacrifice would be worth it. After all they'd done together, though, Carla was determined to see it through with Gibbs.

"Here," she said. "Drink some water."

He shook his head and smiled. It was a sad, frustrated smile. His eyes held an element of hope, even humor, which she immediately loved. She leaned forward to kiss his cheek, but strayed to his mouth, discovering a new desire that surprised them both. Responding, Gibbs tried to move himself higher in the bed, to free his hands again.

"No," she said, putting her face close to his. "Let me show you how."

She calmed him, smoothing his hair.

"Relax a minute," she cooed.

He tried, and did. Gibbs let Carla's lips take his, let her undo the fasteners of his clothes. With each move, she gave him time to adjust.

Each time she offered something, letting him kiss her face and hair, and Gibbs became absorbed by the game. He gave up control, yielding to her administrations. In a way, Carla did too, letting her lips land gently where they might – here and here and here – before returning to seek his mouth's encouragement. Eventually, she crawled out of her nightdress to join him beneath the comforter. Gibbs stirred with the shock of her, then relaxed again as she stroked and kissed his chest, fragrant with the soap she'd used to wash them both.

"There's no hurry," she whispered. "We have time."

Gibbs listened to the sounds of night as Carla removed the last of his clothes. She kissed him further and, stroking him, prompted him to use his mouth the way she wanted.

"Like the French," she said.

Semi-pinioned to the bed, Gibbs submitted to her playful magic. As the swifts settled in the eaves and a wool-wrapped boy lay dreaming on the porch, the two lovers satisfied each other for the first time, free of fear.

ARMY AVIATORS FALL!
Bombing Plane Crashes to Ground
After Spin Near Poe, In Nicholas County
FATE OF AIRMEN NOT KNOWN
Machine Was On Way...to Langley Field, Va.,
When Storm Broke....

– *Baltimore Globe,* October 11, 1921

Chapter 31

General Thomas Mitchell and Colonel Stanley Ford walked together through the Danville fairground. All around them, units of the Twenty-Sixth Infantry were setting up camp. More than one thousand men unfastened packs, pitched tents and rolled out beds for the night, following orders from scores of officers of various ranks, all of whom reported to Mitchell.

As they walked, Colonel Ford's eyes drifted to the Danville depot. A train waited there, its engine steaming. Ford struggled to remain patient with the general, whose attention was focused on all the vigorous activity of the field, on the hurried construction of the temporary camp. The Twenty-Sixth had just disembarked and the general was forced to respond to queries from a steady flow of officers. Ford resented all the interruptions, having hoped that Mitchell would make a faster decision in his favor.

"I'm still thinking about your plan, Colonel," the general told him. "I'll have to run it past the Secretary of War."

Silently, Ford exhaled. He knew the general would be on the line to Washington soon. He could expect no more than this.

"But the whole thing will be shelved if the secretary hands me any question I cannot answer," the general continued. "In any case, tomorrow is still the president's deadline. We have our orders, Colonel."

Ford didn't respond immediately, but waited while another captain approached them, saluting as he came.

"The engineer is asking for permission to continue, General," the man reported. "He asked whether it will be much longer. If so, he wants permission to pull his train onto a side rail."

General Mitchell turned expectantly to Colonel Ford.

"The engineer is to wait for me, Captain," Ford said. "We should be under way within the hour. Make it clear to him that his train is to stay right where it is."

"Yes, sir," the captain saluted and withdrew, allowing Ford to continue his briefing for the general. "This morning, I was up again with Captain Steck," he said. "There are clear indications that the miners on Blair Mountain are standing down."

"Can you give the War Department a written promise, Colonel?" Mitchell asked. "Do we have any contact with their leadership in the field?"

"That's still a problem, sir," said Ford. "Sheriff Gore continues to keep the union negotiator in his jail. Governor Morgan is reluctant to order Gore to free Mr. Kenner. The governor says he fears such an order would 'set a bad precedent'."

"And intervention by the US Army is better?" asked Mitchell, shaking his head. "Quite a knot they've made for us here."

"Yes, sir," Ford agreed. "Admittedly, there is no promise that the workers' retreat from the mountain would go any faster, even if Gore freed their union leader. As I've said, the miner's army is a many-headed organization."

Another officer came to interrupt them. This time, it was Captain Harry Steck with news for Ford.

"Beg pardon, Colonel, but the gentlemen you were waiting for are here," he said. Ford nodded, thanking him.

Mitchell scrutinzed his chief intelligence officer.

"Colonel, the plan you're putting forward is late in coming. I trust you know what you're doing?"

"Yes, sir," Ford answered. "Action by the marshal's office is already under way. But my sense is that it will help us resolve at least half our dilemma here."

"And the other half?" Mitchell asked, one eyebrow raised.

"That's why I'm seeking an extension to the deadline, sir," said Ford. "I know it's a lot to ask. It does appear to me, however, that the miners are standing down."

Mitchell stood, staring at nothing. Ford pressed on with his argument. "Many of the miners are are veterans of the war, sir. Nothing I've seen tells me that they are eager to get into a fight with their Uncle Sam."

"Well, if they do, they'll be giving the Air Service the perfect opportunity to prove itself," said Mitchell. "Frankly, Colonel, I don't share your assessment of these renegades. And I'd welcome the chance to show everyone, both here and in Washington, just what our planes can do."

"I know, sir," said Ford. "I know."

Saluting the general, the colonel took his leave and went to wait on the train.

Carla and Gibbs walked on the softening ground. Nick had run ahead again, but the lovers pressed close together, in no hurry. The surrounding woods had grown gray and cold. Gibbs shouldered the large sack, loaded with blankets, clothes and a little food. Carla carried her own pack, rolled like a horseshoe. Somewhere above the trees, the bruising clouds moved fast as smoke. High, and cracked with light, they left little doubt that a storm was coming.

"Don't get too far ahead," she called to Nick, who climbed the wooded hill before them.

As they approached the battlefield, Gibbs was conscious of the fact that the mountain had been silent all day, that the birdsounds had returned.

"Maybe the soldiers have come through already," he said, trying not to imagine the place above them, a field of half-buried bodies; doctors treating scores of injured.

"No," said Carla. "It isn't that day yet."

They came onto the battered hillside to find the remnants of long-cold campfires, empty pits, strewn with paper – the president's warning. Carla stumbled on a carved tent peg, yanked it up and tossed it into the Sovereign dugout. The shelter's canvas cover was gone and its earthen walls were caving. Looking in, Gibbs recognized some familiar refuse: a broken piece from Darko's pen knife, old matches and cigarette stubs, leather from a tattered boot.

Down the line, Nick scrambled in and out of holes and ran back to show them handfuls of proud treasure – spent shell casings, spilling out and bouncing on the packed earth like brass fingerlings.

"Don't take 'em all," Gibbs warned. "Leave some for other kids."

"Speak of the devil," said Carla, looking up.

Across the gray valley, on the Logan side, three figures dashed into view, moving off-kilter to their distant children's voices.

Gibbs' stitched-up hands began to ache and itch. Carla unwound the bandages. She scrutinized the black cuts and white, criss-crossed sutures.

"Try to keep 'em high," she said. "We're out of tonic."

With odd grace, Gibbs jumped onto a log and, balanced there, stretched his mortified hands into the cool wind. Head tilted back, he raised them up, as if welcoming the clouds, now low and dark.

"How high you want 'em?" he grinned down at her.

"Funny man," she said.

She scrutinized him, stretching on his pedestal, and wished a soothing breeze for him. Nothing, she decided then, could touch her more deeply than her feelings for Gibbs now. As if eavesdropping on her thoughts, he came down from the log and, with his strong forearms, drew her into him.

Impatient with the lovers and their long embrace, Nick scampered off to find new brass.

In Logan, Colonel Ford stepped down onto the station platform. Captain Harry Steck came behind him and stamped out his cigarette. Behind him stood two other men, both well-dressed with expensive hats. The larger man carried a leather briefcase. Otherwise, they wore identical black suits. *Just like the Baldwins,* Ford thought, seeing the gun-bulges in their jackets.

Ford looked up and down the platform, where new troops were off-loading. The planks practically rumbled under their weight, the air alive with the noises of steam brakes, dropped equipment, grinding metal and shouted orders. Men passed their gear down from the boxcars, the officers searching for a place to form up ranks.

Ford found the captain in charge and went through the plan again. Now the colonel ran the gauntlet of doughboy brown, side-stepping duffles and returning men's salutes. Outside the station, he found two taxis and hired them.

At the Logan Hotel, Ford pushed through the revolving door and led the way into the lobby. Here, they found the sheriff, holding forth before a small band of Baldwin deputies. Even from a distance, Ford could see that Gore was drunk.

"I don't *know* where your goddamned captain is!" the sheriff thundered. "Gaujot has betrayed us! He is out there, working for himself someplace! I don't expect to see him again."

Ford and his men closed in on the group. Seeing the two men in uniform, the Baldwin police glanced at each other and backed away from Gore.

"That's your man," the colonel said. One of the plainclothes officers stepped forward, smartly displaying his badge.

"Sheriff Riley Gore," he said, "I'm a federal marshal from the District of Columbia. I have here a warrant for your arrest."

Gore sneered at him, about to speak. Well-practiced, the officer refused to let him.

"The U.S. attorney has filed the following charges, accusing you of conspiracy to violate the Volstead Act, prohibiting transportation and sale of alcoholic beverages."

Several more federal officers appeared, pursuing their orders to search the hotel.

Colonel Ford turned away from the scene. It would be only a matter of time before they found Gore's cache. They'd assign men to take photographs as they hammered it into a pool of bourbon and glass shards. First things first, though. With a contingent of soldiers, Ford would head across the street to the courthouse and its jail. He would get a deputy to unlock the cells of union prisoners and, guarded by the soldiers, get them onto the next train. Only then, Ford thought, would he be able to put this whole damned thing behind him.

It's just a mission, he told himself. *Nothing lasts long, as it is. Not in the Army. Not even victory....*

From the coffee urn, Mary Rising watched Gore's arrest with mild interest. Briefly, she considered going to him, then decided not to get involved. She had her deed. Clearly, the battle on the mountain had ended. She had to find her son and Carla, if she could. In any case, it was long past the time for Mary to be back home.

In the tent camp, hand-lettered signs still marked "Union Ave" and "Easy St," although their once-even rows of white canvases were now marred by missing teeth. Nick ducked his head beneath pinned-up flaps. He examined the cookstoves, mattresses and other valuables that had been too big for anyone to carry. A brown-skinned woman doused a cookfire with her kettle. Nearby, an old man eyed the circus top, sagging on its lines. Families loaded carts with their scant belongings. A young man approached his father, shaking his head.

"No meal," he said. "Not today."

Families bivouacked at the bridge, where union men loaded trucks with goods and canvases. Two women folded and stacked blankets and potato sacks, their eyes searching for the driver. A miner in a worn-out suit stood on a crate, talking loudly. Before him stood a group of hatted newsmen asking their questions. The speaker assured them of "a union victory" before jumping down and heading toward town. The reporters followed, their pencils scratching words into curled notebooks.

Carla and Gibbs passed along the creek bank, littered with rusted chimney pipes, old washtubs and cheap, busted pans. In the water, Carla spotted what she thought was a school of shimmering silver minnows, then recognized them for what they were: shattered porcelain chips, half-buried in the sediment. She stood beside an overturned bucket on which sat an old miner, his skin gray and loose like a ragged work shirt. He looked up at Gibbs and her with envy.

"These're the best times of your life," he said, and pointed at them.

A group of migrating geese passed overhead. Gibbs stopped to watch. Beneath the sea of clouds, the birds repeated their anxious cries, pumping their wings in syncopation. Nick was behind him now. He put his hand on Gibbs' shoulder, like an old friend, and made a sound, something like the geese. Gibbs smiled.

"Time to fly," he said.

Carla shivered and pulled him by the elbow.

"Come on. I want to find Aunt Tildy."

Gibbs found Todd, standing by the desk in Kenner's office. The older brother held the black bell-shaped receiver of the telephone to his ear and tapped its cradle like a telegraph key, before putting it down.

"Lines are cut again," he said. "Just as well, I guess."

The desk was just as they'd found it. No books or papers remained to show that anyone had been there. Todd's face looked better than it had on the mountain. Gibbs went to his brother and clasped him close before pulling away.

"We still in it?" he asked.

Todd shrugged.

"Kenner's out of jail. He was here and offered me a job. In Meridian. I told him no.... I just don't have it in me."

"Where will you go?"

"Jobbing out West, I figure. For a while, at least."

Todd looked around the office, wondering whether he'd forgotten anything. "Dix says you have a better shot at finding work if you got one or two others with you. He's coming along."

Gibbs nodded, went to the window. The men around the bridge were hustling now, packing the last loads. The miners had stayed as long as they could; had fought as hard as they dared. Gibbs had heard some of them talking about the two new camps, hovering over maps drawn in the dirt.

"You start here by following the flags they hung," said one.

Todd stood alongside his brother.

"What about you?" he asked and glanced at Gibbs' bandaged hands.

Gibbs shrugged.

"I'll heal, I guess. I figure I can learn to drive a truck or something."

Later, they walked down to the Main Street, there Lowcoal joined them. Todd and Dix got on board a union truck and waved.

"Say 'goodbye' to Carla for me," Todd called. "And good luck to y'all."

Gibbs and Lowcoal watched the truck pull out.

"You going to the new camp?" Lowcoal asked.

Gibbs kicked the sidewalk boards, pretending to knock dirt off his boots.

"Carla and me," he said. "We'd like to keep fighting, Low. But we'll never be able to go back to Sovereign. A man's gotta look out for hisself."

He looked down, not proud, but Lowcoal reached out and clapped him on the shoulder.

"I figure it this way," he said. "Sometimes, it's important for you to act like you're whupped – even when you ain't."

Gibbs grinned. There was no telling what new hardships lay ahead. Maybe they'd already paid the price.

"What about Ben? And Simms?"

"Took off this morning for Philadelphia," Lowcoal shrugged. "Maybe New York."

"No more union meetings. No more marching off to fight," said Gibbs.

Lowcoal coughed, half smiling. "No time soon, anyhow," he said, then looked up, his eyes alight.

"But, oh buddy! The things we done...."

The two women sat together in the garden, between the wings of the empty mercantile.

"I wish we could stay," said Carla, but Tildy shook her head.

"We all know better."

Carla took her hand.

"I'd like to come back and see this place," she said. "Sometime in the spring."

Tildy smiled. For a moment, she tried to imagine the new beds, filled with life. Instead, an unwanted image came: fresh-dug earth pounded down by soldiers' boots.

"I figure them that owns it will tear it up," she said. "They'll call us vandals, pull everything we planted, tell everyone what awful things we've done."

Carla listened to the sounds of traffic on the emptying street.

"No they won't, Aunt Tildy. I don't think they'll say anything at all."

Carla joined Gibbs on the dampened road. They held hands as they left the town, heading south on foot among scores of bundled others, the anonymous veterans of the brief, aborted workers' war. Carla and Gibbs grew silent, deep in their own thoughts, as they settled into the rhythm of this new march, its long and winding line stretching east into the hills. Later, when the rain had begun to fall, they sheltered themselves using half of Carla's button-down pup tent, which they'd rescued from the battlefield.

"Things might not get any easier," said Gibbs, thinking of the battles they'd survived.

"No," said Carla, not breaking step despite the mud. "I don't suppose they will."

At one juncture, the human river separated, one stream branching right. The other, a bigger group, flowed left toward the union's new refugee camps in Boone. Later – much later – the branches would split again. And again, spreading down a thousand mountainous roads to other camps and towns and distant cities, like arteries of coal coursing through deep shale.

Nick was among the first to hear the drone of engines, a sound that drew him outdoors. Standing with him in the street, Tildy listened to the sky throb with a strange rumble.

"It's gonna rain," she told him. But the rain had already started. Across the street, heavy drops battered the green tin roofs of leaning houses, and Tildy hustled Nick back into the mercantile.

The bombers came, materializing like whining midges. They flew in formation, their crewmen signaling each other through bug-eyed goggles. Looking nervously at the ground, the pilots leveled their machines beneath the sudden swarm of clouds, smokey extrusions dropping from the sky around them, like armored fists.

In symphony, the seven Martin bombers passed over the abandoned workers' camp. A single shell was released by accident. An undocumented demolition bomb, its only innocent victim was the fine, old covered bridge. The blast shook the ground around the camp, and sliced the building like a giant knife. The bomb's effect lifted the bridge, its frame and rafters. Wood siding fluttered down on the camp like playing cards on fire, landing on remaining tents and empty platforms.

As if by vandals, the great miner's community was set ablaze. Flames engulfed the big central canvas where union men had given speeches and women had made good meals. Now, the big tent's acrid smoke spread skyward, springing up like a sudden black elm tree.

All around it, grew a field of smaller phosphorous plumes; odd-colored candles of orange and blue, strangely unbothered by the rain. Row by row, and in well-ordered ranks, the fragile tent homes burned together, in unison.

Leaving the miners' field, the pilots followed their maps and briefings to the mountain. They followed Mitchell's orders and began to release their loads on the abandoned battlefields. Tight and powerful, the aerial torpedoes fell, sending up columns of dirt and flaming firewood, igniting forests on both sides of the valley.

They did not stop. More bombs whistled in, exploding the once-green hillsides. Great blasting cracked the air, fragmenting wooden bunkers, tossing slices of burning debris, twisted shards of shell casings, abandoned weapons and broken tools. After a few minutes, the pilots and their crewmen looked down to see the result of their work. Even they were astounded at the devastation: a landscape as dead as their ordnance testing sites, cratered and pocked as the surface of the moon.

Their materiel spent and fearing the tempest, the pilots signaled to each other and turned toward home. Three planes didn't make it. Midway between Logan and Meridian, their machines proved too fragile for the thunderstorm. They went down in isolated forests, lost for good. Three of the nine crewmen survived and limped back to Logan. But none of them – nor any of their comrades – could ever say where they'd been that day, nor did any of them ever speak about the mission they had run.

It was five o'clock when the soldiers of the Twenty-Seventh Infantry marched into Blair. They slogged in dual rows, their gun barrels high with fixed bayonets. They tracked mud into every ramshackle structure, searching each building from cellar to rickety attic. They found no "red" partisans, only local folks who willingly handed over what weapons they had, a sad assortment of ancient-looking trash.

By the time they reached the mercantile, the regular troops were frustrated, a few of them even angry. They'd been promised a fight with militant miners – hoards of rugged mountain men. Instead, they found a sodden town, populated only by a handful of refugees.

"Someone said there was a war here?" their captain joked. "*Thunderous* was what the general told us! Hundreds of dead and wounded!"

He stood before the mercantile, scowling at Blair's dirty streets and mud-splattered buildings, their roofs half-patched with tin. Still young and untried by any war, the captain had hoped for something better; a storied victory. Sadly, he realized he'd arrived too late. No battlefield to capture, no surrendering flag to take.

The next week was filled with rain. Water came off the battered mountain, choking Blackberry Creek. The devastated strikers' camp swamped over, then joined the river. Every remnant of the tent community at Blair disappeared into the flood – broken boards, burned canvas and countless smaller tokens of people's lives – all buried in mud or carried downstream to the Big Coal River, choked well above its banks for days to come.

Afterword

Prompted by coal-company lawyers, several special grand juries handed down hundreds of indictments in connection with the 1921 "Blair Mountain War," including 325 for murder and twenty-four for treason. There were a handful of convictions.

Franklin D. Roosevelt's National Industrial Recovery Act (NIRA) granted U.S. workers the right to organize unions and bargain collectively across the country. The act was signed in 1933, more than a decade after the Battle of Blair Mountain, but the legal fight continued. When the Supreme Court invalidated the NIRA in 1935, Congress passed the Wagner Act, which strengthened labor's rights vis à vis management, and gave stronger enforcement powers to the National Labor Relations Board (NLRB).

That year, the state of West Virginia banned the practice of county sheriffs deputizing members of a mining company's private police force.

In 1947, two years after the death of FDR, Congress passed the Taft-Hartley Act which fundamentally changed the nature of federal labor law, and seriously hindered the NLRB's ability to enforce it. Having lost its mediation function, the NLRB was largely unable to become involved in labor disputes as it had from its inception (as the National Labor Board) in 1933.

Like the veterans of other wars, men who'd fired guns on Blair Mountain withdrew and didn't talk much about it. Memory of the battle faded even among the people who lived there. After a generation, details of the event were muddled in the collective mind. Few could describe what had happened or fully knew what it was all about. The fight became a vague embarrassment, like a family member doing time in jail.

Since then, far less deep mining is done in the region. Today, relatively few workers can mine incredible amounts of coal using a destructive method known as "mountaintop removal." At this writing, coal-mining firms hold permits to blast the area around Blair for the thousands of tons of carbon buried beneath. Private land preservation and environmental groups are fighting the practice, which disfigures the landscape beyond recognition, leveling the lush, green mountains into a surface as barren as the basalt craters of the moon. This is part of what makes it hard to find and recognize the real battlefield of Blair Mountain today.

About the Author

Topper Sherwood is an American journalist, editor and publisher living in Berlin since 2008. Appalachian Editions is his own imprint, under which he has published several nonfiction titles about history in West Virginia, where he was raised.

CPSIA information can be obtained at www.ICGtesting.com
Printed in the USA
BVOW08s1226080515

399524BV00001B/1/P